SOUL OF A WITCH

BY HARLEY LAROUX

The Souls Trilogy
Her Soul to Take
Her Soul for Revenge
Soul of a Witch

Losers
The Dare (prequel)
Losers: Part 1
Losers: Part 2

Dirty First Dates (short erotica series)
Halloween Haunt
The Arcade
The Museum

SOUL OF A WITCH

Harley Laroux

KENSINGTON
PUBLISHING CORP.

kensingtonbooks.com

CONTENT NOTICE: Content within this novel may be disturbing or triggering for some readers. Reader discretion is advised.

Subjects include descriptions of anxiety and panic attacks, mentions of death/ suicide of a parent, religious abuse, mental and physical abuse by a parent to their adult child, pregnancy, discussion of miscarriage/pregnancy loss, graphic violence and elements of horror, including body horror.

Any character depicted in a sexual scene is at least 18 years of age.

This book should not be used as a reference or guide for safe sex practices. Some activities depicted herein carry significant risk of injury and bodily harm. Kinks within this book include bondage/restraint, impact play, consumption of bodily fluids, public play, ritual sex, blood play, knife play, use of drugs/intoxication during consensual sex, piercing play, extra large penetration, monster dick, and pegging.

*To all my readers who have
waited so long and so patiently
for this book.*

*Thank you for taking this journey
with me.*

WELCOME BACK TO ABFLAUM, dear readers!
   I'm Harley Laroux—author, cat guardian, plant col-
lector, and candle enthusiast. Thank you so much for
picking up *Soul of a Witch*, the third and final book in
the Souls Trilogy!
   This gorgeous print edition from Kensington Books
features an all-new bonus epilogue and beautiful aes-
thetic updates to the cover and interior! Inspired by the
stunning natural beauty of Washington State and my
fascination with all things spooky, the Souls Trilogy fol-
lows three fierce women and the demons who love them,
as they fight to survive in a small town full of monsters,
magic, and mystery. These adult paranormal romances
are extra spicy, each following a different couple as they
unravel the dark mysteries of their town's past.
   In the trilogy's fiery conclusion, timid and inexperienced witch Everly Laverne has spent her life under the
thumb of her cult-leader father. But everything changes

after a mysterious burst of magic leads her to an abandoned coven house, and the powerful Archdemon within. Callum has been waiting for Everly for centuries, and together, they set out to kill an ancient God, destroy a cult, and find a way to protect each other through it all.

Everly's story is a special one to me, not only because it completes this trilogy, but because of the growth she goes through as she finds her power. From a girl oppressed and misled by her family's worship, to a woman with the confidence to challenge a God. This is a story of overcoming fears and letting no one trample your power. But it is also a story of loss, and grief, and how we can carry and honor those feelings within us.

I'm so grateful for the opportunity to share this story with you. I hope you find just as much love, adventure, and excitement while reading these books as I did while writing them.

WITH LOVE,

Harley
Laroux

CALLUM

HELL—2,000 YEARS AGO

A MORTAL MAN once told me, "Only the dead have seen the end of war." But I, being infinite, was doomed to see it all. Every great battle, every raging conflict. The fall of every kingdom on Earth, in Heaven, or in Hell. The endless loss of lives in an ever-churning machine of bloodshed.

The curse of the immortal.

I took up arms, I witnessed the destruction of great cities and the deaths of so many—and yet, I went on. Hell was the domain of the immortals, but even we could be snuffed out.

So many of us were already lost.

There was a soft sound as the flap of my tent was

brushed aside. It was my second-in-command, Kimaris. "A scout has returned, my lord."

"*A* scout?" I turned. "We sent three."

"Yes, *dux*. Only one returned." Her voice didn't betray the pain in her golden eyes.

The fields were covered in ash. Cities leveled. Young ones snuffed out. And still, we went on. Infinite.

I couldn't recall the last time I'd mourned. There was no time for the ceremonies with which we bid farewell to the dead. We couldn't celebrate the freedom of their beings, nor could we come to terms with the horror of their fates.

To die by the hand of a God was to become Theirs for eternity. Your essence, sucked into Its own, the wretched suffering of your immortal being feeding Its gluttonous power. A horror beyond words, beyond what even we demons could imagine.

"How much time do we have?" I said.

"They'll reach us before dawn."

Then we would fight in the night. We were the last line, the final defense before the city of Dantalion. If the High City was taken, then Hell was no longer ours. It would become the realm of Gods.

"Callum . . ." She hesitated, staring at the grass but seeing something else entirely. Something that made her lip curl as she said, "There are Reapers with them."

Sharp, cold fingers of dread gripped my chest. But I kept my face utterly blank. I imagined myself as a chiseled stone, unmovable, unchanging. Unfailing.

"I want every warrior ready. Go through the camp, get them sobered up. We don't have time for their comforts."

"Yes, *dux*." Kimaris turned to go, but there was a final thing to be done.

"The scout," I said. "Are they well? Able to travel?" She nodded. "Take them aside and select two others. I want them to stay back from the battle. If the line is broken, they are to go back to Dantalion and give word. A little time to flee is better than none."

Kimaris looked stricken. "The High City has never fallen," she said sharply. "Never."

"Pride will make us think we're untouchable. But the Gods advance. We are the last line. Dantalion will not fall while I still live." I paced across the tent, snapping my fingers. "Tell them, Kimaris, but let no one else know of this. Keep the conversation private."

A GREAT WHITE fog was growing on the horizon, rolling toward us over the vast plains. Lightning flashed within, briefly illuminating the gargantuan shapes of beasts as they advanced.

Behind me, in the distance, the High City shimmered in the dark, its lights extending far into the heavens. I longed for her warmth, her twisting streets, the shining onyx towers of her keep. But I cast away the feelings; I forced my heart to harden.

If I hesitated, if I allowed myself to long for anything other than bloodshed, Dantalion would be taken.

Hell's army was gathered at my back, demons young and old. Dark clouds gathered overhead, obscuring the night sky and the silver light of the twin moons.

"And so comes the rain," Kimaris said, as the heavy drops began to fall. She whispered, "How many do you think?"

We gazed at the nearing fog. It was faint, at this distance, but I could hear the screams within. Agonized, tortured screams of all those beings the Gods had consumed. Mortal or immortal, it didn't matter. Their souls were locked into eternal torment for the Gods, creatures that thrived and fed upon suffering. Their forms were massive and ever-changing.

Flying before them, like great black shadows, were the Reapers. They were adorned in bones, their multiple eyes glowing beneath their shrouds. Their cries pierced the night, animalistic and hungry. The howls of the Eld creatures mingled with them, the lesser beasts crawling at their masters' heels, gnashing their teeth.

"It doesn't matter how many," I said. "We don't stop until there are none."

Turning my back on the encroaching fog, I faced my warriors. Fangs clipped eagerly, the sound of snapping teeth our battle cry. Many of these demons had sharpened their claws, or fit metal spurs on their fingers. Some held massive weapons made of aether, metal, or stone, their blades shimmering in the night.

Looking upon them, with the lights of the High City glowing at their backs, I could see the end of this war.

Whether I would live to see it, I didn't know. But the end was here.

"Hellions!" My voice roared over the landscape, loud enough to reach even the furthest line of demons. "Some among you have lived as long as I. You've seen the world change, you've seen wars come and cities fall. But some of you are seeing war for the first time. You've seen friends and lovers die, you've seen blood fill the streets of our cities."

They shouted in response, chanting, "Honor the dead! Honor the dead!"

When had I last seen a funeral pyre? When was the last time we'd had enough peace to send the ashes of our kin free to the winds?

As I looked upon them, I saw fear, I saw fury. I didn't see hope. I saw hundreds of beings bracing themselves to die.

Straightening my shoulders, I said, "Dantalion relies upon us and we will not let it fall! I've seen you, fought with you." I paced along their line, meeting their eyes, touching their shoulders. Making it clear they had a leader who was not afraid. "I've seen you tear out the hearts of Gods, drenched in the blood of the Eld! I've seen your viciousness! Today, we go into battle with the names of those we lost on our lips. Honor the dead! But do not forget the living. Do not forget the lives of those beside you, and those behind you. Honor them!"

Weapons slammed, howls broke out across the ranks. Lifting my hand, I drew the edge of my blade across my palm so the blood ran down my wrist. Many of the warriors followed suit, for no demon wanted to give their enemy the satisfaction of drawing first blood.

"We'll see the sun rise on their corpses!" I yelled. "These fields will be fed with their blood! For no creature, no God, will take Hell from its true keepers!"

The cacophony of their shouts and howls was deafening, loud enough to drown out the horrendous screams of our enemies. Stretching my wings toward the sky, I watched them come. The white fog reached out long tendrils toward us, and the screaming grew louder. Massive beings stirred in the darkness.

"Death calls!" I yelled. "But today, you will not answer! Today, you fight, and death will feed on your enemies! Hell is ours!" I slammed my blades together with a crack like thunder, beat my wings, and launched into the air. The first tendrils of mist touched my face, cold as ice and bringing with it whispers of agony.

I bared my teeth. Above me, a massive form loomed.

"Death calls," I murmured. "Death calls."

I raised my weapons and faced the Gods.

THE SUN BEAT down, a blood-red yolk floating in a pale gray sky, as I walked among the fields of the dead.

The odor of burned flesh and rot permeated the air. Corpses riddled the landscape as pools of blood seeped into the dirt. Dead Gods were scattered across the field, their massive forms melting into lumps of quivering flesh, surrounded by clusters of phosphorescent fungal growths. Dying Reapers with ruined wings and broken bodies roared curses at me as I passed.

All around me lay the bodies of my kin. Demons I'd known, fought beside. Demons I'd loved, who wore my metal and jewels in piercings I'd given them with my hands.

One by one, as I found them, I took out the metal

they'd given me. The jewelry pierced through my ears, lips, and eyebrows, covered in glittering jewels—I ripped them out. I didn't feel the pain. Physical pain was nothing in comparison to this.

One wing dragged behind me as I knelt before another body. They'd been gored, but I knew their face. Ryker. They wore my metal pierced through their lip, and I could remember how joyous they'd been when I gave it to them. We'd spent all night in rapture before rising in the morning to fight another day.

If this was what it took to save Hell, perhaps I shouldn't have saved it.

I closed their wide, glassy eyes. Then choked down the pain, swallowed it whole, let it sit like a knot of agony in my chest. I wouldn't stop until I'd seen them all. Every single one. I would not allow even one of my warriors to go unwitnessed into the Void Beyond.

Through the lingering smoke, I could see the High City. Its spires and glittering towers of onyx and emerald pierced the sky like a beast's teeth. Lucifer's great citadel overlooked it all, the tallest of its towers disappearing into the clouds.

They would call me a hero. There would be feasting, debauchery, orgies. Liquor would flow for days. Hell's future was secured, the war was won.

Lucifer would grant me his favor. He would mark me, just like I'd wanted for so long. My ascension would be complete.

Archdemon.

Royal.

Revered.

I wanted none of it.

Turning my back on the city so many had died for, I trudged on. There was a voice in my head, screaming my name like an endless echo. The cries of my warriors were trapped within my own mind.

Amid the swirling smoke ahead, a figure appeared.

It was a woman. Not a demon, not a beast. A mortal woman, with long blonde hair that was damp and dirty. She wore boots and trousers, but the make of her clothing was unlike anything I'd seen on Earth or in Hell. Her head was bowed, her shoulders hunched as she clutched at her side.

I sniffed the air.

Blood, sugary sweet, spring berries and honey, nectar on my tongue . . .

She was a witch.

Witches only sought demons for one purpose—to control us. They would force us to bend to their will if they could discover our true name.

Something about this witch was familiar. Like the face of an old friend, warped by time. But that was impossible. I did not keep company with witches.

Then she lifted her head and looked at me. Her eyes glittered like sapphires, bright and beautiful amid so much gore. We faced each other in silence across the open field, her scent wafting over me like a heady perfume.

Intoxicating, irresistible, the most alluring ambrosia.

Then she spoke, and my entire world changed.

"Callum . . . please . . . help me . . ."

EVERLY

EARTH—7 YEARS AGO

IT WAS FORTY minutes after midnight when the shout came through the trees. "We found her! She's alive! We found Juniper!"

Members of the search party cheered and hugged. Many of them rushed forward, eager to see the missing girl. The distant wail of an ambulance reached my ears, but with it came another sound.

Juniper's screams carried far ahead of her, shaking the excitement of those who had searched this forest for two days in hopes of finding her alive.

My mother stood nearby with her arm around a thirteen-year-old Marcus Kynes. Juniper's mother hadn't come out to search for her, but her younger brother had.

His eyes were wide, his hands shoved into the pockets of his blue windbreaker.

"Is she hurt?" He appeared torn between running toward the screaming and fleeing in the opposite direction. "Why is she screaming like that?"

Mama's gaze met mine. But she looked away again, swallowing hard as she squeezed Marcus's shoulder. A wave of nausea roiled through my stomach, forcing me to close my eyes and count to ten as I took a slow breath.

Did Mama still have Juniper's blood under her nails? Or had she washed it all away, scrubbed clean like the church's wooden floors?

Juniper was wrapped in a heavy blanket as she walked between two men, her arms gripped so she couldn't thrash away from them. People murmured as they stared at her wide eyes and bloody chest.

"She cut herself," someone whispered behind me. "I've always said the Kynes family isn't right. Drug addicts, all of them."

That was the rumor we had been instructed to spread: Juniper had done this to herself. She was a crazy girl from an even crazier family.

Any accusations she made couldn't be believed.

"Monsters!" Juniper screamed. She fought her rescuers as if they were the very monsters she spoke of, throwing herself to the ground and staring back into the trees. "There are monsters! In the trees! They . . . they came out of the ground . . . the mine!" She screamed again, clawing at their hands to pry them off. The ambulance had arrived, and the EMTs had a stretcher ready. One of them prepared a syringe, and Juniper balked, staring at the needle with renewed horror. "No! Get that thing away from me! Stop . . . stop!"

I clenched my hands tight behind my back. Merciful God, why did she *live*?

Juniper's eyes were drooping, her shouting growing weak. Then her gaze fell on me. She raised a trembling finger, and my stomach twisted when I realized her nail had been ripped off.

"You were there," she said. She tried to lunge for me, but her legs gave out. The EMTs had to lift her from the ground. Even with her body betraying her, Juniper kept fighting. "You were there, Everly! You saw . . . tell them . . . tell them, please!"

Her face fell as a warm hand came to rest protectively on my shoulder.

"You should go home, Everly." My father's voice was calm, comforting me the moment I heard it. Papa always knew what to do, what to say. He knew that the right path was not always the easy one.

Sometimes, it was frightening. Sometimes, it required one to do wicked things.

"It was you!" Juniper screamed, teeth bared, weakly thrashing her head as she was laid on the stretcher. "You did it! You left me down there! You're a monster, Kent Hadleigh! You and your bitch daughter! *Victoria*!" Juniper laughed after she screamed my half-sister's name, hysteria overtaking her terror. They pushed her stretcher into the ambulance, but that didn't stop her from looking back at me again and saying viciously, "You watched. You *watched* and did *nothing.*"

THE COURTROOM WAS full that night.

Ever since the old courthouse was converted into the Abelaum Historical Society, the courtroom had only been used for meetings of Society staff and benefactors. At least, that was the ruse we maintained. The two dozen people gathered there were indeed benefactors of the Society. They'd all donated time, money, and loyalty to my father's goals.

Loyalty to my father meant loyalty to the Libiri. Children of the Deep God, worshippers of Its great power. We alone would reap the benefits of Its mercy when It was unleashed. When our goals were fulfilled, our God would be free, this world would change, and we would be granted Its favor.

But tonight, those goals had been shaken. Shattered.

As the congregation huddled in fear in the courtroom below, my family gathered in the attic. The tension in the air was palpable, as if I could sense the wringing hands, shuffling feet, and uncomfortable whispers drifting through the stale air from below. The rumble of distant thunder made me quake, and I stared at the ceiling, expecting it to collapse at any moment.

We had no idea how terrible the Deep One's fury could be. Not yet.

Casting my eyes upward allowed me to avoid the horrendous sight at my feet—my father's captive demon,

Leon, writhing in a binding circle as the wrath for to-night's failure fell on him.

Kent Hadleigh had always been a calm man. Com-posed, collected, eloquent. It made people trust him and put their faith in his leadership. But those of us who were closest to him knew rage simmered just below the sur-face. Righteous anger that he would unleash the moment he was behind closed doors.

Demons could heal from almost anything, but Leon's flesh was raw, crisscrossed with deep gashes. The words my father used to inflict pain sounded so ugly, so full of hatred.

"*Scissa carne*," he chanted again, and Leon made a sound like a throttled scream. "*Cum ardenti sanguine.*"

The smell of burning flesh made me nauseous. My eyes flickered quickly toward my mother as she stood be-side the demon's binding circle, muttering. She'd drawn the circle herself; rings, lines, and runes, carefully assem-bled to contain the powerful hellion within. The spell she uttered bolstered my father's power since he had none of his own.

There was a brief silence, filled only with Leon's la-bored breathing, before my father snapped, "She's fifteen! A fucking *child* got away from you! You expect me to see this as anything other than defiance?"

Beside me, my step-brother, Jeremiah, smirked with sadistic satisfaction. My step-sister, Victoria, looked bored, and her mother, Meredith, did too. The suffer-ing in front of them had no impact, as if the wretched screams didn't even penetrate their ears.

"*Scissa carne!*"

Across the binding circle, I met my mother's eyes. Her blonde hair was tied back, her blue eyes dark with power as she wielded her magic. My mother could craft spells without words; with mere intent and focus, she could summon the elements, make objects move and charm them to behave how she wished.

Meanwhile, to use any magic himself, my father needed the little book currently clutched tightly in his hand. A grimoire, passed down through the generations of our family, allowing each subsequent patriarch to not only wield magic, but to control the demon whose sigil was written within.

No one except a few trusted worshippers knew what Leon truly was. He looked almost human; demons usually did. Given the opportunity, demons would kill us in a heartbeat and revel in our pain. Or worse, they would trick humans with irresistible bargains in exchange for ownership over one's soul.

Once your soul was sold, there was no going back. You would become theirs for eternity, bound to a demon and destined for Hell.

Father said it was a fate worse than death.

Outside the family, people thought Leon was hired by my father from a private security firm. They'd thought the same thing when he served my grandfather, and his father, and so on, all the way back to the source of all this: Morpheus Leighman. The man who started our worship, who discovered the Deep One's presence.

Like my father, Morpheus had not been a witch.

Magic did not come inherently to my father's bloodline. My mother could use it, but I had been blessed with mere whispers of magic, tangled threads of power that I could scarcely unravel, let alone control.

But as my father often said, a young woman did not need power. She needed an obedient mind and a submissive heart.

Finally, Father stopped. He drew in a deep breath, stroking his hand over his short gray hair.

"Return to your room in the house immediately," he said, his voice hoarse as he spoke to the demon who lay curled in a bloody heap on the floor. "You are not to leave your binding circle unless I instruct you otherwise."

Leon's golden eyes squeezed shut before he vanished with a wisp of smoke. My shoulders slumped, tension I'd been unaware I was holding finally flooding out of me. As Mama knelt down, using a rag to swiftly wipe away the chalk lines of the binding circle, Meredith watched her, nose wrinkled in disgust. She detested us. I was proof of her husband's infidelity, proof she could never avoid.

Having my father's wife and his mistress in the same room was a recipe for disaster. Doubtlessly, it was only Father's foul mood that kept Meredith from saying something rude.

"Tidy yourselves up," Father snapped, tapping his hand irritably against Jeremiah's shoulder before roughly straightening his jacket. "All eyes will be on you the moment we step into that room." His gaze fixed on me, so heavy my shoulders shrank. "Keep yourselves composed. We must reassure them we remain in control."

"Yes, Father." My words were so soft, I wasn't entirely sure if he heard me. We followed him out of the attic. Jeremiah was right at his heels, then Meredith, Victoria, and then my mother and I. Mama's hands were cold when she clasped mine as we made our way down to the courtroom.

We should have been gathered in St. Thaddeus tonight. It was the first church to be built in Abelaum, over a hundred years ago, and we had claimed it as a place of worship for our God. But the forests around that church and the White Pine mine shaft nearby were still crawling with state and local police, scouring for clues as to what exactly happened to Juniper. Local police were deep in my father's pocket, but the others were a clear and present danger.

If they found the church, would they find the bloodstains? Would they realize the candles were recently lit, the pews dusted by flowing white robes, the herbal scent of incense still hanging in the air? Would they see my mother's guilt? My father's? My sister's? My own?

Mama's eyes were open, but her mind was in some far-off place. Powerful witches like her could cast their spiritual selves beyond the Veil, into the vast expanse known as the Betwixt, a place outside of time and space.

A skilled witch like Mama could wander there, but it was dangerous. She had never allowed me to attempt it.

Within the Betwixt, one could see and discover many things. One could walk through time, see into the future or the past, connect with spirits and otherworldly beings, even God Itself.

The courtroom doors slammed open, the entire congregation flinching in fear as my father strode down the
aisle toward the podium. The rest of us took our seats at
the front of the room: Meredith, Victoria, and Jeremiah
on one side, my mother and I on the other.

As my father turned to face the room, the congregation fell silent. Soon, the only sound remaining was the
patter of rain on the courthouse roof, interrupted by
thunder.

Father spared us a brief glance. The intensity of his
gaze withered my insides.

"Tonight, we had planned to gather here in worship
and thanks," he said. "Instead, we gather in sorrow, in
repentance. For we have failed our greatest calling."

Murmurs of horror and fear rippled around the room.
Father sighed heavily, gripping the edges of the podium
as he looked down upon us: his family, his flock.

Thunder crashed again, the rumble louder than ever.
The building shook, and Mama's hands flinched. We
could both feel it: a *presence* in the back of our minds.
Like snakes twining up our spines, like worms bur-
rowing into our bones. God saw everything within this
little town, but It was drawn to the magic in my mother
and I.

"Someday, our God will rise," Father said, his eyes
fixing on me with a weighted sense of finality. "It will
choose a blessed vessel, It will walk among us. It will
bless those who have remained loyal, and It will inflict
holy suffering upon those who refuse to believe. But first,
we must fulfill our duty. We must offer three souls."

Someone in the crowd was sniffling, their shuddering breaths making me twitch.

"Juniper Kynes was meant to be the first sacrifice," Father said grimly. "My faithful daughter, Victoria, brought her to us, as gently as one would lead an innocent lamb. But such is the nature of man to fail. Our sacrifice escaped. She defied God, she wasted her bloodshed, she squandered her suffering. So we gather here to beg for forgiveness. And to condemn, wholeheartedly, the great betrayal that has befallen us."

There was a crack of thunder so loud that several people cried out in despair. Some clutched their chests in terror; others squeezed their eyes shut.

"Who among us is the traitor?" Meredith said, her sharp voice grating on my raw nerves. "There is no place within the Libiri for disloyalty. God sees all." She nodded determinedly, and although she didn't glance over at us, my half-siblings did. Victoria's expression was impossible to read, but Jeremiah's narrowed eyes were sharp with suspicion.

But my mother and I had done our duty. Mama guided the sacrifice, I bore witness.

Neither of us could have known Juniper would escape. She'd been thrown into a flooded mine, twenty feet down a sheer muddy shaft, then boarded in and left to her fate.

My stomach lurched, twisting at the sickening memories. The screaming, the blood. She'd begged us to stop.

We should have stopped.

Mama's fingers squeezed tighter in warning. She wasn't a diviner, as my grandma Winona had been, but she still possessed an uncanny ability to sense my thoughts. My fears bled into hers, festering between us like an infection.

"The betrayer will be found," my father said, his words heavy as his eyes combed over the crowd. "The Deep One knows their heart, their disloyalty. Retribution will come. Have faith! God's will cannot be stopped. Juniper may be beyond our reach now, but there are other options from her bloodline." Whispers spread through the crowd, the name "Marcus" dropping from several lips. "Now, I ask all of you to go directly home. Be cautious, keep your faith close to your heart but not your tongues. I will be speaking with the sheriff tonight. Spare your words if anyone asks what you saw. May the Deep One have mercy on us all."

"May the Deep One have mercy," the congregants echoed. My lips were numb as I repeated the words.

As the crowd dispersed, Mama led me out into the hallway. The Historical Society was dark, all the lights turned off except for those in the old courtroom and the entryway. Mama tugged me through the crowd, moving hurriedly, leading me into an empty storage room.

She let go of my hand to pace in the tiny, dark space. I watched her for a moment, waiting for her to say something, but she was wringing her hands silently.

"Mama, what—"

She grasped my arms before I could finish.

"Don't speak of this to anyone," she whispered,

teary-eyed. "I need to tell you . . . Everly, you need to know the truth—"

We jumped as the door was shoved open. My father stood there, his eyes alternating between us, his brows drawn sharply together.

"I need to speak with you, Heidi," he said. "Alone. Now."

She followed my father back down the hall, to the vacant courtroom. The rest of the congregation was leaving, the somber silence of the crowd saying more than words ever could. No one dared to walk to their cars alone. They went in twos and threes, huddled together, glancing cautiously into the deep shadows beneath the trees.

As I waited for Mama to return, a sharp haunting cry pierced the night. Those who hadn't yet left the building froze in place, glancing between each other, eyes wide with fear of what lurked in the dark. The Deep One wasn't the only strange being to inhabit this town. Abelaum was like a vortex; the Veil was thin here, the presence of the Deep One attracting all manner of strange creatures. These creatures were not friendly; they were not the magical fairy-tale beasts from my childhood story books. They were predators, eternally ravenous, supernaturally strong. Humans made for easy prey.

"They should have eaten her."

My sister's voice made me flinch. Before I could turn, she slipped her arms around my waist, embracing me as if to comfort me, her chin resting on my shoulder. But her words were far from comforting.

"Father said it would take powerful magic to hide Juniper from the Eld beasts. Even Leon couldn't find her." She smelled like artificial vanilla, her acrylic nails tapping lightly against my collarbone as she held me close. "How is that possible, Ev? Hm? Because the only people in the family with powerful magic are Dad . . . and your mother."

She laughed as I jerked away from her hold, drawing my sweater tighter around myself. Less than seventy-two hours ago, she had led Juniper into the forest. She'd given her LSD, waited until the hallucinations took hold, then led Juniper straight to St. Thaddeus.

She'd betrayed her best friend out of loyalty to God. She hadn't even flinched when Juniper screamed. She hadn't cried. It was uncanny, but my sister had always been good at playing her part.

It was impossible to know who she truly was. She was fifteen, yet she wore her emotions like masks, picking and choosing at will.

"What are you trying to say?" Even at a low volume, my voice felt too loud. It *always* felt too loud. But I was meant to be seen and not heard.

She smiled at me tightly, as if the action pained her.

"Maybe I'm not saying anything at all," she said innocently. "Maybe I'm just trying to figure out where the hell we went wrong." She stepped closer, that strange expression still frozen on her face. "But you know what? I think I figured it out. Dad made a mistake, sixteen years ago, when he decided to fuck your whore mother."

The words speared into my chest. Victoria waved her hand dismissively, her voice taking on a breezy tone as she said, "But mistakes happen, and God sees them. It will make sure those mistakes are taken care of." She reached up, delicately touching a strand of my blonde hair; a mirror image of my mother's. "You'll never be the daughter he wanted. No matter how hard your mother tries to sabotage me. Maybe you should start giving some thought to who is going to protect you when she's gone. Mommy won't be around forever."

"It's time to leave, girls," Meredith called sharply, waving to us from down the hall. Victoria flicked her brown hair over her shoulder as she turned away, but I remained where I was. Mama was still talking to my father, and part of me didn't want to leave her alone with him.

Victoria's words kept echoing in my head.

Who is going to protect you when she's gone?

WITHIN TWO SHORT years, I had my answer. When Mama took her own life, she left me alone.

And there was no one at all who could protect me.

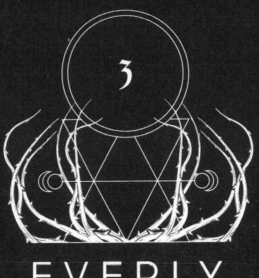

EVERLY

EARTH—PRESENT DAY

FOG ROLLED AROUND my ankles like ocean waves. The forest was dark, but moonlight fell through the pine needles in broken shafts. The dirt was cool beneath my bare feet as I walked, aimless, beneath the trees.

The night was silent. The creatures of the woods fled before me; the crickets' song faded away.

My prey was close. Her breathing was harsh, quick with terror. Her steps were loud and clumsy. She shot panicked glances over her shoulder, growing more frantic every time she saw me.

No matter how fast she ran, it would not be fast enough.

Her boot caught on a tree root, and she tripped, sprawling to the ground. She pushed herself up, facing me, whispering frantically, "Please, Everly. Please, don't do this."

Her glasses had cracked in the fall. Her palms were bloody as she held them up pleadingly.

My chest was hollow and cold. Something was scratching at the inside of my skull, pressing at the back of my eyes. A voice whispered in my head, harsh and demanding, "Kill her. Kill her. Kill her."

The knife in my hand caught the moonlight and glinted. I knew what I needed to do.

"Please, Everly!" Tears streamed down her face. "You need to remember. It's important, please, you need to remember."

I stood over her, tipping my head slowly to the side. Her blood would paint this forest. It would be my greatest work of art.

"Sybil knows the way," she whispered. She said it again. And again.

Her words grew faster. They ran together.

My ears were ringing. My lungs ached. The scratching in my skull wouldn't stop.

I needed it to stop.

I lifted the knife, and she didn't react. She just kept whispering.

"Your blood will feed this soil, Raelynn," I said. My voice didn't sound like my own.

She instantly fell silent. Her eyes were wide, and she was still as stone. Then, slowly, she opened her mouth. Wide. Too wide. Her jaw audibly popped out of place, and she screamed—

I jolted awake.

My sketchbook slipped off my lap, hitting the wood floor with a *thud*. Colored pencils rolled away from me across the desk, falling to the ground one by one before I could scramble to grab them.

"Shit—damn it!" I slammed my head on the desk as I tried to crawl underneath to grab them. For a moment, I sat there on the floor, rubbing my head and feeling sorry for myself.

It was late. The library would be closing any minute. Damn it, I must have been asleep for hours. With a heavy sigh, I collected my fallen items and crawled to my feet, before putting everything away into my bag.

The university library was quiet; the only sound was the rain as it streaked down the large stained-glass window over the entry doors. My head ached, but the memory of my nightmare was already fading. All that remained was that name.

Raelynn. Who the hell was Raelynn?

The semester wouldn't start for another couple of weeks, but I'd spent most of my summer here in the library regardless. I adored the dusty-vanilla scent of the books. I loved the hidden alcoves, vaulted ceiling, and muted light from the old sconces lining the walls.

It was my haven, my little taste of freedom; a glimpse into all the wonders of the world that lay waiting for me.

Waiting for me to get away.

I was on the library's second floor, overlooking the entryway below, surrounded by tall shelves and scattered desks. One of my pencils had rolled out of my reach, and

I narrowed my eyes as I extended my hand toward it. I envisioned it rolling toward me, back to the foot of my seat so I could pick it up.

It didn't even wiggle.

Trying to use magic was like stretching a stiff muscle, or writing with my left hand. It required intense focus, and even then, my control was weak at best.

Gritting my teeth, I curled my fingers as if to draw the pencil toward me.

The pencil flew from the floor, spearing through the air. It pierced into the wall behind me, barely missing my head as I ducked. Shit. I hurriedly yanked the pencil from the wall and winced when I saw the hole it left behind.

Hopefully, no one would notice.

It was late enough that I'd surely missed the last bus. I would need to jog back home in the dark. Most people around here would never dare go out alone after sunset, but I didn't mind it anymore. If I stayed on the road, I would likely be fine.

If I wasn't . . . there would be one final nightmare before it was all over.

A nearby footstep made me jump, but I sighed in relief when William Frawley rounded the bookshelves, a curious look on his bespectacled face. He was one of the librarians, and could usually be found sitting behind the crescent-shaped desk in the entryway, nose buried in a book.

"Are you okay?" he said. "I heard a noise."

"I bumped my knee," I said, wincing and rubbing the

appendage to give credit to my lie. "Sorry. Did I disturb anyone?"

"No one is left to disturb." He chuckled lightly, holding up his keyring. "I was just about to start locking up."

"Ah, damn it, I stayed late again. Sorry." With haste, I shoved the last of my things haphazardly into my bag. "I have a stack of books downstairs too, if it isn't too much trouble . . ."

"No trouble at all." His eyes fell on my drawing pad, and he picked it up before I could stuff it into my bag. I'd been sketching the stained-glass window, the colorful panes glowing with the light of the setting sun. "Is this what you've been working on up here?" I nodded, and his smile widened. "It's beautiful."

As I took the sketchbook from his hands, I said, "Mama used to talk about how much she wanted to paint it. She loved that window. How the sun shone through it, the colors. She always said it was like magic."

William's smile turned sheepish, and he rubbed the back of his neck. "I'm sorry, Ev. I didn't mean to . . ."

"It doesn't make me sad to bring up my mom," I assured him, smiling gently as I put the book into my bag. "It's been five years. It's okay."

Five years since she left this Earth. Five years since she vanished from my life. Five years alone.

It was okay, even though the writhing anxiety inside me said otherwise.

"I'll let you get back to locking up," I said, slinging my bag over my shoulder. "Can I use the self-checkout for my books?"

"Of course. Oh, uh—Everly?"

"Yeah?" I stopped at the top of the stairway. Will awkwardly coughed.

"Some friends and I are going to take the ferry to Seattle this weekend," he said, his voice cracking a bit. He cleared his throat. "We're going to a place called Unicorn Bar. Seems like somewhere you might like, so I . . . uh . . . was wondering . . ."

My stomach churned. I plastered an apologetic smile on my face. "I'm sorry, Will. I'm helping my dad at the Historical Society this weekend. I promised him." Shrugging helplessly, I added, "I hope you have fun though!"

"Don't be sorry, that's—that's totally okay. Yeah, of course. Thank you. Uh, I'll see you later!" He waved, his face bright red.

"See you!" I left him with a wave, making a hasty exit down the stairs. I kept up my smile until I was out of his sight.

I'd had plenty of experience putting on masks, fitting into whatever role was required of me. At twenty-three, I could lie more easily than tell the truth.

Will was kind. Sweet, polite. The kind of guy I would have liked to take a ferry ride to Seattle with.

But that wasn't possible. It wasn't *allowed*.

While most young adults my age were planning to move away from Abelaum and find better opportunities in Seattle or Tacoma, I'd made no such plans. I couldn't. Even if I started walking and never looked back, Abelaum would never release its hold on me.

My father, and his God, wouldn't let me go.

Mama had warned me. Her final words, scribbled on a note I found tucked beneath my pillow the morning her body was discovered, told me the truth she hadn't been able to utter in life.

I am the betrayer. I let Juniper go and shielded her from the demon's sight. This rot cannot be allowed to spread. Take back your power or the Deep One will consume all that you are and make you Its vessel. Sybil knows the way.

That was all she'd written. Like the ravings of a mad woman.

The nightmares started after she died. Her suicide, and the letter she left me, ripped my life apart and left me raw. No longer did I simply fear the suffering my father and his cult would inflict on others; now, I knew exactly how much suffering was intended for *me*.

The Deep One needed a vessel. Mama claimed the vessel would be me. My magic, no matter how wild and untrained, would provide the God with the power It needed when It eventually emerged from Its resting place.

There was no way in hell I would accept that fate. No matter what it took, no matter how much it hurt or how terrified I was, I would rather follow my mother to her grave than become a mindless meat puppet for an ancient deity.

Unfortunately, I had no idea who "Sybil" was, nor how to escape from the God. Her name haunted me, a ghost in my dreams. With every passing night, my nightmares grew more frequent, more vivid. Sometimes, I feared they weren't dreams at all.

They felt too real.

A sharp pain pierced into the back of my skull, like a needle jabbing my spine. Wincing, I squeezed my eyes shut, stumbling forward until I was able to grip the handrail along the stairs.

My palms were cold with sweat. My eyes moved rapidly behind my closed lids, twitching and rolling outside of my control.

Whispers surrounded me. Angry, imperceptible words sent shivers over my arms. A heavy presence loomed over me, filling me with terror.

It would pass. I just had to breathe, focus on the here and now. The smooth wood beneath my fingers, the pouring rain, the distant murmur of conversation and soft turning of pages. I had to remember where I was. Who I was. *Why* I was . . .

My phone vibrated in my pocket, snapping me out of the fog. My eyes flew open, a soft gasp bursting out of me. Rapidly blinking my eyes to get them back into focus, I noticed a text from Jeremiah.

Wrap it up. Me and the guys are bailing soon.

Crap. Dad must have told him I was on campus today. Being stuck in Jeremiah's cramped car with him and his friends was the last thing I wanted to do. Father had been out all day, and he kept my car keys locked in his office, so I'd jogged here earlier and planned to take the bus back home.

As I reached the carrels on the first floor and the stack

of books I'd left there, the back of my neck tingled yet again.

"Hi, Everly."

Marcus Kynes waved as he approached, a small and uncertain smile on his face. "You're here late. Need a ride?"

Marcus captained the university's soccer team now— the same team Jeremiah played for. The two of them had become close over the years. After Juniper was sent away to a psychiatric hospital, Jeremiah took the younger man under his wing.

Father wanted us to keep Marcus close. God wouldn't accept another failure.

Marcus would have been better off staying far away from our family. Still, I was grateful for the opportunity to avoid riding home with my brother.

"A ride would be great, thank you. I just need to check out my books."

OUR BREATH FORMED clouds in the cold night air as we walked from the library toward the student parking lot. Abelaum University was a relic hidden among the trees; an architectural beauty built when the mining town was first booming. Its Gothic towers reached as tall as the pines, its stone pathways carpeted in moss and its gray walls cloaked with ivy. When classes were in session, the windows lining its halls would glow in the night like beacons. But tonight, the multiple old buildings that made up the school were dark, save for the library behind us.

One day, despite everything, my studies would be my ticket out of here. Being a History Major wasn't typically viewed as a recipe for success, but I didn't care. Someday I would leave Abelaum, I would leave Washington; perhaps, I would even leave the country. The God's whispers in my head would disappear, the constant fear of pain and retribution would vanish.

I'd seek a job. I wanted to research ancient languages, surround myself with the beauty and horror of history. Humanity was shaped by our past; all of us were the latest manifestation of a long line of human choices.

Some of us were manifested by choices that were far more wicked than others.

"It was Juniper's birthday last week," Marcus said suddenly. "I wanted to call her, but I guess her number was disconnected after they let her out of the hospital."

We splashed through puddles as we walked, and I pulled up the hood of my jacket to defend against the rain.

And to hide my face from him.

"My mom never wants to talk about it either," he said when I gave no response. "No one does. Everyone just gets uncomfortable when I bring her up."

"I'm sorry, Marcus," I said slowly, but he shook his head.

"I get it. Especially after the accusations she made against your family. I shouldn't have brought it up." He sounded so sad. Confused. "I've just been missing her lately. I never really got to say good-bye before she left."

A familiar voice called out ahead of us. Marcus raised his hand in greeting at the three men walking toward us, and I stifled a groan.

"Look at you being a gentleman and protecting my sister, Marcus," Jeremiah teased as he and his friends—Sam and Nick—approached us. "Don't worry about her though. No one is going to try to kidnap this freak."

Marcus stopped walking to talk to them, but I didn't bother. I headed for the road, determined to walk regardless of the risk. But Jeremiah grabbed my arm as I tried to get past him, pulling me back.

"Hey, woah, don't rush off, *sis*." He said that term of endearment like it was an insult.

"Let go," I said. My fingertips tingled—a subtle warning that I might lose control. "I'm going home."

"I need you and Marcus to help me with something first," he said as Nick and Sam nodded in agreement.

"I can help you out," Marcus said. "No problem."

"Great." Jeremiah smiled; his eyes locked on me in warning. No one could ever call my half-brother *nice*, but there was something genuinely mean in his smile. Something that made me feel like I needed to run.

He tugged on my arm, pulling me close to him as he walked us back toward campus. "I told Coach Shelby I'd grab a couple boxes for him. He said they're in the second-floor storage room in Calgary Hall. Almost forgot to do it."

Sam laughed. He sounded high as a kite, whereas Nick had his hood up and his hands shoved into his pockets. I tried to pull my arm out of Jeremiah's grip, but instead of fighting with me, he put his arm around my shoulders. He dropped his voice, leaned close to my ear, and hissed, "Just do your duty, Everly."

Panic tightened like a vice around my lungs. My trembling hands were so hot, like fire was trying to burn its way out from under my skin.

I willed myself to calm down. I had to maintain control.

If I broke—if the prickling heat swelling in my chest was allowed to keep growing—I truly had no idea how much chaos I could unleash.

We ascended the steps into Calgary Hall. The interior was dark and cold, our footsteps echoing off the stone floors. The doors clicked shut behind us, cutting off the sounds of the crickets chirping and the breeze moving through the trees.

It was silent as a grave.

Jeremiah released my arm and placed his finger over his lips in warning. My world felt as if it were tipping on its axis as Nick handed Jeremiah a knife he pulled from beneath his jacket. Despite the dim light, everything around me was glowing, shimmering with a violet aura of magic.

My control was fragile. Like a balloon about to burst.

Jeremiah turned toward Marcus. My vision tunneled. Time slowed.

The Deep One's demands had to be met. Three souls had to be given. That was our duty. That was worship. It was *faith*.

But when Jeremiah lifted the knife, I screamed.

Everything happened too fast. Sam grabbed me, restraining me as Jeremiah and Nick grappled Marcus to the floor. Sam tried to cover my mouth, but I bit his hand, squeezing my teeth down until I tasted blood, and he struck the back of my head.

"Fucking Christ, you little psycho!" He kept hitting, and I kept struggling, unclenching my jaw only when the force of his blows made me dizzy.

"Jeremiah, stop!" My voice broke as it echoed off the walls. "Not like this, please, don't!"

He straddled Marcus as Nick pinned his arms above his head. Jeremiah cut the blade through Marcus's shirt, moving in a terrifying slow and methodical pattern as his victim yelled, his legs kicking uselessly.

His cries turned ragged with pain as Jeremiah carved the ritual marks into his chest. Jeremiah was giggling like a child with a new toy, his smile widening every time Marcus struggled, every time his cries of pain grew more desperate.

"You know what's funny, Kynes?" Jeremiah said, bringing his face close to the other man's and dragging the blade slowly across his cheek. "Your crazy sister was right. She was right about everything."

Heartbreaking realization made the pain melt from Marcus's face. He looked over at me, and I choked on a sob, an unanswered question lingering in his eyes.

Why?

Jeremiah raised the knife over his head and plunged it into Marcus's chest. Marcus made a small sound, the air knocked out of him. I struggled harder, flailing against Sam's hold until my shoe hit something slick, and I slipped, sending both of us to the ground.

The knife came down again.

Again.

Again.

I was going to break.

Blood seeped across the floor, staining the edge of my dress. Sam's breath smelled vile as it wafted in my face, his grip on my arms tight enough to bruise.

The heat inside me was rising, faster and faster. I didn't have control.

Flashes of purple and orange bloomed behind my eyelids as I squeezed my eyes shut tight. This wasn't happening. I wasn't here. I was somewhere else, somewhere quiet and safe. I couldn't watch this happen again, I couldn't do it, I couldn't, I *couldn't*—

The pressure, the unbearable heat, burst open inside me. For a moment, I was nothing: floating, flying, bodiless. As irreverently free as a gust of wind.

My eyes remained closed as a waft of cold air sent a shiver up my back. My cheek was lying against something prickly, and the scent of damp soil filled my nose.

I opened my eyes.

EVERLY

MY VISION SPUN as I lifted my head from the grass. Trees surrounded me, as did the thick, spiky tendrils of wild blackberry bushes. My clothes were soaked by the pouring rain, my limbs so cold they were numb. My bookbag had spilled open, and my sketchbook lay in the mud, swollen from the damp.

Quickly gathering my things, I climbed to my feet on wobbly legs.

I wasn't on the university campus anymore. The forest surrounded me, the shadows thick and impenetrable. Vague silhouettes loomed in the dark; whether they were trees or something else, I had no way to be sure.

Slowly, I turned around, and my breath caught in my throat.

A house stood before me, larger and grander than any I'd ever seen. Shrouded in darkness, it looked like something out of a fairy tale; a crooked castle that had made its home among the trees. Its three narrow towers stood as tall as the pines, the boughs of which were wrapped around the pale gray stones like a lover's embrace. The windows were dark and overhung with vines, and moss covered the walls. Thick roots protruded from the ground, framing the house's red entry doors with gnarled wood.

Braided thread covered the doors like a spider's web, and dozens of small talismans hung around the entryway. Made of woven twigs, string, and fishbone, they swayed in the breeze, rattling as they knocked together.

I'd seen such trinkets before, usually hung on the doors of Abelaum's superstitious old residents. They were meant to ward off the attention of the Deep One.

This couldn't be real. This had to be a dream, or a trauma-induced hallucination. I lifted my hand to rub my face but stopped. My trembling fingers were sticky with blood, and the front of my dress was stained with it.

Marcus's blood.

My eyes stung, and my throat swelled. Magic had a mind of its own, and mine rebelled like a feral beast. It tried to protect me in the only way it could—by spontaneously teleporting me away from the chaos. Right now, back in Calgary Hall, Marcus was dying, or already dead.

There was nothing I could do. No way I could stop it.

I wasn't supposed to *want* to stop it.

The wind changed, bringing the vile scent of putrefaction rushing in my nose. Nearly gagging, I clapped my hand over my mouth, turning to peer back into the shadowy forest. Amid the darkness of the swaying leaves, something stirred.

Something *big*.

A bone-white skeletal snout emerged from the undergrowth. Milky eyes stared at me, jagged teeth clipping sharply as the beast stepped forward. Its limbs were long and boney, with rotten gray flesh stretched over its misshapen, canid body. A twisted half-spider, half-wolf creature that carried the stench of death upon it.

It was one of the Eld. An ancient, warped species of beast that manifested in places that had endured great suffering and bloodshed. The God's magic had always drawn them here in terrifying numbers; in the night, the forest was theirs, and they would consume anyone foolish enough to step into their path.

Tonight, that fool was me.

The beast wasn't alone. More of them appeared in the darkness, teeth bared, thick, putrid saliva dripping from their jaws. With every step I backed away, they advanced. Their joints popped and crackled as they moved, hunching toward me. If there was ever a time for my magic to teleport me away, it was now.

The fire within me smoldered with fear, but all I managed was a few pathetic sparks.

The beasts lowered their heads. I was weak, vulnerable. Easy prey, with plenty of magic in me to feast upon.

With no choice left, I turned and ran toward the house.

Their grunting breaths were horrifically close on my heels as I sprinted through the overgrown grass. Leaping up the steps, I threw myself at the door, seizing it and throwing all my weight against it. But I swiftly jerked back in pain. Unseen barbs on the backside of the knob had sunk into my fingers, leaving behind tiny puncture wounds that blossomed with beads of blood.

With a burst of light, the lanterns hanging on either side of the red doors flared to life. Within seconds, every window was alight. There was a furious howl, and a flurry of branches snapping. When I glanced back toward the beasts, they had fled.

There was a long, slow creak, then light pooled around my feet.

The house was open.

MY FOOTSTEPS ECHOED off the marble floors as I entered the house. The doors shut behind me of their own volition with an audible click, as if a lock had slid into place. It was surprisingly warm. A large chandelier dangled overhead, suspiciously void of cobwebs. All its candles were lit, bathing the room in a soft glow.

A grand staircase was before me. The wooden steps led up to a landing, upon which sat a statue of a woman holding a dagger in her outstretched hand. The stairs split from there to the right and left, the walls along them covered with paintings in elaborate gilded frames. Clouds of dust poofed into the air as I walked, my head tipped back in wonder at the arched ceiling.

It smelled old; dust, damp, and mold permeated the air.

"Hello?" Only silence greeted me. *Someone* had to light all these candles, but it was so quiet. *Too* quiet. The tapping of the pouring rain sounded so far away.

Goose bumps prickled over my skin. There was a tingle in the air, subtle but distinct. Like the crackle of electricity before a lightning storm.

There was magic in this house.

Pulling my cell phone out of my bag, I groaned in despair when it wouldn't turn on. Completely waterlogged. What the hell was I supposed to do? The Eld would eat me alive if I went outside, but I had no idea what horrors awaited me in here. Father would be furious if I didn't make it home tonight. How could I ever manage to explain this to him?

At least the door was locked, offering me a little protection from the creatures outside. My jacket was drenched, so I peeled it off and slung it over my bag. Meandering around the room, I ran my finger along the surface of a table abutting the wall, leaving a long trail in the thick dust. It looked as if no one had been here for years.

The painting hanging above the table caught my attention. It portrayed six people dressed in black, their somber expressions staring at me. The blue-eyed gaze of a blonde woman in the center of the group drew me closer, and I brushed my fingers lightly against the old canvas to wipe away the dust. She looked so much like my mother; it was uncanny.

Along the bottom of the portrait, an elegant cursive script listed their names. It was difficult to read, and I traced my finger along the text as I tried to discern it.

Thomas Caroll, Rebeccah Anton, Grand Mistress Sybil Laverne—

My trembling finger froze in place. That surname was my mother's own maiden name, which meant Sybil . . .

Sybil was my ancestor. The one Mama had told me to seek out, the one who supposedly held the secret to my escape, was right here before my eyes. Or at least, the memory of her was. Looking to the very bottom of the portrait, I read the words that made my heart clench with both dread and wonder.

Laverne Coven and Family, 1902.

The words swirled in my head like leaves caught in a whirlpool. Grand Mistress . . . Sybil . . . Laverne Coven . . .

This was a house of witches, but not just any. This was my ancestor's house.

How could Mama never mention this to me? How could I have gone all these years never knowing of its existence?

"It's about time you got here."

Jerking back, I whirled around in shock. But no one was there. It must have been my frayed nerves getting to me, making me imagine things.

Pausing for a moment, I concentrated on the lack of weight at the back of my mind. The absence of pain, the voidwhere my anxiety usually lay. It was gone.

I couldn't feel the Deep One's presence here.

Approaching the stairway, I tried my weight on the first step. It creaked, but it felt solid. Despite being abandoned, the house was incredibly well-preserved.

"Is anyone there?" No one answered.

So up the stairs I went.

The halls above were long, with so many turns and locked doors I feared I'd become lost. I inspected every doorknob for more barbs and found none, but I did find several doors bound with rope. Thin black strands had been intricately knotted across their surface, just like the entry doors, in elaborate designs I couldn't make sense of.

It was some kind of old magic. There were runes and Latin inscriptions carved into some of the doorframes, but none of them gave me a good idea of what I was dealing with. It was such a big house; surely it would have been home to dozens of people.

Where had they all gone?

Tap, tap, tap.

A shiver shot up my spine. The sound was soft but distinct, like fingernails tapping on wood. Glancing over my shoulder, I surveyed the empty hallway. A clock ticked somewhere nearby, the old walls creaking in the wind.

The sound was gone.

The sheer size of this place made it impossible to know if anyone else was here, but perhaps I could find a room to rest in until morning. Once the sun had risen, it would be safer to wander out into the trees to find the road.

The thought of returning to my father made my stomach coil in terror. The aftershocks of this night wouldn't be small. I could only imagine the chaos my disappearance would cause, let alone the turmoil that would be unleashed when Marcus went missing too. Or when evidence of his murder was found . . .

"Tread carefully, my dear."

This time, I *knew* I hadn't imagined it. Whirling around, I searched frantically for the source of the voice. It had sounded so close, as if someone was standing right behind me.

"Who's there?" I called out, trying to make my voice sound fierce and bold.

The light was dim. Candle flames danced in the sconces along the walls, as if beset by a breeze. A strange smell, like wet stone, permeated the air.

Then the shadows moved.

They grew, stretching along the walls like long fingers reaching toward me. They bulged and swelled, darkness becoming appendages within a fluttering shroud.

Wisps of shadow and fog swirled to create a wraith-like form with a shimmering blade in one hand. I stared, at first not daring to move, hoping it couldn't see me. But beneath its cowl, silvery eyes locked onto me. Shriveled lips pulled back from blackened teeth, and the creature shrieked, flying toward me with the blade raised.

I turned and bolted, quickly becoming lost within the labyrinthian halls. Portraits glared down at me from every wall, my footsteps terrifyingly loud as I fled. I tried every door, but none of them opened. And despite running until my chest ached, the shrieking cries of the wraith followed me. More joined it; every time I glanced back, another wraith was flying with the pack, or crawling along the walls or ceiling.

Their bodies looked incorporeal; the blades in their hands certainly did not.

With sickening horror, I realized I was facing a dead end. But I couldn't stop. At the very end of the hall stood a large set of doors, wrapped in braided black rope. If those doors were locked, I would be dead.

Throwing myself against them, I grasped both knobs and shoved, glancing back frantically as the wraiths were almost on me—

The doors opened, and I fell inside, landing hard on the floor and knocking the breath out of my lungs. Scrambling forward, I barely made it out of the way before the doors slammed shut, leaving the monsters screaming furiously on the other side. They pounded against the door with so much force that the stone walls shook.

They wouldn't be held off forever. Surely, there was another way out of this room.

My mouth was tainted with the taste of iron, and I reached up to find my lip bleeding. I must have bitten it when I fell. But strangely, I couldn't just taste iron; I could smell it, too. Iron and coal, but also something sweet and pungent. Like the rich scent of a cigar.

As the wraiths screamed and clawed at the wood, I surveyed the room. Shelves stuffed with books lined one side, volumes stacked in piles on the floor. Potted plants, vibrantly green with life, hung from the ceiling and were wedged into every available space between the shelves. Large arched windows occupied the wall directly in front of me, but they were shrouded with heavy curtains. The

light was faint, emanating from smoldering embers in a
fireplace to my left. Beside the fire sat a small table with a
gramophone on top.

To my alarm, the gramophone was playing. The record's crackling jazz melody filled the room; a strange
juxtaposition to the cries of the monsters outside.

Narrowing my eyes, I tipped my head curiously as
I examined the stone floor. There were markings: two
circles, one inside the other, with runes etched between
them.

As the wraiths' shrieking grew more furious and my
eyes followed the strange language beneath my feet, a
cold sense of realization settled over me. I knew what
these markings were. Although I couldn't read them, I
knew what they were used for.

It was a summoning circle. Made to call and contain
a demon.

But if there was a summoning circle, then . . .

My eyes drifted to the far side of the room, to the
shadows beneath the window, and I barely held back a
scream. There, lying upon a massive bed covered in red
velvet, was a man.

He had one leg propped up and the other extended
out, his head resting limply upon one folded arm. His
eyes were closed.

Was he asleep . . . or dead?

Daring to take a few steps closer, I was able to get
a better look at him. His body was long and lean, his
chest bare. He had an angular face, unnaturally poreless
and pale, as if he'd been carved from marble. His dark

hair curled around his ears, just long enough to brush the curve of his neck. It looked soft, like it would slip through my fingers like silk. His feet were bare, and thick black claws curled from his toes. His fingers were clawed, too, lying limp against the soft velvet and leather blankets.

Then I realized it wasn't leather at all. The "leather" was bat-like wings, splayed out across the bed. The thin gray membranes were marbled with black veins, with tiny spines along the top.

This wasn't a human. This was a demon. But he wasn't an ordinary one, no. Mama had told me his kind existed: ancient demons with massive wings and immense strength, royalty among their own species.

He was an Archdemon.

Father used to talk about wanting to summon one, insisting he needed to replace disobedient Leon—who had served the Hadleigh family for nearly a century. But Mama had quickly put a stop to that, and for once, he listened to her. She had said, *You don't summon an Archdemon. You call them. And depending on how unlucky you are, one might show up.*

Maybe facing the wraiths in the hall wasn't so bad after all.

But the demon didn't stir. Not so much as a twitch, or even a single breath.

The wraiths were beginning to cause significant damage to the door. The wood was audibly cracking, the metallic *thunk* of their blades striking the door again and again. There was no other way out; no door, no stairway, no hatch in the floor. Perhaps I could try the window, but that would require climbing on the bed and potentially disturbing the creature lying there.

I was trapped in here—stuck between monsters.

Crack!

The door was splintering. At least a dozen pairs of silvery eyes stared at me through the crack, their shrieks and cries like the howling of wild dogs. Vicious hands clawed for me as they tried to squeeze through—pushing, piling on top of each other, howling ravenously.

As the door fractured and the wraiths poured in, a dark form flew over my head. I was wrenched backward by a hard grip on my shoulder, and I landed on the bed. There was a flurry, like the beating of wings, and what remained of the doors burst outward in a massive explosion that sent the wraiths flying back. The sounds coming from the mass of smoke and shadow were unlike anything I'd ever heard: disturbingly beast-like but terrifyingly human. There was a metallic screeching, like sheets of iron being torn apart.

All the noise abruptly stopped. Dust swirled and settled in the darkness, like milk drifting through coffee. The wraiths were gone—destroyed or vanished, I couldn't be sure.

Only a single tall figure remained. He peered at me over one outstretched wing, fixing me with a gaze that snatched the air out of my lungs.

His eyes were black. Solid black, like the deepest voids of outer space, sprinkled with tiny pinpricks of silver stars.

For a moment, nothing moved except the slowly drifting dust.

Then the demon grinned, baring a mouthful of sharp glistening teeth. He lifted his hand; my eyes tracked it as if it were a weapon he could throw at me.

"Don't run," he said.

The deep baritone of his words rumbled in my chest. My heart was pounding erratically, fluttering like a hummingbird's wings. Frozen on the bed, I didn't move a muscle other than to rapidly blink.

The demon was still smiling wide and excited. His chest was heaving as he sniffed the air, tipping his chin up like a dog on the trail of a scent. His eyes rounded, and his claws scratched on the floor as he turned toward me.

He took a single step, and I leapt up from the bed. My sudden movement made him dart forward, faster than my eyes could follow. He stopped, crouched just inside the broken doorway, panting, as he stared at me.

"I'm warning you, Everly," he said, the words spoken from between tightly clenched teeth. "Do. Not. Run."

There was so much pressure in the air, like I'd sunk to the bottom of a deep pool. Not daring to look away from the demon, I made quick, frantic glances toward my only exit.

"How do you know my name?" I whispered, almost too terrified to speak.

The demon's expression shifted from rapid excitement to irritated confusion.

"Who else would you be?" he said. He rocked slightly on his heels, still crouched. It took me a moment to

realize he was dancing, swaying to the beat of the gramophone. "Everly. Dear, sweet Everly." He spoke as if he
was savoring the words, consuming them, luxuriating in
the sounds. "So . . . very . . . sweet." His teeth parted, a
forked tongue flicking out to swipe hungrily over his lips.
"The very last Laverne witch alive. Only you . . . *only
you* could be here, in this house. You see?"

He spread his arms, as if he'd explained everything.
But I didn't see. I didn't understand at all, and I shuffled
another inch toward the door.

The demon lowered his head, his eyes fixed on me as
he rose slowly to his full height. I was a tall woman, five
foot eight inches without shoes. But he towered over me.
His presence expanded beyond his physical form.

"I'm going to leave," I declared firmly. My mind was
churning chaotically, running through every iteration of
how this scenario could play out. Unless one commanded
very powerful magic, there was no outrunning a demon.
No hiding. No fighting back. But an Archdemon . . . I'd
never seen one before. I'd never even dared to think it
was possible to encounter one.

He shook his head. He was still swaying to the music,
eyes half-closed.

"Mm . . . no. No, I think not." His eyes were fully
closed now, his head tipped back. His fingers moved,
twiddling in the air, as if flying over invisible piano keys.
Moving as slowly and silently as I could, I kept inching
toward the doorway.

Where could I go? Where could I possibly hide?

"Sweet as sugar," he mumbled, though only fragments

of his words reached my ears. "Holy ambrosia . . . so fucking soft . . ."

Finally reaching the doorway, I was closer to him than ever. Trying to keep my eyes on him, while simultaneously watching for any debris I could step on, proved impossible. With one quick step, I sent a splintered shard of wood skittering across the floor.

The demon opened his eyes.

"Drenched in blood," he said softly. Like it was a prayer. "You're too beautiful. It's a sin. A curse. It's fucking poison." He inhaled sharply, deeply, such a massive breath it seemed physically impossible. "Dangerous woman, aren't you?"

His grin returned as I kept backing away. It was wicked. Playful. Like a cat about to pounce on an injured bird. His constant movements were unnerving, but it was far more frightening when suddenly, he went perfectly still.

"I think you should run now, Everly," he said. "Run for your fucking life."

CALLUM

BEAUTIFUL, WICKED, BLOODY woman. Sweet and savory, blood and honey, coating my tongue and making my brain sticky, thick, and dumb.

It had been so long. So goddamn long locked up in this room. No stimulation, no pleasure, no indulgence.

Demons do not merely desire things. We ravenously, violently, relentlessly need. We are wretched, gluttonous, selfish creatures, filled with such a desire to consume that it can destroy us if we ignore it. To survive, a demon must indulge.

And it had been so long since I indulged.

Yet there she was at last. My feast, my bounty. Tender, honeyed flesh.

Just a taste. A little taste. A touch. One little touch of that perfect warm skin, so drenched in magic it made me dizzy. That was all I needed.

Her terror hung heavy in the air like a rich perfume. Her heartbeat was music to my ears. Her blue eyes, so bright, so clever, flickered this way and that like a curious little fox. She was tall and willowy, with blonde hair so long it brushed against her lower back. Her boots were muddy, her dress bloodstained.

Oh, how easy it would be to catch her. But *easy* wasn't satisfying. A game ended too quickly was no game at all.

She was thinking, weighing her risks, mulling over my words; a thousand solutions with a million problems rushing through that beautiful head. Blood pumping, heart pounding. Her pulse was a drumbeat I never wanted to end. Every throb of that frantic little organ made my need worse.

"Run, Everly," I whispered, and she flinched. "Go on. Run, little witch."

Thump, thump, thump. Faster and faster went her heart. It was goddamn intoxicating. I jerked forward, and she stumbled back several steps. I couldn't hold back much longer.

"Run away, run away. Don't let me get my hands on you . . ." Laughing at the increasingly horrified expression on her face, I lifted both my hands and twiddled my fingers at her before covering my eyes with my palms. It was a silly gesture. Insignificant. I knew exactly where she was. "Ten. Nine. Eight . . ."

She sprinted. The sound of her rapid footsteps was like a fist pounding straight into my heart, demanding I go, chase, *catch.*

"Five, four, three . . ." I stretched my wings, shuddering from head to toe. It was too good, too fucking good. "Two, aaand . . ."

I opened my eyes and watched a flash of her blonde hair disappear around the corner as my veins turned black as ink. My physical form lost some of its solidity, my energy swelling, as all my focus narrowed onto one thing: the sweet smell of her magic as she fled from me.

Demons become a little unhinged if we sleep for too long. It must have been at least a couple decades I was in there, lounging the time away. Waiting. Watching. Fighting through the agony of every craving.

But there was no need to restrain myself anymore. I didn't want to hurt her, but . . .

But I did. Just a little. Just enough to break open that beautiful magical mind.

"One," I said and teleported down the hall, manifesting myself again directly in front of her. She skidded to a halt, nearly colliding with me. But she leapt around me, caught herself against the wall, and kept sprinting, leaving a burst of sparks in her wake.

"That's it, girl! *Fucking run!*" I beat my wings, launching myself after her. My feet barely touched the ground; I leapt from wall to wall, claws rending deeply into the wood wainscoting.

When I teleported in front of her again, she lost her footing and stumbled to the floor, and immediately scrambled up in the opposite direction.

"Fight back!" My volume was too loud, a crack

splintering through a nearby window. "Come on, Everly, hurt me!"

Just a little pain. Just a little blood. I needed stimulation before I completely lost my mind. So, I changed my tactic. I stopped chasing and started stalking.

She ran until she was dizzied. Her blood sugar was low, her entire body trembling as she continued stumbling through the halls.

"Don't be shy," I crooned, making my voice drift through the air and echo around her. She had no idea where I was. How far, or how close. But I was close enough to touch: crawling along on the ceiling behind her, like a great lizard, head tipped back as I watched her. "I like magic tricks, witch, so give me a good one."

"Get away from me!" she cried, turning in a complete circle. I was directly above her, shrouding myself in shadow. "I'm warning you . . . if you hurt me . . ."

"Oh, yes, please threaten me." Anger coated her voice, and it made me giddy. I wanted to draw it out, one perfect thread in the web of her fear. "Will I be in trouble? Hm? What will you do to me?"

She ran again, and I *tsk*ed, flying after her. "Don't tease! If you're going to threaten me, do it properly!"

She'd run all the way to the fourth floor, as if the primal knowledge in her brain knew exactly where she needed to go. She was gasping for breath, stumbling every few steps and doubling over. Striding up behind her, I shook my head when she glanced back and cried out in panic.

"Where's your fire, witch?" She'd reached another

dead end, and turned to face me with her back pressed against the locked doors. "Come now, make it big and bold. Try to burn the house down! It will survive, trust me. It's seen far worse than you."

She shook her head. "I don't know what you think I am. But you're wrong. I'm not . . . I'm not . . ."

Tweaking an eyebrow, I stepped closer than ever. Oh, to simply brush my fingers across her cheek. To lean down and breathe in the soft scent of her. To caress my lips across her delicate throat. Would she scream? Would she burn? Would that stunningly vibrant hoard of magic within her finally explode?

"I have no interest in what you're *not*." I crouched, resting my forearms on my thighs as I stared up at her. It was truly impossible to look away. She was as alluring as a comet in the night sky, or a flickering candle in the dark. "Tell me what you *are*. Tell me what burns in your soul, what puts that vicious fire in your veins. Tell me why you run when you know you can't escape."

Her heaving breaths were slowing, her fear becoming cautious curiosity.

"Who the hell are you?" she whispered.

Naughty girl, avoiding my questions. But that train of thought gave me visions of blissfully torturing her words out of her, and that just wouldn't do. I'd swiftly drive myself completely feral if I continued meandering through fantasies.

"My name is Callum," I said. "Archdemon. Elder Warrior of the Onyx Stone Order, Defender of the High City, Prince of the Nine Circles, and guardian of House

Laverne. I've also been called *Magni Deicide*, but that was many centuries ago."

Her face paled, and she said, "*Magni Deicide* . . . the Great God Slayer."

"That is correct. You know your Latin."

She gulped, her eyes flickering about as she looked for another exit. But she was exactly where she needed to be.

"Put a little more force into that door, witchling," I said, nodding toward the locked door behind her. "This house has been empty for years now. The magic which fills this place has fallen stagnant, as magic often does when it isn't used. Stagnant magic can be dangerous. Like the wraiths, for example. The spell that created them was meant to protect the house from intruders, but recognize those who had a right to be here and cause them no harm. Unfortunately, left untended, the spells have gotten rather twisted. But flex your authority a bit, and they'll start to behave."

She stared at me in disbelief. "Did you say *my authority*?"

"Certainly. That's why you're here, isn't it? Come to scope out the family lands, see if the roof has caved in? It hasn't, of course. I've made sure of that." I puffed up a bit, even though maintaining the house wasn't *entirely* my doing. It was a team effort, but my dear, beautiful Everly didn't need to hear that. She needed to be assured of my utmost and unflagging devotion to the protection of this place and everything inside it.

Including her.

Especially her.

Perhaps I'd muddied the waters a bit with my severe lack of self-control, but could I be blamed? When she smelled so fucking good, when she was running around this house like a beacon of sweet magic? I was only a demon, royal or not, and we had needs.

Very increasingly desperate needs.

"I don't know why I'm here," she said fiercely. It gave me shivers, those little glimpses of her fury. "I don't fucking know. I . . . Oh . . . oh my god . . ."

Her eyes widened, her gaze fixed somewhere behind me. I hadn't heard anything creep up, nor could I smell anything other than her intoxicating scent, but still, I glanced back.

I was losing my predatory touch. There was nothing at all in the hallway behind me, but Everly took the opportunity to try to escape again, sprinting away.

"Oh! Naughty, naughty witchling." She shrieked when I teleported in front of her again, waggling my finger at her. "It has been a thrilling game indeed, but I must insist you stop. Your blood sugar is incredibly low, and as much as I would adore to keep chasing you, if you go on further, you might cause yourself harm." I sighed as she backed away again, all shaking hands and adrenaline-induced poor decision making. "If I may . . . show you to bed?"

There was no point in waiting for her acquiescence. Fear caused one to not think clearly, and although I certainly wasn't in my right mind either, I took my duty seriously.

I'd once heard a human say that if they needed to

rip off a Band-Aid, they needed to make it quick. It lessened the pain, or so I guessed. While I couldn't entirely understand why one would desire *less* pain—lovely and stimulating as it was—I supposed the tactic would work well for frightening situations too. Just rip through it. Get it done.

Before she could run again, I snatched her up into my arms. With a flick of my fingers, I opened the door she'd been trying so desperately to get into, launched myself toward the large four-poster bed, and tossed her down upon the mattress.

It was over in a matter of seconds. Just enough time for her to draw in a breath and *scream*.

And by Lucifer's desecrated balls, her scream burned. A firestorm roared out of her, flaring toward me with a massive burst of heat. It was quick, gone in an instant, but I was left staring in awe.

"Don't touch me!" She scrambled up on the bed, pressing herself to the headboard. Her shaking hands were outstretched, palms facing me. "Don't . . . don't you fucking dare touch me again."

Holding up my hands, I gave her a petulant grin. "Terribly sorry, Lady Witch. You should punish me for it. I deserve it, I really do. It's been so long, you see, since I've seen a human. Since I've seen . . . anything . . . alive. Since I've touched . . ." I waited, fully intending to revel in whatever infliction of pain she deigned me worthy of, but it didn't come. Strange.

"Get away from me," she said, lowering her hands and knotting them in the blankets. "Get out. Go."

I didn't move a muscle. Why wasn't she using her magic? She was practically bursting at the seams; without doubt one of the most powerful witches I'd ever encountered. But she was holding back, despite her fear of me.

It made no sense.

"You can do better than that," I said, slowly stalking forward. With every step, her breath came faster. Her fingers curled, digging into the blankets, her jaw clenched so hard a muscle twitched in her cheek. Reaching the edge of the bed, I spread my arms and grasped the tall wooden posts on either side. Her expression was guarded, but she couldn't hide how curious she was as she observed me.

Still, she didn't lash out at me. No magic, no punishment, no pain.

Climbing onto the mattress, I crawled toward her. She watched my movements with growing horror. Her breath shuddered, her eyes darting like a cornered rabbit.

But she was no rabbit, no helpless frightened creature. She was a witch, in possession of such a wealth of power that her energy was like a bonfire compared to everything around her. She glowed; her presence made the air itself vibrate.

When I was close enough to touch her, I sat back on my heels. She'd drawn her legs up, curled against her chest, watching me cautiously. But I was mesmerized by the cupid's bow of her lips, the pink flush on her cheeks, the graceful curve of her neck.

Her scent filled my head as I inhaled. Her magic smelled sugary sweet; it reminded me of springtime in the wilds of Hell. Like damp grass crushed underfoot, young berries drizzled in sap, freshly plucked herbs. It was a scent of comfort, impossible to resist, drawing me nearer like a caress until I was leaning toward her, so close our breath mingled.

Her blue eyes were wide, glittering as she peered up at me. The tension went out of her arms, although her expression remained suspicious, but she watched me differently now. As if she was trying to solve an impossible riddle, or trying to remember something important.

"If you can't reach your magic, a slap will do just as well," I said. Anything, if it meant she would willingly touch me. But she shook her head, slowly at first, then quickly.

"I don't want to hurt you," she said. Dazed, she lifted her hand toward my face. Her long fingers spread, delicate and thin, as they hovered over my skin.

Her hand brushed against my cheek, and an electric current flowed through me. She was *stunning*. Her power was a thousand suns trapped inside her, and when it encountered my own, it flared to life. She exhaled, a sigh so heavy she might have been holding it for a century. Sparks glittered in her breath; heat flooded through her.

She was no dragon, no fire-breathing monster. She was a phoenix, as graceful as the dawn, as soft as she was clever, as gentle as she was determined.

I had waited two thousand years for that touch.

"You're shaking," she said softly. But I was only trying to stay calm, to prevent myself from going feral again and frightening her even more.

I'd spent centuries waiting for a glimpse of her. If I

stared into her eyes much longer, I'd lose myself. I turned my gaze away, staring instead at her raised arm, her hand still tucked so delicately against my face.

Then my eyes narrowed, and she jerked away. But on her upper arm were five stark bruises, pale purple imprints dug into her bicep. Like a hand, as if someone had grabbed her so hard it hurt.

The edges of my vision went blurry.

"Who hurt you?" I hissed. She was trying to edge back from me again but had nowhere to go. She grasped her arm, her palm swiftly covering the bruises, but the sight of them was burned into my mind. Crowding her, arms braced on either side so she couldn't slip away from me, I insisted, "Who fucking hurt you? Give me their name."

"It was just a boy—"

"Give me *their name*, Everly."

"Sam," she blurted. "Sam Hawthorne." Her eyes widened, as if she regretted speaking at all.

Leaping off the bed, I gave her one last fond look before bidding farewell. "Very good, my lady. That's all I needed to know. So long as you stay in this room, you will be perfectly safe until my return. Don't worry." I nodded my head toward the low table in front of the fireplace and the cloche-covered platter on top of it. "The house will provide."

Then, before my rage overtook me entirely, I teleported away.

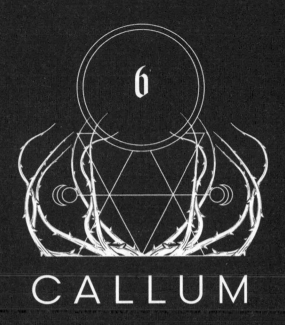

CALLUM

THE SMELLS OF the forest greeted me as I flew from the house. Lightning flashed in the ominous clouds, the air crackling with energy. Cold rain pelted my face and streaked down my wings, but I kept rising, higher and higher through the clouds until I burst above.

The sky was soft as velvet and twinkling, the stars like diamonds catching the light of the full moon.

How fitting, that the night of my release would coincide with the peak of the moon's beauty.

I plummeted into a freefall, streaking through the clouds, through the rain, and over the vast expanse of ancient trees. When I first came to Abelaum, twenty years ago, I hadn't spent much time exploring the town. Now, after two decades of growth and change, the place was nearly unrecognizable to me. But I didn't need recognition to find my way around. Scent and instinct were more than enough to guide me.

Everly's scent led me to a house at the edge of town; a sprawling, metal-and-glass monstrosity of modern engineering, sitting there like a heap of trash carelessly abandoned in the woodlands. Perched in the trees outside, I observed the dark house until sunrise. There were four humans inside, and one demon. But he was young, barely older than a youth. It was easy to hide my presence from him.

One of the humans—Everly's father, I guessed—carried magical trinkets. A protective talisman and a book of spells, a grimoire. But he was not a witch; magic didn't course through him, only the items he carried.

He was the one Everly's grandmother had warned me about. Kent Hadleigh. Leader of the Libiri, a human who absolutely dripped with hubris. It'd be a joy to slaughter him.

But Kent's fate was interwoven with countless others. Killing him would have a severe effect on the balance of the world, which wouldn't please Hell's Council in the least. It would get their attention, and that was the last thing I wanted.

If they found me, they'd take me away from Everly. Lucifer would be petty and claim it was for my own good, but he'd been blind to reality for centuries. He believed that as long as the Gods were out of Hell, demonkind was safe from them. But Gods don't simply cease Their endless hunt for power after one defeat; it isn't in Their nature. They were just as much a threat on Earth as They were when They were in Hell.

Lucifer had been furious when I left Hell to hunt down the Gods that had fled. The war was won; why did I insist on continuing to fight? But in my mind, the battle was far from over. I spent centuries tracking the fallen Gods to all reaches of the Earth so I could destroy them. Most of the Gods I encountered were weak. They sequestered themselves in Earth's forgotten places: underground, or deep in the ocean, or high in the tallest mountains. They were barely able to defend themselves when I eventually ended Their miserable existences.

But this God in Abelaum was different.

Fed by a steady stream of human worship and suffering, the God who hid deep within Abelaum's old mines was powerful. Not powerful enough to emerge from hiding, at least not yet.

I couldn't allow It to get to that point.

But I also couldn't fight a creature like that alone. I needed the strength of another; I needed the kind of magic only a witch could wield.

The man I sought wasn't within the house, so I took flight again. Soaring through the rain, I continuously sniffed the air, searching for the subtle foreign scent I'd noticed on Everly's clothes.

Whoever had bled upon her wasn't the one who'd harmed her; I found that boy in a nearby building, dead in a pool of his own blood. Had Everly killed him? She didn't seem vicious enough, but I refused to underestimate her.

As the sun rose higher behind the clouds and the town awakened, I was accosted by a flood of sounds and smells. Humans were everywhere; filling the streets and shops, speeding down the winding roads in their automobiles. Stinking, laughing, sweating, yelling masses, rushing through their short lives, hurtling toward their inevitable deaths.

Where the fuck was Sam Hawthorne? My rage was knotted up like a swelling tumor. I needed a release, an outlet for my violence.

"Patience, old boy," I muttered. Flaring my wings to slow my speed, I came to perch on the steepled roof of a clocktower and shrouded myself in shadow to keep hidden. Looking down upon Abelaum's streets, I watched the humans scurry through the rain, hiding beneath their coats and splashing through puddles.

Then, the wind changed and I caught his scent. The man whose hands had left bruises on *my* witch's flesh, who'd dared to touch her roughly, who'd dared to touch her *at all*.

He and his friends were drinking in the parking lot outside a nearby liquor store. Reeking of beer and cigarettes, blood and sweat. Soon, the group parted ways. Two of them returned to an automobile, but Sam departed on foot.

He stumbled down the sidewalk toward the lake. The rain was pouring heavily now, so most other humans had retreated indoors. Sam hummed to himself, singing some obscene song. Every vile word that dropped from his mouth fed directly into my predatory instinct. I could smell his blood, his sweat, the stench of his breath. When I unfurled my wings behind him, the breeze must have tipped him off because he paused.

He turned, but it was already too late to scream. My hand clamped over his mouth, muffling his scream as I pressed my claws into his eyes. I lifted him and flew toward the thick, dark expanse of the trees.

He was still screaming when I dumped him to the ground, thrashing in the dirt.

"What the fuck!" he screamed, hands shaking as he reached for his bleeding face. "Fuck . . . fuck . . . What the fuck—"

"No one can hear you," I said, and he froze at the sound of my voice, panting as he turned his head toward me despite being unable to see. "No one will ever hear you again, Sam."

"What the fuck is this, man?" Snot ran down his face, and my lip curled in disgust. "What the hell do you want—is it money? You want money?" He fumbled for his pocket, but I caught his hand, holding his wrist as he cried out and uselessly tried to tug it back.

"Do you know Everly?"

His fingers clenched and shook.

"Everly? Uh . . . yeah . . . yeah! Everly Hadleigh! We're friends, we're— I mean—"

I laughed as he tripped over his words. "Are you sure that's the right answer, Sam? You and Everly are *friends*?"

Wheezing, panting, he frantically whimpered, "How do you know my name? How do you know Everly? Are you her boyfriend or something? Honest to God, man, I thought she wasn't allowed to date. I never meant any of the jokes I made about fucking her, I swear!"

"*Fucking* her?" I crouched, still holding his wrist, bringing it into alignment with my mouth. "Have you *thought* about fucking her, Sam?"

"Come on, man . . . come on, it's— It's not serious, okay—"

He broke off into a ragged scream as I bit off his finger. I'd been undecided between starting with his thumb or his pinkie, but the thumb had such a satisfying crunch. I spat out his blood and the appendage with it, but the taste of it still lingered in my mouth. My excitement doubled as he struggled against me.

"Stop! Stop, please, I'll do whatever you want— I'll— Please—"

"Aw, come now, Sammy, it's just a *finger*," I scolded. "It's not even that bad. It's nothing compared to the whole hand."

I sunk my teeth into his wrist, savoring his cries as I bit through muscle and bone. His screaming was drawing the beasts of the forest; I could see their milky-white eyes in the shadows, their sharp teeth clipping together with hunger. They didn't come out during the day, but Sam's moans of agony were too good to resist.

They didn't dare approach any closer while I was here.

"Now, there's a lesson in this," I said calmly, smacking the palm of his severed hand against his cheek as he shook, still shrieking indiscriminately. "The lesson is that you don't touch what's not yours. Everly is mine. *Mine*." I snapped my teeth near his face, eliciting a sob that made me absolutely giddy.

"Please let me go. Please, I'll never go near her again, I swear."

I got to my feet and tossed his hand away into the underbrush. Within seconds came snarling yips, the excited snapping of teeth as the beasts savored their little snack. Sam's head bobbed about when he heard them, but his ruined eyes wouldn't show him the horrors lurking nearby.

"You can go," I said. "In fact, you should run. Run as fast as you possibly can."

He shoved himself up and clutched his opposite arm. "I'm— I can't see— How can I—"

I wished he could have seen me pout at him, but I'm sure he heard the vitriol in my voice. "Such a poor, helpless thing. How will you ever find your way in the dark?" I chuckled as I circled him, watching his head jerk right and left as he attempted to follow my position. "But it doesn't matter where you run. It only matters that you do. You won't reach home, but you can at least give me a little entertainment."

He ran, or tried to. He stumbled into the trees, gasping, screaming for help, arms outstretched. I thought it was rather nice of me to give him a whole thirty second head start, but I couldn't let him get *too* far away from me. After all, I wasn't the only creature in this forest who wanted to kill him.

But I was the one who did.

EVERLY

THE MORNING BROUGHT thick gray clouds and pouring rain. My feeble hopes of walking out into the woods and finding my way to a road were dashed. With no GPS, not even a compass, it was nearly impossible for me to find my way to another shelter before nightfall.

For another day, at least, I was stuck here. Truthfully, the idea didn't bother me. In fact, I found myself hoping the storm would get worse, that it would keep raining until everything was flooded and I couldn't leave at all.

Despite my terror the previous night, I slept well. The big bed, upon which the demon had unceremoniously tossed me, was more comfortable than any mattress I'd ever owned. The bedroom was large, with several pieces of intricately carved wooden furniture: a low table in front of the fireplace, a wardrobe beside the door, two bookshelves in the corner.

There was a bathroom connected to the bedroom, with a big clawfoot tub in front of a floor-to-ceiling bay window. Potted plants filled the room and the bedroom too. The toilet was old, but at least it worked.

After sleeping in my dirty clothes, I desperately needed a bath to feel human again. But the tub was strange, unlike anything I'd seen before. Instead of a single faucet with a knob for hot or cold water, there were six faucets and more knobs than any bathtub had a right to have. Half expecting it not to work at all, I chose a knob and cranked it.

There was a bang, and the pipes gave a massive groan. Warm, floral-scented water poured from the spout. The next knob smelled like baking cookies; the next poured water filled with pink bubbles. It took me a few minutes of fiddling before I managed to get normal hot water to fill the tub.

An exhausted sigh escaped me as I sunk into the steaming water. Closing my eyes, I let my limbs float freely for a few minutes before I scrubbed away the filth on my skin. The dirt and blood drifted away into the water and vanished, leaving it as clean as when I'd first got in.

Even the water was enchanted.

Why had Mama kept this place secret from me? She'd never spoken of any relatives, except for my grandmother, Winona, whom I'd met only a couple of times as a child.

All I ever knew about her was she was a witch and a diviner; she could see glimpses of the future.

She died several years before Mama did. There was no funeral, or if there was, Mama and I didn't attend.

Even the warm water of the bath couldn't chase away the chill that settled over me. I felt like a boat lost at sea, tossed by the storm, unable to anchor. All I could do was try to stay afloat, try to survive until I could find my way again.

Climbing from the bath, I rummaged through the cabinets until I found a stack of towels. To my complete amazement, they were soft and smelled clean, as if they'd been recently laundered. Wrapping one around myself, I left my dirty clothes in a pile on the floor and went to look in the wardrobe.

Most of the clothes were covered in lace and satin, with bodices designed to lace tightly up the back, as if they'd come straight out of the 1890s. After scrounging around in the drawers, I managed to find a loose white blouse and some high-waisted trousers that were slightly too short for me. Just like the towels, the clothes smelled fresh and clean.

For now, I didn't dare to leave the room. The demon had said I would be safe here until his return. But I couldn't guess when he would be back, and my stomach was rumbling with hunger.

If the demon wanted to kill me, he could have done so last night. Although I didn't trust him, I was certain he didn't intend to cause me harm. He seemed more *playful* than violent. As ridiculous as it sounded, he reminded me of a massive dog who didn't know his own strength. Desperate to play, longing for affection, too excited to sit still.

"You're losing it, Ev." I said as I pulled back the curtains from the windows. The gray, watery day greeted me, and looked down upon a large garden, surrounded by hedges and filled with flowering plants.

It was ridiculous to think of the demon as anything other than what he was: a preternatural predator who would gladly claim my soul and bind me to him for eternity. But I couldn't forget the way he'd looked at me. Wild with need, with desperation, with . . . longing? How he'd trembled when I touched him, a powerful monster quivering like a lamb just from a brush of my fingers. It gave me a strange feeling in my stomach; warm and nervous, but not unpleasant.

I had to be cautious.

With the issue of clothing solved, I turned my attention to figuring out how to get food. There was a bag of old almonds in the bottom of my purse, and after a few cautious sips, I determined the water from the bathroom tap was clean enough to drink. What I really wanted was a mimosa, and a big omelet full of cheese and veggies, but stale nuts and cold water would have to do.

When I returned to the bedroom, something had changed. There on the low table, next to the covered silver platter, was a goblet . . . full of orange juice? Frowning, I picked up the glass and sniffed it, shocked to find it was cold.

"No way . . ." Slowly, I took a minuscule sip. "Oh my god."

It was a mimosa. A fresh, bubbling, sweet-and-sour *mimosa*. Disbelieving, I turned my attention to the elegant silver lid on the platter and realized a tiny stream of steam was seeping from beneath it. Grasping the handle, I lifted it away to reveal a hot omelet, smothered in cheese and stuffed with vegetables, alongside two sausages and a bowl of fresh fruit.

For a moment, all I could do was stare. Then I laughed, although I couldn't be sure if this was truly funny, or if my brain was simply cracking. I'd never witnessed magic that could make food spontaneously appear based simply on one's thoughts.

It was delicious too. Perfectly seasoned, the vegetables buttery and crisp, the eggs soft and creamy. The fruit was so sweet it was like candy, and when I drained my glass, I watched it fill again before my eyes.

Okay, yeah, screw going home.

The champagne eased my nerves, and I settled more comfortably into the cushioned chair near the fire. There was no clock in the bedroom, so I couldn't be sure what time it was, but I guessed it was early evening by the changing light.

Surely, the demon would return soon.

Suddenly, there came a sound right outside the door. My back went stiff as the knob slowly turned. Just in case one of those nasty wraiths had figured out how to properly open a door, I grabbed the poker from beside the fireplace and held it aloft, prepared to strike if necessary.

The door swung open, and my shoulders slumped to see Callum standing there. But I quickly stiffened again, when I realized he was still shirtless and his trousers were unbuttoned.

Why the hell was he standing in the doorway half-naked, holding a tray with a large teapot and two small cups?

"How sweet of you to anticipate my return," he said with a smile that looked rather wistful. It was impossible to tell where exactly his black eyes were looking, but I could *feel* his gaze when it slid over me. Caressing my skin like curious hands.

I lowered the poker and put it away. The demon clicked his tongue in disappointment, but a playful smile remained on his face.

"I enjoy a good beating as much as any other sadist," he said, which was a thoroughly bizarre way to start a conversation. He meandered into the room, carrying the tray. "But I assure you, when it comes to matters of self-defense, your magic will serve you far better than a stick. You are no mere mortal." His expression turned serious. "Why don't you use your magic?"

"Why do you care that I don't?" I shot back.

He stalked closer, his movements too quick and too fluid to appear human. I didn't back away as he bent at the waist and set the tray on the table between us. It was incredibly difficult not to stare at his splayed-open trousers, the thatch of dark hair beneath, and the monstrous bulge contained beneath the cloth.

"Why would a wolf choose not to bite?" he mused, straightening up and clasping his clawed hands behind his back. "Perhaps someone has convinced the wolf that she has no teeth."

"I don't like riddles," I said, and he chuckled.

He took a seat in the opposite chair, crossing his legs and stroking his thumb along his jaw as he observed me. "What do you know about demons? Your father commands one. Do you know how he does it?"

Stammering as I tried to understand how this demon knew anything about my father, let alone about Leon, I said, "He uses a sigil—the demon's true name. It's written in a grimoire. That's how the demon can be summoned and commanded."

Callum nodded. Leaning forward, he took the cups and saucers off the tray and set one in front of me and one in front of himself. As he poured the tea, he said, "Exactly right. Demons have two names. The one we call ourselves, and the one that cannot be spoken, save in very ancient tongues. Our sigil. Every demon knows that if a witch ever finds their sigil, they're doomed to a life of continuous summoning and enslavement. At least until we grow strong enough to resist. Sugar?"

He held up the little sugar bowl, tiny tongs clasped in his hand. Was I still dreaming?

I nodded, and he dropped a single sugar cube into my cup, then dumped five into his own, followed by a generous pour of cream. "A sigil gives one incredible power over the demon it belongs to. A witch like you could make me dance naked in the lake if you so wished. Command me to slaughter thousands. Make me steal from the rich and powerful." He stirred the tea and took a small sip. The delicate cup and saucer looked ridiculous in his massive hands. "Tell me, Everly. Use your imagination. If you had my sigil, what would you command me to do?"

This seemed like a trap, but I couldn't see a way out. I stuttered for several moments, uncertain how I should respond until finally, I threw caution to the wind.

"I would command you to live up to your name," I said. It seemed to pique his interest as he raised an eyebrow. "*Magni Deicide*. God slayer. Is it true? Have you killed a God?"

He dropped another cube of sugar in his tea and slowly stirred. "It's true. I've killed many."

His words snatched the air straight out of my lungs. "You've killed . . . *many*? How?"

"Mm, suddenly very eager for conversation, are we?" He sipped his tea, black eyes watching me over the flower-painted rim. "Why does a witch who barely wants to touch her magic need to know how I killed a God?"

"To prove you're not a liar." Although it was difficult to tell, it seemed as if he rolled his eyes. "If you truly did it, if you're not just trying to trick me, tell me how."

The amusement on his face disappeared. He set down the tea cup and remained leaning toward me, elbows resting on his knees.

"How did I do it?" He said it as if he'd asked himself the same question a thousand times, and the answer was one of the universe's greatest mysteries. "With the lives of 10,000 friends and lovers. With blood. With pain and fury. War is not so different, regardless of where you are in this dimension. Living beings give up their own lives so others of their kind can survive."

He sighed and leaned back in the chair. Callum was so different from the unhinged monster I'd met last night.

Calm and introspective, but there was feral energy lurking just beneath the surface. He continually snapped his fingers, with no rhythm nor reason to it.

"Was that what you wanted to know?" It sounded like he was teasing me. "Or did you want another answer? Something simpler perhaps? There's nothing simple about escaping from a God. Not once It has Its eyes on you."

Frowning, I picked up my cup of tea. The steam wafted in my nose, carrying with it the scent of bergamot and vanilla. It was more bitter than sweet; exactly how I liked it.

"What do you know about me?" I said, mirroring his position as I settled back in my chair. "You already knew my name and my father. What else do you know?"

"I'm beginning to suspect I know more about you than you do yourself." The snapping of his fingers grew louder. "I suppose I should level the playing field. That's something you humans still say, eh?" He rose from his seat, using his foot to shove the chair out of his way. "It's difficult to keep track of language. Humans change things so quickly. Especially with your internets, forums, cellular devices . . ." He crouched, brushing bits of dust and lint from the floorboards. Then, using the sharp claw on his thumb, he pressed the tip against his opposite wrist and drew it across. Thick blood as black as ink dripped from the wound.

He continued, "Demons are adaptable, but Hell changes much more slowly than Earth. I suppose it's easier for us. We don't bother with so many of the petty rules and regulations you humans put upon yourselves. We simply live."

He dipped his fingertips in the blood streaking from his wrist and drew upon the floor. Lines, dashes, and a crescent were drawn out in blood, stark against the caramel-colored wood.

"I regret my poor behavior last night, Everly." His eyes were still focused on the floor. "As an offering of a good will, I would like to remind you that you do indeed have teeth. You could choose to bite, if you wished."

When he stood up, what remained on the floor was a strange symbol: a half-circle with a series of lines and dots within. I stared, speechless, my heartrate ramping up again.

"Do you know what that is?" he said.

"Yes. Your sigil. Your name."

"Perhaps it will help you feel safer. Write it down somewhere, or trace that mark with your fingers, and it will be very easy to compel me to obey you."

Shaking my head, I scrambled for a response, "That's not . . . no. No, that's far too simple. Demons don't just obey."

"We obey easily if we're willing." He looked at me as if he couldn't decide whether he wanted to laugh at me or eat me. Perhaps both. "And you will find I am quite willing indeed."

"A demon doesn't just give up their sigil. *Why* are you doing this?"

The way he lowered his head as he looked at me made my belly do somersaults. "Do I need a reason?"

"Yes! There's always a reason. Shit, I know I'm weak, but I'm not that ignorant. You want something from me. People always want something. There's always a price!"

Aghast at my own outburst, I sharply drew in a breath and fell silent. Perhaps he'd kill me now. Perhaps this was the moment he'd steal my soul, spill my blood, and take me for himself. Out of all the fates that could have befallen me, for some reason, this one barely frightened me. An eternity in Hell couldn't be any worse than an eternity as a God's puppet. Perhaps this was even preferable.

My life had never been my own, always controlled and manipulated by the hands of others. It only made sense my death would go the same way.

But the demon didn't lunge for me. He didn't look angry. In fact, the moment I raised my voice, he looked thrilled.

"You're not ignorant. But you've been intentionally misled. You're not weak." He shook his head, laughing softly. "No, Lady Witch, quite the opposite. You could kill me if you wished, and I don't know how I can convince you of that, but I know someone who can. Your grandmother. Winona."

"My grandmother is dead," I said, wondering if I had any chance of sprinting from the house before he managed to kill me.

"And death has made her more unbearable than ever." He winced and rather sheepishly rubbed the nape of his neck. "She's not fond of that assessment but is very fond of you. And eager to speak with you."

He took a step toward me, hesitated, then held out his hand. Arm outstretched, palm upward, as if inviting me to touch, to hold . . .

To trust.

"What's the harm?" he said. My eyes darted between his face and his offered hand. "If I wanted to kill you, I would do it here and now. The moment you stop fighting fate is the moment you accept death. Take command and choose your path."

I took his hand. "This is all madness."

"Then we'll be mad together."

EVERLY

CALLUM'S HAND WAS warm around mine. The contact between us was the only thing I could focus on as he led me through the halls and down several short flights of stairs.

I couldn't recall the last time I'd held someone's hand. The last time I'd been embraced or kissed.

I'd never even been intimate with another person.

Isolating myself was habitual. Any friendship I formed ran the risk of dragging someone innocent into a horrific underworld they didn't deserve to be exposed to.

As if he could read my mind, Callum's fingers tightened around my own.

"Don't scare yourself," he said. "Remember the sigil. If I misbehave, make me regret it." He winked at me, and that simple gesture turned up the heat on my already flushed skin.

He'd proven himself to be beautiful *and* charming. Perhaps not entirely sane . . . but charming.

Oh, God, what was wrong with me? Demons weren't *charming*; they were predators, tricksters! For all I knew, this one was leading me to my slaughter.

We didn't encounter any wraiths as we made our way through the house, but I could hear them. Distant shrieks echoed in the hallways, setting my teeth on edge and making the hairs stand up on my arms.

"How do all these plants stay alive?" I said, marveling at the number of potted plants we encountered. Many of them were so large they were sprawling from their pots, roots bursting out and tendrils crawling up the walls, encircling the windows in their search for sunlight.

"The land this house is built on is protected," Callum said. "Not only by me, but also by other beings who struck deals with the coven throughout the years. The plants are connected to the forest itself. They're part of the barrier that hides this place from unfriendly eyes."

We reached an area of the house that looked different from the rest. The walls and floors were stone instead of wood, the ceiling high and arched like an ancient cathedral. It was colder here, and I shivered slightly in my thin blouse. Callum led me down another series of short stairways into a wide corridor that ended with a set of tall, narrow glass doors.

His fingers loosened, pulling away. My grip tightened, and he looked back at me in surprise.

"Oh, shit—sorry." I immediately winced at my

apology, snatching my hand away. But I regretted the absence of his touch. It was ridiculous. Foolish, even.

However, the way he was looking at me, it was like he regretted it too. It was a little glimpse of the monster he'd been last night; suddenly eager, suddenly ravenous. The way a starving man looked at a feast he'd been told not to touch.

He stepped closer, leaning down so he could stare directly into my face. It was unnerving to look into those black eyes, even more so when I realized he wasn't breathing.

Did demons need to breathe? Did their heart need to beat, their blood pump, their organs function? Or was it all an illusion, an elaborate costume they put on for Earth and nothing more?

Against my better judgment, I looked down. Down, toward his unbuttoned trousers, toward that one crucial part of him that almost certainly needed blood flow to function.

Or perhaps he was *always* that hard. Damn, it was like a fifth limb down there. Was that normal?

He made a soft sound as he smirked, two fingers tapping lightly beneath my chin to encourage me to lift my gaze.

His voice was a dark, crooning whisper as he said, "If you apologize to me again, I'll eat you." He leaned even closer, so close I could feel the heat of his skin. "I will eat you slowly. I will savor every inch of flesh and suck every tender morsel. I'll savor you like a goddamn dessert."

His teeth clipped together on the final word, and he turned away, proceeding toward the doors. But I was unable to move, unable to think a single comprehensible thought, as the heat of a thousand suns drenched me in a blush to end all blushes.

His snapping fingers brought me back to reality.

"Don't fall behind, my lady."

Barely biting back another apology, I trotted after him.

The tall glass doors swung out as we approached, opening into a courtyard. Flat gray stones lined the crescent-shaped space, and bushes covered with white and yellow flowers bordered the walkway. A massive greenhouse stood at the far end of the courtyard; its blue-tinted glass covered with thick, creeping vines.

The rain was still pouring, splattering across the stones and forming little puddles.

"Stay close," Callum said, his arm brushing lightly against my own. The touch was so quick, so casual, yet it was as stark and shocking as if he'd slapped me.

We stepped outside, and I braced for the cold downpour, but it never hit me. The rain simply slid around us as if we were holding a large umbrella. I looked up to find a translucent dome above us, colored faintly purple and iridescent. The rain struck it and rolled off, and I gaped in amazement.

"Is that aether?" I whispered, hardly daring to believe it.

Aether was a magical substance, naturally occurring, invisible and nearly impossible to control. It was strange and malleable, full of potential. It could allow a witch to create something out of nothing, like a pull a needle out of thin air.

"Yes, it is." The demon glanced at me, a smirk curving his lips. Damn it all, he knew I was impressed. I cleared my throat and nodded, focusing on the path ahead.

A massive tree had grown over the greenhouse door, its sprawling roots sitting on top of the stones. The trunk was gnarled and bent in a way that made it appear like a man was trapped within the wood, his head resting at the apex of the long branches.

"Is there another way in?" I said.

Callum was looking at the tree with a frown.

"No. If this entrance is guarded, the other one will be as well."

"Guarded?" I stepped toward the tree, laying my hand against the wood. It was surprisingly warm. "You mean the tree is guarding it on purpose? It didn't simply grow here?"

"Woodspries do not grow without intention, woman."

The voice was melodic but deep, with a timbre that hinted at a clever tongue and wicked mischief.

The tree *moved*. The human face I'd seen within it was real. The eyes blinked, the head lifted, a torso and arms melted out of the wood. The man in the tree leaned toward me, his eyes like orbs of sap and his pupils like tiny clustered seeds. He had no flesh—he was made of the wood itself, his upper body leaning out of the trunk like a serpent.

Callum regarded him coldly, but the man in the tree only had eyes for me.

"Well, well," he said, repeating the word nearly a dozen times before he inhaled and darted his face toward me. Callum's arm shot out and braced against my chest, forcing me back several steps at the wooden man's sudden movement. I wasn't sure which was more alarming: the being in the tree or the demon's touch.

"Who seeks entry here?" the tree man said, amber eyes roaming over me greedily. "A witch and her demon, peculiar, peculiar, hmm . . . There hasn't been a witch here in a long time, eh? Has there?" He looked off to the side, nodding as if someone else was speaking to him. "Ah, yes, yes. No witches have been here in a great many years . . . ten, fifteen, twenty . . ." His gaze slid back over to me. "Except the dead ones."

"Who are you?" I said. What had he called himself? A Woodsprie?

"I have been called Darragh by some," the creature said. "Not a very clever witch, are you? Never even heard of a Woodsprie." He made a sound as if he'd sharply clicked his tongue. "Terrible. What are they teaching these days?"

"I think you forget, Darragh, how rare your kind is now," Callum said dryly.

Darragh rolled his eyes over to him, giving him an unimpressed look.

"Oh yes, how dare I forget," he said. "The slaughter of my kind. Humans love to cut us down. Cutting, burning, chopping. Laying waste to the forests we once protected. It will destroy them, one day. When the last Woodsprie is dead, Earth will die, too." His gaze darted back to me; his expression suddenly sharper, suspicious. "Who are you?"

I took a deep breath. Time to see if I could indeed claim a little power.

"I'm Everly Laverne," I said, mustering as much confidence into my voice as I could. "I am the daughter of Heidi Laverne, the granddaughter of Winona. And I need entry, if you would allow me."

"He will," Callum said, and the Woodsprie's head twitched.

"Everly Laverne," Darragh repeated my name slowly. He extended his hand, palm up. "Very well. Let us see." I wasn't sure what he wanted until he added, "Your hand, witch."

I thought he meant to read my palm, to see my identity laid out in the fragile lines of my skin. I placed my hand in his, finding him warm but gentle as he drew me closer. His amber eyes were so strange, liquid and glassy. He brought his head down, tracing his nose close to my hand as he sniffed.

"So sweet. A truly intoxicating scent, isn't it?" I didn't know if he was asking me or simply musing, so I said nothing. He lifted his head and his lips drew back, revealing rows of teeth . . . no, not teeth.

Thorns. Thick, sharp, white thorns filled his mouth.

Before I realized what was happening, he put my finger into his mouth. There was a sharp pain as he bit down, and I tried to pull away but his hold was inescapable. Callum growled beside me as something like a tongue swirled over my finger, stroking my skin. The pain was already forgotten as Darragh's mouth suckled around me.

My face was reddening again, but this was more than just a blush. Heat poured through my veins, settling in my abdomen as Darragh met my eyes, slowly withdrawing my finger from his mouth.

"What was that?" I said softly, clutching my hand close the moment he let me go. There was a tiny wound on my fingertip, like a puncture from a thick needle, and blood leaked out.

"I needed a little taste," he said, humming as he swallowed. The tree shuddered, from its branches to its roots, and Darragh gasped. His eyes squeezed shut for a moment before he opened them again, blinking rapidly.

"Oh, that *is* good. Well, well, Everly Laverne. You are who you say. You may enter. And please, don't hesitate to come to me if you need any further assistance." He smiled again, and I could see where my blood had stained one of his thorny teeth. He leaned back as the tree rippled, roots slithering like snakes as the entire structure moved to the side, opening our way into the greenhouse.

"Thank you, Darragh," I said, nodding my head to him as I passed. Callum was right behind me, but instead of following me through the doorway, his hand snapped out and gripped the Woodsprie's throat.

The tree's roots tightened, writhing on the ground. The bushes rustled, even the grass and the flowers shuddered. From deep within the greenhouse came a groan, like a beam of wood about to split as Callum's claws dug into Darragh's wooden throat.

"Touch her like that again, and I'll rip your roots off your body and burn you alive." Callum's voice was a snarl that reverberated around the courtyard, vibrating in the stones beneath my feet. My head pounded, atmospheric pressure rapidly changing and making my ears pop.

Darragh hissed, but his voice was simpering as he said, "I could drink your blood too, demon, if you so desire. No need for jealousy."

Callum narrowed his eyes.

"Consider yourself lucky she enjoyed it," he said, releasing the Woodsprie with a scoff before stalking ahead of me into the greenhouse. Darragh kept smiling with all those sharp teeth as he melted back into the trunk of his tree, then disappeared.

EVERLY

THE GREENHOUSE WAS stunning, like stepping into another world. Brightly colored finches twittered as they flitted through the air, fluttering from branch to branch. There were massive plants, flowers of every variety, and the stone path was covered with moss that was soft and spongy beneath my feet. Vines dangled from above, and the air was thick and humid.

"This is incredible," I said.

"What is even more incredible is your lack of caution."

Callum had stopped ahead of me, frowning as he looked at me. I'd been nothing if not cautious since I got here, so where the hell was this irritation coming from?

"Lack of caution? What do you—"

"The next time a strange being asks for your hand, perhaps hesitate before you give it," he snapped. "Woodspries are fae creatures, they're incredibly dangerous. Yet you let this one savor you without a second thought."

I snapped, "Well, I've never heard of a Woodsprie before. And he wouldn't have let us pass if I hadn't. Besides, I think I can decide for myself who I should give my hand to. After all, I gave it to you first, didn't I?"

In the blink of an eye, he closed the gap between us. I gasped in shock as he snatched my wrist, holding it tightly in his clawed hands.

"You think you know what you want?" he growled. "A little pain makes the pleasure sweeter, doesn't it?" His grip tightened, claws pricking my skin. The sting was ignition for the fire in my veins, but then he brought my hand even closer, toward his mouth.

He opened his mouth and extended his tongue.

His long, red, *forked* tongue.

He twined it around my finger, licking up the blood. I was utterly frozen as he took the digit into his mouth and sucked. The sensation of his lips and tongue contracting around me made my brain short-circuit. All I could think about was heat—suction—pressure, and how desperately I wanted to feel that sensation *everywhere*.

He was so close, so unbearably close, pressing me against the glass wall. His presence was heavy, as if his body was crushed against me even though he was only holding my wrist.

He popped my finger from his mouth. My vision went a little fuzzy at the edges, my tongue incapable of forming words. Inwardly, I was screaming. Not in pain, not in horror, but in unbridled desire. The primal part of my brain was slobbering like a beast, hip-thrusting like a dog in heat.

Holy shit.

He needed to do that again. Immediately.

"Mm, my sweet Lady Witch." His hand moved to cup my face. "Your needs have been so terribly neglected. You'd be far safer indulging your wicked desires with me rather than that wretched fae."

"I . . . I, uh—" Could he tell I was turned on? Was it obvious? Perhaps he could see it on my face or . . . God forbid . . . could he smell it?

"Suddenly so shy," he said. "But the dirty thoughts are there, aren't they? Give them a voice, go on. You can make them real."

There was a pulse between my legs, a need that merely squeezing my thighs together wasn't helping. I dared to look at him, to really look. I dragged my eyes down his bare chest, longing to touch, perhaps to lick my tongue across his skin as he had to me.

Could I create the same feeling in him that he had in me? This same frantic heat?

He chuckled, and I snapped my eyes back up to his face.

"I don't know," I blurted. "I'm a virgin, I . . . I don't know what to say—"

He loomed over me, the unknowable black abyss of his eyes deeper than ever.

"A virgin . . ." he said. "Who desperately wants to be fucked to oblivion."

I wanted to melt into the ground. "I didn't say that. I never said—"

"Don't be afraid to tell him what you want, girl! You have every right to your pleasure!"

My eyes widened, and I whirled around, searching for the source of the shout. It was the same voice I'd heard when I first entered the house, but just as before, no one else could be seen.

"Who's there?" I gasped, and Callum finally stepped back. But he didn't take his eyes off me. The intensity of his gaze was unnerving as he motioned ahead, further down the path.

"Go see for yourself."

I brushed past him, pretending to be unflustered. He didn't know what I wanted. He didn't have the slightest idea. He was *assuming* I wanted to be . . . Goddamn it . . . *fucked to oblivion.*

He was assuming correctly, but I wasn't about to let him know.

The path curved through the greenery until I reached the base of a large tree. The trunk was massive, easily the width of two cars parked side by side. The limbs curved with the domed glass above, the depth of its branches filled with a chorus of birds. Water trickled down its trunk, the little streams splitting around a large stone tablet. There was writing carved into the stone, and I knelt so I could read it.

The first few sentences were written in a runic language I'd never seen before. But at the bottom was inscribed, *May our knowledge overflow like wellsprings.*

"Over here, my dear," the voice sounded again, clearer and far closer. I turned, following another narrow path that curved around the trunk of the tree. There, I found an alcove surrounded by flowering vines, paved with pale stone tiles. Mice peered at me from the grass, their little black eyes blinking curiously as finches flew overhead to observe me, perching on the branches above.

There was a small table with two chairs, formed of intricately wrought iron. An old radio sat on top of the table, its wooden frame and two knobs making it appear like a relic from the 1950s.

"It's a pleasure to see you again, Everly. My stars, it's been so many years."

The voice crackled with static as it sounded from the radio speakers. Staring in disbelief, I stepped closer and twisted one of the knobs to increase the volume.

"Oh, yes, that's much better!" the voice boomed and cackled loud enough to send a flock of nearby finches into flight. "Ha! Now I can shout at you properly. It's taken you ages to get in here! I should have warned you about old Darragh. He's a horny wretch, isn't he?"

The voice was contorted, but I knew it, even after so many years. As I glanced back at Callum, he nodded toward the radio and said, "She can hear you. She's nearby; the radio is merely her conduit."

I sat on one of the chairs, bracing my shaking hands on the edge of the table as I said, "Hi . . . uh . . . would you mind telling me your name?"

"Would I mind?" the voice cackled again. "Put some confidence in your voice, girl! If you want something, you'd better make damn well clear. That's your first lesson. But of course, I would not mind. I am Winona Laverne. I'm sure I look very different from when you last saw me."

"Oh . . . oh, you could say that again." I felt like I couldn't get enough air. "You're . . . you're my grand-mother."

"I am indeed."

"And you're . . . you're dead . . ."

"Quite. But I've found death to be a very fitting end to life. It's peaceful. I can keep to myself and do as I please, and none of the living are any wiser to it. It's a fantastic opportunity to study."

A dozen questions sprang to my mind, swiftly fol-lowed by a dozen more. "You're a ghost?"

"I refer to myself as a hag who's finally shed her mor-tal skin," she said, and Callum scoffed behind me.

"She's a ghost," he said. "Her body lies in the crypt nearby, along with many generations of your family."

"Consider yourself quite lucky you aren't a diviner," she said. "Or a demon, for that matter! Callum can hear me all the time, not just through the radio. He's lucky I'm the only talkative one rotting down there."

"I've been listening to her squawking for years," he said with a heavy sigh.

I was in disbelief. I'd encountered ghosts before, of course. Mama had taught me to be aware of them so I wouldn't be afraid if I saw or heard one. Most ghosts were simply lonely, or a little confused. A few kind words would usually send them on their way.

But this was the ghost of *my grandmother*. The grandmother I'd thought I would never be able to know. As a child, I'd dreamed of her coming to whisk me away, delivering me from a life surrounded by fear and secrecy. In my childish mind, she'd been the greatest witch in the whole world, a master of magic. Wise, kind, and full of knowledge.

"Callum, my dear monstrous demon, I must ask that you leave us for a while," Winona said. "I have important matters to discuss with my granddaughter, and I'm afraid you're simply too distracting for her."

Although I refused to turn my head, I could see Callum smirk in my peripheral vision before he stepped back. "As you wish. I'll be close by."

He stalked away, disappearing amid the greenery. Once his footsteps were out of my earshot, I said softly, "It's all true then? This house . . ." I hardly dared to say it. "This house belongs to our family?"

"The *Laverne* family," she said firmly. "The family of your mother. This place has housed witches within its walls for over a hundred years. Witches from many religions, many cultures, many countries, once gathered here in unity. And now, at last, it shall house a witch again. As for the demon, you don't need to fear him, my dear. I can tell you that with complete certainty." Her voice was calmer now, but she still gave a gentle laugh. "That handsome creature wouldn't harm you even if it cost him his own life. It's all true. This house is your birthright, and all the wisdom and magic within is yours to inherit."

My disbelief finally caved to stunned acceptance.

This place, and everything within its walls, was mine. Everything.

Never in my life had anything truly been mine. Everything came with strings attached, and my father could pull those strings whenever he wished. The very thought that this beautiful, mysterious, magical place could truly belong to me made my chest swell with so much emotion that I couldn't speak.

"I know it's been a very long time, Everly," my grandmother said, her voice infused with static for a moment. "I'm so sorry I couldn't do more for you in life. I tried to reach you. I truly hoped I could save you from that wretched, pompous, self-absorbed prick of a father your mother saddled you with." She sighed heavily. "Your mother was a lovesick fool for Kent. She truly believed there was goodness in him, and by the time she realized otherwise, it was too late. He manipulated her in every way he possibly could. But I know she loved you dearly."

Despite my efforts to remain stoic, my eyes stung with tears. "Do you know that she . . ."

"I felt her life pass on from this world," she said. "I had hoped her spirit might return to the house, but her soul was tired, so burdened with grief. She had no desire to stay. At least, now, her soul is at rest."

We sat there in silence for several long moments. Mourning a mother, a daughter. A life ended with tragedy; a legacy stained with wickedness.

"She helped them sacrifice a fifteen-year-old girl," I said. The words came out choked with pain and shaking with anger. I'd never spoken them aloud. I'd never heard anyone say it. The simple truth. My love for my mother was wrapped in thorns, crushed by the weight of what she'd done.

I'd watched my kind, gentle, patient mother hold down a teenage girl as she screamed in pain.

Grandma remained silent, but I got the sense she was listening. There was a coolness in the air, swirling gently around me like arms embracing me.

"The girl got away," I said. "We threw her down into the mine, but Mama went back for her. She shielded the girl with magic and told her to run. She tried to tell me. She tried to warn me."

My throat swelled. I could scarcely get the words out without sobbing. After Mama's death, when I'd held her letter and read it for the first time, my entire world ground to a halt.

My mother couldn't live with the pain she'd caused. She couldn't forgive herself.

"The girl's name was Juniper Kynes," I said, sniffling as I plucked at the loose threads on my blouse. "We convinced the entire town she was crazy. We destroyed her life. She lost everything." Taking a deep breath, I forced my voice to steady. "Do you know how it works? Our—" I stopped myself before I misspoke. "My father's faith. Do you know what he believes?"

"I do," she said grimly. "The Laverne witches have been aware of the Libiri's activities since the cult's inception. When the God awakened, we knew. We were researching how to keep It contained. But as the Libiri's influence grew, so did the God's strength. One by one, the witches who once comprised this coven were killed. Others fled in fear. Others simply grew old and croaked." She gave another bitter laugh. "I did all I could before death came for me, and it would seem it's paid off. Because here you are at last. Back home, where you belong."

She couldn't have known the impact those words would have. "Home" was such a fraught concept for me. The home I'd known my whole life—the house I lived in with my father, step-mother, and siblings—had never been a comforting place, a safe place. It was an arena, or a stage: a place where I had to walk, talk, and act with care, constantly afraid of doing something wrong. I'd only been allowed to visit Mama's apartment on weekends, but even there, I didn't truly feel safe.

The God was always watching, always whispering. Only since I'd stepped foot in this house had the perpetual sense of being stalked finally vanished.

"You say your mother let that first sacrifice go," she said, speaking slowly. "But yesterday, I felt a great ripple of energy in the air. Something changed. The God stirred."

Nodding, I had to take a moment to compose myself before I said, "Juniper had a brother, Marcus. They killed him yesterday. The first sacrifice is done."

Grief for Marcus, for my mother, my grandmother, even for myself, all hit me at once. My chest ached and all I could do was cover my face with my hands, hiding the hot tears pouring down my cheeks.

"I'm so sorry, my dear." Her voice was gentle and a soft breeze whispered over my back. It took me back suddenly, to being eight years old again, running along the lakeshore to Grandma's waiting arms. One of the few times I was allowed to see her. "You've already seen too much of this wicked world, but it will get far more wicked than this."

"I don't know what to do," I said, using my sleeve to wipe the tears away. I was a mess, but what did it matter? "I want to stop them. I must stop my father but I don't know how. If I just hide here, in this place . . ."

"This house cannot protect you forever," she said. "There will be nowhere to hide if the Deep One is freed, particularly for you. Its eyes have been on you since the day you were born. It wants you, Everly. It wants your power, your physical form. I warned your mother of this, but she refused to see it until . . . well, until you had been born and she realized your father was only interested in having another tool, not another daughter. He used your mother to make himself appear more powerful, wielding her strength like it was his own. You cannot allow him to do the same to you."

"What can I do?" I said desperately, sitting forward in my chair and gripping the radio. "I barely have any power in me. I don't know how to fight this."

A long silence passed.

"Barely any power?" she repeated, her tone incredulous. "Barely any . . . My girl, you could not possibly be more wrong. The power in you is by far greater than any witch I've known."

"That's not possible. I can barely summon a spark." I swallowed hard, sitting back in shame. Perhaps she had expected me to be strong, maybe she'd thought my mother had imparted more of her knowledge to me. "I'm weak."

"Bullshit!"

I jumped in surprise at the volume of her curse.

"You are untrained, not weak! And you've been kept this way intentionally because Kent fears you. He fears what you can become. He lives in terror of the threat you pose to everything he has built, and he will stop at nothing to keep you silent and subservient." Her voice was viciously proud as she said, "But no more. He does not hold the power here, you do. And you have the tools to prove it."

"What tools?" I said. Any moment, surely, she would realize she was mistaken. I wasn't strong, I wasn't someone my father feared. I was a cowardly girl whose greatest power was to run away rather than help a man being murdered.

"This house," she said. "And everything in it. Callum, first and foremost, will be your greatest ally."

"A demon," I said. "But demons are—"

"Selfish, conniving, cruel, wicked, self-indulgent creatures," she said. "Exactly like we humans are. Yet you still find great goodness among humans, don't you? I called Callum many years ago and he answered. He has waited for you ever since."

"He's never met me. He's never known me, so why would he wait for me? Why would he help me?"

"Some questions, I fear, are not mine to answer," she said. "But I will explain what I can, as much as I understand. Callum's sigil was among a collection of demonic names gathered throughout the years by the founding witch of our coven, Sybil Laverne."

With a gasp, I nearly shot straight out of my seat. My knee banged the table, the radio tipped backward, and I scrambled to right everything as I rushed out, "Sybil! Yes! Mama told me her name. She said Sybil knows the way."

"Sybil held many secrets indeed," Grandma said. "She passed away when I was still a young witch myself, so your mother never met her. But Sybil was a prolific demonologist, a talented diviner, and extremely skilled in the ways of spell craft." She paused for a long moment, before saying, "When you were born, I had visions of the many paths of life you could choose to take. I witnessed horrors to end all horrors. I saw glimpses of our world remade, overtaken by a God whose evil we cannot even begin to fathom." Her voice shook, and for the first time, I realized my grandmother was afraid. "I saw you, but your mind and soul were gone. Forced to dance like a puppet on a string, your magic warped and stolen. I knew I did not have many years left, but I had to do something. I had to take drastic measures to change the course of fate."

She drew in a deep breath, and I leaned closer to the radio, eager to hear more.

"In Sybil's writing, I found an Archdemon's sigil. She wrote that it belonged to the oldest demon she had ever encountered, and she had met him purely by chance, here on Earth. She claimed he had come to Earth in pursuit

of fallen Gods, slaughtering them wherever he found
them. He made no attempt to hide his sigil from her,
and instead, laughed at the threat of ever being forcibly
summoned. She wrote that he was far too powerful to
be commanded. Summoning him should never be attempted."

"But you attempted it," I said. "Why?"

"I didn't summon him," she said. "I called to him, he
answered, and I was fortunately able to persuade him not
to kill me. He admitted that I was not alone in attempting to change fate. In fact, he had been chasing a thread
of fate he glimpsed many hundreds of years ago: a vision
he once had."

"A vision? Can demons be diviners, like witches
can?"

She paused for a moment. "I have never heard of it.
Nor had Callum. What he saw . . . even now, I struggle
to believe it."

"What was it?" I blurted. Excitement filled me as I
hung on to her every word.

"He had a vision of a witch. A witch who knew his
name and called herself Everly Laverne."

Of all the things she could have said, that was not
what I expected. "Callum had a vision . . . of me?"

"So it would seem. You had only just been born when
he told me this, but he claimed he had been searching for
you. He had spent centuries on Earth, waiting for his vision to manifest. So when I gave him my name, it was as
if fate had finally begun to align. I told him of the power
I knew you would have. I told him that someday, you

would come to a crossroads and have to make a choice. To submit, to flee, or to fight. There is a path you can choose that will lead you to the end of all this. All the pain and misery caused by that unnatural deity's presence in the world can be ended, Everly. And you are the one who can do it."

"This must be a dream," I whispered, leaning back in my chair. "It has to be."

"A dream, a nightmare, or reality. Regardless, you must make a choice. You can try to hide here but you will not be safe. Callum will try to protect you, but in the end, will be overcome. You can go back to your father, pretend this all was indeed a dream. You can carry on your life as he dictates, enslaved to his will, and eventually, the will of his God. Or you can choose to fight back. You can embrace your power. You can kill a God."

"Kill a God . . . it's truly possible . . ."

"Oh yes. It will not be easy and we have very little time, but I know we can awaken your power. It's practically bursting at the seams already. I would be careful of any more spontaneous teleportations, if I were you. They can sneak up on you when your magic has been left stagnant for so long."

If this was a dream, then I was already in too deep. I couldn't turn away from this.

I sat up straighter in my seat. "Tell me what I have to do."

EVERLY

WITH THE RADIO tucked under my arm, I followed Callum as he led me to the library.

Trailing behind him, I took the opportunity to observe him more closely. His marble-like skin wasn't entirely perfect; he had scars all over, most of them very small but some were larger, puckered and discolored. There were a couple that looked like puncture wounds, as if he'd been stabbed.

He'd known my name centuries before I was even a thought. Over all those years, he'd been searching for me. Waiting for me.

"Blessed Hygieia, this house needs cleaning!" Grandma exclaimed. "The state of it! The dust! The first thing we're teaching you is some proper tidiness spells. Can't have you living in such squalor."

Callum stopped before a set of doors, surrounded

by an elaborately carved wooden frame. "This is it. The Grand Library of House Laverne."

He snapped his fingers, and the doors swung open.

My jaw practically hit the ground as I walked inside. Three floors rose above me, sheltered beneath an arched ceiling covered in a mural of the forest's flora and fauna. Shelves covered every floor, labeled with small golden plaques to denote how the books were sorted. Sconces lined the walls, flames flickering behind frosted glass, bathing the books in warm light.

"The witches of House Laverne were always incredibly studious," Grandma said. "Our kin and companions likely would have devoted all their time to the discovery of deeper knowledge if it hadn't been for the Deep One stirring up bullshit."

Laughing at her expletives, I stopped to stare at a shelf of ancient leather-bound books. As delicately as I could, I pulled one large volume from the shelf and flipped it open. Neat lines of elegant handwritten text covered the pages.

"Why was this place abandoned?" I said. "Why would anyone ever want to leave?'

"The Deep One's growing power made staying here too dangerous. Many of our young witches chose to leave, believing it would be safer to put distance between themselves and the coven, rather than fight to keep the God contained." Grandma sighed heavily. "Your mother was one such witch. She left and never looked back. I fear I may have driven her to it. Having a diviner for a mother was not easy for her. I tried too hard to control her, to change the course of her fate. The coven was dying and she was a bright, talented young witch. She did not want to spend her life hiding in a forest."

As I made my way up a spiral stairway to the third floor, a strange object caught my eye. From a distance, it appeared like a large mechanical wardrobe. Numerous gears and springs turned and pumped all over its surface, and it ticked as if a thousand clocks were contained inside, all keeping a different time. It was at least ten feet tall, set into the wall, composed of brass and iron. It had two doors, but they were sealed, with no handles or keyholes in sight.

"This is the heart of the library, the vault," Grandma said. "Grand Mistress Sybil built this to protect our most precious knowledge. All of her research into the Gods is contained within. Not even a ghost like me can penetrate its magical barriers."

"How does it open?" Cautiously, I brushed my fingers over the bronze surface, and it was cold to the touch. "There are no keyholes."

"Sybil's grimoire is the key. It was lost after her death, and taken by the Libiri. I believe your father currently carries it."

Despair rushed through me. No wonder my father guarded that grimoire so carefully. "Then we can't get in. Mama always said grimoires were impossible to steal."

"That isn't technically true, although they are certainly *difficult* to steal. A grimoire cannot be stolen from the one who carries it by force or deceit. But grimoires are tied to the family they came from. All claims of ownership are trumped by the fact that you are a Laverne witch, and that book has always belonged to us. You'll be able to steal it, if you can find a way to do so safely."

My father treated the grimoire like it was the most precious thing he owned. He never allowed anyone else to hold it, even touch it.

"He sometimes locks it in a drawer," I said, my hands shaking as I contemplated what I had to do. "Or in his briefcase."

"You'll find your opportunity," Grandma said. "You're a clever young woman. Kent underestimates you, and you can use that to your advantage."

But I barely heard her. The wraiths in the halls and the beasts lurking in the woods—those didn't scare me as much as my father did. They didn't scare me as much as leaving here and feeling the God's eyes on me again, poking around in my head, probing for weakness.

Would It see I was a traitor? Would It know how deep my blasphemy had become?

Sweat broke out on my forehead and cold chills went up my back. My lungs were tight as I stumbled, bracing one hand against the wall. Setting down the radio as I shook, I pressed my back to the wall and closed my eyes, willing the dizzying nauseous to stop.

"I can't go back," I said breathlessly. "I can't. You don't understand, my father won't— He won't—"

With a rumble like thunder, Callum was suddenly perched on the railing in front of me. But I was still trying to simply breathe in a normal pattern, instead of frantically gasping for air.

"I don't want to go back." I was disgusted with how

desperate, how pathetically frightened my voice sounded. "He won't trust me after this, he'll be suspicious. He won't let me go, Grams, he won't *ever* let me."

"He can't keep you," Callum said. The viciousness in his voice snapped against my panic like a rubber band, shocking me out of it. He stepped down from the railing, moving with a feline-like grace as he came over to me.

I lifted my eyes, looking at Callum with a mixture of shame and defiance. Was this what he'd hoped for while he was waiting for me? A woman who hyperventilated at the thought of facing her own family?

He reached out, and his clawed fingers brushed along my cheek, wiping away a tear. Then they trailed down, tracing over my arms until he eased them apart. He took my tightly clenched hands, slowly straightening my locked fingers. His movements were so gentle, so unexpected, that my panic melted away into fascination.

"If you need to go back, I'll be waiting for you," he said. "I'll be watching. If your father tries to keep you, I'll ensure you escape. I'll bring you home."

"Home . . ." I whispered. "I don't know if I've ever really had a home."

"Home is wherever I can keep you safe," he said. He was still holding one of my hands, embraced between his palms. Irrationally, I longed to lean into his touch. I wanted to press myself against his chest, and finally, after so long, just be held.

I wasn't supposed to trust him. Yet, when I looked into those jet-black eyes . . . I did.

EVERLY

FOR THE REMAINDER of the evening, I explored the library. The sheer volume of books was astounding, and it wasn't long until I amassed a stack of fascinating tomes. For hours, I was curled in one of the cushioned velvet chairs, consuming the literature like it was the only sustenance I needed.

At some point, food and drink appeared on the table beside me: a creamy bisque, mug of tea, and pitcher of water. Whether the house provided it or the demon brought it, I couldn't be sure, but my stomach was satiated and so was my mind.

Callum made frequent appearances to check in on me, although he said very little and didn't stay long. But he remained nearby; watching, lurking. I could feel his presence in the air, in tingling pressure that crept slowly up the back of my skull.

I had all the magical knowledge I could desire at my fingertips. I consumed books of spell craft until my head ached and my vision grew blurry, but I didn't stop. There was a frantic need within me to absorb all the information I possibly could.

When I was too tired to sit upright anymore, I wandered out of the library in search of Callum, hoping he could escort me back to my room. But I only took a couple of steps down the hall, my arms full of books, before an open door caught my eye. Few doors were left open in this place; I couldn't resist peeking inside.

It was a small sitting room. Nudging open the door with my shoulder, I stepped onto an elegant, plush rug covering the shining wood floor. A large fireplace was to my left, and the moment I stepped inside, the stack of wood within caught flame, swiftly chasing the chill from the room.

Velvet furniture was set before the fire: a chaise longue and several chairs. To my right, on a slightly raised dais before a tall open window, was a grand piano.

Quietly closing the door behind me, I settled on the chaise lounge with my books. It wasn't long before my tired eyes grew heavy, the steady rain lulling me into drowsiness.

Only when my book slipped from my fingers and hit the floor with a heavy thud did my eyes suddenly fly open, finding the room dark and the fire burning low. Hours must have passed, but it wasn't only the light that changed while I slept.

I wasn't alone.

Moving slowly, so as not to make a sound, I turned my head. The curtains were drawn, but I could hear the rain tapping against the window and the distant rumble of thunder.

The chair beside the fireplace was occupied. Only the silhouette of massive wings was visible in the dark.

With half-lidded eyes, I stared at the dark shape, knowing he was staring back. Neither of us said a word, neither moved.

The demon inhaled slowly, and I resisted the urge to shrink down and close my eyes. My heart pounded as the chair creaked, and he rose, a looming specter that seemed to glide toward me.

It was so dark I couldn't see his face. He reached for something, and a moment later, a soft, heavy blanket draped over me.

"Your mind is restless." The demon spoke softly, igniting goose bumps along my arms.

"It always is. I don't usually sleep this much."

I was used to long nights, aching eyes, and drowsy days. When the world was asleep, that was when I found freedom.

There was another long beat of silence.

Then he said, "When my mind will not calm, music helps me. If you would like, I can play for you."

Perhaps this truly was a dream. The difference between waking and sleeping seemed utterly insignificant in the dead of night, in that tiny room with a demon at my side. Silently, I nodded, and watched his shadow cross the room to sit on the bench before the piano.

His clawed fingers moved soundlessly over the keys, exploring them, as if refamiliarizing himself with something long forgotten.

Then, he began to play.

The melody that poured out of his fingers could have been written by an old master of the instrument. Slow and gentle at first, it soared into a complex crescendo. His fingers moved with inhuman speed and ease. The song was unlike anything I'd ever heard, and yet, it was familiar too. Like a memory from early childhood, impossible to remember clearly but imprinted on my mind.

It wasn't long before I was asleep again.

WHEN I AWOKE the next morning, I was alone. But a blanket lay over me, and my books had been carefully stacked on the table nearby.

It wasn't a dream.

Hesitant as I was to wander the halls alone, I desperately needed to find my way to a bathroom. Cautiously, I poked my head out into the hall, looking to and fro for any wandering wraiths. I'd left Grandma's radio in the library, but I could feel her presence nearby in a lingering scent of patchouli and a cool, directionless breeze. It made me feel a little bolder.

"Callum?" I winced the moment I called out. I really didn't like raising my voice, but this house was so vast and I didn't trust myself to find my way alone just yet. There was no answer, and I took a few cautious steps down the hall toward the staircase. "Callum? I don't really know how to summon you, but uh . . . appear, please?"

A prickly feeling went up the back of my neck, and I glanced over my shoulder. Nothing but a long, empty hallway. My fingertips tingled, heat trickling through my veins. My magic was so close, more accessible than ever before. But the weight of it was intimidating, like waves crashing against the walls of a dam, threatening to break through.

Turning back around, I came face-to-face with black eyes and sharp teeth.

Sparks burst from my mouth as I shrieked, stumbling backward. Clapping my hand over my mouth in disbelief, I took deep breaths for several moments to calm my racing heart, glaring at the demon who'd snuck up on me.

"You called?" he said, giving me a crooked smile that was hardly innocent.

It was remarkable I hadn't pissed myself. Folding my arms, I grumbled, "You should wear a bell so you don't give me a heart attack."

"A bell? Like the ones humans put on their cats?" He tipped his head to the side curiously, seeming to give the idea some thought. "Only if you promise to drag me around on a leash. Then I'll gladly wear your collar."

My face bloomed with heat. That was *not* the kind of thought I needed right now, but it was too late—he'd planted the seed and all I could think about was this monstrous being crawling toward me on his hands and knees as I pulled the leash taut.

The demon drew in his breath, suddenly turning his face away from me. "Stop that, Everly."

"Stop? Stop what?"

"Stop fantasizing." His voice was sharp, but not with anger. It was desperation. "It arouses you, and that is incredibly . . ." He paused, his throat visibly moving as he swallowed. ". . . distracting."

Part of me was embarrassed he could tell. But another part of me, in a deeper and practically unexplored part of my mind, felt a sudden rush of power.

"Where were you?" Maybe conversation would distract me from the fantasies still roaring through my mind.

"I was clearing the house of wraiths for you, Lady Witch. The halls are now safe for you to wander. I would suggest familiarizing yourself with the layout, but remain cautious. This house holds many secrets, and not everything is as it seems."

The idea of being able to finally explore these halls safely, whenever I wished, brought an immediate smile to my face. "Thank you! I will, I'll be careful. Maybe I should make a map, if my sketchbook isn't completely ruined . . ."

"It isn't," he said. "Your books are a bit waterlogged but readable. You have some interesting choices in literature."

He said it so casually, with a mischievous smile. Shaking my head in disbelief, I said, "You went through my bag?"

He blinked slowly, as if my irritation confused him. "Yes, I did."

"That's *private*." I sighed in exasperation. "You can't do that."

"Private?" He laughed as he repeated the word, but his smile faded when I didn't unfold my arms. "I see. I won't go through it again."

The concept of privacy seemed utterly lost on him. But my bladder still needed relief, so instead of trying to explain any further, I said, "Can you point me to my room? I can find my— Oh, shit—"

The next thing I knew, I'd been flung onto his back and was clinging to his wings for dear life as he sprinted through the halls. Faster than I could snap my fingers, I found myself standing dizzily on my feet outside the bedroom door.

"It would not be kind to leave you to wander when you need to relieve yourself," he said. His actions had, once again, come dangerously close to voiding my need for a toilet. "You'll find breakfast on the coffee table. If you need me, simply call."

And with that, he was gone again, disappearing like a guard dog that suddenly got a whiff of a nearby cat.

After taking care of my business and washing my face, I found another platter of food waiting for me on the table near the fire. As I ate my breakfast—coddled eggs with wheat toast and a mug of coffee—I stared mindlessly at Callum's bloody sigil on the floor.

Something so precious, so intimate, yet he'd given it to me without any hesitation.

As curious as I was, I wasn't yet brave enough to ask him about the vision he'd supposedly had of me.

How could something like that happen? How could a demon in Hell receive a premonition about a witch who wouldn't be born for thousands of years?

It was the kind of thing that happened in books, not real life.

I didn't believe I was capable of much. But one thing I certainly wasn't capable of was simply rolling over and giving up. Finding this place had provided me with opportunities I'd once thought were impossible.

No matter how much it frightened me, I was going to fight.

But without knowing how to use my magic, my fight wouldn't last very long. Before leaving last night, Grandma told me I needed to start practicing my magic whenever I had an opportunity. She said I needed to build my confidence; using magic should feel as natural as breathing.

Yeah, right. It felt about as natural as breathing underwater.

Leaving my breakfast on the table, I walked from my chair to crouch near Callum's sigil. His blood had settled into the wood, giving it a dark brown stain. It would be wise to keep his mark close to me, somewhere safe.

Retrieving my sketchbook from my bag, I pursed my lips when I saw my stack of swollen books stored beside it. Most of them were innocent: textbooks I'd selected so I could get a head start on my studies before the school semester began.

But a small paperback with a dramatic cover was

doubtlessly what Callum was referring to when he said I had *interesting choices* in literature.

Ravaged by the Duke of Shadows was the type of book I read late at night while hiding under my bed covers. If I couldn't live out my fantasies in real life, then reading was the closest I could get.

Victoria had taunted me relentlessly when she found out I read these smutty books. While she was going through a different boy toy every week, I was daydreaming about gruff, growly book boyfriends who could only touch me in my dreams.

Goddamn it, why did Callum have to see that? I wanted to crawl under the bed in shame and never come out.

With a groan, I fished a pen out of my bag so I could carefully recreate the demon's sigil within my sketchbook. Taking my time to ensure every line and dash was positioned just right, my hand flowed through the marks as if I already knew them by heart.

The sudden, unbidden memory of Callum's hands stroking gently down my arms gave me an involuntary shiver. A sigh escaped me as I thought of how carefully he'd uncurled my clenched fingers, warm hands and sharp claws touching me tenderly.

There was a creak outside the door, and I paused. Although I'd finished drawing the sigil, my pen kept tracing the design, over and over. It was involuntary but comforting. Even as I lifted my eyes toward the door and spotted the shadow of someone beneath it, my hand kept moving.

If there was ever a time to experiment, to try to flex my power, it was now. It felt forbidden, like I was doing something inherently wrong. But instead of ignoring the heat, instead of trying to bury the jittery feeling in my chest, I allowed it to spread. A chill went up my spine, and a subtle but sweet scent filled the air. Like strawberries crushed in sugar.

As I traced the sigil, I formed my intention as clearly and confidently as I could. *Open the door. Come to me.*

The door swung open. Callum walked in, taking his time as he softly shut the door behind him. He stopped halfway across the room and clasped his hands behind his back.

"You needed me?" he said, and my mouth went so dry it may as well have been stuffed with cotton.

There was anticipation in his voice. He was shirtless still, and I was getting the feeling he simply never wore one; perhaps it was difficult for clothing to accommodate his wings. But I had no complaints about the view.

The intricate lacing on his trousers seemed purposefully designed to make me stare exactly where I shouldn't.

"I wanted to test it," I said softly, my pen finally held still on the page. "I wanted to see if it would work. If you would really come."

A small smile curled the corner of his mouth. "It's wise you've begun practicing. I assure you, I find it very difficult to ignore your voice. Even when you're not stroking my sigil."

Snatching my hand away from the page, I awkwardly looked away. Now that he was here, I didn't have a clue what to do with him.

Well . . . that wasn't entirely true. I certainly had *ideas* of what I could do with him, but they were wild, nonsensical . . .

"Don't lose your nerve now." His voice was a dark croon that made my stomach do a spontaneous backflip. "You can be far rougher with me, if you wish."

Good God, it was suddenly so hot in here. I was practically sweating through my clothes. A thousand unbidden fantasies exploded into my brain, awkward mashups of my own dreams and the ones I'd read in books. I didn't dare give voice to the things I wished for.

Why did my throat have to close like I was having an allergic reaction to my own desires? Had I gone so long pushing away what I wanted that having the opportunity to seize something for myself was frightening?

But Callum was patient. In fact, my hesitancy seemed to excite him more.

"Come now, Everly. Take control, or I may end up taking advantage—"

"Get on your knees." It was the first command that popped into my racing mind, and I honestly expected him to laugh at me. But instead, this massive, clawed, fanged demon sank to the ground and knelt for me.

"Aren't you curious?" he said. The way his lips parted around those soft words was mesmerizing. "Don't you want to know how powerful you are?" He lowered his head, placing his palms flat upon the floor as he sat on his heels. "Don't you want to find out how far you can command me?" My breath was throttled in my throat as he crawled toward me. On his hands and knees. "Don't you want to see . . . experience . . . the things you can make me do?"

EVERLY

MY EYES WERE wide, and I was frozen in place, my back rigid against the chair. My magic had never been so awake, so wild, so alive.

The demon reached my feet and rose on his knees. He gripped the arms of the chair as he leaned toward me, his scent surrounding me, intoxicating me. Iron, like blood, like smelting metal. Oakmoss, like damp earth, like a whisper of smoke on the wind. He smelled both soft and dangerous, with a wicked promise in his eyes.

But whether that promise meant pleasure or pain, I had no idea.

His lips moved, barely a sound behind his words. "What would you have me do?"

The heat rising on my cheeks quickly spread to the rest of my body. How could I ask for something when I wasn't even sure what it was?

He shivered as I traced his sigil with my finger. His claws punctured the chair's fabric as his grip tightened.

"Take off your clothes," I said.

He stood up slowly, almost lazily. "As my lady wishes."

Every muscle in his chest was defined, his shoulders thick, dark veins standing out against his pale throat. His body looked *designed*, as if every muscle, every scar, was there with intention.

As he reached for his trousers, loosening the lacing, goose bumps prickled over my skin and I forgot how to breathe. His bulge was clear, impossible to ignore. Why did it look so *massive*? It had to be an illusion.

He dropped his trousers. It wasn't an illusion at all.

"Oh . . . my God . . . that's . . ."

He wasn't wearing any underwear—why would a demon even bother? Like a fool, I'd honestly expected to be met with the sight of a very normal, at least vaguely human-like penis.

That was *not* what was in front of me. Not even slightly.

His shaft was thick, at least the size of my clenched fist, with a tapered head that had a swell of muscle at the base. Thick ripples ran along his length, like swollen veins. The base was bulbous, two large swells on either side of his shaft.

"You won't fit," I babbled. "Holy shit, there is no fucking way—"

His grin widened. "Was that your intention? To make me fit inside you?"

He was a predator built to hunt, to kill, to *take*. Besides the God Itself, I had never met a being as powerful as Callum.

I'd just commanded a demon prince to strip off his clothes, and he *obeyed*. No hesitation, no argument, no anger. It made me giddy as much as it frightened me. It made my head tingle and excitement roil through my stomach.

He was watching me raptly. Waiting. Wanting.

"You're scared of me." His tone was amused but gentle. Surprise flickered over his face when I shook my head.

"My mother warned me about demons." I dared to stand and take a step closer. Then another. And another. "She told me you were all selfish beings."

His fingers twitched at my approach. Self-control, barely maintained. "Your mother was right."

"She said you're dangerous."

"Absolutely."

"That you're killers. That you manipulate humans to get what you want. Our bodies. Our souls." I was right in front of him now, the closest I'd ever been to naked flesh. I thought suddenly of all the times I'd averted my eyes, every time I'd looked away from something I longed for. Every time I stifled myself because that was what I was told to do.

"You should believe it. All of it."

And I did. I just didn't care.

"I was told not to play with dangerous things," I said, reaching up, my fingers hovering over his chest.

Not close enough to touch, but close enough to feel the heat radiating off his skin. Close enough to feel the tension vibrating between his flesh and mine, growing more violent the closer I came. "But my mother is dead, and my father is wicked. So I think I'll play how I please."

He was perfectly still when I touched his throat. I traced my fingers along the contours of it, the thick cords of muscle that framed a prominent Adam's apple. So close I could smell him, warm and earthy, like the way the sun felt on a cold day, or the softness of green moss growing on stone. He was something wild, something that didn't fit into the world around him.

He didn't belong, and yet here he was. Just like me.

He made a soft sound, not quite a moan but more than merely a breath, as my fingers stroked over the alcove at the base of his throat.

His wings retracted, tightening against his back. His fingers curled; his lips parting slightly. Those subtle tells were the cracks in his monstrous guise, and I wanted to press my fingers into them and rip them open.

"Why aren't you breathing?" I said.

"I can smell you. *Constantly.* Your skin, your sweat. Every change in your hormones, every chemical reaction in your brain. Your magic—I can't escape it. It's intoxicating. It's irresistible. Every instinct in my brain demands I give in to it. So, I hold my breath."

"And what would happen? If you gave in?"

"I might hurt you, without meaning to. I might not be able to control myself."

He said this all very matter-of-fact, as if it were entirely normal to be so overwhelmed by the smell of
someone that you'd lose control. It should have been terrifying, a giant red flag for my safety.

But as he stood there shuddering with the effort to
hold back, waiting for me to give him permission before he even touched me, I was so turned on I felt feral.
Nothing I'd read about, no porn I'd watched, had ever
been so erotic as simply knowing how desperately he
wanted me.

"Start breathing," I ordered, and his black eyes widened. "I want you to inhale, as much as you can, and
hold it."

"Oh, you are wicked, aren't you?" he said. His nostrils flared, and he breathed in, a shiver running over his
naked body as he did. His cock twitched, standing rigidly
at attention as he held the scent of me in his lungs.

"How does it feel?" I whispered as he closed his eyes
and shook his head from side to side, humming.

"Like honey on the tip of my tongue," he said, his
words creating a pulse in the air that made my ears pop.
"Like a knife at my throat. Or the first drink of liquor
after a very long dry spell."

He opened his eyes, and I was lost in their beauty
once again. Orbs of black marble with veins of gold. It
was like he'd been decorated, fitted with jewels and precious stones like the death mask of some ancient king.

"Can you control yourself for me, Callum?" My voice
sounded strange, even to my own ears. The softness that
usually infected my words was gone.

The demon nodded, never ripping his gaze away from mine. "I can."

Stepping closer, I reached up on my tiptoes to bring my lips to his ear. This was madness. This was me looking death in the face and laughing.

"I want you to lose control."

His movement was quick. The next thing I knew I was sprawled in the chair, and Callum was bent over me. His chest was heaving with deep gulps of air, and a tremor ran through the taut muscles in his arms. His claws were gripped so tightly into the armrest they tore the fabric.

He sucked in a breath, slowly shaking his head. I slid my hand up his arm, and his veins turned black, as if ink was spreading beneath his skin where I touched him.

"You need to think very carefully about what you're asking of me," he said, so tightly it was like the words pained him.

"I've been careful all my life and look where it's gotten me."

His arm was shaking under my hold. I'd never felt a rush like this.

"I'm done being careful," I said. "I'm not fucking content being silent and sweet and permissive." All these years I'd spent keeping my head down, being obedient and faithful. Choking down every desire, gagging myself with my own fears.

As Callum hovered mere inches away from my mouth, I said, "Can I trust you?"

"Yes." He kept his teeth clenched as he spoke. "My

loyalty is to you, and you alone. I relinquished fealty to Hell for you. I waited . . . for so . . . fucking long . . ."

There was a sound of snapping wood, and the back of the chair was suddenly loose. The heat of his skin was feverish.

"Why?" I had to know, I needed to understand. My heart pounded, a coil of heat sitting deep inside me.

Carefully, so carefully, like I was made of the thinnest glass, he took my hand. He brought my fingers to his lips, kissed them. He bowed his head and pressed his brow to the back of my hand, growling viciously, "Fate took everything from me but offered you in exchange. Who am I to deny what fate provides? You know I saw you. I heard your voice and you were calling my name. Demons do not dream of witches, Everly." On a sharp exhale, he continued, "But you've overtaken my dreams. A woman I don't even know. Taunting me like a nymph playing a game of chase. Always years away from me . . . until now."

I pulled back my hand, and when he lifted his head, I kissed him.

He surged forward to meet me, pressing me in the chair as his tongue parted my lips and slid inside. The forked sides moved independently, consuming me, while his arm encircled my back and pulled me closer. His touch was pure luxury, his breath flowing into me. He grazed his clawed hand along my jaw, stroked his fingers through my hair before gripping it at the nape of my neck and holding tight. He tugged my head back so he could angle his kiss deeper.

When he parted from me, I was dazed, like warm putty in his hands. I'd had quick kisses before; I'd made out with strangers in bars before fleeing, too timid to do anything more. But this time, I didn't want to stop. I wasn't going to run away.

"Oh, my dear Lady Witch . . ." His voice vibrated against me with a satisfying rumble as he sank his head against my neck and kissed behind my ear. "I want to do such filthy things to you." I shivered at the touch of his teeth, those sharp fangs barely skimming me. "Mm, but you've never been penetrated before, have you?"

"I . . ." Anxious shame swirling in my stomach. There were only two ways people had ever reacted to me telling them I was a virgin—either with bizarre fascination or mockery. I didn't want it to matter, but it always did. Apparently not even demons were exempt. "No, I never have been. I've never . . . I've never had sex with anyone."

"I like the way you say that." He tipped my head back further and his tongue traced along my throat, the forked sides sliding over my flesh. "Like you're defiant. Like it's a challenge. It makes no difference to me, darling, except . . ." He loosened his hold and let my head come forward. This close, the size of him was even more apparent. It was terrifying, to think that *that* was supposed to fit inside *me*. "I'll have to take my time with you so I don't injure you. I'll have to stretch you slowly, one finger at a time. I'll make that sweet pussy drip for me."

My mouth uselessly opened and closed, left absolutely

dumbfounded at his words, like my brain was about to short circuit.

"You've had a little taste now," he whispered. "You've had time to think. I told you to consider carefully. So, are you still so certain you'll let a demon corrupt you?"

I nodded. There were a million doubts in my mind but not one was stronger than my certainty. I'd been desperate for a way out, desperate for freedom, and this . . . this was it.

He grabbed my hips and tugged me forward, right to the edge of the chair. My arms flailed, gripping tightly against the armrests as I stared at him between my legs. He tugged down my trousers, pulling them off my legs and tossing them aside. I hadn't shaved in ages—why bother if no one was going to see it?—and self-consciousness quickly reared its ugly head.

"You're so soft," Callum murmured, caressing his hand over my thighs. The sharpness of his claws made me shiver, but he was moving carefully, inspecting every inch of me. Maybe if I'd planned on losing my virginity today, I would have worn something sexier than navy blue panties.

Callum dipped his head, running his tongue along my skin and making me quiver. "Mm, sensitive little thing. You've played with yourself before, haven't you?" He paused, mouth just inches from my panties, sending goose bumps prickling across my legs. "Tell me how you like it. Tell me what you think about when you push your fingers inside yourself. Tell me what makes it feel good."

I'd never put those thoughts into words before, never tried to articulate to anyone what I wanted, let alone what *felt good*. I'd read descriptions in books that sounded like heaven, I'd watched porn that had me sweating from how hot it was. But verbalizing it, putting those desires into words, was something I had no idea how to do.

He didn't miss a beat. As my mind turned into a hurricane of embarrassment and uncertainty, he kept delicately touching me and said, "Soft or hard?"

I watched, mesmerized, as his claws left thin red lines down my flesh. "Hard."

He gripped one leg and pushed it up, folding it close to my stomach while shoving the other leg to the side. I was splayed open for him now, curled in the chair.

"Gentle? Or rough?"

I gulped, but I knew what I wanted. "Rough."

"Oh, Everly . . ." He chuckled softly. "I did hope you'd say that."

He shoved my other leg up, pressing my thigh close to my chest just as he had with the other one. But when he stood up, hands no longer gripping me, I was left confused as to why I still couldn't lower my legs.

Slim black ropes were wrapped around my limbs, binding my calves to my thighs to keep them folded up. There were also ropes around the armrests, binding my legs to them too, forcing them to stay spread open. Callum leaned his hands against either side of the chair, looking down at me as he ran that wicked forked tongue over his lips.

"Wrapped up like a little present," he said. "Just for me."

"How did you do that?" I gasped.

"I created them," he said simply. "Magic is simply influencing the chemical compounds around you, nudging the atoms to do what you want. Influencing aether takes practice and time. But I've had a lot of time."

"Teach me how," I said suddenly. "I want to learn how to do that."

His grin remained, one hand lazily reaching down to lift my chin. "One lesson at a time. Someday I'll teach you how to tie me up as nicely as you please, but today's lesson is about pleasure. How pleasure can be ecstasy, and how it can be torture."

With one hand still holding my chin, the other disappeared lower, outside my range of vision. His claws stroked over my panties, and a single finger came to rest on my clit. My breath hitched as he moved the digit in a slow, firm circle. Embarrassment demanded I close my legs, but the ropes wouldn't allow it. They kept me spread and his grip on my chin kept my eyes on his.

"You're so beautiful," he said, his voice low and rough, but reverent. His finger pressed a little harder, a little faster. "Perfect for me to ruin."

His finger kept playing, rubbing my clit with a single-minded determination; he was going to make me come, and he hadn't even gotten my panties off yet. A second finger joined the first, massaging me, and the additional stimulation had my bound legs twitching.

"A little appetizer before the main course," he said,

dark eyes staring into mine as my mouth gaped open in shock. "I'm not taking these panties off until you've soaked them."

I moaned helplessly. He never let me look away, not even for a moment. When my toes curled and my cries became more urgent, he hummed and moved the hand on my chin lower, to my throat.

"Let me see how pretty you are when you come," he said. "Go on. Come for me."

The buildup had been slow and steady until my peak. Then, it was like my body shattered, tensing, shaking, every bit of me taut until—*fuck*—bliss. Muscles limp, my core vibrating, my bound legs straining as the orgasm crashed into me. I'd made myself come before, but when it was by someone else's hand, the experience was stunningly different. Breathtaking.

"You are too exquisite. You smell so fucking good."

In a daze, my vision blurred, I nodded mindlessly through the aftershocks. He tore my panties away and jerked my hips toward him.

He knelt between my legs. His face was so close; he'd be able to see everything, and I wanted to cover my face with my hands.

"Please!" I gasped, and he went still, arching up a single eyebrow in question. "Please, I want . . ." I couldn't form the words. "I'm sorry, I need—"

"Ah! What did I tell you?" He was practically vibrating with excitement, his movements becoming quicker. "Didn't I warn you about apologizing? Hm?" I whimpered again, nodding. "Well, I'm so sorry to say, but I'm

a demon of my word. I have to punish you for that."
The ropes tightened, and my arms were pulled up by an
invisible force, extending them above my head along the
back of the chair. Ropes slithered around my wrists like
serpents, locking me into place.

Softer now, the demon said, "If you want your punishment to stop, ask for mercy. Repeat it for me now, say
the word."

"Mercy," I said, the word feeble.

"There's my good girl. Remember that." The room
grew dimmer, until Callum was nothing more than a dark
silhouette looming over me. "What did I say would happen if you apologized to me again?"

Gulping in apprehension, I said, "You said you'd
eat me."

His laughter filled the space, echoing unnaturally off
the walls. "Oh, yes. I'm going to eat you alive."

Then he leaned forward and his mouth closed over
me. His tongue stroked over my clit, my labia, my entrance—then pressed inside. The heat and suction of his
mouth, combined with the entirely new sensation of a
forked tongue twisting inside me, left me gasping.

"Oh, God . . . Callum!" My toes curled as perfect
orgasmic bliss flared through me again. The ropes subtly glowed violet against my skin, digging in as I fought
against them, unable to move. His tongue pressed deeper,
stroking inside me until my eyes rolled back, probing in
and out.

"This is what happens." His voice rumbled around
me despite his mouth being occupied, like he was speaking

directly into my head. "To naughty witches who try to play with dangerous things."

I cried out, trembling in ecstasy. When his mouth finally left me, I was panting, my head light. He stood up, leaned over me, and squeezed my face with one hand as he held up two fingers with the other.

He retracted his claws, then slipped his hand between my legs . . .

The noises he drew out of me were so lewd that my face burned. He stretched me slowly, gently, and when his fingers were sunk in as deep as they would go, he drew them back and pressed in again.

"That's it, let your body relax."

My pussy was squeezing, *clenching,* grasping at his fingers. My muscles were spasming outside of my control, and when he added a third finger, I groaned loudly with every inch he pushed inside me.

"It's so tight," I gasped, then squealed as he lowered his head again and flicked his tongue over my clit. Back and forth, over and over, the forked sides working me from every angle as his fingers thrust into me.

By the time he lifted his head again, I was half-lucid with pleasure. He was tall enough that he needed to kneel again to line up his cock with my entrance. My eyes were wide as he rubbed his thick head over my clit, drawing more pathetic noises out of me.

"I'm too big for you," he said, and I whined, protesting his assessment even though it was obviously true. "I'd rip you open, darling."

"Don't care . . ." Shaking my head irrationally, I tried

to make my voice authoritative but completely failed. "Please fuck me, I don't care if it hurts."

"I care." He kissed my thighs; first on the left, then on the right, then another kiss just above the soft hair between my legs. "We'll have plenty more opportunities to open up this beautiful body, Everly. I want to savor every second."

Dripping wet as I was, his cock slipped easily inside. At least—his head did. But the moment he pressed a little more, the aching stretch made my breathing deepen. A little more, and I was groaning, then whimpering.

"Shit . . ." I grit my teeth, watching with rapt fascination as his monstrous organ squeezed a little deeper inside me. But he wasn't even halfway in, and I was beginning to believe if I took anymore, he would rip me in half. "Callum, I-I don't think—"

"I know." He was so tense he shook, his hair dangling in his face as he gave me a sharp grin and moved inside me. Shallow thrusts, but they were shocking nonetheless. The way my body clung to him, my inner walls squeezing with every penetration. "I'm not going to break you, not this time. Take it for me. Take the pain, take the pleasure. Let yourself feel it."

The intensity of him inside me, our bodies locked into one overwhelming union, made my eyes roll back every time he moved.

"I'm going to mark you," he said, his words rapid, his pitch kicking up with an excitement that seemed beyond his control. "I'm going to come all over those pretty lips . . ." He grabbed my blouse and tore, the fabric ripping easily in his hands. "All over this gorgeous body." He snarled as he shuddered, moving erratically. "I'm not going to break you this time. But you broke me the moment I laid eyes on you."

He pulled out of me and stood, his hand wrapping around his thick shaft. He stroked himself roughly, fast and hard, until spurts of pearlescent cum dripped over my face, my tits, my pussy. His black eyes were so far away, as if for a moment, his essence left his body and floated through some other reality. But then he returned, and he bent over me as if in prayer, body trembling, murmuring breathlessly.

"My beautiful thread of fate. My lady. My mistress."

The words wrapped around me just like his ropes, holding me in comfort.

CALLUM

AS SOON AS I vanished the ropes from her limbs, Everly disappeared.

Luckily, it wasn't another instance of spontaneous teleportation. She shut herself in the bathroom, mumbling something about cleaning up. Within a few minutes, the pipes groaned, and the sound of running water emanated from behind the closed door.

Usually, I was the one making a swift exit. Although I'd neglected my desires for the past few decades, prior to that, I was a fiend for pleasure. But humans were clingy, and I didn't have the time nor desire. Sticky skin, their arms around me, murmuring words of praise and affection—I shuddered at the thought. That was why I was always sure to quickly leave after an encounter, lest these humans think there was some kind of coitus-induced bond between us.

But every time I paced toward Everly's bedroom door, I couldn't bring myself to leave.

The rush of hormones and happy chemicals that flooded her as we played were fading now; I could smell them growing faint. From experience, I was aware such a drastic change in hormone levels could result in a human not feeling well, depressing one's mood until the body was in balance again.

She needed sugar, alcohol, and food. Those things usually made humans feel better.

With that thought in mind, I teleported down to the kitchen. There was plenty of food here, kept perfectly preserved, thanks to magic. Now that a witch was in the house again, the herbs in the windowsill planter box were growing, and doubtlessly, the garden behind the green-house was full of fruits and vegetables once more. Facing a plethora of teas, wines, meads, potions, and poultices, I frowned at the dizzying options.

"Winona," I said, and the air stirred as her ghost came near. "What does one give to a woman after fuck-ing her?"

"What does one— WHAT!" Ghostly hands smacked my head. "You wretched demon! Have you killed the poor girl?!"

"Killed? I've never killed a mate." I frowned, waving my hands to shoo away the furious wisps of her spirit. "You said yourself she should take the pleasure she wanted. And need I remind you that the human vaginal cavity is made to stretch to accommodate—"

"I swear, if you dare try to explain childbirth to

an old grandmother, I will curse you to never be erect again."

Immediately, I shut my mouth. While I didn't believe ghosts *could* cast curses, I wasn't going to risk it. She was still grumbling, but things were moving about on the shelves as if she was searching for something, sending canisters and little pouches of herbs floating down to the countertop.

"I don't understand your anger," I said. "Would you have preferred she penetrate me instead?"

Whispered curses floated through the air. "It certainly would have been preferable."

That was fair enough. I still didn't *understand*, but humans worked in mysterious ways. "Well then, we'll try that next time."

The explosion of cursing that followed my declaration told me perhaps I should stop talking entirely.

Regardless of Winona's irritation, she gave me what I needed. At her instruction, I selected a crisp biscotti from its jar, laying it on a plate with a variety of fresh fruits. Meanwhile, Winona was combining a variety of herbs in a bubbling pot, and when she deposited it into a teacup, the scent was vile.

"This tea smells like piss," I said. Another ghostly smack was delivered to the back of my head.

"Make sure she drinks all of it." A soft breeze whispered through the air, masking the gross smell with the somewhat milder scent of lemongrass. "The last thing that poor girl needs is to get pregnant."

With a scoff, I said, "She's not a full-blooded witch; her father has no magic. Such a thing is nearly impossible."

"You know how much magic is in her. Full-blooded or not, we can't risk it."

"As you say, then." With a shrug, I let her have her way. Collecting the plate and the gross-smelling tea, I couldn't help chuckling as the old ghost grumbled one last complaint at me.

"Wretched demon waited two thousand years for that woman and couldn't even keep it in his pants for forty-eight hours. Typical."

EVERLY WAS STILL in the bath when I returned to her bedroom, but the door wasn't locked. She jolted upright as I walked into the bathroom, staring at me with her arms crossed over her naked chest and her legs pulled up.

"Haven't you ever heard of knocking?" she exclaimed. Why the hell was she bothering to cover herself? I'd already seen all of her, I'd been inside her.

Humans were so strange.

"You need sustenance." I set the plate of fruit and biscotti on the small glass table beside the tub. "And your grandmother says you must drink this. Blame her for the taste, not me."

She stared at the things I'd brought her with suspicion. The way her eyes darted around reminded me of a cornered rabbit, searching constantly for an exit. Usually such a display of fear would turn me on, but from her, it made me uncomfortable in a way I wasn't used to.

She should have been running wild through an endless summer. Naked limbs and wild hair. Unbridled smiles and laughs that were too loud. She should have been bursting with all the power and hope inside her.

Instead, she was muted. A fire struggling to survive in the rain, a masterpiece with gray paint thrown over it. It made me long to throw kindling on her flames, shelter her heat until it grew so strong nothing could vanquish it.

It was dangerous to feel that way. Fate taught me better than to feel such things.

"You brought this for me?"

She was obviously hungry; I could hear her stomach growling as she stared at the fruit.

"Your body needs fuel to recover," I said. Picking up a sliver of orange, I offered it to her, holding it close to her lips so the smell could tempt her. "Go on. You're shaking. The food will help."

Never taking her eyes from my face, she ate the fruit from my fingers. Her lips touched me briefly, an electric current shooting between us that made her wince, then softly smile as she chewed the food.

If only I could see into her mind, read her thoughts like a book. So many years had passed since I first saw her face, but in all that time, I'd tried not to imagine what she would be like. Listening for her name, through century after century, watching the human world change and countless generations pass by—never finding her. Always wondering, but never daring to hope.

That first taste of food whet her appetite, and she ate enthusiastically. She eyed me with uncertainty when I dragged in a chair from the bedroom, positioning it so I could keep my eyes on her.

"You really don't understand what privacy is, do you?" Her lips twitched with a suppressed smile.

"To be free of observation or disturbance by other people," I said, reciting the definition easily. I was perfectly fluent in most human languages. The ones I didn't know, I could easily learn by listening to it for a couple of days. Propping one leg atop the other so I was a bit more comfortable, I said, "But I am not *people*. I'm your guardian."

"*Self-declared* guardian," she said. But she didn't tell me to leave. She took a sip of her tea, made a face, and put it down again.

"Your grandmother insists you drink it," I said. "I suppose it's a method of birth control."

She suddenly looked as if she was going to spew out the tea she'd just choked down. "It's—what? That's possible? For you to . . . oh, God."

"Calm yourself. Winona is showing an overabundance of caution. It is likely wise of her, but don't let it frighten you. Such pregnancies are extremely uncommon."

Despite my assurances, she gulped down the rest of the tea. As she chewed a mouthful of fruit to wash down the taste, I was distracted by the shine of the juice upon her lips. Her face hid her emotions, but her eyes gave it away.

"Something is still worrying you," I said. More discomfort poured into me, demanding that I fix whatever was causing her distress. It made me fidget, and I began snapping my fingers to keep calm.

She stared out the window, at the streaking rain, her heart fluttering like the wings of a frightened bird.

"I have to go back, don't I?" she said grimly. "I have to go back to my family to steal the grimoire, if we're going to get into the vault."

"You don't have to do anything you don't want to. The decision is yours alone. No one will force you. There may be other opportunities to steal the grimoire, without making your presence known to your family. Besides, Winona is only guessing that whatever is contained in the vault will help us. Even she doesn't know exactly what lies within."

Although I didn't say it aloud, the situation was certainly complicated. Her father was clearly a cautious man, and I couldn't steal the grimoire from him myself. Nor could I kill the man, as much as I wanted to, thanks to the wretched iron talisman he carried. Any attack I attempted on him would be turned against me.

Everly shook her head, determination on her face. "This whole situation is going to make my father extremely paranoid. I don't think he knew Jeremiah was going to kill Marcus; he would never have allowed a sacrifice to be so messy. People are going to ask questions, there's going to be investigations. He hates that." She gulped, finally looking at me again. "He might stop leaving the house with the grimoire. He might lock it up somewhere. I need to be close to him to know what he does. To steal it, I need him to let his guard down."

"As I said, the decision is yours alone. Whatever you choose to do, I will assist you."

She looked at me curiously. She and I wore similar armor, and I didn't blame her for her caution.

When I left Hell behind, I was running from the pain

that came with every long night and burning sunrise. Pain I couldn't escape in the depths of liquor or the heights of mind-altering potions. I took humans as lovers but never claimed their souls. I avoided other demons, and over the years, my name was forgotten.

I did everything and anything I could to disappear. I pursued no friendships, I offered no love. And yet, one glimpse of her, and I was broken. I was weak again, aching. All the raw pain I'd buried was clawing to the surface.

She didn't need magic to destroy me; she could do so with delicate caresses and kisses light as feathers. She could make me pour out my pain and then fill me with more.

Yet, I'd let her do it. Even if it meant the death of me. If this was the final joke cruel fate would play, then I would laugh along with it.

"I choose to go back," she said. Her words shook, but they were brave. "I'm going to steal the grimoire, and get into that damn vault. And then . . ." Her fingers tightened on the edge of the tub. "You and I, we're going to kill that thing."

The fierceness in her voice made me want to kiss her again. Every second I wasn't touching her filled me with the most blissful, agonized longing, but I would gladly suffer for her. Bowing my head, I said, "As my lady commands, so it shall be done."

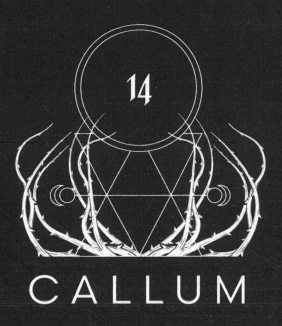

CALLUM

OUR PLAN WAS simple, although I loathed carrying it out. Returning Everly to her family felt wrong.

"I know how to handle them," she insisted, trying to assure both me and her grandmother, who didn't seem fond of the idea either. "My father will be suspicious, but he'll keep me close to have his eye on me. That will give me the opportunity I need."

"And if it doesn't, I can remove you from the situation immediately," I said. "I'll be close by and watching carefully."

"Don't let her out of your sight, Callum," Winona said. "There's no telling what Kent or his horrible children will do. The first sacrifice has been made, the God is stirring. It will be watching."

The reminder of the Deep One's watchful eye had me on edge. The wretched creature was still trapped underground, too weak to survive in the outside world. It needed the darkness, cold water, and mud of the mines to keep Its massive, unnatural body from falling apart.

Creatures from other dimensions shouldn't have been able to survive here, and yet, these Gods had found a way.

Its physical form was trapped, but Its psychic influence wasn't. It could still extend Its influence into vulnerable minds, gleaning knowledge and sapping energy. Without proper training, Everly was susceptible to Its attacks.

But she was determined, confident she could steal the grimoire from right under her father's nose. I only hoped she could manage it before the God stole her mind instead.

INSTEAD OF FLYING Everly back to her family, I showed her the path through the woods. The rain had ceased that morning, and the forest was thriving after the downpour. Using her sketchbook, Everly recorded the path I showed her, drawing a map that would lead her from the coven house to the nearest road.

She seemed at ease beneath the trees. She hummed as she walked and stopped frequently, to admire a blooming flower or to watch a deer and her fawn slink away into the trees.

I didn't share her sense of calm.

From the moment I stepped foot outside the coven house, I was being watched. The air was thick with the scent of loam and sprouting grass; but beneath the forest smells was another, faint but familiar.

Sharp and prickling at the back of my throat, like iron and smoke.

We walked on, passing through a dense section of woodland that was teeming with wildflowers. Their scent filled the air, a heady perfume that could swiftly make a human drowsy if they weren't careful.

"The flowers are enchanted, aren't they?" Everly said. Her nose wrinkled as she sniffed. "The smell of them is so potent."

"Not enchanted, but certainly magic. Darragh has command over this forest. He knows every tree, every plant, every root. The forest protects the house, and in return, the coven protected the forest. At least, while there was still a coven present."

A violent twitch ran up my back, and I paused. Somewhere behind me, deep within the trees, a twig snapped. The birds were silent. The air was strangely still.

Everly noticed my hesitation. "Is something wrong?"

"Nothing at all. We should move quickly, before the flowers get to your head. They'll have you walking in circles if you breathe their toxins for too long."

But something was wrong indeed.

BEFORE WE PARTED ways, Everly tore both her map and my sigil out of her notebook. Folding them up and storing them within a small plastic bag she dug out of her purse, she buried them in the woods close to her family's house.

"You'll be watching, right?"

She'd come up with a simple story to explain her

disappearance, but there was no guarantee her family would believe her. But the only evidence of deceit was now buried, safely stowed away for when she needed it.

"Always." Combing my fingers through her hair, I gripped the long locks and pulled her close, kissing her tender mouth. Her body was tight, tense and uncertain for a split second before she melted against me. "Remember this, darling. Even when you can't see me, I'll be there. No one can harm you. No one else can touch you."

"No one else?" A little grin took over her mouth, and I longed to kiss her again. "Besides yourself, you mean?"

"Certainly."

"As if you own me?"

Still gripping her hair, I pulled her head back just a little more, letting her feel the ache of my hold. "I could not own you any more than one can own the ocean, or a storm, or a forest fire. Those are not things one owns; their beauty and power cannot be claimed in such a way. But they can be chased. And they can be worshiped."

When she exhaled, sparks flashed in her breath.

"Then I'll see you soon?"

"I swear it."

I loathed watching her go, and loathed it even more when I heard the raised voices of her family at her arrival. But her absence was for the best. That prickling feeling was creeping up my neck again, and I knew with certainty this time . . .

I was being hunted.

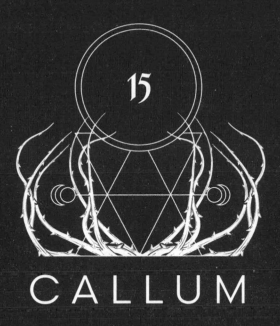

CALLUM

AS THE SUN dipped below the horizon, stretching the shadows and casting the woodlands into gray dusk, I was hunting.

But I wasn't the only one. Somewhere beneath those very same trees, another demon was hunting me too. It was unlikely she had any intent of hurting me. Sneaking around her in circles, masking my presence so she could no longer pinpoint exactly where I was, was no doubt going to infuriate her to the point she wished she could hurt me though.

I'd never played nice with authority figures. No demon had ever turned down an invitation to be a member of the Council, none had ever refused Lucifer's mark. It was an honor, a true accomplishment, something most demons would envy.

But not me. To say Lucifer had been displeased with me would be an understatement.

But that was hundreds of years ago. Surely the bastard had forgiven me by now.

Laughing to myself, I said aloud, "Surely not. Lucifer isn't the forgiving type, is he?"

"Not in the least."

Her voice was close behind me, but I didn't turn. I just grinned, nodding my head and shifting from foot to foot, considering if I should make this even more difficult for her and run.

Maybe it was better to behave. After all, she knew about Everly. Until I heard what she had to say, I at least had to attempt good behavior.

"Leaina," I said. "My, my. I've really gotten Lucifer pissed, haven't I?"

Her footsteps didn't make a sound as she stepped out from behind the trees. She wore red, as usual, a beautifully stark color against her deep brown skin. Her tightly curled hair formed a halo around her face, which was professionally kept emotionless. She had a single silver ring pierced through the center of her lower lip, set with an onyx stone, and multiple jewels studded her ears.

The lip ring was Lucifer's mark. He pierced every member of the Council, an act of intimacy and loyalty, a form of welcoming them as one of his closest confidants.

"A pleasure to see you, Callum. As always." Her voice was perfectly even, and I shook my head, clicking my tongue.

"Please drop the niceties. You're not pleased to be here or to see me. I'm hardly a pleasure. No need to lie."

She sighed, her wings stretching comfortably before

she leaned against the tree behind her. Leaina: Lucifer's right hand, his most called-upon member of the Council. After I refused my offer, she rose to prominence with a single-minded determination to prove her loyalty.

"You're right," she said, producing a thick black envelope from somewhere on her person and holding it up. "I'm not pleased to be here, Callum. Again."

"Ah, fuck." I exhaled heavily. "You have a file."

"*Your* file." She opened the envelope and withdrew the sizeable stack of papers from within. "It seems to always be growing larger."

"My apologies for not being more boring."

"You were boring enough for the last few decades." She withdrew a pen from her jacket and gave it several quick clicks. "But that's changed quickly, hasn't it? You fell off the radar for years, and now you return with a bloody bang."

She withdrew a sheet from the file and held it up. A missing person poster for Sam Hawthorne. I smiled, and she slipped it away again.

Her voice was sharp, clipped. "You're responsible then?"

"You wouldn't be here if you didn't already know I was."

She tapped her pen rapidly on the back of the file. "You know I still have to take the appropriate procedures."

"Fine, fine. Go on then. Scold me."

She glared, but she was the one who wanted to follow *procedure*. "Alright. Let's review, since you've taken responsibility. You tortured and killed a human. He was not attempting to summon you nor were you currently bound to his service. The killing was not in defense of yourself nor in defense of another—"

"It was in defense of another."

She glanced up in surprise. "Was it really? Was Mr. Hawthorne in the process of harming someone when you accosted him?"

I grit my teeth. My claws ached with the want to *make* her leave. But I couldn't. "No."

"Were you obligated to kill Mr. Hawthorne by the orders of a summoner who held power over you? Or were you obligated to do so by the terms of a soul bargain?"

"Don't fucking insult me, Leaina."

"I'll damn well insult you if that's what it takes," she hissed. "You were seen clearly on security cameras, Callum. Wings, claws, all of it. You were recorded snatching him off the street, gouging his eyes out, and *flying off with him.*"

"That's unfortunate." Security cameras . . . huh. I hadn't thought of that. That wasn't really a worry when I'd locked myself up in House Laverne. "I'm sure you've already taken care of it?"

"Obviously. I've been running all over the place trying to ensure your mess doesn't get out of hand." Every tap of her pen was chipping away at my patience. "Let's talk about the coven, Callum. Let's talk about your witch."

"Let's not. Tell the Council to close their eyes and look the other way. They're good at doing that about any of their actual responsibilities. Can't imagine why it's so difficult to do it when it comes to me."

"You know *very* well why. We've been lenient through the centuries. Letting you run all over Earth on your God-hunting crusade. We've looked away from far more than we should have. But this witch . . ." She flipped through several sheets of paper. When I saw Everly's photo on the page she turned to, something vicious raised its head in me. "Everly Hadleigh, also known by her mother's surname, Laverne. Twenty-three years old. The daughter of Kent Hadleigh and Heidi Laverne, a powerful witch in her own right as the daughter of Winona Laverne. Everly has quite the impressive pedigree." She looked at me pointedly. "You haven't claimed her soul yet."

And there it was. "No. I haven't."

"But obviously you intend to. *Hastily.*"

We paused, tense silence growing between us. I had to choose my words carefully.

"I'm in no rush. Frankly, I'm more concerned with claiming her for myself, before I claim her for Hell."

Leaina flashed me a quick, exasperated smile. "Claiming her for yourself and claiming her for Hell are one and the same. Surely, you'll find it in your best interest to have her soul bound to yours. The power that would give you would be . . ." She paused, and for the first time in this wretched conversation, I heard something truly sincere. "It would be astronomical. Almost unheard of."

"As I said, no rush."

I was already sick of standing here and trading tense smiles. Hell's Council was made up of six of the oldest and strongest of demonkind. I'd almost been one of them, invited to join the Council once the war was over and I was being called a "hero."

But while the rest of the Council was eager for Hell to forget the horrors of the war against the Gods, it was impossible for me. Like so many others who had fought, I couldn't forget even the things I desperately wanted to.

I remembered it all. The blood, the pain, the torture, the hundreds of lives lost. Demons I'd known, demons I'd loved, lying dead around me as far as the eye could see.

That shit couldn't be forgotten, and it couldn't be allowed to happen again.

But Leaina was insistent. "You know the laws, Callum. You know why they're there, why these *very few* rules we have are necessary. Lucifer is willing to make an exception for you but *only* if you claim the witch's soul. We can't take the risk of a half-demon being born to a mother who isn't even bound for Hell. *Especially* when that mother is so powerful."

"Getting a bit ahead of things, aren't you?" I said. "I've only just fucked her, Leaina. Calm down. Tell Lucifer to worry about his own seed rather than mine."

"Callum." The warning in her voice was evident, but I really didn't care. After all, *she* was the professional.

"Boo-fucking-hoo. Lucifer has plenty of other ass-kissers, he can afford to lose one."

She rubbed a hand over her face, scratching her claws along her jawline. "You need to return to Hell. Immediately."

"No, I don't think I will."

"You need to come back. You're not well."

"Not well? Really? Is the Council suddenly concerned for my health after all this time?"

"We've been concerned ever since you began this *fixation*. Centuries of obsessing over a witch you envisioned for only a few minutes. A witch who hadn't even yet been born in linear time." She huffed in exasperation.

This conversation wasn't going anywhere, but I'd known it wouldn't before we started. "Tell the Council that while I appreciate their concern, it's unneeded. I'll take care of what's mine."

"I need something more than that, Callum." Despite her obvious irritation with me, I could hear her concern too. She was a fierce demon, loyal, one I'd known for a long time. But our loyalties lay in different worlds. "Lucifer won't accept that, and Bael and Paimon won't interfere if he chooses to come after you."

"Then he can come and have it out with me himself."

She looked like I'd slapped her. She roughly tucked her envelope back inside her jacket, her claws ripping the paper as she did. "Madness. Utter fucking *madness*." She stalked away, brushing roughly against my side as she did. "Mark the witch. Claim her. If you want any hope of keeping her, if she truly means so much to you, then do it. When Lucifer comes, he won't be as kind as I've been."

EVERLY

AFTER SPENDING MY last few days in the coven house, my father's home felt dead. Like bleached bones, left in the sun until they were cracked, brittle, and dry.

Sitting in the hard wooden chair before his desk, wringing my hands in my lap, I waited for my father to acknowledge me. He sat there flipping through paperwork, signing a sheet here and there, checking notifications on his phone.

I was merely one more unwelcome item on his to-do list.

When he finally sighed, his pen clicking with ominous finality before he set it down, my stomach churned as if I was going to be sick.

Just stick to the story. Simple. Easy. You've done nothing wrong.

"I'll ask you once again," he said. "Where did you go?"

My mouth was so dry, my tongue stuck to the roof of my mouth as I tried to speak. "I woke up in the oak tree in the park. Near Mama's old apartment. I-I don't know how, Dad. Really, I don't. Jeremiah scared me and I guess my magic must have—"

His scoff cut me off. "Your *magic*? Everly . . ." He pinched the bridge of his nose between his thumb and forefinger, closing his eyes for a moment. "I've told you before, countless times, that attempting to use magic could kill you. You're not a witch, not like your mother was. The magic in your veins is weak, practically un-usable. You've not only endangered yourself, you've endangered *everything* we have built."

"I know. I'm sorry. I didn't mean to do it. I don't even understand how it happened." Drawing in a shuddering breath, I forced my eyes to well with tears. "I was so scared. I'm just glad to be home."

The back of my neck prickled with the uncomfortable feeling of worms squirming under my skin. God's gaze upon me. Watching me. Judging me. As if It could sense my lies.

My father's eyes bored into me, narrowing.

After moments of uncomfortable silence, he said, "Marcus's funeral is in just a few days. You will be at-tending, along with the rest of us. Afterward, Leon will bring the sacrifice's body to White Pine, where he will be dedicated to God." He leaned toward me over the desk, his hands clasped upon the stack of papers in front of him. "If you don't maintain your composure, there will be severe consequences. We need to ensure there will be no more *accidents*."

He unlocked a drawer on his desk and took something out, setting it before me. It was a pair of thick glass cylinders, open at both ends, with faint, shimmering veins running through them. He pressed an invisible mechanism and one of the cylinders sprang open, its two halves connected with a hinge.

"This magic of yours must be brought under control," he said. "Hold out your arms."

Dread filled me, but I obeyed. The moment he enclosed one around my wrist and it clicked into place, something sharp punctured my skin, digging into the soft spot on my inner wrist. Pain shot through my arm, as if my bones were splintering into dust. Screaming in panic, I tried to pull away, but my father had a tight grip on my arm.

He locked the other cuff onto me. Agony filled me, so intense that I blacked out as I curled over the desk. Perhaps I was still screaming, perhaps I was silent; for the next few minutes, I truly didn't know.

When I came back to reality, I was sitting limply in the chair, my forehead dripping with sweat, my chest heaving. The pain had faded to a dull ache, and when I looked down, the glass cuffs were sealed tightly around my wrists.

Beneath the glass, bright red blood was pooling.

Shaking, my voice weak, I said, "What the hell are these?"

"Watch your tongue," my father said sharply. "They will keep your magic under control so we don't have another incident." He waved his hand dismissively as a wave of dizziness nearly made me black out again.

Trying not to panic, I said, "When can I take them off?"

"When you've proven yourself trustworthy. Until then, this is what is best for your safety. For *our* safety. God knows there's enough risk to us already, thanks to Jeremiah acting so rashly." He sighed heavily. "Furthermore, I've withdrawn your enrollment at the university."

My breath caught, sinking into my throat like a fish-hook. My eyes stung, vision blurring.

"Please don't." The plea burst out of me before I could stop it, but to do anything else would have been suspicious. Running away would end my studies regardless, my hopes of a degree—but what did a degree matter if humanity itself came to an end? Still, if I didn't protest, he would wonder why. He had chosen to take this away specifically because he knew how much it would hurt me.

"It pains me to do it, Everly, but you can't be trusted." He scoffed as tears rolled down my face. "I've told you before it's a frivolous waste of your time. You have duties of faith to attend to instead. What exactly did you think you were going to do with that ridiculous degree any-way? History, of all things." He shook his head at me, as if my choice of degree was a personal insult. Even though I'd chosen it because of him. Even though he was the one who'd fostered my love of ancient things.

The fact that he'd managed to have any influence on me at all made me angry.

The tears came to me a little too easily, but that was what he wanted. To see me hurt, shaking in regret, pleading for mercy. I barely cared anymore what I had to say or do to placate him.

"I could have worked at the Historical Society," I said, sniffing as I reached for the tissues on his desk. "With you."

He smiled at me as if I were a very stupid little child. "I don't need another secretary, Everly."

Not a thing he said should have been able to hurt me, and yet those words were like knives stabbing between my ribs.

I buried my face in my hands and sobbed. It didn't take much effort to sound authentic; I had plenty of pent-up tears to spill.

"I'm failing God," I cried, face still covered with my hands. "I feel so weak, so—so useless! I can't control my magic and it's letting you down." Lifting my tearstained face, I looked into my father's eyes. "Can't you teach me to be better? You know magic, you have the grimoire, you . . . you could teach me how to control it. So this doesn't happen anymore."

My desperation came across as sincerity, and my father's face softened. He reached into his jacket, and as my heart pounded, he drew out the grimoire and held it up.

It was a small book, thin and bound in leather. Faint but elegant text marked the cover, Latin words roughly translating to *Magical Work and Conjuring*. My mouth

SOUL OF A WITCH   163

practically salivated at the sight of it, wild fantasies bursting into my mind. I envisioned myself snatching it from his hands, sprinting from the room, down the hall, out the front door. Callum would be waiting for me, he would protect me from Leon, protect me from my father. He would fly me away on those massive wings—

"This grimoire is my most valuable tool," my father said, snapping me from my thoughts. "But my second most valuable, Everly, is you. A young lady such as yourself does not have any need to access magic. That power is for God."

"I don't understand. What use does God have for me?"

Tucking the grimoire away, my father regarded me in silence for several long moments before he said, "Someday, when our God rises from the deep and remakes this world, It will need a vessel. It will need a body filled with power, a mind filled with faith. It will need *you*."

My heart hammered. Even already knowing the truth, to hear him say it was stunning. "Me? I'm . . . *I'm* supposed to be the vessel?"

"One of your siblings will give up their life to fulfill our oath to God. One will remain to lead the Libiri when I am gone. And one will carry the God Itself. You, your brother, and your sister all have a greater purpose in the Deep One's plan."

He rose from his chair, coming around the desk to grasp my hands.

"I think it's time you witnessed God's greatness for yourself. When your mother had her doubts, I suggested the same thing. What she was shown through God's great power completely changed her outlook. It soothed her fears."

What the hell was he talking about? What did it mean to "witness" God's greatness?

"After the dedication of Marcus, you and I will go to St. Thaddeus. You'll see." He cupped his hand under my chin and lifted my face. I'd looked into eyes far darker than his and seen more light than I ever saw in him. "You will witness the grace of God."

EVERLY

TO OFFER OUR sacrifice, the Libiri gathered deep in the woods.

Condensation collected on the pine needles above, the little droplets growing heavier until they dripped down, creating an unsteady rhythm of rainfall. The guttering bonfire we huddled around only did so much to drive away the chill.

Two dozen worshippers in white cloaks and stag-skull masks shivered together under black umbrellas. Our family didn't wear the masks, which were meant to symbolize both our innocence and our honor.

We were to be as innocent as fawns, as faithful as a doe, and carry ourselves with the pride of a stag.

It was late in the night. My mind was wrapped in a fog I couldn't shake, but I was thankful for it when Marcus's body was brought to us, carried by my father's demon. His body had already begun to decompose, a distinct scent of formaldehyde and rot wafting around him.

He'd been dug out of his grave, still dressed in a stiff black funeral suit.

Muttered prayers and thankful murmurs surrounded me. They rattled my head like buzzing mosquitoes.

I had to stay strong. I had to play my part and wait for my opportunity.

Callum promised he would be watching. If I needed him, I could call his name and he would come. That thought was my only comfort as Jeremiah and Leon took Marcus to the mine shaft, where they would throw his body down to the Deep One.

As the other congregants dispersed to return to their homes, my father led me down another path. Not toward the road, where our vehicles were parked. But deeper into the forest, toward St. Thaddeus.

The church loomed ahead of us. St. Thaddeus was a dilapidated beauty, caving in on itself while clinging to elegance. The massive stained-glass window above the doors was covered in grime, but within it, I could faintly see the image of a maiden holding a knife, standing in the sea.

The thud of our shoes on the old boards were as heavy as my heart. The caved-in roof allowed the rain to seep in from above, pooling between the broken pews. Ahead of us, the pulpit was surrounded by mounds of wax. The remnants of candles burned down through the decades.

I could hardly breathe as I stood before the pulpit. I

wanted to flee into the night's darkness, even if it meant facing monsters. But I had to endure. I had to stay.

I needed the grimoire.

I swallowed hard, swaying on my feet as my father took a seat on one of the foremost pews. The old church creaked and groaned around us as rain dripped in. My eyes were drawn to a dark corner of the ceiling, where the shadows were so thick it was like a black cloud.

There was a face within the darkness. Callum.

My breath caught, but I had no time to rejoice. My father was speaking.

"When your mother and I first met, she already knew of the Deep One's existence," he said. It was the first time I'd ever heard him give even a passing reference to his early days with my mother. He and Meredith had already been married. "But she was resistant to Its power, she didn't trust that our God would fulfill Its promises to us. But witches like your mother, and like you, are blessed. You have the ability to commune with God when the rest of us do not. It can see through you. Even speak through you."

My horror must have shown on my face, because he clicked his tongue in sympathy. "Do not be afraid. You've been prepared for this all your life." He reached out his hand, and without any other choice, I went to him.

That creeping feeling wouldn't go away. Like fingers brushing up my back, tangling in my hair, squeezing my skull.

Let me in, let me in, let me—

Father took my hand.

"Close your eyes," he said, and I obeyed, shuddering in the dark. "Let God speak to you."

There was a sudden strong smell of seawater. The cold air was sticky. When I licked my lips, I could taste salt. Then I could smell . . .

My stomach lurched. There was a rotten stench, putrid and cloying in my throat. My breath came faster as a stifling weight pressed down on me. It squeezed the air out of my lungs.

It was silent—no, not entirely so. I could hear something. A subtle sound, slow and unsteady.

Drip . . . drip, drip . . .

Water . . . but it wasn't the rain.

Everything else faded away. The touch of my father's hand, the cold air whipping through the church, the damp clinging to my skin. All that remained was the drip, slow and distant.

Then . . . a breath. Cold and sudden on the back of my neck.

"No," I whispered the word like a frantic prayer. "It's not real. It's all in your head, Everly."

"Oh yes, child. All of it is in your head, as am I."

My eyes flew open as I stumbled back in panic. Sunlight blinded me, my senses assaulted by a dozen new things all at once.

I was standing in the middle of an open field, surrounded by tall, lush green grass. Flowers of every shape, color, and variety grew around me—hundreds of them, covering the landscape like confetti. Their scent hung heavy and sweet in the air.

A tall figure, dressed in white, stood in the grass watching me.

It was beautiful beyond words. So elegant, so perfect, that I felt completely insignificant. Small, ugly, and foolish. I couldn't bear to lift my eyes, but in my peripheral vision, I could see Its face was constantly morphing, changing subtly and slowly.

The face was unfamiliar but this feeling was not. Like a hand was gripping the nape of my neck, both holding me down and dragging me closer.

"Come to me, child. Do not be afraid."

Against my will, I crawled through the grass. Trembling, gasping, too fearful to do anything other than obey, I approached the being. The God . . . *my* God . . .

How was It so beautiful? I could spend all my life kneeling at Its feet, basking in the glory of Its presence, cutting off my fingers one by one just to please It.

My vision flashed, like static cutting through a TV broadcast. For a split second, the beautiful world around me entirely changed.

The field became smoldering embers littered with bones. The grass was gone, the trees—dead. The dirt crawled with maggots, writhing, feasting upon the flesh of corpses. And the bodies—there were hundred. Thousands. Milky eyes rolled in rotting heads. Intestines ripped out by beasts, who roamed the landscape in broad daylight. And over it all stood God, but God was not beautiful. It was—

The horror vanished. Everything was perfect. Serene. God was gracious as It smiled upon me, a smile I couldn't look at but could *feel* like warm arms around me.

"Do you see? The world as it could be?" It said. Its voice was strange, as if It were not one but hundreds of people, all speaking in unison. "The world as I will remake it?"

My vision flashed again, and I screamed. The deity before me was not a beautiful humanoid creature but a beast—a massive, indescribable monstrosity, with shapes and colors I had no words for. Its body was gargantuan, completely overtaking the land. Massive gray tentacles with grasping tooth-lined suckers coiled around me, pungent with the scent of rotting fish. It was covered in dozens of eyeballs, rolling in their sockets, reddened, pupils shaped like diamonds—

Gone. But my memory of it was not. This place, this vision—it was all fake. A mere illusion created by the deity.

This beautiful place was what my mother had been shown. Perfect. Peaceful. A world she would have longed to raise her daughter in.

But the truth was different. And I had no idea why I could see it, why my mind was able to break through the hallucinations caused by the God's control . . .

But I could. And It knew.

The sky darkened. The grass withered. My vision flashed rapidly back and forth, until the two realities were one and the same. The desire to hurt myself, to inflict pain on my own body, wrapped around my brain and squeezed, demanding I obey.

"You will give in. You will submit or you will suffer. Death is not the worst fate that can befall you, rebellious girl. Your disobedience must be culled from your mind."

I screamed again, curling up into a ball as I clutched my skull, certain it was going to split apart. I had to get out . . . had to find my way back to reality . . . out of my mind . . . but where . . . where could I go . . .

Like a beacon in my bloody, rapidly morphing vision, a silver light twinkled. It was distant . . . so, so far away . . . but I could reach it. I could crawl . . .

"You will not escape me, witch. You are already mine. You cannot exorcise that which is already a part of you. I see all. I know all. Your house in the woods will not protect you. Your demon will not defend you. Your magic will not serve you."

The agony was indescribable. But I dragged myself along the rotten earth, cheek against the dirt, fingernails clawing for grip.

"It's all in your head," I said, again and again, even though my throat was so raw. "It can't stop you. It's just in your head."

I squeezed my eyes shut. I willed myself to feel the heaviness of my body, like trying to force myself to awaken from a dream. I kept searching for that silver light, glimmering, beckoning me closer.

Suddenly, with a gasp, I ripped away from my father's hand. I lost my footing, fell hard on my side, and lay there gasping, shaking in horror.

My father's steps pounded across the floor, rattling my head. He crouched beside me, gathering me into his arms.

My shaking stopped. I went as still as a rabbit striving not to be seen, frozen in the gaze of a predator as he held me close. I could smell his cologne, the powdery scent of detergent on his clothes, the slight whiff of the scotch he'd drank before coming here.

And rot. Salt water and mold. The God clung to him like a noxious cloud.

Did it cling to me too? Was I already infected, already claimed, as the Deep One insisted?

Was there no way out for me?

"There, there, my precious girl. I know it's overwhelming." My father's hand stroked my hair, his voice low and soothing. "Your mother reacted in the same way. She would want you to pursue the joy of a world made new."

I could only nod. Anything to make him believe me.

His words quickened excitedly. "Things are already set in motion. The first sacrifice has been made, and the second will arrive soon. Raelynn Lawson is returning to Abelaum. You must meet her. The God must look upon her. It must see." The way he grasped me seemed frantic, so unlike his usual mannerisms. Like he was desperate. Like he was afraid. "It must see that we will not fail."

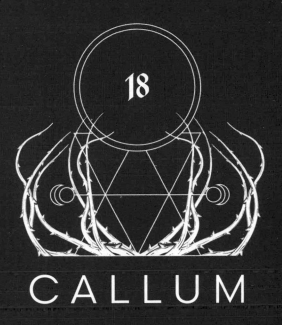

CALLUM

LUCIFER WAS COMING for me. Of that, I had no doubt. So apart from watching cautiously from a distance, I stayed away from Everly until that night.

She slept for hours, through the morning and into the evening, regaining her strength. Her dreams were fitful, but I nudged my energy against her mind, calming her swirling thoughts.

She didn't wake until her sister pounded on her door, informing her that the family was going out for the evening and would return late.

"Better not go running off again," her sister said. Everly managed to play nice and keep her mouth shut, but as her sister departed, there was a distinct scent of something burning in the air.

Waiting until her family departed in their large, shiny vehicles, I occupied myself with fantasies of their deaths.

Ripping them limb from limb, scattering their entrails, and fucking my witch in the remains. Everly would look gorgeous bathed in the blood of her enemies, and these people she lived with were enemies indeed.

Once the others were gone, I returned to her bedroom window.

The moment her family departed, she scurried to the kitchen, gathering food like a squirrel stashing nuts for the winter. Fruit, bags of chips, a bowl of soup, and a plethora of cookies.

Perhaps her family was not providing her with enough food. The urge to chase them down and kill them nearly overtook me once more.

Patience, old boy, patience. They'd get what was coming to them.

Slowly, I eased the window open. She didn't even notice as I crawled through the window onto her bed. She was seated at her desk with a small canvas before her, which she carefully drew her paintbrush across before popping a grape into her mouth.

I didn't want to scare her. Most demons had a little psychic power and could influence the brains of other living things to experience certain sensations, so I reached out and nudged her mind, as I had the previous night.

Her body jerked, and she scrambled up from her seat, clapping her hand over her mouth to hold in her scream when she noticed me standing behind her.

Well. So much for not scaring her.

"Oh my God . . ." She uncovered her mouth. "I thought you were . . . shit . . ."

She stepped closer, pressing herself against my chest and letting out a heavy sigh when I embraced her. Even a few days without touching her had been too much. The way her tense body melted against me was sheer heaven.

If I could have swallowed her whole, just to have her live beside my heart, I would have.

"I haven't had a chance to get the grimoire yet," she said shakily. "They're watching me so carefully. They're suspicious. And they have the next sacrifice. Or they will soon. A girl named Raelynn." She shuddered and shook her head. "I can't watch anyone else die. I can't do it, I can't."

"Don't dwell on what may or may not happen." I was far more concerned by the cursed magic locked around her wrists, and whatever the hell had happened in that cathedral. "These cuffs—do they hurt?"

"Not so much." She drew back, staring at the glass bindings. "At least, not anymore."

I drew her arm closer so I could have a better look at the damn things. The air around them vibrated with subtle energy, and despite being made of glass, the items smelled strange, like metal.

"You must be extremely careful with these," I said. "They're vampiric. The harder you try to use magic with them on, the more of your power they'll sap, and the stronger they'll become. Vile things."

It enraged me to see them on her. No one should have been binding my witch, save for me.

"Easy enough," Everly said, clearly trying to sound

hopeful. "I won't try to use magic at all, which . . . isn't hard for me."

"Says the woman who spontaneously teleports." I took her into my arms again, and she gasped softly when I lifted her off her feet, carrying her back to the bed. Her bed was rather small, the soft green sheets and blankets tidily arranged, just like the rest of her room.

From what I had observed, the rest of this house was painfully sterile. White walls, white carpet, white furniture. Unnaturally bright, crisp, and clean. But Everly's room smelled like pine and paint, like sweet magic and soft skin. Her belongings were scattered about on shelves or piled into corners: books and canvases, wooden knick-knacks, and little glass figurines.

She was tense as she sat between my legs. She refused to lean into me, instead curling in on herself and shuddering for a moment. How I longed to read her thoughts, if only to know instantly what was bothering her so I could destroy it.

If I were to claim her soul, then I—

No, no. Although the temptation was there, to bind myself to another living being, to intimately feel their pain and terror every waking moment, to feel with certainty when they died . . . no.

Every binding, every connection, was an open wound, and I couldn't bear any more injuries.

"What happened in the church?" She was so close to me, and yet she felt so far away. "The God spoke to you?"

She nodded, pulling up her knees and wrapping her

arms around them. "It got in my head. I thought I could shut It out, but It was too strong. It—" She shivered. "I still feel It. I still hear It. Like It lives in my head. I'm scared, Callum. What if It never goes away?"

"I won't allow that to happen. The God's presence in your mind is an illusion. It is reaching you with psychic power, nothing more. Don't think of It. Don't give It any more of your thoughts. That's exactly what It wants."

Could I truly protect her? Or would I fail her like I'd failed the others?

This room was a treasure trove of information about her; many of her books were massive volumes on history, languages, or ancient civilizations. But the ones closest to her bed had colorful elaborate covers, many of them featuring couples intertwined in each other's arms.

She sputtered when I picked up one of the paperbacks, opening it to her marked page. "W-wait, um, that's, uh—"

"Literary pornography." I smirked as I read the first passage on her marked page.

"It's not *porn*!" She looked scandalized I'd even say the word. Grasping her face, I dragged her closer, giving the silly little thing a shake.

"There's nothing wrong with what you like. Humans have such a ridiculous habit of shaming each other for what they enjoy. Erotica, porn, sex, unusual fetishes— so long as the participants are willing, there is no shame in it."

She looked confused. As if the concept of living without shame was new to her.

"Is there something in here you don't want me to see?" I settled against her headboard with the book spread open between my fingers. "The pages smell like you." Her face flushed a deep crimson as I scanned the page. "Ahh, so you like to read about a woman in charge, eh? Are you imagining yourself in such a position, or on the receiving end?"

"Oh, I, uh—both? Uh, yeah, both, I guess. I've never really been with another woman, but I'm curious." She tucked back her hair, squirming awkwardly as I read. "I don't know if I'd be any good at it though. Being in charge, I mean."

She said it with such a defeated shrug that I burst out laughing. "Well, you've never *tried* it, have you, darling?" She shook her head, and I put aside the book. "Would you like to?"

Her eyes widened. "Try it? W-with you?"

"There's no one better." Although I tried to maintain my calm, I was practically foaming at the mouth for this.

"My father's demon is downstairs." She lowered her voice. "He'll know you're here."

"He certainly won't." Nuzzling my face into her neck, I inhaled the sweet scent of her, and a deep growl rumbled in my chest. "If anything, all he'll smell is you. He'll think you're pleasuring yourself."

Her breath hitched before it slowed and deepened. "I-I don't want him to think that."

"Mm, are you sure?"

She wasn't. She arched her back, pressing her ass against me, and giving me better access to her neck. Fuck, she was such an innocent little thing and yet so ravenous. She'd been starving for years, and one taste of the bliss she'd been denied was all it took to awaken her.

Everly was working herself up just from grinding against me. But I had a different plan for her; as much as I longed to feel her warm pussy clinging around my cock, her body was going through enough already with those cuffs locked on her. It was sapping her strength.

"Your grandmother was pissed at me for fucking you," I said. "Nosey old ghost thought I might injure you."

"You *told* her?" she yelped, then quickly clapped her hand over her mouth, aghast at her volume. "Callum, that's— Goddamn it. That's *private*!"

"Please, darling. In a house full of ghosts, nothing is truly private," I said, chuckling at her mortification. "Besides, I made her a promise that I would give an equal opportunity to you to return the favor. Not that I wasn't going to do so regardless."

How could I resist? The very thought of this woman taking command of me was almost enough to make me cum without a single touch.

"What exactly do you mean?" Curiosity and confusion filled those beautiful eyes as I grabbed her face and kissed her, but she was smiling when I pulled away.

"It's your turn on top," I said. "I showed you how. Now you get to try it yourself."

For a moment, she stared at me in confusion. "Woah, woah, you want *me* to . . . you want me to fuck you? Like, actually?"

It was adorable to see her so flustered. Smirking, I nodded my head. "I've thought of nothing else for days."

I was careful to gauge her reaction, and beneath her nerves, only desire lay. If she wasn't interested, I would have abandoned the idea without complaint; I was perfectly happy to be versatile. But her excitement made me more ravenous.

She rubbed the back of her neck. "Callum, I don't exactly have the equipment to do that."

Springing eagerly to my hands and knees, I said, "Don't move a muscle. I'll be right back."

My departure wasn't long. Knowing exactly where I was going, I teleported there and back again in a matter of minutes, my only delay being that I had to hide briefly to ensure the store employees didn't see me. Hell's Council usually arranged for demons who spent time on Earth to have access to human money, but such access for myself had been cut off long ago. Doubtlessly thanks to Lucifer's petty scheming, trying anything he could to make me return to Hell.

Everly jumped when I returned, reappearing in her bedroom with a bang as my feet hit the ground. I held out the box I'd stolen, watching the stages of confusion on her face as she figured out what it was.

"That's a— Oh wow, okay, that's a penis. With . . . a harness?" Her face couldn't have turned any redder. She held up the toy with its adjustable straps, the length and size of it comparable to her forearm. "It's a strap-on. Got it."

Her eyes kept darting between me and the toy, growing wider with every pass.

"You want *me* to fuck *you* . . . with *this*?" Her voice cracked, and I couldn't keep myself from laughing. "It's . . . Callum, this thing is *massive!*"

"Afraid you'll hurt me? You don't need to worry, darling. Consider this your free pass to take out your frustrations."

She lowered her eyes.

"I've never really considered myself to be very, um . . ." She licked her lips, swallowing hard as she looked at herself in the mirror hung upon the wall. "Very dominant."

"It's entirely up to you," I said, standing close behind her. "If it doesn't intrigue you, tell me no."

"It does intrigue me."

Her whisper sent goose bumps prickling over my skin. She was still staring at the mirror, and in the reflection, her gaze met mine. Was she imagining what it would be like? Could she envision me beneath her?

I sank to my knees before her. "I ask only that you re-mind me what it means to feel something, my lady. However you wish to do that, I leave it to you to decide." But I knew by now that uncertainty made her freeze, and I didn't want to make her nervous. So I kissed the back of her hand and suggested, "If you're worried that you might hurt me, I am more than happy to prove I crave any pain you would be so kind as to grant me."

She reached out slowly, brushing her fingers over my face. "You want me to hurt you?"

"You understand the desire, don't you?" Leaning into her hand, I gave her my very best I'll-be-a-good-boy look. "It's easier to slap me down here, isn't it? Try it, go on."

She didn't move. She took her time contemplating, then said, "You killed Sam, didn't you? I saw the missing person signs."

"Sam went for a walk in the woods," I said innocently. "At night. Very foolish of him."

She drew her lips between her teeth, suppressing a smile. "You shouldn't murder people, Callum."

"Punish me for it then."

She tapped my cheek. I refused to call it a slap. To give her a little encouragement, I snapped my teeth at her hand, fangs clipping together just inches from her fingers.

This time, her slap rang out loudly enough to echo around the room. Within a split second, horror, fear, and then excitement flashed across her face. When she saw my grin, her arousal smoldered, flaring like gasoline poured on a flame.

With a groan, I said, "That's it, darling. Harder."

The crack of her hand rang out again, the sting blooming across my cheek. My bliss pushed even higher, and I laughed, reveling in the pain and the way her eyes brightened at my sounds.

"No need to be gentle." I rolled my head back, gazing up at her. "I want all the pain my lady can inflict."

She straightened up, her expression unreadable as her clever eyes examined every inch of me.

Then she lifted her bare foot and pressed it against my chest.

"Lie back," she said, and I obeyed. My cock was rock

hard and aching; I was dizzy with need. Skirting the edge of madness to please her.

She straddled my chest and used one hand to grip around my throat. Her fingers didn't extend far enough to throttle me, but simply the weight of her hand was enough for me. She reached beneath her soft pajama pants and grinned when an unbidden growl burst out of me.

"That's what you want, isn't it?" she murmured. She rolled her hips, and I salivated at the thought of burying my head between her legs. "Will you beg for it?"

"You're a cruel girl, aren't you?" I could turn the tables on her easily. I could pin her down and have her screaming my name within seconds. But the struggle to earn her approval and her permission was far more pleasurable.

Blame it on a lifetime of living as nothing more than a machine built to kill, a warrior encouraged to be as vicious and violent as possible. Pain was a familiar, understandable comfort. Control was necessary for life itself. Without someone to counterbalance my baser desires, I was no better than any other wild beast.

"A little sadist hides behind that pretty face," I said as my hips thrust up mindlessly. She laughed, and my cock twitched with desperation as her delicate fingers tightened their grip.

"How can I resist when desperation looks so sexy on you?" She didn't say it like it was a line, like she was trying to flirt. She said it as if it was fact, as if she'd only just begun to understand how her own desires tied into mine.

I couldn't *make* her dominant. I couldn't force her to feel confident in her power. I could only guide her in the right direction, and let her make the journey.

"You're powerful enough to kill Gods." Her hand moved slowly, her eyes fluttering as she pleasured herself. "Yet you're allowing me to push you around. Why?"

"You give me what no one else can," I said. I lost myself in the scent of her arousal; mind hazy, body on fire.

"What do I give you, Callum?" Her voice was a siren's song in the fog rolling over my mind. As I bucked my hips again, her nails pressed demandingly into my throat.

"Someone to please. Someone to serve." I could feel her fingers as they moved, hidden by flannel as they pumped in and out of her. Her eyes were half-lidded, the air around her shimmering faintly.

"I've never met a demon who *wants* to serve a human."

It was likely she hadn't met many demons at all, but I wasn't going to argue.

"When a demon becomes a warrior, we are trained to be violent." I struggled to string together enough cohesive sentences to explain. "We are encouraged to abandon any efforts at civility or domesticity. We live to destroy. But destruction needs boundaries. Every weapon needs a handler."

I didn't expect to see such gentle understanding in her eyes . . .

Right before she lifted her arm and backhanded my face.

"Fuck *yes*, darling. Hurt me." My hips thrust up and

nearly threw her off balance. Her legs squeezed against my sides, and she moaned when my struggling pushed her fingers deeper.

"You need someone to control you," she said, and I quickly nodded. "Do rules make you feel safe?"

The question made me bristle, and my pride wanted to deny it. But her asking was innocent, and she was right. Lucifer's commands had once made me feel safe, until I lost my faith in him to lead. My commanders' control once comforted me, until I rose through the ranks more swiftly than I was prepared for, and suddenly, the control was in my hands.

Control came with responsibility. It made me not only a leader but a protector. A master over my warriors but a servant to their well-being.

I didn't want to think about that. I didn't want to dwell on all the ways I'd failed.

"Callum."

Her voice brought me back to reality, and I recalled she'd asked me a question.

"Nothing is safe," I muttered. "But if I can't be safe, I can at least be useful."

Some things were better left unsaid. It worried me how easily I could blurt things out to her.

She gyrated her hips, grinding herself against me. I clenched my hands into fists so I wouldn't seize her and flip her.

"You get to be useful by being my seat while I get off." Her voice trembled, already on the edge. "Don't touch. Don't struggle. Just watch."

"At least let me fucking touch you—" I snarled, only for her to slap me again and send me spinning off into floaty bliss.

"Do as I told you, Callum. If you're good, maybe I'll fuck you like you asked."

Every time her tongue formed my name, it made me shiver. She didn't need to force me to obey. My pleasure came from my sacrifice: from foregoing what I desperately wanted for the sake of obedience.

I lay there salivating, drunk on arousal as she got herself off. I watched her in awe, cursing as much as I begged. Her legs clenched around me, her breath shuddering, as I writhed beneath her.

I would accept her torture willingly, thankfully. The only sounds coming out of me were animalistic growls of desperation.

Everly withdrew her hand from between her legs, holding up her two fingers as she watched my face. The digits glistened with her arousal as she brought them to my mouth and slid them inside. Closing my lips around her, I sucked. She watched me with fascination and gasped when I clenched my teeth, not hard enough to hurt but enough to tease.

"I want to try it," she said. "I want to fuck you."

She was holiness and blasphemy all in one. A goddess of desire and innocence.

She allowed me to undress her slowly, taking my time to worship every inch of her. Kisses she responded to with praise, but smacked the back of my head when I would nip at her skin, giggling when I did it anyway.

"I would build a temple for you if I could," I said, dragging my nose along her skin as I inhaled. "Lock you away like a gilded goddess and worship at your feet for eternity."

"I bet you say that to everyone you're with," she said.

Clutching her hips, I planted a kiss beside her navel.

"I've been alive too long to speak idly," I said. "I've uttered those words to no one else."

Grabbing the toy from the bed, I tightened the straps around her hips, ensuring it was comfortable and secure. She swung it playfully, laughing when her cock slapped against my cheek.

"Did you get lube?"

Pressing my lips to the tip of her cock, I said, "I make my own."

She inhaled as I took her into my mouth. My jaw stretched around it and my saliva thickened as I sucked, coating the surface. She didn't take a single breath as she watched me, only exhaling when I drew back and grinned up at her.

"Wow." She was barely able to bring her volume above a whisper. "That was— You're— Holy shit."

Stroking the forked sides of my tongue around her cock, I said, "Fuck me, Mistress. Please. Where do you want me? On the floor? Or on the bed?"

She straightened her back, seeming to remember who was in charge here.

"On the floor," she said.

Obediently, I turned my back to her, lying on the carpet. She knelt between my legs, her hands moving over me gently, appreciatively. The head of the toy nudged against me, but she was clearly hesitant to push any harder.

Reaching back, I spread myself open with one hand and arched my back, impaling myself on her. She swore softly as I groaned, working her cock deeper.

It had been ages since I'd been penetrated. It was agony and ecstasy rolled into one, the most overwhelming catharsis. "Fuck, you feel so good."

"Watch your mouth," she said softly, and my back tingled at her tone. Quiet but authoritative, still a little uncertain. But with far more confidence than I'd ever heard from her. "It's not very respectful of you to swear at me, is it?"

Telling a demon not to swear was like telling a fish not to swim. Growling at her request with obvious defiance, I was surprised to feel her hand tangle in my hair, gripping the locks and shoving my head down. She pressed deeper until her hips were flush against me.

"It's not very respectful of you," she repeated. "*Is it?*"

"No, my lady, it isn't respectful." Her words were accompanied by a hard thrust, the sensation practically making my eyes roll back. It ached in the best of ways, and if she kept moving this slow, I was going to make an absolute whore of myself in my desperation for more. "Fuck me harder, please, come on—"

She giggled, causing a wave of heat that had my over-stimulated body shaking. "Do you really want it that bad? Such a needy boy."

She sounded so painfully sweet that I groaned. I was

practically rabid, swiftly losing all decorum as she moved her hips, drawing them back before punching forward. She was clumsy with the strap, but every awkward, eager movement only served to turn me on more.

"I like hearing you groan," she said. Her fingers pulled my head up, enthusiastically rough, her other hand pressing down between my shoulder blades. Her heartbeat was quickening, pattering hard and fast. Her breath was coming in quick, excited gasps. "If you want it harder, ask me nicely."

"Fucking hell, if you keep talking to me like that, you're going to make me come on the damn carpet, Everly."

Her laughter in response was mockingly sympathetic.

"Aw, it's *so hard*, isn't it?" she crooned. "Is that all it takes to make you come? Just having your ass filled by a pretty girl's cock?"

I wasn't sure where she'd found this filthy mouth, but I was more than happy to let her keep talking. Arching my back and lifting my hips toward her, the toy was angled perfectly to push me over the edge the second she gave me permission, which I doubted she would grant unless I managed to get my rambling tongue under control.

The only words I could manage to speak were breathless oaths, swearing everything to her if she would only please, *please* give me more.

"Please, I'll do anything you want. Anything you fucking ask, just . . . fuck me harder, please, just fucking kill me—"

"Killing you would be merciful," she said. "You can't suffer if you're dead. But alive . . ." She tugged my hair, shaking my head back and forth as if *I* was the weak mortal and she the demon. "Alive, you get to endure whatever I decide to give you."

She thrust into me, keeping a pace that had my cock leaking on the floor. Releasing my hair and dragging her fingernails down my back, she gripped my hips, finding her rhythm.

I could have truly died in that moment. My mind ascended to some other plane where all I could comprehend was the tight feeling of her moving inside me. My cock was grinding against the floor, the rough abrasion of the carpet stinging just enough to hold me back.

"Do you want to come?" she said, leaning over my back, her voice soft and sweet and *so teasing*.

"Yes," I snarled, and she tugged at my hair.

"Yes *what*?"

My claws raked through the carpet, tearing it even more as she *tsk*ed in disapproval.

I could have taken her cock for hours, but I was also a greedy bastard who was so worked up I felt more like an animal than a demon as I said, "Yes, Mistress, please, let me come."

She kept fucking me. I was about to start begging in earnest when she finally commanded, "Come for me, demon."

My teeth clamped on my arm, clenching so hard I drew blood. I wasn't sure if it was truly words or only snarled groans pouring from my mouth, but every sound was in worship of her.

IT DIDN'T FEEL right to leave Everly alone, but her family would be home any minute. Climbing back out her window and watching her snuggle into bed by herself made my chest tighten with an unpleasant assault of irritation and loneliness.

"You'll be close by, won't you?" she said, leaning close to the window as she spoke to me. "If something goes wrong tomorrow, you'll be there?"

My skin prickled. A creeping feeling on the nape of my neck told me I was being watched, and it stretched my nerves almost to their breaking point.

"I'll be close, darling," I said, leaning my chin on the windowsill. She kissed my forehead, to my surprise. It certainly wasn't a gesture I was used to—gentle partners weren't something I'd ever sought.

Whips, chains, and pain could undo me. But soft words and softer touches could tame me just as effectively.

"We'll meet at the Historical Society tomorrow," I said. "I'll distract your father while you take the grimoire. I may not be able to kill your father, but I'll gladly steal you from him."

Her eyes lit up. "You'll take me home?"

"I'll take you wherever you wish to go."

With a look of bold determination, she kissed me. My hand cradled the back of her head, pulling her closer. As her tongue parted my lips, a growl rose out of me, and my cock twitched, ready for round two.

But that persistent feeling of being watched distracted me. When Everly parted from me, I couldn't help a quick glance over my shoulder in the direction of the trees.

Nothing. Not a soul to be seen.

But there was a familiar scent on the wind. One that filled me with alarm.

"I'll see you tomorrow," I said, cupping her face one last time before I sprinted away toward the trees. She'd been about to say something; I cursed myself for not lingering to hear it. But I was on high-alert.

Someone was here, and their presence was powerful enough it caused a change in air. The wind grew colder, the shadows darkened. Beneath the trees, the crickets didn't chirp and the creatures of the night refused to emerge from their burrows. Crouching low in the shrubbery, I surveyed my surroundings carefully.

But not carefully enough. I heard the footsteps behind me in the same moment that magical bindings snapped around my limbs and darkness descended over my vision.

19

EVERLY

THE NEXT MORNING, I woke up with absolute certainty of what I had to do. There would be only one chance. If I messed it up, if I was caught, I wasn't sure if I would ever find an opportunity again.

Frankly, I wasn't even sure if I would survive. If my father caught me stealing his most precious possession, would he let me live? Or would he kill me on the spot? Pay off the police, the investigators, and portray my murder as a horrible tragedy?

If I allowed myself to dwell on my fear, if I allowed it to control me, then I would wallow here forever. I'd remain frozen until God Itself rose from the deep and took away my ability to make choices at all.

Callum had given me confidence I had never expected to feel. The way he reveled in any show of power I gave, how he craved and praised any authority I dared to demonstrate; it made me feel strong.

But I had a problem. Dad had locked away my car keys, and I needed to be able to make a quick getaway. Unfortunately, that meant I needed my sister's help.

My knock on her bedroom door was a little louder than I meant it to be. When Victoria ripped the door open, she looked absolutely pissed.

"What the hell do you want?" she said. She had her hair straightener in one hand and a face mask on. Cheerful pop music played from her speakers.

"Oh, just wanted to see if you were going into town today," I said, not daring to set foot in her room. She'd probably have a fit if I touched anything.

"Yeah, I'm *obviously* just getting ready for a night in," she said, rolling her eyes as she sat in front of her vanity. "Why does it matter to you where I'm going?"

"I thought maybe you could give me a ride into town," I said, trying to sound as innocent and hopeful as I could.

"Did you forget how to drive or something?"

"Um . . . no." *Patience, Everly, just be patient and polite.* "Dad took my car keys. So . . . yeah."

She snorted. "So, you got yourself into trouble and now it's on me to haul your ass around? No thank you."

"Come on, RiRi," I said, daring to go for the throat and use the pet name I had for her as a kid. "I just want to go get a coffee real quick. I thought I'd take one to Dad at work."

Our father had several meetings at the Historical

Society that day. There was a conference that weekend, something about land management and the preservation of historical buildings, so of course, he had to be involved.

"You want to take Dad a coffee? God, you're such a kiss-ass." She put on a mocking, high-pitched voice that sounded nothing like me, thank you very much. "Aw, boo-hoo, Daddy took away my car keys and won't let me go to school anymore. My life is so sad!"

I had a sudden intrusive thought of slapping her face as hard as I'd slapped Callum's last night. Despite the satisfaction it would give me, I resisted.

"It'll be a quick trip," I said. "Please? I'll even tell him it was your idea."

"Mm, no thanks. I'm not trying to have Dad think I'm trying that hard." She sighed, reached for the fuzzy pink bauble on her keys and tossed the ring over to me. "Just take the Mercedes. I don't care. Have it back by two, Everly, do you understand? I swear if it's one minute later, I'm going to tell Mom you're the one who put ghost pepper oil in her eye cream."

"I'll have it back by two and not a second later," I said, leaving before she could change her mind. She'd get her car back eventually, but certainly not by two. Once the police hauled it out of the lake I planned to drive it into, she could drive wherever she pleased.

My plan was simple: head down to the Historical Society, and while Dad was distracted running in and out of various meetings and phone calls, grab the grimoire, and run. Drive up to the forest near House Laverne, hide the vehicle, and meet up with Callum to get back to the house by nightfall.

Perfect. Simple. Not scary at all.

God, I was fucking terrified.

It was a relief to see numerous vehicles parked in the lot as I arrived at the Historical Society building. Plenty of people meant plenty of other suspects. Waiting in the car for several minutes, I kept my eyes open for Callum. Although I hoped it wouldn't be necessary, he would ensure my father was distracted while I got the grimoire.

But five minutes passed. Then ten.

Callum didn't appear.

Frowning, I got out of the car and whispered his name. Had I misunderstood the plan? This was the only day we could hope to pull this off while my father was distracted with his meetings. Looking around impatiently, I called his name again.

Nothing.

I was running out of time; I couldn't wait around for him any longer. Maybe he was already inside, keeping my father distracted. My hands were now clammy, and my chest tight, but I couldn't let fear control me.

With two lattes in hand, I walked straight in the front doors.

"Oh! Hello, Miss Everly!" The secretary, Janet, waved to me cheerfully from behind the desk. She was a graduate from Abelaum University, blonde and curvy. Exactly the type my father usually went for. "Are you looking for Kent? Mr. Hadleigh, I mean?" She gave me a sweet but slightly nervous smile. "I think he's still up in his office. But you better hurry to catch him, he has a meeting in five minutes."

"Oh, gosh, I'll hurry then!" I waved to her quickly and headed up the stairs, toward my dad's office. The more rushed my father was, the better.

Rapping quietly on the door, I waited until I heard him mumble "Come in" before entering.

He looked up from his desk, clearly surprised to see me. "Ah, Everly. I wasn't expecting you." He frowned. "How did you get here?"

"Victoria let me borrow her car," I said, adding quickly, "She wanted me to go get coffee for her since she's still getting ready for . . . well, I don't know what she's getting ready for. But I figured if I was already out, I'd bring you an Americano."

Giving him the most innocent smile I could muster, I held out his beverage. He still looked surprised but took it without hesitation.

"Well, that's kind of you," he said. "Unfortunately, I only have— Shit!"

Right as he lifted the cup to his mouth, the loosened lid allowed hot coffee to pour down the front of his shirt and jacket. He swore again as I scrambled, apologizing profusely as I helped him pull the jacket off.

I could feel the weight of the grimoire in the inner pocket as I draped the jacket over the back of his chair.

"The lid must have cracked," I said forlornly as he vainly tried to sop up the stain from his white shirt with tissues. "Do you want me to go home and grab a change of clothes—"

"No, no, don't bother," he snapped. "I'll just ask Janet for my— Well, I likely have a spare coat in the closet downstairs. I'm going to be late for the damn meeting." He left the room, urging me out the door. "God, this stain. Give me a few minutes, the meeting will be quick. You and I can grab lunch afterward, eh?"

"Oh . . . yeah . . . yeah, sure!" I tried not to sound too panicked as he hurried off toward the stairway. Shit, the last thing I needed was for him to immediately come looking for me after his meeting. I thought I'd have a little time to get away first.

I'd have to make this quick.

The moment he disappeared down the stairway, I rushed back inside his office. The building only had security cameras around the perimeter, outdoors, so I wasn't worried about being recorded. As I rifled through his jacket, I found the grimoire in his pocket.

I could barely breathe as I took it out. I didn't expect such a swell of emotion, such an instant and undeniable feeling of *rightness*. I held years of my ancestors' studies, their devotion to their magic, their blood, sweat, and tears. Their hands had touched these pages, scrawled these words.

Hurriedly, I shoved the book into my bag. Unlocking the window, I pushed it open, hoping to make it appear the thief had entered and exited that way. Shutting the door behind me, I walked as swiftly as I dared toward the stairs.

I just needed to make it out the front door and to the car. Once I was behind the wheel, I would drive north, taking every backstreet I knew. Callum would be watching; he would be waiting for me.

Finally, at last, I would be free. I just needed to get out the damn door.

I didn't even make it down the hall.

"Bastard couldn't even show up for his own meeting . . ." My father was striding toward me up the stairs, looking more perturbed than ever. I quickly backed up, freezing when he lifted his head. "Are you all right, my dear? You look like you're going to be sick."

Shit.

"Oh! No, I'm fine. Totally fine." I nodded, forcing my mouth into a smile. "I was just going to . . . um . . . sit in the lobby. Until you were done."

"Well, I'm just about ready. As it turns out, Mr. Fedderman can't even manage to show up for the meetings *he* schedules." He wrapped an arm around my shoulders, giving me a squeeze before he continued toward his office. "Let me just collect my things."

Oh my God, I was dead. I was really dead. This was it. He'd throw me down to the God, he would know I was a traitor. My head jerked around as I considered sprinting, then my eyes fell on a stack of cardboard boxes shoved against the wall, piles of old books inside them.

I didn't have another second to think. As my father disappeared into his office, leaving me outside, I shoved the grimoire into one of the boxes and leapt back, hoping I looked casual as he emerged.

"Everly." His voice was cold, his eyes narrowed. "Where is it?"

I hadn't been prepared for this. I licked my lips, stuttering, "I don't know what you're talking about."

The words sounded natural, even flippant. But the problem with being a liar with a suspicious father was that nothing, not even the truth, was ever enough.

He grabbed my arm in an iron grip, tugging me back toward his office. He slammed the door behind us, shoving me so roughly I had to catch myself on the desk.

"Where is my grimoire?" His face was red, his voice raised, his hands clenched into fists.

"Dad, I don't have it," I insisted. He was blocking the door and there was no way around him. No way I could make a quick escape without trying to physically fight him, and that wasn't going to happen.

If I could use my magic . . .

But I couldn't. I fucking couldn't. As if warning me not to try anything, the cuffs tightened, squeezing my wrists until I feared my bones would break.

"Give me your bag," he ordered. I handed it over, and he ripped it from my hands. I scrambled out of his way as he dumped the contents on his desk. A tube of chapstick and a pen rolled to the floor as my things were spread out for his inspection.

Luckily, I'd made sure to leave nothing of value inside.

He tugged at the bag's lining, opening every zipper before he tossed it aside.

"Strip," he said. "Now."

My mouth gaped open as I stared at him in shock. "You want me to . . . what? Dad, you can't—"

"Now, Everly!" His voice filled the tiny office, and I flinched as he took a step toward me. But there was no way. No. Especially not today, of all days, when my body was covered with little scratches and bruises from Callum's hands.

"No," I said softly. "Dad, please, you're overreacting—"

"This is not an overreaction!" he yelled. "That grimoire is imperative to the continuation of our society and you know it, Everly! Do as I say." He lowered his voice to a hiss that chilled me straight through. "Obey me, or I'm calling Leon here to make you."

God, where was Callum? I needed to get out of here. Everything had gone wrong. My eyes kept darting toward the window, hoping to catch a glimpse of my demon flying to save me.

But he didn't come.

My fingers shook with rage and indignation as I reached for the edge of my shirt. I tried not to think about it, tried to imagine I was anywhere else but here as I hurriedly pulled off my shirt and then unbuttoned my jeans.

With my clothing laid on the desk, wearing only my bra, panties, and socks, I spread my arms. "There? See?" My eyes stung with humiliation as he looked at me, and stung even more when his mouth curled into a sneer.

"What the hell is this?" he said. He brushed my hair away from my neck, and I jerked away, arms folded over my chest. But I knew he could see. The bruises, the hickies, scratches, and little red marks. "Who have you been with?"

"It's none of your business," I whispered.

"It's well within my rights to know who the hell my daughter is whoring herself out to!" He grabbed my arm, again, his fingers digging in. I wondered suddenly if he'd leave a bruise of his own, a bruise Callum could see.

Would Callum find a way to kill him too?

"William Frawley," I said. I hated to drag his name into this at all, but it was the only way. He was the only person who made sense, someone my father hopefully wouldn't consider too much of a threat.

My father laughed. It wasn't a *nice* sound, it wasn't humorous. It was cruel.

"Oh, Everly." He shook his head. "Don't be foolish. You think you have time to invest in this nonsense? Time to be spending with some . . . some *boy*? A boy who wouldn't even love you? Understand you? Truly *know* you? Do you really think anyone outside this family could possibly accept who you are? What you're capable of? What you've *done*?"

He looked at me with revulsion.

"Dress yourself and go home. *Straight* home. Don't leave the house for any reason."

He wrenched open the door once I'd dressed myself, leading the way back downstairs. My face was still hot, my hands shaking with adrenaline as we passed the cardboard box I'd shoved the grimoire into. Dad led me all the way outside, and when we reached my car, he said, "I'll be driving right behind you. Straight to the house."

EVERLY

AS MY FATHER ransacked my room, pulling clothing out of drawers and tossing books from my shelves, I kept telling myself I was innocent. I didn't know where the book was. I'd never touched it.

I was good. I was obedient. I wasn't a liar.

Dad stubbornly refused to tell the rest of the family what had happened. Meredith became more and more irritated, until she was following Dad around the house, shrieking at him to tell her what the hell was going on. My siblings thought it was hilarious to watch, until their own bedrooms were next to be torn through.

Only when the house was entirely turned upside down did Dad leave, declaring he was going back to the Historical Society. He'd doubtlessly rip that place apart too, but his fury was slowly melting into fear.

If Leon found out he no longer had the grimoire, there was a good chance we'd all be killed.

The moment my father left, I locked myself in my room. I needed to get out now, while I had the chance. The grimoire was still out there. I needed to get back to the Historical Society, find the box before my father did, and run.

But night had fallen, and I had no vehicle. Callum had promised he would be nearby, but I hadn't seen a sign of him all day. I'd been so certain he would appear when my father caught me; I'd believed he would somehow sense my fear and come.

Sliding open my bedroom window, I leaned out into the night and whispered, "Callum! Callum, where are you?"

Only the chirping crickets answered me. The distant trees moved in the breeze; the grass swayed. Frowning, I said, more loudly this time, "Callum!"

A figure suddenly appeared from the darkness, and I jerked back so hard I banged my head on the window frame. But it wasn't Callum. It was Leon.

His gaze practically glowed in the dark as he strode through the yard on silent feet. Shit, how much had he heard?

He stopped walking, taking a moment to regard me slowly.

"Considering sneaking out the window?" he said as instant denial rushed to my tongue. "I wouldn't bother, girl. If the Eld don't get you, I'll have to."

I sunk onto my mattress, staring at him out the

window. He narrowed his eyes for a moment, stepping closer, his nostrils flaring as he sniffed the air.

Could he smell Callum on me? On my window? On my bed?

But all he did was scoff in disgust and back away, saying rudely, "Fucking witches . . ." He kept muttering as he walked away, disappearing into the darkness, and I finally breathed a little sigh of relief.

But my relief was short-lived. Where the hell was Callum?

Despite the risk, the day after my attempted theft, I made a call to the Historical Society. I kept my questions as casual as I could with Janet, not wanting to raise her suspicions as I asked if the cardboard boxes on the second floor were still there.

"Oh, those were donated," she said. "Some guy picked them up this morning."

"Some guy?" Hope bled out of me. I wanted to scream. "What was his name? Who did he work for? Where was—"

But Janet just said, "I don't know. Did I do something wrong?"

Practically choking on my words, I said, "No. You're good. Never mind."

The grimoire was gone, sent away to who knows where, and the more questions I asked, the more suspicion I would draw to myself. But it was Callum's absence that worried me more than anything else.

Maybe I shouldn't have trusted him after all. Maybe my grandmother was wrong, and all this time, the demon had just been waiting for his opportunity to abandon me.

Even for me, who loathed trusting anyone, such a thought made no sense. Callum had no reason to go back on his word or make empty promises.

The way he'd held me . . . the things he'd promised . . . perhaps I was being naive, but I trusted him.

But that made my fear even worse. Because if he wasn't here, like he'd sworn to me he would be, then what the hell happened to him?

DAYS PASSED.

There was no further discussion about the missing grimoire, but it was clear my father had not found it. He and Meredith were constantly on edge, watching me with suspicion every time I dared to set foot outside my room. When they weren't watching me during the day, Leon was stalking around the house at night.

There were no opportunities to escape. Desperate, I tried everything I could think of to get the cuffs off my wrists. Perhaps, with them gone, I could teleport again. But whatever magic they held made them unbreakable, even when I locked myself in the bathroom, wrapped my wrist in a towel, and slammed a hammer as hard as I could against the cuffs.

The pain was agonizing, but the glass didn't crack.

In a daze, I lay curled on the cold bathroom floor, waiting for the agony to subside. The sound of water dripping from the sink faucet was so loud it made me twitch, and I covered my ears to make it stop.

But it didn't.

Drip, drip, drip.

Was I losing my mind? My wrists were so swollen, so reddened, it looked like they were infected. A slimy feeling crept up the back of my skull, and I squeezed my eyes shut as the sensation of ragged fingernails dragging along my spine made me shiver.

Let me in.

Something wet touched my cheek, and my eyes flew open. There was cold water all over the floor.

Drip, drip, drip.

I looked up.

The ceiling was *writhing.* A mass of thick, gray tentacles coiled over each other as cold, viscous liquid dripped onto my face. I tried to scream, scrambling on my hands and knees for the door, but no sound came out. My fingers slipped on the doorknob, slick with the putrid slime covering my hands. My mouth filled with the taste of rot, and I gagged as something wriggled in my throat.

Doubled over, I retched until bile spattered across the floor. But something was still in my throat, filling it, choking me, cutting off my air. My head felt like a balloon about to burst as I used the sink to drag myself to my feet. My eyes were wide, bloodshot and terrified, as I stared into the mirror, opening my mouth wide—

A thick tentacle, covered in blinking eyeballs, protruded from my throat.

Without a sound, I screamed as the tentacle reached out of my mouth, curling around my head. The suckers latched onto me, piercing my skin, squeezing tighter and tighter until—

"Everly! Hurry the fuck up! I'm trying to get down to Main Street before all the parking is gone!"

My brother's voice was accompanied by his fist pounding on my bedroom door. Standing in front of the mirror, clutching my head in my hands, I blinked slowly before drawing in a shaking breath.

The illusion was gone, just as quickly as it had come. Opening my mouth wide, I peered into my empty throat . . . then promptly vomited into the sink.

More pounding, this time on the bathroom door. The handle shook. "What the hell are you doing? Dad wants you at the festival, so get your shit together!"

"What festival?" I barely managed to croak out the words.

"*Art Fest*, dumbass!" Jeremiah said. "You know, that stupid thing you've been dragging us to every damn year since you started college?"

Groaning, I tried to force my mind and stomach to settle. But my thoughts kept flying away from me, swirling like leaves in a storm.

Art Fest was a staple of Abelaum life, held every year to feature both student artists from the university and local artisans. There were booths selling everything from jewelry, to paintings, to hand-made soaps. It was always crowded, with people filling the streets until late into the evening.

Forcing myself to stand up straight, I managed to open the door. Jeremiah stood there, and his lip curled at the sight of me. "What's wrong with you? Are you sick? I better not fucking catch it if you are. I've got soccer practice all week."

"Not sick," I said. "Give me five minutes and I'll be ready."

At this point, disappearing into a crowd might be my only hope of escape. At the least, it was my first opportunity to get out of the house in days, and I couldn't let that slip away.

Art Fest was one of the few ways I was allowed to make money outside of the allowance given to me by my father. I sold my canvases, or the hand-painted tarot cards I spent months perfecting. Every penny I made was saved toward my future freedom.

Although I was in no way prepared to sell anything today, I collected the merchandise I still had from last year as well as my folding table and loaded it into Jeremiah's car as quickly as I could. My jacket covered the cuffs on my arms, but couldn't hide how pale my face was or the dark circles under my eyes. I was still reeling, dizzy from the God's attack, but I had to stay alert.

If the opportunity presented itself, I needed to be ready to run.

I didn't like the look Jeremiah had on his face when he got into the driver's seat, cranking up the music loud enough to hurt my ears and vibrate the leather beneath me as he sped down the road toward downtown.

As he was forced to slow his speed the closer we got

to Main Street, he turned to me and said, "So, are you ready for it this time?"

I didn't bother to look at him as I answered, "What are you talking about?"

The tires screeched as he whipped into a narrow parking spot, startling the woman parked beside us as she tried to get her crying baby into a stroller. My plan was to exit the vehicle the moment I had the chance, but before I could reach for the door handle, Jeremiah grabbed my face.

"Jeremiah, what the fuck? You're hurting me—" I tried to pull back, but I was crushed between him and the door as he leaned out of his seat to crowd my space. His windows were so tinted, no one walking by could see what was happening within.

"I don't know what you're fucking planning," he snarled. "But you're not going to mess this up for me. The second sacrifice is ready to go, Ev. Dad and I have a plan, and tonight, we're going to make it happen. Raelynn Lawson is going to *die*." His eyes were wide with excited glee, and his voice was cruelly mocking as he continued, "Don't be a little crybaby this time. I know you have something to do with the grimoire going missing. I don't believe your bullshit story about teleporting and being passed out for days." His fingers dug in, squeezing my face so hard my eyes filled with furious tears. "Whatever it is you're trying to do, it's not going to work. When Victoria brings the little lamb over to meet you, you'd better suck it up and play along. Do. Your. Duty."

He roughly pushed me away, knocking my head against the window. He shoved open his door but remained close by, watching me like a hawk as I got my table and merchandise out of the trunk.

That was why they had allowed me to come. So I could serve as the Deep One's eyes and ears when the sacrifice-to-be was paraded in front of me like a calf at auction.

If I ran now, right now, how far would I get before I was caught? Would I manage to get back home, dig up my map and escape? Would I be able to reach House Laverne before nightfall? Would I—

Sudden, sharp, stunning pain pierced into the back of my neck. For a moment, I thought I was going to pass out as visions assaulted my mind, blinding me completely.

Blood and viscera, endless cries of pain, rattled in my head until I wanted to bash it against the concrete if only to make it stop.

It stopped as suddenly as it began, and I stumbled, catching myself against the side of the car.

"Hey, watch it!" Jeremiah snapped. "You're gonna scratch the paint!"

What was wrong with me? A strange sensation lingered, even after the pain had passed: an itch on the inside of my skull. As if something was *in* my head.

Something had changed the night my father took me to St. Thaddeus, and I dreaded to think what that meant.

After finding my booth and setting up my things, my hopes of managing an escape were swiftly dampened.

Even when Jeremiah stepped away, Leon stalked through the crowd past my table, giving me a warning glare. He looked human today, with pale green eyes and declawed hands.

"Callum, please," I whispered, hands wringing on my lap. "Please hear me. Please come."

Every shout made me jump, every customer that stopped and wanted to chat made me feel like screaming. Then, to my horror, I spotted Victoria approaching with her "friends."

One of them was named Inaya. I'd had a few art classes with her and she was likely the only person who was *actually* friends with Victoria. Or at least, friends with the version of Victoria she got to see. Inaya was always kind to me, always sweet. But she wasn't who I was worried about.

My stomach crumpled like discarded paper when I realized the second sacrifice was standing right in front of me.

Raelynn was a small woman, with large black-rimmed glasses and oversized clothes. Between her big boots, horror-themed T-shirt, and *Official Mothman Fanclub* pins covering her bag, she seemed like the kind of person I would want to be friends with.

But when I looked at her, my mind wasn't filled with visions of friendship.

I'd seen her before, in my nightmares.

A terrifying, all-consuming desire to *hurt her* overtook every other thought in my head. I wanted to slit her throat, watch her choke on her own blood. I wanted to carve into her skin, hear the sweet music of her screams as I—

Fuck. No, no, no, that wasn't right, that wasn't *me*.

All I could do was try not to let the horror show on my face as they came to my table. Raelynn's eyes were wide as she looked at the paintings I'd brought—*gouge them out, poke out her eyes, burst them like grapes*—but then she noticed my tarot deck and her face lit up.

"Did you paint all these yourself?" she said, and I nodded, forcing myself to smile at her enthusiasm.

"She paints every single one," Victoria said, her voice sarcastic and her words slightly slurred. "That's why she's locked in her room all the time." She leaned against my table, taking a long sip from a plastic bottle she was carrying. Doubtlessly, it wasn't water she was eagerly gulping down. "Everly, this is Raelynn. Raelynn Lawson."

She could still be saved. *But she should die in agony.* There was still time, I still had a chance to get away, to ensure no one else was hurt. *But you wouldn't betray your God, would you, Everly? Do your duty, do your FUCKING DUTY—*

"Nice to meet you, Raelynn," I said, forcing my voice to be calm and steady despite the bile rising in my throat. This poor girl had no idea, no fucking clue. What if I just blurted it out? What if I screamed at her to get away, to run and never look back? But my tongue was *tight*, like a cramping muscle.

It was just like with Juniper. Just like with Marcus. It was the same nightmare over and over again.

"You should pull some cards for her, Ev," Victoria said, tossing my sample deck toward me. I could lie, but the cards wouldn't. Why the hell Victoria wanted me to pull for Raelynn, I couldn't understand. Was she taunting me? Testing me?

I nearly dropped the cards multiple times as I shuffled the deck. Maybe I could warn Raelynn, somehow. Even if I couldn't tell her directly, even if the Deep One kept me tongue-tied, there had to be a way.

I smiled, and as steadily as I could, I said, "Come a little closer, Raelynn."

There was an eager smile on her face as she stepped closer to the table.

"It's Rae," she said. "I mean, my friends call me Rae. You can call me Rae."

"Rae." I repeated her name with intention, with purpose. A name carried power, and even with my magic entirely inaccessible to me, I hoped she could somehow feel my warning. "I like that. Somewhere between masculine and feminine."

If only I had been blessed with the gift of telepathy, or any form of psychic power at all. If I could implant the idea in her brain that there was danger here and she needed to leave, perhaps it would be enough. Concentrating my thoughts toward her, I tried to somehow impart my message.

You're in danger. You need to leave. You can't trust Victoria. You can't trust any of us. Leave. Leave. Leave.

But instead of telepathically implanting a message,

I received one in return. It was only a split second, the briefest of visions. But it was undeniable.

It was a vision of Raelynn's hands, with her chipped black nail polish, holding the grimoire. *My* grimoire.

Nearly gasping, I barely kept my reaction under control. How was that possible? Why? When? This woman who'd only just arrived in town, who didn't have a damn clue what was going on, *had my grimoire?*

Setting my cards back on the table, I cleared my mind, discarding the fear and the confusion. Those feelings couldn't help me right now and they couldn't help Raelynn either. If I was to warn her, then I needed the cards to be true even if my tongue couldn't be. Taking a deep breath, I pulled the first card.

The Tower.

My eyes darted to Victoria, but she wasn't paying attention. She was too busy nursing whatever liquor she had in that *water* bottle of hers.

Laying the card on the table, I explained, "Change. The life you knew, your strong tower, has been dramatically changed. It is no more." I wanted to tell her about the chaos this card could signify, but I could only hope the flames consuming it were enough to get the message across.

As I reached for the next card, a chill went up my back. A whisper? Or just the wind? My neck prickled. My fingers twitched. The murmuring of the crowd created a constant background of conversation and laughter, so I forced my attention back to the deck.

The next card was the Ten of Swords. How could I dare to explain this with Victoria standing right there?

Betrayal was coming. Someone Raelynn trusted would stab her in the back.

Picking up the next card, another cold chill washed over me. Something felt *wrong*. Like the onset of food poisoning; my body knew something vile was inside it.

Rip her open, dig your hands into the warm entrails, let the blood soak beneath your fingernails just like your mother, just like your filthy whore mother!

The card almost slipped out of my fingers.

Another customer asked me for a price, and I leapt to help her immediately. But I left the final card face-up, hoping desperately that the sight of Death would be enough to impart a warning to Rae.

The three women left as I fumbled through the sale, my panic rising with every second. What the hell was happening to me? No matter how deep of a breath I took, it didn't feel adequate. My skin was clammy and cold. Even when I sat in my chair again, my head kept spinning.

Raelynn Lawson had the grimoire. When I concentrated on that thought, I was overwhelmed with mental images of Rae picking the grimoire out of a pile of books, Inaya wrapping it in brown paper, Rae's fingers tracing the pages.

Never had I experienced a psychic premonition like that.

I needed to get out of here, I needed to go *now*. I had to find out where Rae lived and get the damn thing back. I had to warn her, I had to do *something*.

They would kill her. They'd sacrifice her, take the grimoire, and then there would be nothing to stop the Libiri from making the final sacrifice. Nothing to stop them from setting the God free, and nothing to stand in Its way as It infested my mind, took over my body, and claimed my power for Itself.

My power . . . *my* power. Even if I couldn't control it, it was there. It was within me, and this God was ravenous for it.

It came again. The intrusive thoughts, the visions, the bloodlust.

She's mine, she's mine, she's mine! Bring her to me!

Gasping for air, I shoved myself to my feet. My vision was fuzzy at the edges. There were whispers all around. And the screaming . . . God, the *screaming,* as if a crowd of hundreds was in the woods, yelling until their throats were raw.

Feeling as if I was walking through waist-deep water, I stumbled away. Nearly blind, I shoved through the crowd, trying to keep my thoughts focused. *Get back to the house. Dig up the map. Hike to the coven house before the sun goes down.*

The sun was setting. Dusk was already here.

"Everly. Everly!"

My head was swimming. The sound of my name was so far away. The faces of the crowd blurred sickeningly as I stumbled through them, single-minded determination keeping my feet moving as my brain disconnected.

"Callum," I whispered, the crowd blurring before my eyes. "Please, Callum, please find me . . ."

Get home. Get the map. Run.

It would be dark. The Eld would be hunting. I had no way to defend myself.

Home. Map. Run.

There was no other choice.

"Everly!"

A hand closed tightly around my upper arm, jerking me back, and I screamed in alarm before my father's face filled my vision.

"Come with me." He dragged me, my feet tangling as I stumbled to follow. The screaming in my head wouldn't stop, and it made it impossible to hear him. Something about the sacrifice. Something about Jeremiah.

Raelynn. Something about Raelynn.

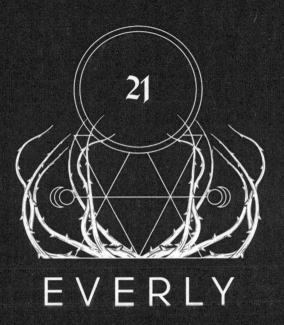

EVERLY

BY THE TIME my father dragged me to his SUV, the hallucinations had stopped. But they left behind an exhaustion so intense I thought I might pass out right there in the passenger seat. My eyes were heavy, every part of my body ached.

What was happening to me?

Groaning, I clutched my head in my hands and pressed my forehead against the window. The glass was blessedly cold on my hot skin.

". . . try not . . . fight it, Everly. It's only . . . blessings . . . the pain will . . ."

His voice kept fading in and out. But the calm acceptance in his tone made my panic rise, killing my desire to sleep, even as exhausted as I was.

When we arrived at the house, my heart was beating so hard it hurt. This was my last chance, I had to run, I had to . . . somehow . . .

"Don't fight it." My father opened the passenger door, catching me before I could fall. My muscles refused to work how I expected them to, my arms locking up while my legs were nearly limp. "When the second sacrifice is offered, you will feel God's presence even more intensely. Let it happen."

It was already happening. I was being overtaken. And Raelynn . . . Jeremiah had said they were going to kill her tonight . . .

"Oh no . . ." My voice caught on the words as my father shushed me, helping me walk into the house. I was too disoriented to struggle as I was guided to a chair at the bar in the kitchen, where I could see Meredith and Jeremiah seated on the couch in the living room.

More words I couldn't understand swirled around me. Staring at the white carpet until my brain stopped spinning, I poured all my tired effort into clearing my head. Going limb by limb, muscle by muscle, I reminded myself that I was in control. Curling my fingers, my toes, rolling my shoulders.

A subtle scent of woodsmoke filled the air. I thought it was Callum. I thought the demon had come for me after all. He wasn't a liar, he hadn't abandoned me, I wasn't alone—

But it was only Leon, called here by my father.

There was something *different* in the way his golden eyes moved over us, assessing the humans before him one by one. My father gave him orders, showing him pictures of Raelynn and ordering him to orchestrate her disappearance. Kidnap her. Dump her car off the coast. Make it all look like it was just an accident.

SOUL OF A WITCH

Gripping the edge of the countertop until the marble dug painfully into my fingers, I tried to maintain my focus. I could find a way out of this. I could stop them before they killed her.

But then, Leon did something he'd never done before. Something he'd never been able to do, because my father carried the grimoire and would cause him pain if he dared to step out of line.

After staring at the photos of Raelynn for several seconds in silence, the demon lifted his gaze to my father's and said, "No."

My eyes widened as I shifted in my seat. My father sputtered, lifting his voice as he demanded Leon obey. But he had no power to enforce his commands. My father couldn't use magic without spells, his tongue couldn't recall the words to weave enchantments without the grimoire in his hands.

He was powerless. Only the talisman around his neck protected him now.

The rest of us weren't so lucky.

The demon snatched Jeremiah from the couch, gripping him by the throat as he hoisted him into the air. Meredith screamed, and Father began to shout as Leon squeezed, claws digging into my step-brother's throat. His face was vicious, contorted with fury as he snapped his sharp fangs.

My father sounded panicked as he yelled, "Put him down! Obey me! Obey at once!"

"Obey or *what*?" Leon's voice was strong enough to rattle the windows and shake the walls. "What will you do? What will you do without your precious grimoire?

Did you really think I wouldn't figure it out? That I wouldn't notice?"

Jeremiah wheezed, clawing weakly at the demon's hands. His face was reddening, his lips turning blue.

"After all these years, did you really think I'd let you slip up for even a second, Hadleigh?" Leon roared. His eyes kept darting toward me. Me, the only person present who could theoretically stop him, was also the only person who had no desire to do so.

If he slaughtered us all, perhaps it would be better that way. Perhaps that was how this could all be brought to an end. Even if he couldn't kill my father, if he killed the rest of us . . .

Our eyes met. His bright with fury, mine stinging with tears and exhaustion. It was only the briefest of moments, but I saw fear in the demon's eyes, and I knew it wasn't fear for himself.

It was Raelynn. He was . . . afraid for Rae? Did he care about her?

Was he *saving* her?

Turning away from me, Leon said, "Dismiss me. Now. And I'll let your son live."

Jeremiah was twitching limply in his grasp. Meredith was screaming at my father to do something. So he did. He dismissed the demon, and Leon vanished with a sound like a bubble bursting.

A LONG GAP of silence followed Leon's disappearance, punctuated by Jeremiah's gasping breath.

I slipped awkwardly out of my chair, stumbling into the kitchen so I could seize a glass from one of the cabinets and fill it from the sink faucet. As I gulped down the tap water, I was certain I was going to be sick.

Something struck the back of my head, startling me so much the glass slipped from my fingers, shattering on the floor. I whirled around, arms flung up defensively, creating a burst of heat that exploded in Meredith's face, sending her stumbling back with a shriek.

She had her arm upraised to hit me again. Her eyes were wide, practically bulging with fury. Jeremiah was still on the couch, clutching his throat and groaning. Father was in the doorway, watching me with a heavy frown.

"Everly . . ." He said my name as a warning, but the buzzing in my head blocked him out. My arms were aching, my skin *burning* beneath the cuffs. Wedging my fingers against the glass, I tried to tug them down, desperate for relief.

"You wretched girl," Meredith hissed. "You couldn't even manage to defend your own brother. You'll go teleporting all over creation, but you won't raise a hand to protect your own family?"

As if I could. As if I, after being locked in cuffs against my will, my magic stifled, my power denied to me, could possibly do *anything* to protect my family, let alone myself. Staring at the shattered glass on the floor, I willed myself not to say anything.

Just keep your head down. Don't talk back. Don't argue.

"Do you have nothing to say for yourself? You ungrateful, selfish, stupid little—"

Her hand whipped toward me, another slap coming straight for my face. Much to Meredith's surprise, I didn't let her hit me.

I caught her wrist midair.

"Don't fucking hit me." Shoving her hand away, I braced myself dizzily against the counter, trying again in vain to tug the cuffs off my wrists.

"Go to your room, Everly," my father said. He was clearly trying to remain neutral between us, but his voice was tight with impatience. "We'll discuss this later."

"There's nothing . . . nothing to discuss." I grit my teeth, willing myself to stay conscious despite the agony in my veins. "Get these . . . get these things off me . . ."

But Meredith didn't stop. "We've sheltered you, we've fed you! I let you into my house, you little bastard bitch!"

She tried to hit me again. This time, she barely managed to lift her arm.

She was flung back, her body slamming into the cabinets so hard she bounced off them before falling to the floor. My arms were extended, palms toward her, fingers curled. Around the edges of the cuffs, blood was welling.

They were all staring at me. Eyes wide, mouths agape. My father's hand was outstretched, and he moved slowly toward me, like one would approach a frightened animal.

"Calm yourself down," he said firmly. "We can talk about this—"

"You said she couldn't use her damn magic, Kent!" Meredith shrieked, sitting on the floor and clutching her side, as if she was grievously injured. "And now she— Deep One, help us— Her eyes . . ."

When I reached up to rub my eyes with the back of my hand, it came away bloody. Holy shit . . . that wasn't good . . .

"Stand down," my father said calmly, daring to take another step toward me. But I backed away rapidly, stumbling toward the front door, keeping my hands outstretched. "Don't make any rash decisions. The more magic you attempt to use, the worse it will get."

But I was beyond his orders. I'd die if I stayed here.

MY FATHER COULDN'T stop me. The moment I was outside the house, I ran. Despite the blood blurring my vision, despite the sharp and deadly cold in my lungs, I fled into the dark.

Underneath the trees at the edge of our yard, beneath the tangled roots of a massive blackberry bush, I dug my few possessions out of the soil. Using my bare hands, clawing at the earth until it was packed beneath my fingernails, I could have cried with relief when I unburied the precious contents of the plastic bag. Callum's sigil and my hand-drawn map to House Laverne. I kept them both clutched close to my chest and kept moving.

As I hugged the edge of the road, my breath formed clouds in the cold air. It wasn't raining, but little droplets of moisture kept hitting my face, warning me there was more to come. Every time I saw headlights approaching, I scrambled into the shadows beneath the trees to hide.

It would take me all night to reach the house. Hours and hours of walking through the cold, the dark. I kept stopping as I doubled over, dry-heaving, the pain around my cuffs growing worse and worse.

The night was quiet, the air heavy with dew. Fog lay thick beneath the trees and crept along the twisting road. As I neared downtown Abelaum, I stuck to the roads on the outskirts. The streetlights were a comfort, and within the yellow glows of light, I felt safe.

But as the road curved along the lake and plunged into the trees, that feeling of safety vanished.

The night was utterly silent now. The chirping of crickets stopped. The occasional hoot of an owl could no longer be heard, the clicking of fluttering bats was absent. The only sounds remaining were my footsteps as they crunched on the dirt beside the road, and the subtle rattle of the wind through the autumn-dry leaves.

Snap.

I went still. Patchy clouds drifted over the moon, covering the only illumination I had. The trees towered over me. The air smelled of pine, loamy soil, damp leaves . . .

And rot. A sickeningly sweet, cloying stench prickled in my nose.

A low growl emanated from the darkness beside me. I turned toward the sound. The darkness was impenetrable, but I didn't need my eyes to know what lurked there.

I was being hunted.

There was more rustling, snapping branches and crunching leaves. As I backed away, standing in the middle of the vacant road, the beast stepped out of the shadows. Its long, skeletal limbs stretched toward me, claws clicking and grating upon the asphalt. Putrid saliva dripped from its maw, sharp teeth jutting from its rotten jaw at all angles, like shards of glass growing from the blackened bone.

More beasts crept out of the darkness. Heads low, white eyes fixed upon me as they advanced. They came from every angle, surrounding me, giving me no choice but to retreat toward the trees on the opposite side of the road.

I couldn't fight them. I couldn't hide.

One of the beasts lunged for me, its long limbs easily launching over the distance between us. Its jaws audibly clipped together as I spun, nearly losing my footing as I dodged its attack. My moment of clumsiness was exactly what the rest of the pack was waiting for.

With a chorus of horrific yelps and shrieking cries, they attacked.

Their teeth snapped at my heels as I plunged into the woods, sprinting through the dark. The sounds of them were all around me, loud enough to drown out my own panting breath and pounding heart. I feared that if I slowed even a little bit, I would lose my momentum and collapse entirely.

They would eat me alive.

Blackberry thorns tore at my clothes and branches whipped my face. My arm was outstretched, my only defense against the massive trees I couldn't see until they were too close.

One of the beasts clawed my leg, tripping me. I was

sprinting so fast it launched me forward, tumbling end over end and knocking the air from my lungs.

Gasping and coughing, I scrambled onto my hands and knees. I was surrounded. The beasts' eyes glowed unnaturally in the dark with a pale green luminescence. Rotting gray tongues eagerly licked their dripping maws. Their ragged breath was quick and ravenous as they sniffed the air.

My circulation had been gone for so long my limbs were like deadweight. But my fingertips were hot and tingling. My swollen veins looked like they were going to burst through my skin.

The cuffs were supposed to prevent any and all magic. As if they were punishing me for even thinking about it, blood seeped from beneath the glass.

I lifted my hands. My fingers were like claws, trembling in agony.

Sparks cascaded around my fingers, illuminating the snouts of the beasts as they closed in.

I wasn't going to die like this.

The darkness was overtaken with blinding white-hot light. It seared through my body, tearing me apart, crackling through my arms. A cacophony of screams and animalistic cries surrounded me, and there was a terrible sound of *snapping*.

The light died. Embers remained.

A blackened forest swayed before my fading vision. I collapsed, the dirt warm beneath my cheek as I stared at the charred corpse of a beast. Flaming pine needles rained around me, a storm of embers that I couldn't even feel when they landed on my skin.

It was so hard to breathe.

No one could hear me. No one knew where I was. No one . . . except . . .

My papers lay beside me, covered in ash. Dragging my arm through the dirt, I unfolded them. The paper tore under my weak hands.

His sigil. The one thing I needed to summon an Archdemon, *my demon*.

He'd promised me his help. He promised . . .

Laying my bloody hand over the mark, my throat was too raw and my mouth too dry to give voice to the words. But I mouthed them anyway.

"Come to me, Callum."

CALLUM

THE PRISON I was locked in was comfortable. There were no windows, but the cavern was spacious. The bed was covered with black silken sheets which smelled of Lucifer's cologne: cinnamon and clove, a hint of black pepper, and a sharp scent of copper. He couldn't resist reminding me who was responsible.

It was so quiet that I kept whistling to myself, snapping my fingers so I wouldn't go mad in the stifling silence. Cruel to do that, honestly. Lucifer knew I loved music, I loved sound. Taking it away from me was a petty attempt to flex his power.

My cell was thoroughly protected with magic and perfectly designed to contain a being as powerful as me. Lucifer was no fool; he knew what he was doing. He also knew he couldn't get away with it for long.

To contain a demon against their will was repugnant.

To imprison a demon who had done nothing wrong—
and I maintained that I had not—was one of the most
heinous acts a demon could commit against their own
kind. Without a trial before the Council, Lucifer could
not keep me imprisoned here for long.

It had already been *too* long.

Everly was waiting for me. Locked in those vile cuffs,
alone, doubtlessly confused as to why I hadn't been there
when I said I would.

My emotions became more erratic with every passing
hour. Time passed differently in Hell than it did on Earth,
but I'd been kept from her for days.

I couldn't feel her, couldn't smell her.

What if they'd hurt her? What if she'd attempted to
steal the grimoire without me and find her way back to
the house alone?

I hurled an elaborate jeweled sphere across the room,
and it shattered into powder against the stone wall.
I seized a wooden table next, smashing it against the
ground until it split into pieces. "Lucifer! Goddamn you,
show yourself!"

He would have no peace until he did, I'd make sure
of it. Everything I could get my hands on in that room,
I destroyed. My yelling was loud enough to vibrate the
stones, but just to ensure he heard me, I picked up a large
metal statue from near the sealed door and beat it repeatedly against the walls. The metal bent under the force of
it, but I didn't stop.

"You're a fucking coward, Lucifer! I'll make sure the
entire citadel knows you have me in here! Lucifer!" I

struck the stones so hard they cracked, leaving a crater where my fists landed.

Finally, I felt his presence. My head grew tight, like an overfilled balloon: a sure sign he was close.

Then, from the darkness, his voice rumbled, "You're a horrible bastard. You know that, don't you?"

"Certainly," I snarled, facing the door with my fists still clenched. "Yet you still made the foolish mistake of bringing me inside. Face me, Luci. You owe me that much."

There was a derisive snort. "You've spent too much time around humans."

"And you've spent too much time around simpering fools whose only interest is kissing your ass. You can't keep me here. This is against my will."

His growl made the stones shake beneath my feet. There was a flash like lightning, and suddenly, he stood before me, looking thoroughly displeased but as beautiful as ever. He kept his dark hair short now, although in his younger years, he'd let the tight curls grow into a massive mane into which he would braid metal and gems. Tattoos covered nearly every inch of his flesh, save for his face, and he wore more elegantly crafted piercings than I could count. His umber skin had a slight shine of oil, the scent surrounding me like a baker's kitchen at Christmas time.

"You can't keep me," I repeated as his claws flexed and his black eyes narrowed. "Unless I've committed a crime."

"You've done exactly that," he said tightly. "Or have

you already forgotten you slaughtered a human without cause?"

"*I* did not kill him," I said quickly. "The Eld beasts did."

"Did you really think you'd get away with it on that technicality? You gouged out his eyes."

"Which did *not* kill him."

"You cut off his hand."

"Again, that did not result—"

"You disemboweled him, Callum!" When Lucifer raised his voice, I swear the entire High City could hear him. Just lovely. Now they all knew I was running around Earth gutting people.

But I, ever the vision of saintly patience, said, "When I left him, he was still alive. Screaming, yes, and a bit mad with agony but, nevertheless, he was alive. Can't help what happened to him after I left."

He practically swelled with rage.

"The Heavenly Host contacted me," he said, and for the first time, a sliver of alarm pierced through me. "They're concerned, you see, about certain strange activity in the human realm currently causing significant threat to the balance."

"At least someone is paying attention," I said. "Do you have any idea what those wretched humans are doing—"

"*Yes*, Callum, believe it or not, I do take my position seriously." He sighed, standing several yards away from me. He didn't dare to get any closer. "Those humans, the Libiri, have known about that God for over a century.

You know how the beasts operate; don't pretend you don't. You think all it will take is their three sacrifices, and the God will be free? It will be nothing more than quivering flesh. A fallen God can't even create Its own body without the sacrificial energy of hundreds, if not thousands."

"It won't create a body," I said. "One has already been prepared for it: a young witch."

His mouth curled in derision. "Ah, yes, of course. Your precious witch."

"Jealousy isn't attractive on you, Lucifer."

"I should rip out your tongue."

"I'd grow a new one, even more sarcastic than the last."

He snapped, lunging forward with a snarl. But he didn't come close enough to touch me. He held himself back, restraint kicking in at the last possible second.

"Do you have any idea how close I came to sending a hunter after you?" he snapped. "*Years* you've spent locked up in that house, talking to ghosts, waiting for your fucking hallucination to come to life. *Madness.* You're fucking feral."

"I'm not."

He looked as if he wanted to kill me, and I would have loved for him to try. Perhaps he'd been stronger than me when I left Hell all those years ago, but the difference between us was far slimmer now.

"Two thousand years ago, you envisioned a witch in the middle of a field full of your dead friends," he hissed. "You've searched for her ever since. Across centuries,

Callum. And for what? To kill one more God? To feel the thrill of slaughter again? You won't even claim her for Hell."

"I'm not obligated to bind myself to anyone." I choked out the words, bitter as they were. I had to get out of here. I'd been away from Everly for far too long.

"Oh yes, of course not. Callum, the great and terrible, who has no friends, who takes no lovers. Who will not bind, nor mark, nor claim another living thing." Lucifer shook his head, and I recoiled when I saw tenderness on his face. "That war broke you. I know. All these centuries I should have kept you close, but I thought you would get it out of your system—"

"Stop speaking to me as if I'm a youth!" I lunged forward, and he leapt out of my range with a soft, disapproving chuckle.

"Yet you're still making the foolish decisions of one. Wasting your loyalty on an untrained witch, as if she won't perish like every other human. As if she could ever understand the thousands of years you've seen, the pain you've experienced. As if she could ever be more than a passing fascination."

"Passing fascination?" I echoed, laughing low under my breath. "You've sat in your onyx tower too long; it's softened your brain. Everly is not, and has never been, a mere *fascination*. She is my reason, my logic. *She* is my one and only God. Think I'm mad if you wish. There is nothing left for me in this existence except for her, and I would sooner rip myself apart than allow you or any other being to stand in her way."

"I will not risk bringing hybrid spawn into existence without a guarantee it is Hell's and Hell's alone," he said. "Do you understand me?"

"As I said, jealousy isn't—"

"You need to learn to shut your mouth." His hand darted out, grabbing my face and digging his claws in. To think I once loved him. To think I once wanted nothing more than to accept his mark and be taken into the Council.

"Claim her," he said viciously. "I want her marked, I want her soul bound. Do you understand me?"

"You won't make me your pawn in whatever pissing contest you're in with the Heavenly Host," I said, although it was rather difficult given his tight grip. "Who I claim is personal. That choice has always been *personal*."

"Perhaps for common demons. But we are not common, are we, Callum? The destruction creatures like you and me can inflict upon the world is unprecedented, and Heaven knows it. You don't want the angels involved, trust me."

My jaw clenched. There was an odd tingling in my abdomen, a sensation like fingers grasping at my skin and tugging. It made me think of Everly's fingers, so soft and warm as they caressed me. Realization pulsed through me and the tugging intensified.

I was being summoned.

"The angels won't touch her," I said. "Nor will you, Lucifer. You've seen me fight. You've seen me go to war." Shuddering at the sensation of the summoning, I grinned up at him. "What makes you think I would hesitate to bring about the apocalypse itself if it means keeping her safe?"

He bared his teeth at me. "Are you threatening me?"

He may as well have asked me if I was prepared to be a traitor to Hell itself. But I was. His question didn't frighten me, as he hoped it would. The clawing hands were growing stronger now, and I was being pulled back and away. Lucifer finally realized what was happening, but it was too late.

He couldn't do a damn thing to prevent me from being summoned.

"I'll see you soon, Callum," he said, right before I vanished, my spiritual form ripped away and sent flying, plummeting into the human world.

THE FIRST THING I noticed was the smell of ash. The next thing I noticed was blood.

The forest looked as if it had been hit by a small bomb. Young trees had their trunks snapped in half, their carcasses lying burned on the singed forest floor. The buildup of leaves beneath my feet was still smoldering as I stepped forward, gazing through the haze of smoke. The burnt bodies of Eld beasts lay around me, some still twitching, jaws snapping.

Then I saw her.

Everly was curled at the base of a tree, her arms outstretched to grip the massive roots. Her body was coiled, hunched over, shaking violently. Her hair was drenched with rain and mud, and her arms . . .

Fuck.

The glass manacles were still locked onto her wrists. Blood seeped from beneath them, thick and dark, putrid with the magical poison swirling within. It was impossible to fathom how she'd used magic despite them—the amount of power, the sheer brute strength required to overcome the enchantment in those cuffs, was astronomical.

It should have been impossible.

But the more power she poured out, the more fiercely those wicked devices would sap it from her. They didn't just stifle her magic, they absorbed and poisoned it.

To judge by the destruction around me, Everly should have been dead.

She lifted her head. Through her sopping wet hair, one eye fixed upon me. So many blood vessels had burst in the whites of her eye that it was almost entirely red.

"Callum . . ." Her voice was hoarse, barely above a whisper. "Help me . . ."

Fury and fear filled me as I rushed to her side and wrapped my arms around her, holding her close. I wanted to scream, to rage, to punish everyone responsible. She said nothing, but her breathing was ragged; it wheezed in her chest. Every movement made her whimper.

She'd needed me and I'd failed her. My beautiful witch had fought alone.

I cupped her face, her skin cold against my palm. I barely recognized my own voice as I said, "Everly? Keep speaking to me. Please."

Her eyes wouldn't focus on my face. Her lips moved, but she was too weak to make a sound.

It was as if I was back on the battlefield again, surrounded by blood and the screams of the dying. Watching those I loved slip away.

No. Not again.

With singular focus, I launched myself into the air and over the trees, flying back to the coven house as swiftly as I could. The doors flew open before me. Flying through the twisting halls, I took her to the piano room, where the small space and large fireplace could keep her warm.

"What happened?!" Winona's voice crackled from the large antique radio in the corner. The fire flared to life the moment I entered, and I laid Everly gently on the bearskin rug before it. "Who put those infernal devices on her? Callum! What in the name of Venus—"

"They're killing her," I said, tearing off her coat and ripping through her shirt so I could get a better look at the cuffs. They were so tight, they'd sunk into her flesh. She shook violently, her eyes rolling in her head, imperceptible whispers dropping from her lips as sweat drenched her face. "They're fucking killing her, Winona! How do I— Fucking hell—"

"You need the key, Callum, the *key*! They're enchanted, you won't be able to—"

"There's no goddamn time! Fuck!" Grabbing the closest thing to me—a small, polished wood table—I hurled it across the room to shatter against the wall. Then I crouched over her again, taking in the blood, the pain, the smell of infection. "I have to crack them. It might break her wrists . . . I have to . . ." Her eyes fluttered as I held her face. "Everly. Listen to me. Can you hear me?"

"Break . . . break them . . ." Her words were barely audible. "Don't care . . . just . . . please . . ."

"She's not strong enough," Winona said, her voice thick. "She's lost too much blood, Callum. She doesn't have any strength left."

I was a fool, a fucking *fool*. I'd let her go back, I'd left her alone, I'd failed to keep her safe. I should have been able to protect her. What fucking good was my strength if it couldn't even be used to protect those I cared about? What use was my power when those it should have sheltered were dead?

"Callum."

Everly's soft voice drew me back. She barely managed to lift her arm to touch me. "You came back. You came . . ."

"I swear to you I will never leave your side again," I said.

"She's dying, Callum."

I roared in response to Lucifer's voice, grabbing another nearby piece of furniture and hurling it in his direction. He dared to follow me here, he *dared* walk into this house and invade this moment? I'd kill him, I would rip him to *fucking* pieces—

"Get out," I snarled. "Before I kill you."

"You would step away from your precious dying witch to try to kill me? A waste of time." He scoffed. "You want to save her, you know how. You have a solution."

My hands clenched into fists. Everly's head lolled to the side. Her beautiful blue eyes were glassy. I wanted to burst apart. I wanted to scream. The pain of seeing her like this was worse than any battle wound I'd endured.

"Perhaps you'll run away from her too," Lucifer mused, and I grabbed the chair beside me to launch it at his head. He knocked it away with his arm, shattering it in midair, then brushing a bit of lint from his suit. "A bit tender there, are we? You weren't the only one to survive the war. There were others, but your pain was so much *greater* than theirs, wasn't it? They simply couldn't understand."

"Shut up!" I couldn't think. I knew what I had to do, I *knew*, but the thought made me so violently terrified I was frozen in place. Watching her die in my arms while I cowered in fear.

"He's right, Callum." Winona sounded so calm, so blessedly reasonable. "Claim her soul. Bind her to you. It will give her the strength she needs."

Bind her to me.

It was irrevocable. Unchangeable. A soul bargain could not be broken. Only the most extreme and violent of circumstances could severe it.

Her strength would become mine. And a little of mine would become hers. From this day, until the end of eternity, we would be bound together.

I'd claimed human souls before. Far more than I could count. They lived, they died, I escorted them to Hell. Humans assimilated well to life among demons. After a few decades, they were nearly imperceptible from us.

I couldn't even feel my ties to those human souls anymore. They didn't frighten me because they could no longer hurt me. Time and distance had rendered those relationships nearly moot.

But if I bound Everly to me, I would feel her pain. Her fears, her worry, her suffering. Her power and pride. All that she was would be connected to me, and the longer we remained in close contact with each other, the more intense that connection would become.

Claiming her meant ripping open old wounds, breaking down the defenses I'd so carefully built around myself. It meant facing the agony again. The pain and terror of having someone I could lose.

But if I didn't, I would lose her here and now. The pain was already there. There was no hiding from agony.

Only the dead see the end of war. Only the dead can rest.

Lifting Everly's limp body to hold her close against my chest, I snarled, "Get out. Both of you, get the fuck out of here and leave us alone."

CALLUM

A SOUL BARGAIN required both participants to consent. But Everly's eyes were far away, her breathing shallow and sporadic, the warmth gone from her limbs. Cradling her against my chest, I brushed the damp hair out of her face.

"Everly. Listen to me." Her eyes fluttered. Her pupils twitched; they focused on me. "It will kill you if I break the cuffs, but you will die if I don't. You need strength."

"Not strong enough," she whispered. As if she'd known it all along, as if it were confirmation of what she'd feared.

I gripped her tighter, shaking her. "No, no, listen to me. You have strength in you that's greater than my own but your body is failing you. I can lend you my strength—" *But it terrifies me. But it's the one thing I've feared above all else.* "But I need you to agree. I need you to say you're willing." She nodded, eyes rolling back. I shook her face again and demanded she look at me. "Say you willingly offer me your soul. You have to mean it, Everly. Please."

Her lips moved soundlessly. There was no more furniture nearby for me to smash, no outlet for this sickening fear.

She was all I had left. For so long, my vision of her was the one and only thing that spurred me to continue. To bother to stay awake and not simply sleep away the pain for eternity.

She was my hope.

My faith.

She was everything.

Bowing my head, I clutched her hands and realized this was the closest I would ever come to a human prayer.

"I bind myself to you, from this moment until the end of eternity. I offer you my obedience, my loyalty, and my protection, in exchange for your soul. I offer this willingly. I offer this desperately. Stay with me." I slapped her cheek lightly to keep her awake, and her eyes widened as she drew in a deep breath. "Repeat it back to me, darling, come on. You're not fucking dead yet." She squirmed, a little of the fierceness coming back to her. "Come on. Say it. I offer you my soul . . ."

She licked her lips, blinking her eyes repeatedly as if she couldn't see me clearly.

"I offer . . . offer you . . . my soul . . ."

She'd already lost too much blood, but there was no other way to proceed. Manifesting a knife out of aether,

I brought the sharp blade down, tapping the flat side lightly against her chest. She didn't flinch, she didn't shake. There was no fear in her eyes as I told her, "I need to scar you. My sigil in your flesh. I'll be gentle . . ."

But she shook her head. "I didn't ask you to be gentle."

Certain she was delirious, I said, "It will be quick, just deep enough to mark."

She laid her hand against my neck, nudging me closer with a demanding press of her fingers. "Talk to me . . . like before . . . like that night." She sucked in a shuddering breath and her words grew steadier. "Tell me that I can take it for you."

My eyes widened as I realized what she meant. That first night we'd fucked, when her strength had blossomed with just a little encouragement.

Her mouth tasted like blood and ash as I kissed her.

"If you can feel pain, that means you're still alive," I said, and she nodded against me. I trailed my hands over her body, feeling the ripple of her muscles beneath her skin, the softness around her hips and belly. "You're a warrior, Everly. You can take the pain, you can endure it, I know you can." With one hand tangled in her hair, I gripped the long blonde locks near the roots, smiling when she winced and then offered a small smile in return. "That's it, that's right. The pain means you're alive."

When I pressed the tip of the knife into her flesh, cherry-red blood welled around the blade and streaked down her skin. The sweet scent of her magic filled the air, heady and as intoxicating as liquor. It was remarkable every demon within a hundred miles hadn't been drawn to her by now; but they'd have no chance at all if they pursued her.

She was mine. Entirely, wholly, irrevocably mine.

"Take it for me," I murmured. Her face contorted with pain and her eyes rolled in her head, dangerously close to passing out. But as the ancient demonic runes bound us together, our strength mingled. I felt a rush of her pain, then bliss. The most perfect, stunning pleasure. Heat tingled through my veins. Hidden within her struggling body was a knot of magic so great that it made me shake.

She was not the only one made stronger by this bargain. I was too.

Blood smeared across her skin, but with every cut, she smiled a little wider, even when her eyes narrowed with pain. Warmth came back to her. The cuts were deep enough to scar but only barely, and she looked so beautiful with those stark red lines crisscrossing her stomach.

"It's done," I said gently. The knife vanished from my hand as I allowed the manifestation to dissolve. She was trembling violently, and she felt feverish, sweat beading on her forehead.

"The cuffs," she growled. "The fucking cuffs . . . please . . . shit . . . ."

Crouching over her, her legs splayed around my waist, I gripped one of the cuffs and warned her, "It's going to hurt."

She was nodding, squirming, every inch of her tense with anticipation. "I know. It means I'm alive."

She screamed when the glass cracked in my hands. Barbed spikes tore out of her wrists as I pulled the shattered bits of glass off her flesh. The skin beneath was blackened with bruises, purple and yellow splotches marring her.

"You're almost there," I said, locking my hands around the other cuff.

I hated to hear her cry. Having to hurt her was agony, but I had no choice. My mind kept drifting into the past . . . to all the lives I was too late to save. All the beings I'd watched slip away.

I wouldn't lose her too.

"It's okay," she whispered. "Just do it. It's almost over."

The sound of breaking glass was nearly drowned by the shriek that escaped from her. The cuffs' wicked barbs were finally out of her, and life came back into her face. She held me breathlessly, clumsy hands caressing my neck as trembling legs wrapped tighter around me.

She looked like a wild creature, something untamed that had crawled in from the woods and now lay looking at me like a succubus. Bloody, face smudged with dirt, body covered in bruises and those fresh cuts on her stomach.

"Where were you?" she said. "You left me . . . you left for so long . . ."

"I was taken." I burrowed my face against her neck, as if I could impress into her body how sorry I was. "Lucifer took me to Hell and I couldn't escape until you summoned me. But he can't take me from you again. Not anymore." I trailed my fingers through the blood, the cuts that bound us as one. She smelled so sweet, and my head was light with all the magic in the air.

"I was so scared." Her voice was weak with exhaustion. Her eyes drooped, her heart pounding steadily at last.

"I'm so sorry, my lady." Laying my head against her chest, I listened to its beat, reassuring me with every throb that she was still with me.

FOR THE FIRST time, Everly slept in my arms.

She was limp and warm as she lay against my chest before the fire, a blanket draped over us and the bear-skin rug beneath us. She slept for hours, regaining her strength. I was content to simply hold her, watching as the sun rose through the open windows and filled the room with pale light.

She shifted her weight as she awoke, lifting her face to look at me. My arm was curled beneath my head so I could see her.

"Tell me about your vision," she said. "Tell me about the first time you saw me."

She drew back when I stiffened, as if to separate her body from mine. Instantly, my arms tightened around her, demanding she stay.

"It will be easier to tell you if you're close to me," I said. Despite being the one event that had guided my actions for many centuries, this memory wasn't one I preferred to recall.

To my relief, Everly settled down again, laying her palm flat on my chest and resting her chin on top of it, so she could watch my face. Casting my eyes upward, I tried to lose myself in the swirls of carved wood on the ceiling.

"Hell had been at war with the Gods for decades," I said. "We don't know where They came from, or how They made their way through the Veil to gain entrance to Hell. It's always been suspected They broke through from another dimension. A predatory species, hunting for sustenance. The Elder creatures were drawn to Them because of the immense magic They contained, and so the Gods amassed an army of wretched things. They wanted our worship; They sustain Themselves with the attention and devotion of other living things. But what They wanted above all else was our suffering. Our pain. Our fear. A God is well-fed when It has hordes of other living things in terror of It. But demons do not worship. We do not obey. Our loyalty is to ourselves. So we fought."

Even now, I could recall how it felt when the Council called for warriors. When Hell was threatened, and all we had ever known hung in the balance. Even the Heavenly Host was convinced demonkind had finally met our match.

"That was many centuries ago," I said. "I was a different demon then. Younger, still powerful, but I hadn't yet ascended. That's what we call it when one of us becomes an Archdemon. Ascension."

I'd wanted that more than anything. I'd already spent several centuries hunting souls on Earth, growing my power.

I had hundreds of lovers. I spent my days hopping between clandestine demonic parties on Earth to making my debauched way through Hellish clubs every night. My memories of those days were so faint now. Like a different life.

Whoever I'd been back then had died in the war.

"The fighting went on for years. Every time a God killed one of us, It captured our being. Demons don't have souls, not exactly in the way humans do anyway. Demons, like angels, instead have an energy that comprises our consciousness, similar to a human soul but simpler. Our *being*, we call it. The burst of energy that makes us alive. The Gods were taking it when They killed us. The consciousnesses of the demons they killed were forced into an eternal, spiritual suffering."

Even now, it sickened me. So many were forced to suffer for so long after death. There was no greater torture for a demon than the loss of our freedom.

"I volunteered to fight to prove I was valiant. That I was fierce and loyal and deserved my ascension. But I watched my warriors die. Dozens of them. Then hundreds. Then thousands. I lost count. I couldn't remember all of their names, their faces. And fuck, I tried."

The words grated in my throat, and I fell silent until I could compose myself.

"We were slaughtering Them, but it cost us greatly. We were told the end of the war was near. That the Gods had begun to flee from Hell and were instead hiding on Earth. But many still remained, and They were moving toward the High City. Dantalion, the seat of the

Council, and the Onyx Citadel, home of Lucifer, Bael, and Paimon, the oldest among our kind."

It choked me how greatly I'd idolized them back then. How I'd longed for Lucifer's attention, how I'd pushed myself to be even more vicious, more bloodthirsty, more cunning, if only to have his approval.

"I fought that final battle. I positioned myself and my warriors between the Gods and the city. We were the last defense. We . . . were victorious."

Saying it sounded like a lie.

"More than half of those I fought beside were killed. The demons who fought with me that day were among the greatest of Hell's army. I'd known them, many of them, for the entirety of my life. We'd marked each other . . ." Seeing her frown of confusion, I explained, "Demons mark each other with piercings, gifts of metal. To pierce another's flesh and leave a mark of your affection is one of the greatest symbols of devotion our kind has."

"But you have no piercings," she said softly.

Keeping my eyes fixed upon the ceiling, I didn't dare look at her. To look into her eyes was to see that moment again in all its horror. A battlefield covered by the dead, and in the midst of it all . . .

"I ripped them out," I said. "When I found them dead, I ripped out the metal they'd given me. I couldn't live with the reminder." But I still had them: the jewelry, the bloodied piercings. I'd carried them with me through all these centuries, hoarding them like a dragon's precious treasure. "That was where I saw you, Everly, in the morning after that last battle. I'd survived, but I felt dead. You called my name."

Still, centuries later, I didn't fully understand it. Demons had never been known to receive visions of the future. We were not blessed with gifts of premonition, as some witches were. Yet I'd seen her, I'd heard her, as clear as day.

"What did I . . . what did the vision say to you?" she said.

"You told me your name and begged for my help."

She sat beside me. The blanket was still draped around her shoulders, but I longed for her skin-to-skin contact to return. Reaching out, I wrapped my arm around her waist so I wouldn't have to go without her touch.

"What kind of help?" she said, picking at her cuticles instead of looking at me. I noticed the redness around her nails; how abused the skin was.

It had been so long, but every word she'd said to me was seared into my brain.

"You said I had to keep fighting. And that you would find me."

Her frown deepened, and I grasped her hand. Her fingers curled toward her palm, like a frightened reptile retreating into its shell.

"And what was it about me that made you so determined to help that you searched for me? For centuries . . ." She shook her head, scoffing as if she didn't believe it, even now.

"It was not merely that one vision that convinced me," I said. "The day I saw you was the day I lost everything

I had left. Almost all of those I loved were dead. The demon I'd been, who could pass his days with frivolous parties, who sought nothing more than pleasure and power, was destroyed. No, I wasn't convinced immediately. But I swear, you haunted me. Everywhere I turned, I would see your face. In crowds, in dark corners, whether I was in Hell or on Earth. Fate had thrown me a lifeline that I'd refused to grasp, and it wouldn't stop reminding me of it. I needed a purpose; I needed a reason to live. You gave me that. What else did I have to go on for?"

Her eyes were filled with flickering firelight. She brushed a few loose strands of hair away from my face, leaving her hand there against my cheek for a moment.

"I don't blame you for not trusting me," I said, and she looked stricken. But it was true; she was only afraid of offending me. "Give me time, my lady. This is all I have. You are all I have. I know that may scare you." Her eyes flickered around my face, searching it. "But I've fought this war for two thousand years, waiting for my commander. If I am ever meant to see peace again, it will be through you. If anyone can bring this war to its end . . ."

"Me," she whispered. Such a simple word, full of so much fear, drenched in disbelief. "You really think I can . . ." She shook her head, laughing softly. "You think I can kill a God?"

Taking her wrist, I caressed my fingers over the mottled bruises and the swollen wounds from where the cuffs had bit into her. "The manacles you wore have been used for hundreds of years to completely and totally render witches unable to use their magic. Not only did you continue to use magic in a myriad of ways while wearing them, but you laid waste to an entire pack of beasts. You burned an acre of forest to a crisp in mere seconds." Bringing her wrists close to me, I kissed her bruises. "You are far more powerful than you have ever been allowed to believe."

EVERLY

FOR THE ENTIRE next day and following night, I slept. Fitful dreams filled my sleep, visions of fire, memories of pain.

In the brief moments I would wake, Callum was standing over me. Sometimes close, right at my bedside. Sometimes in a chair near the fire or standing by the window, gazing out at the rain. But he was always near, and his presence gave me comfort.

Despite the Deep One's vicious efforts, my soul was no longer destined for Its merciless eternity. With just a few words and the cuts from Callum's knife, my fate had changed entirely.

I belonged to him, and my soul was destined for Hell.

Slowly, I sat up, feeling like a corpse rising from the grave. Pale sunlight streamed in the open windows. My grandmother's radio was set on the table near the fireplace, and it crackled with her voice.

"It's good to see you awake at last," she said. "Callum has gone out to the garden to fetch a few herbs for me. I'm preparing a tincture that will help those scars heal cleanly."

Immediately, my hand clutched at my stomach. I'd been dressed in clean clothes, made of soft, loose linen. But beneath the cloth, my skin was tender. Holding my breath to brace myself, I lifted my shirt and peered down. Elaborate lines and circles covered my stomach, surrounding Callum's familiar sigil carved over my navel.

Abruptly, I lowered my shirt and hugged my arms around myself. My grandmother *tsk*ed softly, and I felt the sensation of a hand rubbing my shoulders.

"Oh, my dear, do not be afraid," she said. "Many people throughout history, witches or not, have given their souls to a demon. An afterlife in Hell is not the terror you've been led to believe. It is an entirely new world; you will not be abused there. Some witches visit Hell even before their deaths. I've heard it's a fascinating place."

"Have you been there?" I said, desperately eager for her reassurance. So much of my life felt beyond my control; I was stuck on a rollercoaster with no brakes, unable to see the twists and turns of the track ahead.

"I have not. But your ancestor, our Grand Mistress Sybil, traveled there many times."

The reminder of Sybil made me groan. "The grimoire. I *lost* the grimoire, Grams, I—" I sighed, thinking suddenly of naive Raelynn carrying that book around. "But I know where it is."

"Then you haven't truly lost it, have you?" she said, keeping her voice fiercely upbeat. "You've been through enough in these past few days. You need your rest, and a bath by the look of your hair. When you've healed, you will try again. As long as you're alive, we have not failed." There was a soft sound, like the shifting of dry grass. "Callum has returned. I'll leave you to rest, but I'm sure he'll be up to check on you soon."

Before she could go, I said suddenly, "There was another demon here, wasn't there? Callum was angry . . ." The memories were so vague, but I was certain I'd seen another demon, with massive feathered wings, standing over me as I writhed in pain.

My grandmother's voice was grim as she said, "We were visited by one of Hell's oldest and most powerful demons, Lucifer. He demanded Callum claim your soul, and Callum tried to refuse—until he had no other choice."

A thousand questions fought for attention in my mind. "Why would another demon care what happens to my soul?"

"You're powerful, Everly. And Hell craves power. The dedication of your soul to Hell helps to ensure the ongoing security and longevity of that world." It seemed as if there was something more she wanted to explain, but instead she said abruptly, "I'll prepare the tincture for you. You'll find clean clothes in the wardrobe."

With a final crackle of static, she left the room.

Despite my clean clothes, the rest of me was still filthy. The wounds on my wrists had been cleaned and bandaged, but my hair was clumped with dirt and tangles, my skin spotted with mud. My body ached as I got out of bed, stretching my stiff arms and legs. To my surprise, despite being drowsy and sore, I felt far stronger than I expected.

Far stronger than I had felt *before*.

I drew a bath, filling the large porcelain tub with water that smelled faintly of cedarwood. Steam surrounded me as I stepped into the bath, sinking into the water with a groan. Carefully, I unwrapped the bandages from my wrists, allowing the wounds a bit of fresh air. The bruising was extensive, but the tears in my skin had already healed.

After scrubbing myself clean, I drained the tub and filled it again with fresh water, closing my eyes as I soaked. But it wasn't long before a strange feeling made me open them again.

It was the sensation of being watched, but not by the God. Frowning, I looked all around the room, searching for the source of my unease. The large window beside the tub looked out upon a gray rainy day, and as I peered down into the yard, I spotted a figure standing beneath the trees.

They were shrouded in a red cloak, standing out starkly amid the dark greenery. They were tall, easily as tall as Callum, and instead of a face . . .

It was the skull of a horse.

A chill went up my back as I stared into those empty

eye sockets. The being didn't move, but I knew with absolute certainty they were watching me.

The bathroom door quietly swung open, the subtle
click of claws on the tile announcing Callum's arrival.
He was already standing in the room when he knocked,
drawing my attention away from the window.

"Someone is out there," I said.

The demon didn't seem alarmed as he nodded. "I
know. He is one of the fae; Darragh told me he was coming. It's been a very long time since magic like yours has
been unleashed in their forest. You've caught their attention, my lady. The fae are curious creatures, but cautious
too. It is the duty of the Old Man to ensure you don't
mean his kind any harm."

"Old Man?" I jerked my head toward the window
again, but the horse skull had vanished. Rising halfway
from the bath in alarm, I pressed my face closer to the
window, looking all over the garden for him.

But the haunting figure was gone.

"That's what Darragh calls him," Callum said. "I
suppose he has other names, too. But demons don't fuck
with fae. We certainly don't seek out their names. It's bad
form."

Frowning, I sank back into the water. "There's so
much I don't know. The fae. Heaven and Hell. The Gods.
I feel lost." It frustrated me to be so naïve, so *ignorant*.

"A hunger for knowledge can be more valuable
than knowledge itself. People take what they know for
granted."

I turned away from the window and faced him.

The night he rescued me, flying me here through the dark, through the rain, I'd seen a different side to him. Something beyond the feral monster who pursued me like a ravenous wolf, who could shake the stone walls with his voice.

That night, he'd been afraid. Afraid for *me*. Even in the depths of my pain, I'd felt the way he held me. As if he was prepared to fight death itself to keep it from taking me.

"This isn't the first time you've claimed a human soul?" The moment my words emerged as a question, I felt like a fool and shook my head. "Of course it isn't. You've been alive hundreds of years . . . thousands . . ."

The silence stretched. It grew thick, heavy with tension.

"It's been a very long time since I claimed a soul," he finally said. The words were slow and careful, and he looked away as he spoke. "Claiming a soul binds that life to yours. Over time, and with distance, that bond can fade, but it can also grow stronger. I've claimed more human souls than I can count. More names than I could ever remember. There was once a time when such bonds didn't terrify me. That was very long ago."

In that haze of pain and exhaustion, I'd heard the arguments. The shadowy figure—*Lucifer*—demanding my soul be claimed. Callum's voice breaking when he realized it was his only choice to save me.

"Did it terrify you? Claiming me?" Callum's head snapped toward me at my question, and I flinched.

"Yes," he said, after a long pause.

"Then why did you do it?"

His expression fractured, and I *felt* it. A pang of uncertainty shot through my chest like a bolt. Then came the rolling wave of fear, a ripping terror that could hardly be encompassed by words, so shockingly intense I gasped.

The feelings left me as suddenly as they appeared, and Callum said, "That's part of it . . . the emotions. For most humans, it would merely be a hint of my feelings, but your magic amplifies it. What I feel may bleed over to you and vice versa."

He still hadn't answered, but it was clearly on his mind. He looked as if he were trying to solve a puzzle, and his frown didn't dissipate until he met my eyes again.

In the blink of an eye, he was standing over me, with his hands braced against the edge of the tub.

My eyes drifted over him with appreciation. The lean muscles, tight with anticipation. The hard set of his jaw, the intensity of his eyes. My brain turned to mush every time I saw that taut, lickable chest . . .

Lickable? Oh, God, Everly, get yourself together, girl.

"I have no reason to live without you," he said, his sharp teeth clenched. "Perhaps what I've done was incredibly selfish, but I would save your life again. I swore to protect you, and now, I'm bound by the demands of our bargain to do so. No matter what it takes. No matter what I must sacrifice. No matter who I must kill. For you, I would burn this world and the next."

His words snatched the air from my lungs. It was impossible to disbelieve the sincerity in his voice, the *viciousness*. His hands tightened on the edges of the tub, and I jumped when a crack appeared on the porcelain edge. He winced, standing up slowly as he clenched and unclenched his fingers.

"Whether you choose to stay in this house, or leave, I will follow you," he said. "If you choose to face the God, or don't, I will be by your side. Whether or not you can find it in yourself to trust me, I will not leave you. This obsession might mean the death of me, but that is an end I will meet gladly. Humans have their deities, their great and powerful Gods, guiding them to live and die. I have you."

Words were completely lost to me. I could only stare at him, this powerful being who seemed so much larger than life, who vibrated with a deep and ancient energy. My demon. My protector.

From within the pocket of his trousers, Callum withdrew a corked glass vial, filled with honey-colored liquid. "Your grandmother prepared this. She said it should be applied to your wounds, to help them heal. If you would allow me."

Nodding, I stepped out of the bath. Black eyes seared my skin as I reached for a towel and dried myself, squeezing the water from my hair. The way he looked at me caused heat to pool in my abdomen.

Glimpsing myself in the large, framed mirror leaning against the wall beside the tub, I paused. I tried not to pay too much attention to my looks. I'd never had Victoria's grace or seemingly effortless beauty. I didn't have much skill with makeup, and honestly didn't like wearing it. I'd always been plain; painfully average. Too tall and too skinny, as Meredith frequently pointed out to me. Jeremiah used to say I looked like a giraffe, and that insult still lived on my hunched shoulders, as if I could make myself smaller.

Now, with scars on my body and bruises on my arms, I didn't know how Callum could look at me like that. When he looked like a Greek statue brought to life, not even his scars could diminish his looks.

Biting my lip, I turned away from my reflection. That mirror would have to go, so I wouldn't have to see myself every damn time I came in here.

Callum stepped closer behind me, taking the towel and tossing it aside. He wrapped his arms around me and I fought the urge to hide my face.

"Why do you look at yourself with disdain?" he said, his tone truly confused. "As if any part of you is shameful. As if this beautiful body wasn't perfectly designed to appeal to every single one of my senses. This soft skin, tender and warm." His lips brushed against my ear, while his claws caressed up my arm. "The sound of your voice, sweet as a siren. The sight of you is enough to make me a beast with need. And the *smell* of you . . ." He gripped me tightly, sinking with me to his knees on the thick rug in front of the mirror. As I knelt before him, he leaned close over my back. "Intoxicating. The taste of you?" His forked tongue stroked along my neck, his eyes closing for a moment. "Divine."

He uncorked the bottle of golden liquid and poured some of it over his fingers. His hands moved slowly over my abdomen, working the oil over the scabbed cuts. It was a firm touch, but gentle enough not to hurt my wounds.

"These scars are our bond," he said. He watched me in the mirror, fascination softening his dark eyes. "They tell the story of your survival. They're the regalia of a warrior."

It was impossible to tear my eyes away from the sight of his hands caressing my skin. His movements were so slow, so reverent.

"Gorgeous, every inch of you," he murmured. "I adore the way you react to me, the sounds you make, the way you feel. So soft and yet so strong."

His words filled me with a warm feeling, and I squirmed, unable to bear looking in the mirror a moment longer. But he immediately reached up, grabbing my face and pulling my gaze back.

"Don't look away," he said. "You're exquisite."

He dipped his fingers into the oil again, then lifted his hand, allowing it to drip over my chest. Shining droplets streaked over my breasts, and his fingers chased them, grasping me and squeezing. This gentle appreciation, the tenderness of his hold, was so unfamiliar to me it was overwhelming.

He hummed gently, his body rocking against mine. His hard length pressed against my back, tenting his trousers. I longed for the brutal ache of him inside me, demolishing every thought until nothing was left but pleasure.

"Relax," he said. "You're safe with me."

He massaged me, moving from my stomach to my breasts, then my shoulders, my back. I was jelly in his hands, nearly limp as he moved me.

"I can feel your anxiety," he said, speaking close to my ear. "How it sits inside you like a knot, how your brain feeds it lies to keep it alive. Let me help you."

Everything felt so new, so unfamiliar, so strange. And yet . . .

"I trust you," I said. He met my gaze in the mirror, and his eyes made me think of the sky just before dawn. Those vast depths kissed with light and warmth.

"Do you trust me to give you pleasure?" he said. "Or to give you pain?"

"Both."

I wanted every experience he could give me. I'd spent my life behind locked doors, and now those doors were flung open, and I intended to indulge gluttonously.

An eager grin revealed his sharp teeth.

"Stay where you are," he said. "I'll be right back."

He vanished, the absence of his arms leaving me cold. He returned, carrying something in his hand.

A leather flogger with numerous soft tassels.

My eyes widened as he dragged the brown leather tails through his fingers.

"There is an entire world of sensation waiting for you," he said. He trailed the flogger across my shoulders. "A spectrum between pleasure and pain that you cannot even imagine. I intend to show you all of it. To guide you on a journey of indulgence toward whatever bliss you desire."

He guided me so that my back was resting against his legs. Slowly, teasingly, he caressed the tassels over my breasts, igniting a storm of goose bumps across my skin. I shivered when the leather brushed over my nipples, the buds swiftly hardening.

With a gentle hand on the back of my head, Callum pushed me forward. "Brace your hands on the mirror's frame," he said. "Watch while I use this flogger on your back. See how beautiful you look, how every expression on your face is a masterpiece."

Part of me wanted to melt into the floor in embarrassment. He couldn't mean it, not truly, because I was—

"Everly." His voice was sharp as he leaned over me. "Get those thoughts out of your head. You're not allowed to disparage yourself."

My face turned red, but I forced myself not to look away as he stepped back. He used the flogger lightly at first, tapping it against my back and trailing it up my spine. When he brought it down with a little more force, I gasped.

"How does it feel?" he said, swinging the flogger in his hand as he waited for my response.

Meeting his eyes in the mirror, I said, "Amazing. That feels amazing."

I lost track of time. The flogger's soft tails nipped at my back—sometimes sharp, sometimes heavy, sometimes teasingly soft. Callum wielded the tool like it was an extension of his arm. Every time I looked away from my own reflection and back at him, I found his eyes fixed on my face.

Watching me, learning my reactions. He would bring the flogger down, then he would pace, keeping his eyes on my face all the while. The soft sound of his feet brushing over the wooden floor made my back prickle with anticipation. The skin on my shoulders was already bright red.

Warm and tenderized, like a feast prepared to be eaten.

The flogger snapped, stinging like a million tiny pinpricks. I cried out, a loud moan more than a scream.

The flogger was tossed aside. Callum ran his fingers through my hair, pulling it back out of my face so he could touch my cheek. My arms shook, still braced against the mirror's frame.

"There you are, darling," he said. He cupped my chin, lifting my face as he crouched behind me. His wings framed me as if they were my own. "Look at yourself. Look at your eyes, how soft they are. Look at your mouth." He traced his thumb over my lip. Without thinking, I opened my mouth for his finger, letting him press down on my tongue as I suckled softly. "All your worries, all your fears, cannot hold you forever. But I can. And I fully intend to."

I barely recognized my own face. So close to the mirror, my eyes appeared more black than blue, more demon than human.

Lowering my trembling arms, I braced them on the floor and arched my back, pressing myself against his hard length. His fingers were still in my mouth, and I stroked my tongue over them, holding his gaze.

The light in his eyes became an inferno. With quick, sudden movements, he seized the nape of my neck and bent me forward, so my cheek was pressed against the soft rug. He pulled up my hips, bringing me to my knees, bent over with my ass pressed against him. I was positioned at such an angle that I could still see myself in the mirror, squirming against him with a desperate need.

"Be a good girl," he warned me. "Ask nicely for what you want."

"You gave me pain," I said. "Now I want pleasure."

He scratched his claws up my reddened back. "I want you to watch yourself while I fuck you, Everly. If you look away . . ." His grin turned truly wicked. "I'll punish you."

His words were twisting me into knots of arousal, so desperate I wanted to whine, squirm, beg—but he'd already beaten all the fight out of me.

As he entered me, my pupils swelled, dark pools consuming the blue until it was merely a slim ring in each eye. I was unable to stop the moan he forced out of me as he sheathed himself fully inside.

God, it was— This was—

"Holy shit, you feel so . . . so good." My words shook, my pitch keening higher. He was so deep inside me, the pain should have been far worse. But I was soaking wet, tingling with magic, my body so relaxed that the ache of him filling me up was stunning.

He watched me in the mirror as he drew himself out before slowly filling me. Again and again, those slow thrusts drove me wild.

"Callum, that's— Oh, God, you're going to make me—"

"You're not coming yet." He chuckled, his hips tight against me, buried in me. "Not until I say. Not until I've fucked every last whimper out of you. You won't have a brain left in your head when I'm done with you."

As if he knew every nerve and weakness in my body, he made good on his word. Every time I thought I was going to tip over that blissful edge into orgasm, he pulled me back.

But only barely. Only just enough that I was teetering on the edge, moaning with abandon. My body was alight, and every touch, every movement, every *word* felt so delicious.

The demon hummed appreciatively. "That's what I like to see. Not a thought behind those eyes besides how fucking good you feel." He pulled my wild hair out of my face, tenderly stroking my cheek. "I swore to take care of you, Everly. In every single way you need caring for."

I was trembling on the edge, desperate for release but too tired to fight for it. He played my body with the same ease he'd played the piano, my pleasure rising to an impossible crescendo. He pulled me up, wrapping his arm around my chest and grasping my throat. I was overcome by the sight of myself held tightly against him, his claws piercing into my skin, my abdomen bulging slightly with every thrust of his cock.

His voice was deep enough to shake my bones as he said, "You're mine. You've *always* been mine. Even when this world is nothing more than ash and dust, your soul will belong to me." His black eyes stared into mine, and

I was falling deeper, deeper into that endless void. "Other humans would break from taking me like this. It's like you're made for me, crafted by fate itself."

He grasped my chin, keeping my head up. Lost in need, I opened my mouth and whimpered, placated only when he pressed two fingers onto my tongue. Closing my lips around him, I savored the primal taste of flesh and sweat. My vision blurred.

His hand moved between my legs. The touch of his fingers as he thrust inside me was all it took. My body coiled, gasping and weeping from the sheer overwhelmingness of it all. I could *feel* his thick cock pump inside me as he came, filling me until he dripped down my thighs.

25

EVERLY

RAELYNN LAWSON'S CABIN was on the outskirts of town, at the end of a dirt driveway, hidden among thick pine trees. It hadn't been difficult to find her address. After showing Callum how to use a cell phone, he made one quick call to the university and managed to charm Raelynn's address out of them within ten minutes.

It was a little unnerving how very human he could sound when he wanted to.

Despite Callum sensing no one on our approach, I stood in the shadows of the trees as he searched the yard and the interior of the cabin. Not that I could see very much of him. Even under normal circumstances, he moved too fast. But when he was trying to be sneaky, as he was now, he was all but invisible. A flitting shadow.

After several tense minutes of waiting, Callum teleported beside me with a tiny pop that made me jump.

"Another demon has been here," he said, instantly moving to stand far too close to me. Too close, or not close enough. He put one arm possessively around me, claws pricking dangerously through my denim jacket. "Smells like your father's captive hellion."

"Leon? He's been here?" At Callum's nod, I shook my head in disbelief. "I thought he would have gone straight back to Hell."

"He escaped your father?" I briefly explained what had happened. "Perhaps he's taken a liking to the woman. All the better for us if he chooses to pursue her. Having a demon keeping an eye on her might dissuade the Libiri from attempting to capture her."

"It buys us time," I said grimly.

He'd broken the cabin's sliding glass door to allow me access inside, leaving shattered glass upon the deck. Stepping inside, I froze at the disapproving glare of the house's current inhabitant. A fluffy calico cat stared at me with bright yellow eyes, before giving a loud meow and jumping down from its perch on the kitchen counter to rub around Callum's legs.

"I see you're already on good terms with the guard," I said. Callum smirked as he picked up the feline, using a claw to scratch beneath his chin.

"Cats are everywhere in Hell," he said. "Although they live longer there, and therefore, become much cleverer. Dangerous little beasts."

As Callum made friends with the cat, I headed straight for the bedroom to rifle through Raelynn's things. But my search was fruitless. There was no sign of the grimoire anywhere.

"Crap, it isn't here," I called.

Callum appeared in the doorway; the cat was still rubbing around his ankles. "Calm your mind. You sensed the grimoire before; perhaps you can do it again. Let your magic aid you."

It was difficult to reach for the very thing I'd been taught to avoid, but I tried. Returning to the cabin's main room, I closed my eyes. I allowed my limbs to slacken, rolling my head to stretch my neck. I'd never been good at relaxing, but I needed to clear my head.

"There's magic here," Callum said, his voice close behind me. "It's faint, but I keep getting whiffs of it. Human magic smells sweet, like honey or sugar." His chest pressed against my back, one hand wrapping beneath my chin and tipping it upward. "Deep breaths. Do you smell it?"

I could scarcely think of anything other than the touch of his hand. The way he held just a little too tightly, fingers digging into my skin, body looming over mine. All I could smell was the warm, rich aroma of him.

Callum laughed softly. His lips brushed against my cheek as he said, "So easily distracted."

He stepped away, and I was left breathless. But he was right. A sugary-sweet scent was in the air, and when I opened my eyes, I swore I saw something like shimmering gold smoke around a bookshelf.

I knelt before the shelf, rifling through the mess of

books and papers stacked upon it. Finally, I grasped a small leather-bound book.

The world seemed to stop as I drew it out, brushing my hand across that familiar cover. My fingers tingled as I opened it. Grand Mistress Sybil's handwriting filled the pages in elegant Latin text, her drawings and diagrams rendered with elaborate attention to detail.

Dad had complained multiple times that carrying the grimoire felt like holding a sheet of ice. But as I held it close, I swore the book pulsed in time with my heart.

As if it was happy to be found.

I WAS ALREADY flipping through the grimoire as I followed Callum out of the house. My Latin was a little rusty, so I read slowly, but eagerly. Everything I'd wanted so desperately to learn was right there in my hands.

I paused as I stepped off the porch. Callum only made it a few paces before he noticed my hesitation and turned. "What's wrong?"

"There's a protective enchantment in here," I said, reading slowly as I mentally translated the Latin text. "A ward, meant to discourage the presence or entrance of beings with ill intentions." After carefully reading the spell several times, I faced the cabin. "I'm going to cast it. Or try to . . ."

I'd never cast a true spell in my life, but there was no better time to try. Even though my last attempt at using magic had been agonizing, I didn't feel afraid as I spread my arms, concentrating upon the spell's intended purpose.

Protect this house. Protect its inhabitants. Prevent anyone who would cause harm to its inhabitants from entering here.

"*Lanua cunctis hostibus clausa est,*" I said. My pronunciation was far from perfect. While the words were important, they weren't nearly as important as the intent behind them. "*Hostes huc intrare non possunt.*"

A sense of relief flooded through me, and my hands steadied. The air around my outstretched fingers shimmered slightly.

There was no visible change to the cabin, but it *felt* different. Tucking the grimoire into my bag, I said, "I have no idea if that worked, but maybe it will help her."

When I turned around, Callum was staring at me.

"How did it feel, my lady?" he said. "To cast your first spell?"

Pride filled me, so thick and sweet that my eyes stung. The rush of emotions was unexpected, and I lowered my head so he wouldn't see it on my face.

"Like breathing for the first time," I said. It felt like nothing I'd ever experienced before, and yet it felt familiar too. Like a sensation from my dreams, manifesting in reality.

Callum gave me a sharp-toothed smile. "Then let's cast a few more, shall we?"

EVERLY

BEHIND HOUSE LAVERNE, at the very end of a cobblestone path that meandered into the trees, stood a beautiful mausoleum carved of stone. An old graveyard surrounded it, overgrown with fauna, headstones and elegant statuary spread out beneath the trees.

The mausoleum was large in comparison to the little graveyard it watched over. The pale stone was webbed with bronze veins, and its square structure was crowned with a dome of elaborate stained glass. Weeping angels reclined between pillars set into the outer walls, arms outstretched in despair, beautiful faces veiled.

Callum looked as if he could have been one of those angels brought to life—if said angels were wicked instead of beseeching, full of mischief instead of mourning. Fingers laced, we made our way down the cobblestone path.

"Is Grams buried here?" I said, pausing to brush away dirt and vines from a crooked headstone. The year of death was 1902, and my eyes practically bugged out of my head at its age.

"She is. I buried her myself," Callum said. "The moment she died, her ghost was banging all over the house demanding to be buried. Do you have any idea how picky she was?" I certainly didn't. "She wanted me to sing hymns. Me! A demon! Singing *hymns*!" He shook his head, huffing with such disbelief one would think he'd been asked to prance naked between the headstones. "But I did it. I don't understand human death customs, but it made her stop nagging me."

He turned to stare at me as I snickered, trying not to completely lose it at the thought of Callum standing out here with Gram's shrouded corpse, singing Hellenistic hymns.

Callum folded his arms, claws tapping irritably on his bicep. "I see my suffering amuses you. It's only fair you amuse me in return."

"Oh?" I turned from admiring the elaborate gravestone before me, giving him an innocent look. "Did you bring the strap out here? That certainly seemed to entertain you."

He tried to maintain his grumpy glower, but the corner of his mouth twitched. "Never should have given you a taste of that. Give one little inch and you take—"

"It was *much* bigger than one little inch, Callum."

One moment, he was standing near the graveyard gate; the next, he had snatched me up and pressed me against the wall of the mausoleum.

"My, my, you've gotten bold, haven't you, darling? Perhaps you forget whose pretty little neck is most vulnerable to throttling between the two of us?" To prove his point, his clawed fingers pinned me by the throat. He didn't stifle my air, but slightly squeezed the sides of my neck until my head swam and I caught my breath, gasping in his hold.

"I may be weaker than you," I dared to say. "But you would beg me to throttle you and whine if I didn't acquiesce." His eyes flashed dangerously. "So, who's more vulnerable between us really? The witch or the desperate, horny demon?"

"You must be trying to provoke me." His voice lowered in warning. "Such a determined little witch would do well to remember her safeword if she wants to proceed."

"Mercy," I said, "is not something I'll be asking for."

"That's exactly what I wanted to hear." He lowered me to my feet and stepped back. "Get to work then, witch. There's a horde of wraiths waiting for you in there. It's time you dispatched them."

My face fell. Fear slithered up my spine. "Wait, you want me to go in there—alone?"

"Certainly. A witch so bold and confident as you shouldn't have an issue destroying them." He waved his hand flippantly, and I glared as I realized what he was doing.

If he thought he could gain the upper hand by getting me to beg for his help, he was sorely mistaken. Even with my stomach flipping in trepidation, I drew in a deep breath and said, "Fine. It's not a problem at all."

Striding toward the chained doors of the mausoleum, I told myself not to be afraid. The sooner I began practicing my magic, the better—and what better opportunity than this? Killing shrieking, blade-wielding wraiths . . . in a graveyard . . . not scary at all.

Stopping in front of the doors, I glanced back at Callum. He folded his arms, nodding his head toward the door as if to say *Go on*.

What a dick.

I grasped the lock and it sprung open in my fingers. The doors swung inward, creaking on their hinges. A rush of stale, dusty air rushed out to greet me. The walls were lined with statuary standing in rounded alcoves with tall, narrow windows illuminating them from behind. Gleaming copper beams supported the domed ceiling, like rows of crosses lining the long narrow path ahead.

In the dreary light, wisps of shadow drifted silently through the gloom. They hadn't noticed me—at least, not yet. Gulping at the sight of them, I fumbled to pull the grimoire out of my bag and hurriedly flipped through the pages.

There were plenty of spells that sounded unpleasant: flogging, flaying, ripping, and burning spells. But were these meant to be deadly? Or was I only going to irritate the monsters, encouraging them to attack?

Unfortunately for me, I didn't have time to give it any more thought. Callum slapped his hand loudly against the wall of the mausoleum, nearly making me jump out of my skin and instantly drawing the attention of every wraith present. A dozen pairs of glowing silver eyes turned toward me, shrieks echoing in the air as they realized an intruder was in their midst.

"You're such an asshole!" I snapped. A wall of billowing flame manifested before me as I flung my arms up in panic, so massive and so hot I flinched away from it, causing the barrier to dissipate instantaneously.

My concentration was already shattered as I sprinted out of the way of the encroaching wraiths, only to find myself surrounded. Using one of the copper columns as a shield between myself and them, I tried to read one of the spells in the grimoire as rapidly as I could.

"*Convertat ossa . . . ossa sua ad . . . ad pulvis!*"

Why the hell did nothing happen?!

"What a unique spell to choose," Callum said. He was leaning against the door frame, watching with rapt attention as I fled around the interior with the wraiths at my heels. "Turning one's bones to dust would indeed be an unpleasant way to die. If one had bones in the first place."

"I don't need your sarcasm!" I yelped, stumbling and nearly falling flat on my back as two wraiths flew forward, their ragged robes billowing around them as they slashed their blades toward me. Still with no time to think, I defensively put up my arms and a thrum of power pulsed around me. The wraiths were pushed back, but only barely.

This wasn't working. My focus wasn't strong enough for any of the spells I attempted, and I couldn't read while being pursued.

Callum was now examining his claws, staring at them with extreme focus. "You're going to exhaust yourself running in circles."

"Shut. Up!"

I flung two useless balls of flame toward the pursuing monsters, but the fire dissipated into harmless smoke. A deadly blade swung down, coming within inches of my face—

Only to be stopped by Callum's hand.

He stood over me, arm outstretched, gripping the sword as if it was made of wood.

"When fighting with magic, it's imperative you understand your enemies," he said. His fingers tightened, veins blackening in his arms. "Wraiths are barely corporeal. Their forms are extremely fragile; therefore, using the element of air would be wisest."

He forced the wraith back, then seized another. His claws tore through their bodies easily, rending them into pieces of ragged fabric that screamed as they disappeared.

"Or I could get myself some claws," I said. Sarcasm wasn't the right choice.

One of the wraiths slipped around him and came at me. With a terrified shriek, I swiftly threw everything I could think of at it: bursts of air, poofs of fire, even a strange ball of freezing cold water that I wasn't entirely sure how I manifested. The grimoire slipped out of my grasp, and I scrambled for it, seizing it from the floor right as the wraith descended toward me and I realized I'd made a grievous error.

Callum had the same realization. He crossed the room in a split second, gripping the wraith by the back of its cloak and ripping it away from me. Lifting it into the air with one hand, he slammed it continually against the stone floor.

In just a few seconds, he'd destroyed every wraith. They weren't even a threat to him.

But with our enemies dispatched, the demon's dark attention turned on me.

"What a tragedy," he said. His face was cast in shadow, but I could feel his eyes on me. "The bold but ill-prepared witch fell victim to her enemies. Shocking."

"You told me to go after them!" Drenched with embarrassment, I huffed as I shoved the grimoire back into my bag.

"Hubris can be even more deadly than fear," he said, circling me slowly. His claws clicked on the floor with every step; an ominous sound within that enclosed, echoing space. "I told you to dispatch them; I did not tell you how. You could have asked. You chose not to."

"Well, I didn't know I was supposed to!" I was all bluster now, snapping back at him for no reason other than to have the last word. Turning for the door, I only made it a few steps before something snapped around my wrist and yanked me back.

A black rope wound around my wrist, holding me tight. The other end was in Callum's hand, and he coiled it around his palm, dragging me closer.

"Where do you think you're going, witch?" he said. "Your lesson isn't over."

He coiled the rope again, forcing me to take a few more stumbling steps toward him. Any attempts to yank my arm back were useless; neither he nor the rope were budging.

"Allowing yourself to be so panicked and distracted before going into battle is not only foolish, it's lethal," he said, dragging me even closer. "You are a clever woman with a powerful mind. You're above such rash decisions."

His scolding was having an effect I didn't expect. It was arousing.

Had I hit my head the night he rescued me from the forest? I'd always been the definition of a Goody Two-shoes, desperate to follow the rules, eager to repent at the slightest suggestion I'd done something wrong. But that stern tone of disapproval in his voice was setting off fireworks in my head.

"Let go," I said. Bracing my legs, I thought I could resist being pulled any closer. I was wrong.

He wound the rope around his hand yet again. He tweaked up an eyebrow in challenge as I stumbled forward, swearing at him all the while.

"Let yourself go," he said.

Grasping the rope, eyes narrowed at him in fury, I closed my eyes to concentrate. But it didn't help; it just filled my mind with visions of Callum's sardonic smile, fantasies of him scolding me before coming up with some diabolical way to punish me.

Spanking me, perhaps.

My eyes flew open when I was able to imagine such a scenario a bit too vividly.

"Lost in your thoughts?" Callum teased. "You're far too easy to distract. It gives your enemies more than enough time to take advantage of you."

This time, he tugged the rope quickly, forcing me all the way until I had to catch myself against his chest. He grasped my face as I struggled against him.

"Mercy?" he asked softly.

"No." I wasn't prepared when his claws tightened on my jaw and forced me to stand still.

"Pride has no place in your training." His voice was sharp, drenched in authority. "If one of my warriors continually allowed pride to stand in the way of their learning, I would ensure they had no pride left to lean on." His hand tightened, forcing me up onto my tiptoes as I grasped his forearm. "Perhaps I should do the same to you."

Delicious fear somersaulted in my belly. All those erotic books I'd used for years to fuel my fantasies were throwing me into overdrive now that I had a real-life fantasy unfolding before me. But my nervous, awkward mind was determined to screw me over even more, and the urge to laugh bubbled up in my throat.

My brain had decided to malfunction and *laughter* was the only response I could manage.

Callum's eyes widened at the sound of my sudden, nervous giggle, then narrowed when I slapped my hand over my mouth in shock.

"Does that idea entertain you? If you're craving discipline, I'm more than happy to oblige."

More ropes appeared, slithering over the ground and coiling up my limbs. In a matter of seconds, I was overtaken and suspended in the air. The ropes behaved as if they had a mind of their own, but I knew it was all Callum's doing. He directed them subtly, with little movements of his fingers or with merely a look. They slid under my clothes in an invasive exploration that made me glare at him venomously.

With my limbs helplessly spread, I could only watch as he slid his nail down my blouse, cutting the buttons loose one at a time.

As a member of the itty-bitty titty committee, I rarely wore a bra unless I really had to. So, when he pushed the fabric apart, he paused for several long moments to appraise me.

"Beautiful . . ." He murmured the word like a prayer, hands squeezing my breasts before pinching my nipples between his fingers.

The ropes tightened as he sliced off the rest of my clothes. Pulled backward, I was bound to one of the T-shaped copper columns. My arms were spread, wrists bound to the horizontal beam above. The rope braided itself around my chest, hips, and legs with expert precision, supporting my weight without pinching.

"What a pretty picture you make. A virgin on a cross." He surveyed me like an art critic, eyes narrowed, claws thoughtfully stroking his face. "Is it prophetic? Or perhaps symbolic? Will you cry for God?"

"Never. And I'm not a virgin anymore. You made sure of that."

"You're close enough." His fingers traced the contours of my body; taking his time, exploring me, pausing when he noticed a physical reaction from me. "You still blush like one. Just look at those lovely, pink cheeks."

He brought his mouth dangerously close to mine. I thought he would kiss me. He didn't. Instead, he hovered there, a grin on his face as he pressed his thigh between my legs, forcing them apart. The ropes tightened again, squeezing against my clitoris until I saw stars. Tensing my muscles, I attempted to lift myself, to somehow ease the tension of the rope, but it didn't work.

"Are you whining at me?" He slipped two fingers beneath the rope and tugged it repeatedly, making a horrendously embarrassing cry burst out of me. "I'm sorry, but if you don't learn now, I'm afraid you won't be nearly so lucky next time. So, what have we learned, Everly?"

"That you're a dick," I gasped, and he shook his head.

"Wrong answer."

The ropes between my legs loosened, but they didn't disappear. They coiled down my legs, repositioning them so my ankles were bound behind the column. This forced my legs to remain spread apart, my muscles quickly feeling the strain of my position. As I hung there, huffing and puffing, Callum held up two fingers so I could see his claws disappear.

"Where do you think I'm going to put these?" he said, twiddling his fingers in my face. "I'd bet you want them in your pussy, don't you? Making you drip all over my hand."

With no other options available besides uttering my safeword—which I had no desire to do—I nodded my head, hoping my cooperation would inspire him to pleasure me instead of punish me.

This was a wicked game I was bound to lose, but I wanted to play anyway.

"Please . . ." My voice was soft and desperate, but instead of looking at me with pity, Callum only grew more excited.

"I'm afraid begging won't help you now." His tongue slid over his lips, as if I were a piece of meat hanging before him.

His fingers dipped into my arousal as he stroked the digits over me. Whimpers burst out of me as he teased my pleasure to a frenzied height.

He withdrew his touch at the last possible moment, when I was certain I was going to fall apart in orgasmic bliss. Crying out in despair, I struggled against the ropes until they dug into my skin, and I had to stop, panting to catch my breath.

"What have you learned?" He repeated his question, painfully calm and condescendingly patient.

The fact that I was supposed to *learn* something from this had completely left my mind. All I could think about were the sensations assaulting me—the weight of my body against the ropes, the refreshing ache of air filling my lungs, the pulsating heat between my legs.

"I learned I'm not very good at magic."

Callum went very, *very* still.

"Would you care to repeat that?" His low voice told me I shouldn't have said it at all.

"I learned, uhm . . . I learned that . . ." I couldn't

think of the right words when he had my body so torn between pain and pleasure.

But that was the point, wasn't it? When the God assaulted my mind, It inflicted confusion. Terror, pain, bliss—It used those feelings like a weapon.

"I can't get distracted," I blurted, grasping at my sudden realization. "I learned I can't let myself be distracted, and I need to— Ahh—"

His fingers were between my legs again, but it wasn't my pussy he was teasing. He reached further back, probing my puckered hole. I whimpered as he pressed one finger into that tight ring of muscle.

"It's not discipline if you don't suffer," he mocked. His fingers were slick with my arousal, and the intrusion felt strange at first. But as he worked his finger in and out of me, I lost the ability to speak. He forced lewd sounds out of me that I hadn't been aware I was capable of making.

"I will not allow you to use your mistake to disrespect yourself," he said. "You lack skill in magic because you've never practiced. You do not lack potential nor power; don't think for a single second that you do."

"Y-yes, you're right. I'm . . . fuck—" My voice broke as he eased a second finger inside my ass. It was tight enough to be uncomfortable, but slick enough not to hurt. My brain was going to short-circuit.

"Your control over magic will improve with time." He was as calm and composed as if we were merely taking a stroll through the garden. "Your lack of experience is by no means the lesson I want you to take away from this. *Listen* to me." He gripped my face, moving his fingers inside me as he forced me to hold his gaze. "What did you *learn*, Everly?"

He withdrew his fingers, and I groaned as he spat on them, lubricating them before entering me again.

"I learned . . . I can't . . . I—"

"Deep breath, darling." His voice was rough, merciless. "Take a slow breath and calm yourself down. I know it's hard to take." He pressed his body closer, gyrating his hips against me so I could feel the hard length of him. The stretch of his fingers in my ass was *almost* too overwhelming to be pleasurable—the result was a brutal ascent toward orgasm, edging closer with every thrust of his fingers.

"I need to learn about my enemies," I babbled, spilling the words out as quickly as I could before the thoughts fluttered away again. "I need to be patient and not rush . . . Shit—" The way he was pressing his hips against me applied pressure to my clit, and my vision grew hazy.

"That's it, you've got it. Good girl. You'll remember that for next time, won't you? No more rushing your enemies, no more running into fights without a damn clue what you're doing. You're too precious for that, understand?"

"Y-yes, yes, I understand—"

"You're going to slow down and think. You're going to be confident in the magic you carry. You're going to use that clever brain of yours, and when you've mastered it, I promise there's nothing in the world that can stop you."

I was falling apart for him, and he didn't stop, didn't let up even the slightest bit as he pushed me over the edge.

As I came down from bliss, shaking and whimpering, Callum held my face and said, "Snap your fingers for me. Show me you can." I obeyed, snapping my fingers repeatedly until he told me to stop.

"I'm going to silence you now, because you're going to come for me again, and while you do, I want you to think only of searing that lesson into your brain. No whimpering, no whining, no begging. Understand?" When I nodded eagerly, still drifting on that pleasure high, he added, "If you need me to stop, snap your fingers."

My mouth snapped shut. My jaw muscles were drawn tight, my teeth clenched together, my sounds held captive behind my sealed lips. It was psychic magic; the demon was nudging my brain to make my body obey.

Callum sank to his knees, and with his two fingers probing my ass, he swirled his tongue over my clit. A cry rose in my throat but didn't make it past my lips as he closed his mouth over me.

The mausoleum was shockingly quiet. Only the lewd sounds of Callum's tongue and fingers remained. My body shook, limbs trembling as the ropes held me tight and secure. All I could do was soundlessly scream his name as he brought me to orgasm again.

DUSK HAD FALLEN by the time my demon carried me back to the house. Clinging to his back, lying between his wings with every muscle limp and weak, I listened to him talk as I drifted in and out of sleep. He was telling me everything he knew about wraiths: their strengths, their weaknesses. Half the words, I was able to log away in my brain for later.

The other half drifted in one ear and out the other.

I enjoyed listening to him. The timbre of his voice was soothing, deep and rumbling. At first, I wasn't entirely sure what the warm, swollen feeling in my chest meant. It was comfortable; like how I felt on those rare nights when the rest of my family would leave me at home alone and I could simply listen to music, lying on the floor and staring at the ceiling for hours of contented bliss.

Was this feeling . . . safety? That was certainly part of it.

But it was more than that too. I was half-asleep as he carried me in the front doors, and his voice softened, but I was glad he didn't stop talking.

How many years had he spent talking only to himself, before he found someone who wanted to listen?

"You should eat something," he said. My tired eyes fluttered open for a moment, and I groaned, nuzzling my face against his neck. "What do you need from me, my lady?"

"Play," I said softly, and he chuckled.

"I hardly think you have the energy to play anymore," he said, but I shook my head.

"No, I want *you* to play," I said sleepily. "The piano."

I was shocked by the tenderness of his voice. "Of course. As you wish."

He laid me on the chaise longue in the piano room,

leaving the curtains open so I could look out at the night sky. The fire lit itself, and I snuggled into the blankets. Callum sat on the bench and traced his fingers over the keys, rocking his head from side to side as if imagining a melody.

When he played, it felt like a waking dream. The melody was unfamiliar, but I swayed to it as if I'd known it all my life.

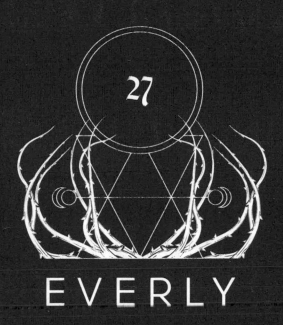

27

EVERLY

THE MASSIVE VAULT door appeared even more daunting today than the first time I'd seen it. Little puffs of steam and random sparks flew from the mechanism, as if the entire apparatus was aware the grimoire was near and was excited to be reunited.

Callum had gone into the forest to check on something Darragh had mentioned to him and had yet to return. The Woodsprie had been expanding a magical shield into the woodlands around the house to discourage the Eld from intruding too close. But something in the forest to the northwest kept breaking the barrier, so Callum had gone to investigate.

He wasn't happy about it either. He'd grumbled all morning, arguing with Grams about whether or not the vault should be opened while he wasn't in the house.

"It's nothing but a load of books and papers in

there," Grams insisted. "Certainly nothing to fear. Your precious witch won't come to any harm if she's out of your sight for a few hours."

He still wasn't convinced by the time he left. I wasn't sure if I was flattered he was so concerned, or ashamed he felt I couldn't defend myself without him.

He wasn't wrong, either. My time spent in the mausoleum yesterday had certainly increased my confidence to *use* magic, but I was far from skilled. I didn't yet have the technique to use it confidently.

But as Grams said, I didn't expect to find anything in a library that was particularly threatening. At worst, maybe there was another wraith hiding in there. As a precaution, she taught me a spell to conjure ripping winds, strong enough to tear a wraith to pieces. We practiced in the foyer before heading to the library, and Grams wasn't satisfied until I could manifest the spell without even uttering the words.

It wasn't easy, and my technique was sloppy. The magic I conjured was too strong, swiftly spiraling out of my control. The wind I summoned would often become a firestorm, swirling with hot licking flames that singed my hands.

"We have leather gloves somewhere in this house," Grams said as I winced at another blister on my palm. "Your great Aunt Cynthia was a skilled fire witch. Her things will likely fit you."

"If I had better control, this wouldn't happen," I grumbled, applying ointment to my palms from a jar in the kitchen.

But Grams scoffed. "Fire is the most dangerous and difficult element to conjure. Even incredibly experienced witches still wear protective clothing to use it. Regardless of age and skill, mistakes will happen. Such is life."

By the time I was standing in front of the vault, I was confident I could summon the spell if I needed it. With the grimoire clutched tightly in one hand and Grandma's radio tucked under my arm, I stood before the massive sealed doors and took a deep, steadying breath.

Hopefully, beyond these doors lay the secret to destroying the God. We didn't have the luxury of time to truly hone my skills; we needed a trump card, something to give me an advantage despite my limited experience.

Sybil had believed whatever was within this vault was worth protecting, even if it meant locking it away from her comrades. The thought filled me with anxious hope as I laid the palm of my hand against the door, and there was an audible click from within.

The gears turned faster, steam billowing out. Stepping back, my mouth hung open as the door trembled, then slid open, the massive metal vault splitting in two as it moved along invisible tracks set into the floor.

Darkness greeted me within. But as I stepped inside, two lanterns hanging on either side of the door flared to life, surrounding me in their flickering glow. I was standing on a metal platform, looking over the railing into the sea of black beyond. Metal stairs led down on my left, and I followed them as they curved along the stone wall. More lanterns lit as I passed them, slowly illuminating the room.

The space was shaped like a cylinder, with shelves set into the stone walls. Books were squeezed into every available space, along with piles of papers and hand-drawn maps. Dust motes drifted through the lantern light, and when my foot left the final step, a great chandelier overhead came to life. Two crescent-shaped desks were in the center of the room, facing each other like a ring split in half.

"It's like someone was only just here," I said, looking over the notes and open books on the desktop. A feather quill lay discarded upon a large sheet of yellowed paper, a sentence of Latin text left half-finished. I summoned a little flame in my palm, using it to illuminate the fading text.

"It has been demonstrated that aether causes significant damage to . . . to the . . ." I frowned, unfamiliar with the term scrawled before me. "Hellkite . . ."

"It is an old word for the creatures we now call Gods," Grams said, her voice echoing in the strangely quiet space. "It was long believed the Gods originally came from Hell itself, like Reapers. Now it is known They came from somewhere else entirely. Another dimension, most likely."

"But how?" There was a peculiar smell in here; beneath the soft odor of dust and old pages, there was a scent that cloyed in my throat, faint but unpleasant. Like old fish and stagnant water. "How is it possible for creatures to pass between dimensions?"

"Unfortunately, I don't know." My grandmother sighed, and I set the radio on the desk. "Perhaps we will find the answer here."

A wide hallway with a low stone ceiling led out of the room, but I couldn't see into the darkness within. Summoning another flame, I tried to send it floating down the hallway to illuminate my way, but it kept guttering out when it went more than a few feet in front of me.

"Damn it!" I hissed, accidentally burning my fingers. Putting them in my mouth, I said, "Do you know what's down there?"

Grams replied, "Another study room, I believe."

Lanterns came to life on the walls as I stepped down the hallway. Perhaps it was only my imagination, but their light didn't cast as far as the ones in the first room did. The smell of stagnant water grew stronger.

Halfway down the hall, I paused. There was a room ahead of me, but I could see nothing within, darkness shrouding everything.

But I could *hear* something: a strange, rasping rumble. My footsteps sounded different too, and I realized it was because there was water on the floor. My boots splashed through a shallow puddle as I entered the larger room.

Lanterns flared to life, illuminating a strange structure in the center of the room. It was round, built of stone, about three feet tall. A bronze lid was affixed to the top with a single thick hinge. It was ajar, revealing the deep inky blackness of a narrow shaft leading straight down. Thick metal rungs led into the dark, and I shuddered as I peered down.

"What the hell is this?" I whispered.

Seizing one of the lanterns from the wall, I held it over the shaft. But its light didn't reach the bottom. If there was anywhere in this vault to hide something top secret, it would be down there.

Tying the lantern to my belt, I shouted, "Grams! There's a lower level back here! I'm going to check it out!" The radio crackled faintly, and a cool breeze rushed around me as I pulled back the bronze lid, opening it fully. The metal rungs were slippery as I made my way down, covered in a greenish-brown substance that looked like algae.

The air turned damper and cooler the further I went. After climbing about twenty feet, I reached the bottom, and my boots were on solid ground once more. Holding up the lantern and encouraging its flame to brighten with a bit of magic, I peered into the gloom.

It was a cavern. A narrow tunnel in the far wall led deeper into the Earth, but I ignored that for now. Three simple wooden tables, stained and darkened with age, stood before a chalkboard covered with minuscule writing. Beakers, corked vials, and all manner of strange glass laboratory equipment covered the tables, with ancient pages of fading text scattered everywhere.

Stepping closer, I raised my light to examine the specimens floating in murky glass jars. Some of them looked like nothing more than mutated lumps of flesh, bulbous and discolored, covered in tiny bumps that looked like . . . *eyeballs*.

Another jar held the familiar skull of an Eld beast, its

thick fur and jagged teeth still intact. Others held strips of seaweed covered in neon green pustules and similarly afflicted fish. Making my way to the end of the last table, I came to a glass terrarium, sealed with a cork covered in red wax, filled with a cluster of pale mushrooms. A tangle of white threads extended around the inside of the glass like a web, and the threads were growing thickly near the base of the cork.

As if looking for a way out.

I had to narrow my eyes and step close to read the writing at all. Not all of it was in Latin; some of it was written in the strange runic script I'd first seen in the greenhouse. There were lists of herbs and minerals, with some crossed out and some circled. My eyes moved rapidly over the words, my excitement growing despite struggling to translate the messy writing.

. . . *break the flesh barrier* . . . *infuse* . . . *poisonous to the Hellkite life force* . . .

Sybil had been looking for a way to *poison* the God. And somewhere down here, amid all her research, I was certain she'd found it.

Sprinting for the ladder, I nearly slipped several times in my enthusiasm to reach the surface. As I scrambled out of the shaft, I called, "Grams! You're not going to believe this! I found—"

Thump.

The sound came from behind me, from somewhere deeper within the room. I envisioned a wet piece of meat slapping against the stone floor when I heard it.

Then came the *scraping*. A slow, wet rasping. As if

something drenched and heavy were being dragged across the ground.

Turning, I peered between the tall shelves, searching the shadows. A cold feeling of dread prickled over my skull, and I was immediately certain I needed to get out of the vault.

But it was too late.

From between the shelves emerged a creature, the likes of which I'd never seen. It was big—easily ten feet long, and as tall as I was. It had a long, seal-like body and wriggled itself across the ground like a snake. It used clawed front limbs to drag itself forward, its pale pink flesh covered in slime that streaked across the stones. Its bulbous head was crowned with a cluster of eyeballs that looked like peeled grapes. Its mouth was agape, unable to fully close because of the massive needle-like teeth that jutted from its upper and lower jaws.

It was between me and the hallway. Its head bobbed about, making warbling vocalizations that turned my stomach. Backing away, one slow step at a time, I realized the creature seemed to be blind. None of its gray eyeballs focused on me . . .

At least, not until my foot caught on the edge of a table, jostling it and sending several books falling to the floor.

Then the creature lunged.

It moved far faster than I ever would have anticipated. It lashed out, one of its front limbs knocking painfully against my ribs and sending me sprawling to the floor. It kept coming, its jaw gaping open wide enough to swallow me whole. I seized everything I could get my hands on to throw at it: books, empty ink bottles, discarded candles. It whipped its thick body around, using its tail end like a cudgel to slam me against the wall.

Distantly, I could hear my grandmother calling to me from the radio, the static sharp as it drowned her words. My back was to the wall and there was no direction I could run. I lifted my hands in panic, sparks flying from my fingertips as pathetic poofs of flame billowed away from me.

Its jaws were descending, and there was no escape.

I needed a weapon. I needed fangs, as massive as this beast's own teeth.

I wasn't going to die in my own fucking house.

For a moment, it felt as if my head were splitting in two. My lower jaw was trying to rip itself off my body. I was screaming, and my vision flashed crimson.

In the blur of red, I lunged forward, acting on instinct alone. I snapped my aching jaws, again and again, drenching myself in thick, wet redness. I was aware of a horrible shrieking, and a smell that was as pungent as molten metal. Warmth filled my mouth and drenched down my front. I tasted rot and something sweet. Stretchy sinew ripped between my teeth—

And suddenly, arms were around me. A strength that I couldn't overcome held me down as I thrashed, jaws still snapping pointlessly as the reddened world faded. My gasping breaths turned to sobs of confusion. The fury and terror that demanded I keep struggling receded, leaving me as weak and limp as a baby bird.

I recognized the stone-like arms clinging to me. I knew Callum's voice as he spoke frantically in my ear, saying, "Calm down, Everly, calm down, it's alright. It's dead, you've killed it. You're all right."

CALLUM

"IT WAS ONE of the Eld," Winona declared. "Formed out of the corrupted carcasses of deep-sea fish, to judge by the looks of it. Nasty business. But truly a remarkable way to discover you can shift, my dear. Our magic provides, even when we least expect it."

Winona was handling the situation with remarkable calm, and frankly, it infuriated me. My vision was still tunneled, blurred at the edges. Everly kept trying to get up from her seat and pace, and I wanted to tie her down so I could finish tending to the open gash on her upper arm.

The cut on her cheek. The bruising across her back. The split lip. All the little injuries taunted me, showing me in no uncertain terms how close my witch had come to dying.

Again.

Blood drenched the front of her shirt and stained her mouth. Blood from the beast she'd slaughtered, ripping it apart after she magically transformed her own jaw into that of her enemy.

She was still shaking, even as she nibbled at a frosted lemon cake and sipped a hot cup of tea. She kept fidgeting as I cleaned the wound on her arm, continually reaching up to rub her jaw, occasionally reaching into her mouth to run her finger over her teeth.

I'd heard legends of witches who could physically change their own bodies, morphing their physical forms like demons could. It was incredibly rare. I'd never seen it myself.

Until today.

Her wonder and curiosity had turned to terror, and I'd felt it. Even miles away, in the northern reaches of the forest—I'd felt her. That sudden shift in her emotions had immediately brought me back.

Flying into the vault and finding her there crouched over the beast, drenched in blood with a mouthful of fangs, had stunned me. If it weren't for that, she would be dead. I would have been too late. My oath to protect her would have been broken, and although her soul would live on, how could I forgive myself?

"I can't keep depending on my magic to simply provide," she said, her voice shaking as I secured a bandage around her arm. She would heal quickly, thanks to the enchanted medical supplies. "I need to be able to use it when I need it, not simply hope for a miracle when I'm desperate."

"You will," I said. "It will take time and patience."

"The first of which we have in short supply," she said. Glancing toward the radio as I dabbed at the blood around her mouth, she said, "Where does that tunnel in the vault lead?"

"I'm not entirely sure," Winona said thoughtfully. "That place has been sealed for so long, I'm not sure anyone in the house really knew what was inside. But if I had to guess, judging by Sybil's fascination with studying the God, it may be an entrance to the mines."

"That would explain why such a powerful Eld creature was able to get in," I said. "A beast like that needs a great deal of corrupt magic to form."

"Does the tunnel give the God access to the house?" Everly said.

Winona was silent for a moment. "It's unlikely. The protective spells around this place extend into the ground as well as the air. The God would have to stretch Its energy excessively to enter. Without being able to easily move Its physical form, the God would struggle to penetrate the barrier with psychic energy alone."

Everly's eyes were vacant with shock. Her heart was still pounding. How could I have been so foolish to leave her alone? I'd known there was risk, and yet, I'd left her anyway.

I hated myself for it.

"I don't understand how it happened," she said. "I just remember thinking . . . if only I had teeth like that, I could defend myself."

"You shouldn't have had to defend yourself." I pulled

her hand away from her mouth so I could clean the scrapes on her knuckles. "I was wrong to leave and let you go in alone. I should have been there."

"You couldn't have known."

"I should have." The words came out with a snarl, and she stared at me, making me bristle under her gaze. "I failed you. It's not acceptable. I failed the oath I made to you."

It was a sickening feeling, truly. The thought that she'd been so close to death, from such a ridiculous thing. To die in the safety of her own house, left alone by the one being who should have been protecting her above all else.

"You should punish me for it. You never should have been left alone."

She shook her head, her face softening. But I didn't want her to be soft. I didn't need gentle reassurances.

I needed the reminder that consequences came without mercy. I'd dared to allow myself to grow lax and that simply wasn't acceptable.

"Oh, stop pouting, Callum," Winona said. "It is a dangerous world we live in, and Everly defended herself well. Remarkable, truly remarkable . . ." She went on muttering to herself.

My energy was so heightened. I could barely sit still, and I couldn't force my mind to calm. I needed to be alone with my witch. I needed her voice, her touch.

"It's not your fault, Callum." Everly grasped my arm, and I froze. She noticed my stiffness and softened even further, gentling her voice like I was a wild animal that might flee from her at any second. "It's okay."

Those words were like torture.

I couldn't have known. Nothing I could have done. I gave all I could.

Bullshit. Fate had ripped everything from me and yet somehow that wasn't enough for me to learn my lesson?

"If that tunnel leads down to the mine, we would benefit from having a map before attempting further exploration," Winona said, oblivious to my suffering. "Those flooded passages are like a maze."

"We could check the university library," Everly said. "They probably have the original building plans for the mine somewhere in storage."

She still had her hand on me, keeping me close. It both comforted me and intensified my guilt. Her affection, which I longed for above all else, wasn't something I deserved.

"I need to get down into the laboratory again, as soon as possible. Sybil found something, I'm sure of it. A way to poison the God. But . . ." She paused, chewing her thumbnail. "Many of her notes are written in a language I don't understand, one I've never seen outside this house."

"Sybil was known to frequently write in code, particularly toward the end of her life as she grew more paranoid," Winona said. "But if we can decipher her writing . . ."

"Then we may find a way to get the upper hand," Everly finished for her. The determination on her face would have made me proud, if I weren't so wrapped up in my own guilt.

But I could see that field again. I could smell the dirt drenched in blood, the smoke, the stench of rot. The screams of the dying.

Everly was watching me. Although I couldn't meet her eyes, I hoped she would understand my shame. My regret. How desperately I needed an outlet for this simmering anger before it boiled over.

"Grams, could we have some time alone, please? I need to talk to Callum."

Finally, at last, I'd get what I deserved. Everly didn't know enough spells to hurt me, but I could guide her, I could tell her how.

The room was warmer now that the ghost had left. Everly had stopped shaking, and the focus had returned to her eyes. But with that focus came concern and worry.

"Callum. Look at me."

She was bloodstained. Battered. Bruised. Staring at the cut on her lip, I stood with my hands behind my back and didn't say a word.

"You're angry," she said.

I needed to get those clothes off her, dress her in something clean so death couldn't touch her.

"At myself, yes," I said. "I knew better than to leave you."

"You were doing your duty to protect this house."

"I knew—"

"*Stop* arguing." The authority in her voice rattled me. She folded her arms, drawing herself up to her full height. "Am I not your mistress?"

My fingers snapped, anxious energy seeking an outlet. "Yes. Yes, my lady, you are."

"These games we play are only acceptable if we are not using them to harm ourselves, or to cause true harm to each other," she said. "You feel guilty. You feel responsible. You want that guilt to disappear and the only way you can think of is with pain."

"You couldn't truly harm me. It's merely a—"

"*Yes*, I could," she said fiercely. "And you know it. I will not allow you to use me to hurt yourself. That's not what I want."

She crossed the room, taking a seat in the high-backed chair beside the fire, facing me. She'd removed her muddy boots, but the tight corset of her white shirt was streaked with crimson. She raised her chin and crossed her legs.

Every inch of her embodied the mistress of this house as she said, "You're demanding what *you* want. Not much of a punishment if you want it, is it?"

I didn't have an answer for her. A distressing cocktail of emotions swirled in my chest. Protests and arguments tried to claw out of my throat.

"If you want to make it up to me for your absence—which I do *not* blame you for—then you'll do as I say."

Growling in frustration, I clenched my fists. "Everly, you don't understand. When a warrior fails—"

"A warrior listens to their commander." She did not raise her voice; she lowered it. That was far more intimidating.

When had I last encountered a being that could truly shake me to my core, who could make me question everything? I wanted to be strong, and yet, with her blue eyes fixed upon me, I wanted to give in. To be weak, for just a moment.

The tempest inside me was merciless. *Defy. Obey. Flee.*

Instead, I stood there, waiting. Watching her and her alone.

"Whatever your wish, my lady, I will obey."

She clicked her tongue, shaking her head. My mind was in chaos, scrambling for answers, for something to satisfy both her and my own stubbornness.

"Don't withdraw from me." She sounded sad, like she pitied me. Damn it, I didn't want her sympathy, but this wasn't about what *I* wanted. "Listen to what I'm telling you and try to understand why. Otherwise, we're not communicating."

She was right. My mind was at war with itself but I could still see the wisdom in her words.

My nails dug into my palms, the pain keeping me grounded. "I'm listening, my lady. I'm angry. I feel wretched and fucking useless. Like I've failed you in the same way I failed so many others." It was like pulling out the words with fishhooks as I said, "I want to obey you. I want you to bring me back to myself, regardless of how you choose to do that."

It terrified me to be vulnerable, to be weak—even with her. But only she could guide me back to a state of calm.

"I'm with you, Callum," she said. "I'm not leaving you. You're not alone."

I almost begged her to stop. Stop the reassurances, the kindness. Stop before it stripped me raw. Instead, I bowed my head, accepting her words like a whip's lashes.

Her fingers curled around her chin, pushing her lips into a delightful pout that made me long to kiss her.

"Undress," she said.

There wasn't much clothing to remove, as I hated wearing restrictive garments in the first place. With my trousers tossed aside, I stood naked before her, clasping my hands behind my back yet again.

Her gaze fixated on my cock. Arousal swirled through her like a sudden storm, and she squeezed her crossed legs together.

"Are you *always* hard?"

"It would take a concentrated effort not to be," I said. "Particularly in your presence."

I longed to rip that filthy clothing off of her, to kiss every bruise on her, to make her forget her fear in my arms. But to obey her was to suffer, and that was what I deserved.

She lifted her hand, pointing to the shining wood floor in front of her seat. "Kneel and restrain yourself."

On my knees before her, I paused. "How would you prefer I be restrained?"

She smiled, and my cock pulsed at the sight. "With rope, of course. Bind yourself. Hands behind your back, and keep your legs spread."

I manifested my ropes and coiled them around my body. My arms were bound behind my back, connected to a rope that looped around my neck. If I squirmed my arms too much, it would cut off my air, effectively forcing me to stay still. With intricate knots, I bound my thighs to my calves, preventing myself from being able to rise from my knees.

My head remained bowed, awaiting the first hint of pain, eager for agony to chase my guilt away. But it didn't come. Instead, Everly rose from her chair and crouched in front of me. Her delicate fingers tucked beneath my chin, and I winced as she lifted my head.

"You can't watch me every second of every day, Callum. I need to be able to do things on my own, too."

Shaking my head, I insisted, "I can certainly try. You're too precious to risk."

"Every day is a risk," she said. "To *live* is to risk dying, always. You have my soul. My afterlife is already yours."

"Not if the God takes you from me."

Her eyes were soft, yet so radiant. They drew me in, even when I wanted to look away in shame.

She closed her fingers around my cock. There was still uncertainty in her movements, clumsiness from lack of experience, but that only made me love her touch more. The thick veins in my shaft throbbed against her hand.

"This isn't punishment for failing to protect me." She leaned forward, and I groaned aloud as she spat on my cock, spreading it over me with her hand. "This is punishment for trying to hurt yourself."

She kept stroking me, slow and steady, building the pleasure but taking her sweet time to do it. She gave me a condescending smile as I bent forward, choked sounds forced out of my throat by the rope as it tightened.

"Sit up straight," she said. "I like to see good posture."

"Fuck, Everly, you don't understand what you do to me—"

"I didn't tell you to speak."

She kept stroking, slowing her pace every time my shoulders desperately hunched forward. When I dared to thrust my hips into her hand, demanding more in a moment of weakness, she slapped the palm of her hand against my cock.

The sting made me groan, precum leaking from me. My breath shuddered as she grasped me again, moving so painfully slowly. Pleading words tried to escape me. They manifested as furious whimpers that made her giggle.

"Don't you like it?" she teased. She lightly stroked the very tip of my cock, making me twitch. "Do you want more?"

I nodded rapidly. But her smile was too wicked to be reassuring.

She leaned close enough that I felt the warmth of her breath. She withdrew her hand from me, slick with her saliva and my own precum, and reached around to stroke the lubrication over my hole.

"Fuck yourself," she said. "Squeeze two fingers inside your ass and make yourself moan for me."

As I obeyed, the movement of my arms tightened the rope around my neck. My muscles were taut, and the penetration burned, but I savored the pain. My fingers squeezed past the knuckles and a strangled sound choked out of me.

Everly was watching me with wide eyes. Her breathing quickened as I groaned, and she cupped my face in her hands.

"Such a good boy," she murmured.

I shook my head, nearly rabid with desire, pain, and longing. "Not good. Fucking failed you."

She spoke so tenderly, so goddamn *gently*. "You're doing so well for me, Callum. Obeying me even though it hurts. Mm, I like that expression on your face. Like it's too much . . . and not enough."

I leaned into her hand, shuddering as I pumped my fingers. She stood up, and another throttled sound escaped me as she stood there holding my head. Encouraging me. Praising me.

"That's it. Push them a little deeper. Now all the way out . . . and push them in again. So good."

My cock was leaking on the floor, and every thrust of my fingers made it worse. I was aching to be touched. But she stepped back and sat in the chair again; a victorious queen on her throne, drenched in blood. She spread her legs, resting the crook of her knee up on the arm of the chair as she pulled up her skirt.

She tugged her panties to the side. Fuck, she looked delicious. Pink and glistening with arousal, soft blonde curls covering her. The keening sound I made was humiliating, ravenous with desire. The whimper of a dog who's been denied food.

She curled her finger at me. "Crawl to me, demon."

Every movement tugged the rope around my throat, keeping it tight. I knelt at her feet, and she guided my head closer, bringing it to rest against her thigh.

"Keep fucking yourself."

I was going to lose my goddamn mind. The blood staining her clothes, the sweat on her skin, the sweetness of her arousal—I could smell it all. It made me tingle as if I'd inhaled a drug, my veins running so hot that my vision grew blurry.

Turning my head, I clamped my sharp teeth into her soft skin. She gasped, withing in the chair, hands clenching on the arm rests. But her gasp of pain dissolved into a moan of pleasure as I broke the skin.

The magic in her blood was so sweet. Like honey filling my mouth.

"Careful . . ." She gripped my hair, guiding my head closer to the apex of her legs. I closed my mouth over her like I was starving, straining against the rope around my neck. I lapped my tongue over her clit, savoring her, encouraged by every little groan and whimper she gave me.

She was panting, her hand fisted in my hair.

"Keep your fingers deep inside," she said, her voice faint with pleasure. "Don't stop until you make me come."

Her control calmed my mind. The beast inside me that wanted to rage and destroy needed a master who could soothe it, contain it, *tame it*. All the failures that weighed on me, all the memories I tried to forget, were buried instantly by one desire.

Obey her. Please her. Serve her.

She shuddered beneath my tongue, her eyes fluttering closed. She rolled her hips and I moaned against her, making her squirm in ecstasy.

When she came, her thighs squeezed around my head. Her muscles pulsed, and she trembled, gripping my hair so tight it ached.

My face was wet with her, and I licked the taste of her from my lips, my chin. She sat there for a moment in silence as she recovered, breathing slow and deep, a little smile on her face.

She straightened up slowly, tucking her wild hair back from her face. She lay her hand against my cheek for a moment, murmuring, "You're such a good boy. You use your tongue so well. Are you still fucking yourself for me?" I nodded, cock aching.

Then she said, "Retie your wrists in front of you."

I repositioned my arms. My cock jutted up between my fingers, my claws twitching with the need to touch myself.

"Pleasure yourself for me," she said. "But don't come until I give you permission."

I obeyed, grasping my cock in my bound hands and stroking. Rebellious thoughts of discarding these ropes and seizing her, throwing her onto the bed, and fucking her mercilessly made my hands begin to shake.

"Be good," she said, and I was weak for her, *again.*

Pricking my claws into my skin, I groaned at the sting, but it helped me remain in control. I'd had countless lovers, both dominant and submissive, beings who could play my body like an instrument; but Everly made me feel things I hadn't experienced in centuries.

She was too pure, too sincere in her intentions. Her face hid nothing; I saw her fascination, her desire, her pleasure. Her fingers tightened on the arms of the chair, and I wished they were still gripping me instead.

I was riding the edge of orgasm, mercilessly close to losing control, held back only by my determination to obey. My eyes were locked on her, waiting, pleading silently for her lips to move and her permission to come.

"Mistress . . . please."

She smiled, the expression so sudden and unbridled that I groaned, bowing my head as I kept stroking. My claws had dug in so many times that blood streaked my hand, but that only made me more feral. A beast consumed by ravenous need.

Finally, like a blessing from a goddess, she said, "Come for me, Callum."

My mind fractured; the growl that came out of me was purely animalistic. My seed spilled across the floor, pearlescent in the firelight. My body was in rapture, seized for a moment in perfect bliss as I curled forward, unable to keep myself upright. My forehead came to rest against her bare foot, dangling from the chair, and I kissed her warm skin as I said, "Thank you, Mistress."

"You're not done yet. Clean up the mess you made."

Every inch of this room smelled like her. The rug, the drapes, the furniture—and yes, even the floor itself as I lowered my head to obey her command. Still tightly bound, the ropes dug in as I moved, bent over my knees to lick my own cum from the floor. Her foot pressed lightly on the back of my head, and I stroked my tongue along the wood to get every last drop.

For a moment, my cheek lay at rest against the floor, her foot still pressing me down. Like a ship in the aftermath of an ocean's brutal storm, I drifted, quiet but tired, full of relief.

It had been decades since I'd last felt so calm; centuries, perhaps. I'd forgotten the sensation, how it melted through my body, soothing the writhing energy inside.

Her foot moved, and she softly called my name. Lifting my head, I allowed her arms to guide me closer so I could rest on her lap instead. Kneeling at her feet, my wings were limp at my sides, my face buried against her thighs as her fingers stroked through my hair.

"Did I please you?" It ached to hear myself sound so vulnerable.

"Yes, Callum." Her voice burrowed into my very being, surrounding my heart like cradling hands. "You did so well."

For the first time in nearly two thousand years, I felt an emotion I swore I'd never feel again. I tried to beat it down, tried to smother it with fear, but it was useless.

I'd learned long ago that love could not truly be killed.

29

EVERLY

AS EAGER AS I was to get back down to Sybil's laboratory and dig through her notes, Callum insisted I couldn't
until I was confident in my ability to protect myself. I
needed training; I had years of magical knowledge to absorb, and a very short time to do it.

Grams warned me the training would be exhaust-
ing—I still wasn't fully prepared.

The weather was clear, so I took the radio out into
the yard, to the rose garden behind the greenhouse. A
fountain trickled nearby, crowned with a statue of a
faun spouting water from its mouth. The roses were in
bloom, the fruit trees were blossoming, even the vegetables were growing. The season didn't matter to these
plants; magic sustained them, and they were tended to
by Darragh.

Callum accompanied us, remaining quiet throughout

my lessons but watching me carefully, occasionally giving his input to adjust my technique or change my stance.

"Keep your feet planted firmly on the ground," he said, as I attempted to shatter a row of crystal goblets set atop the garden wall. "As you release the spell, shift your weight forward as you exhale."

He made it sound so damn easy. At least I had leather gloves now; I'd found them locked in a chest in one of the other bedrooms, alongside a grimoire written by Aunt Cynthia, my grandfather's sister. I'd never known the woman existed, but her grimoire now sat on my bedside table, filled with her notes and experiences using fire magic.

"Let the heat build within your chest," my grandmother said, the radio turned up as loud as possible. "Focus it there as you breathe in, then release."

Widening my stance, I inhaled deeply. Heat gathered within me, throbbing in my chest like a ticking bomb. My hands twitched. My legs felt unsteady.

When I shifted my weight, I was off-balance. Bolts of fire shot over the wall and exploded in the sky, with a bang loud enough to hurt my ears.

"Again," Grandmother said. "Steady yourself."

Again and again, I tried and failed. Some of the explosions were massive and fiery; others were barely more than sparks. I burnt several rose bushes to a crisp. I singed the grass around my feet until it was blackened.

We were at it for hours, and my excitement dissolved into frustration.

Then fury.

What the hell was wrong with me? Why couldn't I control it? Why was it so goddamn hard?

"Your shoulders are too tense," Grandmother said. "You must relax them. Flow through the motions."

"I'm trying!" I snapped. My hands clenched into fists. Every breath was quick and shallow as anger filled me, and with it, came panic.

What if my father had been right? My magic was wild, and I wasn't strong enough to command it. I was just weak . . . stupid . . . ignorant . . .

Flinging my hands forward with a yell, scorching bolts of flame flew from me like arrows, and the goblets exploded into sparkling shards of glass. My heart was hammering, my breath coming in quick shallow bursts. Flames surrounded me, licking my face as if I was standing in the middle of a bonfire. The fire grew hotter and more vicious with every second, my chest so tight I could barely breathe.

Suddenly, cold water splashed into my face. I sputtered, my fire instantly doused, my hair and clothes now soaked. Callum stood beside the nearby fountain, shaking droplets from his hand.

"Perhaps it's time for a break," he said, folding his arms.

I wiped the water from my face, biting my lip. The tips of my hair were singed, and my clothes were dirtied with soot. The surprise of being splashed with water had at least halted my panic attack, but anxiety was still tight and roiling in my chest.

My grandmother chuckled. "You are indeed a fire

witch, with that temper. Anger is more productive than fear, but just as difficult to control. Your mind is your greatest weapon, Everly, but it can also be your greatest weakness."

"And what the hell am I supposed to do about that?" A wave of exhaustion made me squeeze my eyes shut. I wanted to sit down somewhere quiet, before more angry words burst out of me. Perhaps it would be better to dunk my whole head into the fountain and simply never come up.

Grams was only trying to teach me. I was the one failing.

She was silent for a moment, and my shame grew until I wanted to cry.

At last, she said, "Callum, would you show her the meditation room? Learning to guard her mind and calm her thoughts is imperative if we're going to make any progress."

CALLUM LED ME into an area of the house I hadn't explored before. The stone walls were covered with creeping vines; grass and flowers were growing through the ancient floor. The air was cool and smelled like dust. As if no one had been there for a long time.

We were both silent. My doubts were choking me. How could I possibly hope to fight against a being as powerful as the Deep One if I couldn't remain calm enough to practice? I was trapped in an endless cycle of anger and fear: fear of failure, then anger at my fear, then more fear of my own anger.

It was a whirlpool, sucking me down, drowning me. Too powerful to fight.

Ahead of us, down a short staircase, was a familiar sight: a doorway sealed with black rope that dissipated slowly as we approached. The doors swung open, the ancient hinges creaking, and we entered a large, open room. There were no windows, but elaborate tapestries and vines hung from the concave stone walls.

"Take off your shoes, and your jacket," Callum said.

The smooth stone floor was cool under my bare feet. Stepping onto a large, richly colored carpet, I curled my toes in its plush surface and sighed.

Overhead was a massive mechanical model of the solar system. The planets were formed of brass, with shining copper arms moving them slowly through their rotations. A backdrop of stunningly painted constellations covered the ceiling.

"This is the meditation room," Callum said as I stared in astonishment. "While you are free to meditate anywhere in the house, this place was built for exactly that. The spell work within these walls is meant to promote peace, calm, and focus. Every day, before you begin your lessons, come here first."

The effect was subtle, but I did feel calmer. My churning anxiety had faded, leaving me exhausted. My muscles ached, and my face stung as if I'd been sunburned.

"Why don't you look at me?"

Startled, I finally did look at him. "Sorry! I mean . . ." I grit my teeth, but I was unable to come up with anything more than another lame apology. "I'm sorry I lost my temper. I'm sorry I couldn't finish the lesson today. I couldn't do it."

He frowned, tipping his head curiously to the side. "You *did* do it. You broke the goblets. You summoned fire. As for your temper . . ." He chuckled as he folded his arms. "I like seeing you in a rage. It's sexy. The way your power fills the air is divine. But offer an apology to your grandmother. She'll understand your frustration. I'm sure every young witch went through something similar."

Tears welled, and I immediately looked away again. In a blink, Callum was at my side, cupping my face, tipping my head up. "Sshh, you're alright. Don't look away. Everly." I met his gaze, straining not to let a single tear fall. "Training will exhaust you. It will push you to your limits. There's no shame in the work you did today."

My throat was tight, but I said, "I wish I knew what it was like to know other witches. To train with them. Be surrounded by them. But I've always . . . always . . . been alone. Ugh!" I scrubbed my hands over my face in frustration. "I shouldn't feel sorry for myself. This is ridiculous. I have work to do, I need to study—"

"Not tonight." Callum gripped my arms, preventing me from storming away. "No more tonight. You're exhausted. You've given all you can. Stop." He placed a finger over my lips, silencing my protests. "Make yourself comfortable. You need to clear your head."

He stepped back, giving me space as I wandered to the center of the room and sat cross-legged on the round green carpet. Straightening my back, I closed my eyes and took slow, deep breaths.

This was the opposite of relaxing. I didn't have *time* for this. I thrived on keeping myself busy; it was the only way to keep anxiety at bay. If I wasn't studying, I was jogging. If I wasn't jogging, I was reading or painting.

I needed to be down in Sybil's laboratory. I needed to be out in the garden practicing, or in the library studying, or running up and down the stairs until my lungs burned and my brain was too tired to worry anymore.

"So much tension." Callum grasped my shoulders and squeezed. His breath was warm on my neck, his cheek brushing softly against my own. "Relax your body. Every muscle. Let your bones go limp."

His claws scratched lightly over my scalp before he gripped my hair, easing me backward until I was lying flat on the floor. Arms and legs splayed, eyes closed, I released a heavy breath. My brain grasped at my swirling worries, clinging to them, determined not to let go.

Callum moved down my body, rubbing my arms, massaging my muscles. He worked down my legs, to my feet, then back up again, kneading at a slow pace as he spoke to me softly.

"Let your mind slow down. You don't need to be thoughtless. You only need to let your thoughts go. Allow them to pass through and disappear."

Easier said than done.

His touch was so soothing. My thoughts stalled, and I began to feel as if was floating.

"There you are, darling. Let yourself drift."

My worries didn't seem so important anymore. I ached too much to move; weariness weighed me down.

Callum kept massaging me, speaking to me gently, his words like a lullaby.

I opened my eyes just enough to see the twirling planets overhead. The mechanism spun with a slow and steady tick, lulling my mind into a state of half-sleep.

Drifting . . .

Almost dreaming.

The thoughts that floated through my mind took greater form: images of people, familiar voices, pungent smells I could have sworn were real. They played like a movie, whether I focused on them or not. But when I did finally allow my attention to hone in on them, I saw a face I'd never expected.

Juniper Kynes.

The girl who got away was now a woman, covered in scars and tattoos, with dark eyes full of anger. She carried a gun on her back, and at her side, an unfamiliar, golden-eyed demon.

My eyes flew open, although I hadn't even realized I'd closed them again. I lay there gasping softly, and Callum's face appeared as he crouched over me.

"I . . . I saw something," I choked out. "Something real."

EVERLY

FROM THAT DAY on, I spent every morning in the meditation room. Callum would join me, using his voice and hands to ease me into that dream-like state of relaxation.

Sometimes, I had visions. Sometimes I saw nothing at all. My grandmother warned me that regardless of what I saw, I had to remember these apparitions were merely possibilities, not guarantees.

"Even I have fallen into the trap of attempting to change the future based upon things I envisioned," she said. "But you must resist the temptation. What you see and what eventually may come to pass can be very different things."

Most of my visions were vague: merely still images or fragments of conversations. I saw Raelynn once, with Leon beside her, and it gave me hope she would live.

Too many people had already been hurt by my father and his Libiri. Even one more life lost was unacceptable.

My grandmother made it clear meditation served another purpose besides keeping myself relaxed: I had to learn to guard my mind, how to erect mental barriers in case the God attempted to attack me again. It would be difficult for Its mental influence to reach me within this house, but even so, my encounter with It in St. Thaddeus had left me vulnerable.

"The creature knows exactly how to reach your mind, how to frighten you, how to trick you," Grams said. "Although this house is well protected, an unguarded mind can still be vulnerable to influence. If It can find a way to harm you, Everly, It will."

What a reassuring thought.

Still, after several days of consistent meditation, I was getting better at it. Simply breathing still didn't settle my anxious thoughts, but it could help me keep steady until they passed. My grandmother suggested a metronome to help me focus, and some mornings I would lay on my bedroom floor, losing myself in the slow and steady tick.

It started to feel as if I was more in control. As if, maybe, my mind was finally safe.

At least . . . it felt safe when I was awake.

My nightmares had returned.

It helped that Callum was usually there when I fell asleep. He would sit on the bed with me, or close by. He didn't sleep himself and was often too restless to lie down. But he would hum softly, or rub my back as old records played at a low volume on the gramophone.

Perhaps it gave me a false sense of security.

A storm moved in one night, bringing with it lightning and crashing thunder. Rain pounded the windows. Callum had put on one of his favorite records for me to sleep to, the gentle crooning of the Ink Spots filling the room as I drifted off.

When I awoke, hours later, the rain was still pouring. The record had stuck, the same two words scratching as they played again and again, "I don't— I don't— I don't—"

I stumbled out of bed and across the room, switching the gramophone off. In the silence that followed, as I blearily rubbed my eyes, I could still hear music playing. But it was far away and so faint. Like it was deep in some other part of the house.

Callum was no longer in the room. For some reason, his absence gave me a strangely queasy feeling.

I should have gotten back in bed. But now that I was up, that uncomfortable feeling led me inexplicably toward the door. Opening it, I poked my head out into the dark hallway, looking up and down. Lightning flashed, illuminating the empty corridor.

"Callum?"

There was indeed music playing, and strangely, it sounded like the exact same record that was currently sitting in my room. I stepped out into the hall, leaving the door ajar behind me.

"Callum?" I raised my voice a little louder. The demon had sharp hearing; there was no doubt that if he was in the house, he would hear me.

Why wasn't he answering?

The floorboards creaked beneath my bare feet as I made my way down the hall and toward the stairway. The music wasn't coming from above but from below. On the same floor as the library.

A strange certainty that I needed to be quiet settled over me as I descended the stairs. Thunder rumbled as I reached the next floor, accompanied by another flash of light. In the sudden illumination, I spotted a figure walking ahead of me down the hall.

A chill ran over my skin as I stopped walking. Without any light, I could no longer see the stranger ahead of me in the dark. Her back had been to me, her hair long and pale blonde.

"Mama?" I whispered her name into the dark. With another flash of lightning, I caught a glimpse, right as she turned and entered the library, the door quietly clicking shut behind her.

The music was closer now.

The library door creaked as I pushed it open. The wind and rain made it seem as if there were imperceptible sounds all around me, emanating from the shadows. Following the music, I made my way to the upper level.

The vault was open.

Only a few flickering candles were lit within. The air was so still. Something told me I wasn't supposed to be in here, at least not alone. I needed someone with me, but . . .

But I wasn't alone. Mama was here.

Taking one of the candles from the desk, I held it

up to illuminate the way as I crept toward the back of the vault. Its flame fell upon the hatch leading down to Sybil's laboratory, which someone was barely holding open, staring at me with wide eyes through the gap.

The moment my light fell on her milky-white eyes, Mama vanished, down into the dark.

I had to follow her. I *had* to.

There was an odd sensation at the back of my skull. Like fingernails scratching. Like roaches crawling under my skin.

Holding my light in one hand, I pulled open the hatch. A dusty, floral smell rushed out, like dry roses left in an old graveyard. Leaning over the edge, I listened. The music was coming from down there. But faintly, over the sound of the music, was something else. Straining to hear, I leaned closer.

It was whispering. Someone was whispering my name.

It didn't sound like my mother.

Something grabbed my hair in a sudden, unbreakable grip and *pulled*. I tumbled down, screaming as I fell until I landed hard on the dirt floor. With the air knocked out of my lungs, I lay there, my candle gone out, completely blind in the dark.

The music stopped. But I could still hear the whispering.

"Come closer, Everly. Come, come, come, my dear sweet girl. My child."

"You're not my mother." I scrambled to my feet. Extending my hands, I turned in a complete circle, feeling frantically for the ladder so I could get out of here. But as my eyes adjusted to the dark, I realized there was no ladder.

It was gone.

Pressing my back against the cold dirt wall, I could see something crouched near the entrance to the tunnels. Long, wet blonde hair hung in its face. Dirty, gnarled fingernails tapped upon its knees.

"Come closer," it whispered. "And you'll see."

Shaking my head, I tried to summon fire. Sparks cascaded away from me, but my efforts were useless, unless I could somehow get my mind under control.

This was a nightmare. It had to be. This was all in my head.

I had to make it stop.

Slowly, the hunched being that looked like my mother stood. Its proportions were all wrong. Too tall, its limbs too long, its rib cage too wide.

"Perhaps you do not love your mother," it hissed. Its head was still low, so I couldn't see its face. It lifted its hands, running its grotesque fingers through its hair. The long blonde tresses fell away, leaving behind silky black strands.

My breath caught.

It looked at me with Callum's face. But his eyes weren't black. They were white.

"Come to me, Everly," he said. "I have something to show you."

Again, I frantically shook my head. I needed to calm down. My breath was coming too quick and panicked, my thoughts moving too fast.

Callum raised his hand, curling his finger at me. "Don't make me come get you."

Dread shot through my veins. Sucking in a deep breath, I forced myself to hold it before fully exhaling. Again and again, I gulped in air until I felt light-headed.

"You can't touch me," I said. My voice was too frightened, too uncertain. I tried to think only of the ticking metronome, filling my mind with its repetitive tone.

The thing took a step toward me, tipping its head to the side. "You don't believe that. Your mind is full of doubts."

This was a dream. Only a dream. I could wake up, and this would all go away.

Callum laughed eerily. "Are you really dreaming? Or do you only wish you were?"

My chest was tight with fear, but I could control this. I could wake up. The God had found a way into my nightmares, but It was in *my* head and I could force It out. These were only thoughts, figments of my imagination. I could control them, I could *make them stop*.

The creature with Callum's face abruptly stopped walking. Its lips curled, revealing black-stained teeth.

"Get the fuck over here, Everly," it snarled. "You know who I am."

"I know exactly who you are!" I said, raising my voice. "You're a liar! You're not Callum! You're not—"

There was a flurry of motion, and everything changed. I was no longer underground, staring at the thing wearing Callum's face. I was sitting up in bed, my hands gripping the sheets, my skin cold with sweat.

Callum stood at the foot of the bed, his hand out-stretched toward me. His eyes were wide with concern, and they were black, as dark as the deepest reaches of the night sky.

Scrambling across the bed, I flung my arms around him. He held me tight, soothing me, his hand stroking over my hair. He sat on the mattress, gathering me close, saying, "I'm right here, it's okay. I never left, Everly. You're all right."

I wrapped my arms around his neck, burying my face against his chest. "It had your face, Callum. But I made it leave. I did it."

"Of course you did, darling." His hand cupped my face, and I was finally able to close my eyes again as I relaxed against him. "I knew you could. I knew you'd find that strength. Easy now. It can't hurt you. You're in control."

At last, I felt as if I was.

EVERLY

IT WAS TIME for us to further investigate Sybil's laboratory and delve into the tunnels beneath the house. We
needed to prepare ourselves, and since no records of
those tunnels existed in the original building plans for the
coven house, we needed to search elsewhere.

That meant going back to Abelaum, to the university's
library. There, we would hopefully find the old Leighman
Mining Company maps and possibly figure out how these
tunnels connected to the larger mine, if they connected
at all.

But first, Callum had another lesson to teach me, one
he deemed absolutely necessary before we ventured out
of the safety of the coven house.

We met in the meditation room at noon. The demon
had told me to dress warmly but comfortably, and
be prepared for a little rain. "A little" was a bit of an

understatement, as the sky had been pouring all day and night. But the meditation room was sheltered and dry, so I wondered why it was a concern.

"If you can master teleportation, you can master any magic," Callum said, pacing in front of me after I'd stretched and relaxed for a while. "It is one of the most complex and difficult abilities to learn, for demons as much as witches. It requires entirely disassembling and reassembling your physical form, while maintaining your concentration over the distance you need to travel."

Nodding, I tried to put myself back in the mindset of a student at the university. Losing myself in ancient languages, enthralled by the wisdom of my teacher . . .

I was enthralled by much more than his wisdom, but I didn't have time to get distracted, as he frequently reminded me.

"To start, you'll want to be in tune with your body," Callum said. "As you practice and grow more comfortable, it will be as easy as walking." To demonstrate, he took a step toward me, but that single step carried him the entire distance of the room, and I jumped to find him standing right in front of me. He grinned and did it again, teleporting around me, each step another jump through space until he stood in front of me again.

"Your turn," he said. "Focus on your limbs, starting with the tips of your toes and your fingers. Let your muscles soften. Imagine your physical body as mere particles, vibrating together, magnetized to each other. But they can be pushed, pulled, manipulated. They can flow like sand."

Closing my eyes to concentrate, I imagined my limbs drifting into the air, fragmenting away like cherry blossoms in spring. I imagined the ground vanishing from beneath my feet, my body floating, weightless and free as the wind . . .

"Very good."

There was a split-second sensation, as if my body was being sucked through a straw. Then my eyes flew open, and I was stumbling forward, pulled toward the Earth by the heaviness of gravity—

Callum's arms braced around me, keeping me upright. Lying against his chest, blinking my eyes rapidly, I tried not to lose myself in the way he was looking at me.

Like he was excited. Like he was proud.

"You'll try teleporting a distance this time."

He stepped back, leaving me swaying slightly on my feet as he strode about ten paces away before turning to face me again.

"Again. Except this time, come to me. Maintain your concentration on where I'm standing. You must envision it with as much clarity and intention as you can muster."

Giving my limbs a good shake, I closed my eyes again. But I held the image of Callum in my mind: how the stones intersected beneath his feet, how the light angled across his chest, and the tapestries framed his face.

Then I was light again; a little breathless, a little dizzy. The sensation made me want to giggle, but then my stomach dropped, my feet thumped to the stones, and once more, Callum's arms wrapped around me, preventing me from falling face-first to the floor.

He was smiling slightly, the expression small enough I wondered if he was trying to hide it.

"Excellent work."

My heart buzzed with pride. Flustered now, my next few attempts weren't as successful, although I did manage to teleport entirely across the room and slam my head against the wall in the process.

"Mm, once again, you are very easily distracted," Callum said, snapping his fingers as he paced, and I rubbed my sore forehead. "Try again. Fail this time, and you'll be in for worse consequences than a little bump on the head."

He looked as serious as ever, but I could see the mischief in his eyes.

"Consequences?" I said. "What do you mean by that?"

He curled a clawed finger at me. "Come to me, Everly. Try again."

In the blink of an eye, I crossed the room. The air rushed out of my lungs, my head prickled with chills. But I didn't stumble. I didn't fall. I stood mere inches away from him, gazing up into his face with a victorious smirk.

"The threat of consequences is helpful for you, eh?" He snapped his fingers again and vanished, reappearing on the opposite side of the room from me. "Again, Everly."

Again and again, I teleported after him. Every time I stumbled, or misplaced my feet, or flew too far, he would count.

"That's three. Four. Going to make five, then, are we? Six."

"What the hell are you counting?" I finally blurted. A slow, wicked smile spread over his face.

"I'm counting how many swats you're going to get over my knee when you're done," he said, and my mouth dropped open.

"You . . . you think you're going to *spank* me?" He simply waited, staring at me. "And what makes you think I'm going to let you?"

"You've practically fallen over my knee several times already," he said. "I think it's the logical progression for your sloppy attempts."

"Sloppy?" I gasped and teleported toward him again. While I would have loved to do so flawlessly, I overstepped my intentions once again and wound up *behind* him.

He gave me a stinging slap on the ass before he darted away from me, teleporting to the opposite side of the room. I was pursuing him determinedly now, stumbling frequently, but at least I was keeping up. Every time I lost my balance, moved too far or too little, he'd give me another swat. They were playful slaps, teasing me into such a state that I was puffing in exasperation as I chased him.

"I didn't even stumble that time!" I yelped, stomping my foot after another swat. Callum was across the room, squatting on the balls of his feet as he laughed at me.

Rubbing his hands together, he said, "Your ass bounces when I smack it. How am I supposed to resist playing with it?"

Quickly blowing a loose strand of hair out of my eyes, I teleported to him again. Somehow, he caught me in midair. I swore our bodies were melting together. Heat and skin, flesh and blood.

Callum held me close, arms tight around me. Face to face.

"Is this how you trained your warriors?" I whispered.

"Exactly the same," he said, his expression carefully controlled. "Except I used a whip instead of my hand." I giggled, then laughed harder at the mock offense on his face. "Oh, do you think it's funny? Won't be so funny when your ass is red, eh?"

He tossed me over his shoulder, allowing me to dangle there as he smacked my backside repeatedly. I squirmed, kicking my legs and squealing. It was impossible to wiggle out from his hold.

But it wasn't impossible to teleport.

I vanished from his arms and reappeared on the far side of the room. Breathing heavily, I pushed my loose hair out of my face and stuck my tongue out at him as he widened his eyes in surprise.

"Well, well. A fast learner, aren't you?" he said. "All right. We'll try something harder. The great tree inside the greenhouse." He vanished before I could say a word, and I closed my eyes in concentration.

The greenhouse. The great tree with its scarred bark and massive roots, limbs curving along the crystalline interior of the glass dome. I could see Callum standing before it, birds flitting by his head as bees buzzed through the air, and I caught my breath for a moment.

When I inhaled again, the scent of flowers, greenery, and damp dirt rushed in my nose.

"I did it!" I practically shrieked as I jumped up and down, pumping my fist in the air. "Hell *yes*! I can't believe it . . . I can't . . ."

I paused when I noticed the way Callum was watching me.

He kissed me. A slow, deep, lingering kiss. And when he pulled away, the hand that had gently touched my cheek moved to grip my chin.

"Don't you dare doubt yourself again," he said. "Or I'll start using the whip." I smiled at that, and he shook his head. "Insatiable, aren't you? I give you a little taste of wickedness and suddenly you can't get enough."

"You gave me a taste of what I deserve," I said, and his dark eyes brightened like a solar eclipse. "And now I want more."

The branches rustled above us, and Callum snarled, "Stop fucking watching, you perverted tree!"

"Now *that's* not very nice!" Darragh whined, his voice emanating from somewhere within the branches. "Don't mind me, just go on with whatever you were doing."

"Bedroom," Callum whispered, before he teleported again. After taking a moment to focus myself, I followed, teleporting myself to my bedroom. I flopped down on top of the bed, which wasn't *exactly* where I'd intended to appear, but close enough.

It made my desires obvious at least.

"I can't reward you quite yet," my demon said, standing at the foot of the bed. He held up my bag in one hand. "You'll need this. Your next teleportation will take you outside the house."

I took the bag, slinging the strap over my shoulder. Scrambling off the bed, I took my position in front of him, continually readjusting my bag because my nervous hands couldn't stay still.

"Don't be afraid," he said. "You need to be confident you can get back to the house without me, if necessary, and teleportation is the safest way to do so. Try teleporting to Abelaum and back again. But remember, you must have a very specific location in mind. You must picture it vividly, with as much detail as you can. Both getting there and getting back."

"To Abelaum? Oh . . . okay."

The places I knew most vividly in Abelaum were *not* places I wanted to risk randomly showing up in. But then, I thought of the perfect place. My favorite coffee shop: a quiet cafe tucked away down a narrow street, the brick facade coated thickly with vines. The front door had a bell that jingled when you opened it, and when you walked past you could smell the pastries baking, rich butter and yeasty bread, hot coffee and sweet cream . . .

Something wet hit my face, and suddenly, I was standing in a downpour.

Hurriedly pulling up the hood of my jacket and tucking back my hair, I stepped out of the shadows of the alleyway into which I'd teleported. People hurried by on the sidewalk, rushing to get indoors and out of the rain.

I peered through the windows into the coffee shop. Baristas bustled back and forth behind the counter, and patrons sat at tables reading and playing board games as they sipped their drinks.

But then, there at the table just inside the window, I saw them.

Victoria and Raelynn. Together. Sipping coffee, chatting with big smiles on their faces.

My heart nearly stopped. My first instinct was to flee, to *immediately* teleport back to Callum. But I knew what this was. I knew exactly what Victoria was doing, because I'd seen her do it before.

I'd watched her call Juniper her best friend. Watched her play the long game as they grew closer and Juniper's trust ran deeper.

Only to stab her in the back in the end.

She was going to do to Raelynn exactly what she'd done to Juniper.

The wind whipped rain into my face, catching my hair and pulling it from the safety of my hood. Lifting my head so I could hurriedly tuck my hair away again, my eyes met with the woman sitting at a corner table, behind Victoria.

My palms went cold and clammy.

My stomach lurched, terror bursting through every inch of me as adrenaline pumped from my frantic heart.

The woman in the corner, staring at me as if she wanted me to drop dead, was Juniper.

Juniper, who'd looked at me with such desperation as an ambulance took her away. Juniper, who'd screamed the truth only for no one to listen. Who'd seen my mother's wickedness. Who'd witnessed my cowardice.

Who'd been thrown down to God and *lived*.

She rose slowly from her chair, her eyes locked on me with vicious intensity, and I turned and sprinted.

Dodging down the rainy sidewalk, I was certain I heard the cafe's bell jingle as the door was shoved open. *Shit, shit, shit!* I didn't dare stop, my mind too addled with surprise and fear to concentrate on teleporting. I turned down every street—right, left, left, right, left—constantly glancing over my shoulder.

But with every turn, Juniper was behind me. Moving quickly and easily through the crowd, hood up, eyes locked upon me.

The look on her face was murderous. She wasn't a frightened teenage girl anymore. This was a woman who'd looked death in the face and wasn't afraid to do it again.

With every fiber of my being, I knew she wanted to kill me.

But after another quick turn, I was facing a dead end. A narrow alleyway was before me, wedged between three buildings. The fire escapes were out of my reach, there was nothing I could hide behind. With my back to a brick wall, I faced the mouth of the alley . . .

And willed myself to disappear.

I imagined myself vanishing into the brick, my body clear as glass, my breathing utterly silent. A cold feeling settled over me, but I refused to let it shake me. I held my concentration as Juniper appeared at the mouth of the alley.

She paused, and although I felt like she was staring right at me, her brow furrowed with confusion. She approached slowly, looking around with every step. She kept coming closer . . . closer. Beneath her jacket, I could see the handle of a knife holstered on her belt.

Why the hell had she come back to Abelaum? She had left years ago. She knew the true danger that lurked here. Yet she'd returned . . .

But of course. Her brother. Marcus.

They'd killed him, and it summoned her like an angel of vengeance.

She stopped just a few feet away from me. Her frown deepened, and she reached out, muttering softly, "No fucking way . . ."

My magic shattered, and her eyes widened in shock as I reappeared. I shoved her back, magic pummeling her chest like a cudgel so I could run, but her hand snapped out, grabbing the strap of my bag. She was so strong, her teeth bared with the effort to drag me back toward her.

I tugged with all my might, ripping open my bag and sending my possessions tumbling to the rain-soaked ground. It gave me the seconds I needed to get away. I fled out of the alley, dodging into the first sheltered door-way I spotted.

"Back to the house," I whispered desperately. "The house, the house. Back to Callum. *Please.*"

I wasn't proud of myself for literally begging my magic to work—but it did, and the next thing I knew, I was stumbling into the foyer of the coven house.

"Callum!" No sooner was his name out of my mouth than he appeared before me, clutching me with concern. The radio was in the kitchen, and my grandmother called out, "What on Earth is happening out there? Everly! Come, speak to me at once!"

IN TRUE GRANDMOTHERLY fashion, Grams wouldn't let me explain until my rain-soaked body was wrapped in a blanket, seated in front of the kitchen's hearth with a hot cup of tea in my hands. At least by the time I was comfortably warm, I could manage to get the story out without the words shaking too much.

"A woman out for vengeance is a very dangerous thing," Grams said. "And you've had visions of her accompanied by a demon . . . that makes her even more of a threat."

"It doesn't matter who accompanies this woman," Callum said. He was leaning against the counter, arms folded, wings rigidly tense. "Anyone who attempts to harm my witch will not live. We will be rid of this problem by tonight. It will not take me long to find her—"

"No!" Callum stared at me. "Don't go after her. She won't harm me, she—"

"You said she pursued you *viciously*." Callum pushed away from the counter, stalking closer to me. "She is a threat to you. Why ignore a threat when I can dispose of it?"

"She doesn't know where I am." Memories of that night in St. Thaddeus, when Juniper was cut and marked for the God, kept replaying in mind. The screams . . . fuck, those horrible screams . . . "She's not a threat to me right now. Not here. She has no reason to come after me."

"Vengeance is a powerful drive," Callum said slowly. He was displeased, and the air around him shimmered with furious power. "Do not allow guilt to cloud your thinking."

Holding his gaze, I said with as much fierceness as I could, "Do *not* go after her. Leave her alone. She's been through enough."

His fingers twitched. He looked away from me, jaw clenched.

Then, softly, he said, "As you command."

EVERLY

IT WAS STRANGE to set foot on the university campus again. Even with my hood up and sunglasses on, I felt too exposed.

What was even stranger was seeing Callum look so human. He'd disguised himself for our outing—no wings, no claws. He'd shrunk his towering height to a somewhat modest six foot two inches. But his eyes were the most shocking change. Caramel-colored pupils made his boyishly handsome face look even younger.

He had offered to go to the library alone, but when I asked what he would do if the librarian refused to give him access to the Leighman Company records, he said, "Then I will persuade them to cooperate."

Knowing that Callum's methods of persuasion were likely to involve death and dismemberment, I made the decision to go with him then and there.

"I never said I would kill your little librarian friend, Everly," he said as we made our way across campus. It was the third time he'd tried to assure me, and the third time I was not even slightly convinced. "Persuasion can take many forms. Mild torture is far more effective than death."

Stopping abruptly, I turned and looked at him, folding my arms. "No torturing either! This is why I came with you. You think you can handle every situation with violence."

He looked at me skeptically. "Every situation *can* be handled with violence. It's not a theory; it's a fact."

Stepping closer, so I could maintain eye contact with him, I said, "No torture. No violence. Behave yourself."

A shadow flashed over his eyes, and his lips stretched into a grin. "As my lady wishes. I'll be a perfectly well-behaved boy."

Somehow, I doubted it.

Despite my fears of being spotted by someone who knew me, walking into the library still made my heart flutter with happiness. The familiar sights and smells, the polished wood shelves warmed by the late afternoon sun, the roasted-coffee aroma of the library cafe—God, I'd missed this.

"Oh, good. It's just William today," I said as we lingered in the entryway and I took a careful look around. Callum craned his head toward the librarian's desk, not being even slightly subtle as he stared.

"You mean that small boy with spectacles?" he said. "What's good about him?"

Small boy. I barely stifled a laugh. Will was twenty-three years old and gangly, certainly not small. But it was rather satisfying to hear the hostility in Callum's voice. It validated my decision to come with him, first of all. But it was also an ego boost to have this powerful demon with the good looks of a high fashion model sounding jealous over me.

"He's my friend," I said, clasping his arm to draw his attention back to me. He was glaring at Will as if the man had insulted him, and I reached up to turn his face toward me. "Stop staring, you're going to scare him." When his eyes narrowed even further, I grasped his jaw, shaking it as I insisted, "No torture. No murder. Behave."

"Your rules are cruel."

But he made an obvious effort not to stare as we approached the desk and Will finally looked up from his paperwork.

"How can I help— Holy shit! Everly?!" Will leapt out of his chair so fast he nearly tumbled it over. "You're— Oh, thank God, you're alive! I've been so worried, everyone has been so—"

Pressing a finger to my lips, I leaned over the desk and whispered, "Please be quiet, Will. No one can know I'm here."

Lowering his voice to a stage whisper, Will cautiously peered around and finally noticed Callum standing beside me.

"Victoria said you vanished," Will said, slowly breaking his glaring contest with Callum. "She said you . . .

well, she thought you were having some kind of mental breakdown."

"Victoria doesn't know I'm here and I need to make sure she doesn't find out either. Whatever my family has told you, please trust me that they're lying."

His eyes searched my face, wide with concern. "I knew they treated you like shit. I'm so sorry, Ev. If there's anything . . . *anything* I can do to help you . . ."

Callum made a sound that was either a scoff or a laugh, and Will's eyes darted between us suspiciously.

"Who is this?" he said, the distaste obvious in his voice. I stepped closer to Callum, putting myself between the two of them.

"This is Callum," I said. "He's my . . . uh . . ."

"Fiancé." Callum brushed past me, extending his arm to Will and engulfing the man's hand within his own. "Pleasure." He hardly sounded pleased.

"Fiancé," Will repeated, glancing between Callum and I. "Right. I'm Will. Pleasure, I guess."

Callum did indeed make Will look very, *very* small.

"Listen, Will, I don't have much time," I said, getting between them again before they could start spitting at each other like angry cats. "I'm looking for some old documents from the 1890s. Building plans from Leighman Mining Company. Is there anything like that kept here? Even in storage?"

Will appeared deep in thought for a moment before he sat again and rapidly typed on his computer.

"We do have documents from Leighman Mining," he said. "They're not categorized though. Seventy-seven preserved documents in a single file, stored in . . ." He frowned. "The rare books depository. That's odd." He chewed his lower lip. "Look, Ev . . . I want to help, I really do, but I could lose my job letting you in there."

"I know. I hate putting you in this position, I just really need your help. *We* need your help." Encouraging him to play nicely, I gave Callum a sharp nudge with my elbow.

My demon sighed. "Yes, Mr. William, if you could assist us, that would be just peachy."

It took considerable effort not to wince at that, just as I'm sure it took Callum considerable effort to say something at least vaguely polite.

Luckily, William didn't take much to convince.

"Okay, okay. I'll be right back. I'm going to get the key and tell Sarah I'm going on break." He left his chair and disappeared through a door marked *EMPLOYEES ONLY*, leaving Callum and I standing side by side at the desk.

"My fiancé?" I said, the moment Will was out of earshot. "That sounds so serious. It would have made more sense to say I'm your girlfriend."

Callum growled with irritation. "You humans and all your various terms for your lovers make no sense. Calling you my girlfriend would imply a lack of certainty on my part, would it not? A lack of commitment?"

"Not necessarily. Some people stay boyfriend and girlfriend forever, and are entirely committed to each other."

"Regardless. Fiancé carries the significance I wanted it to. Makes the point clear."

"What point is that?"

"That you're mine." He crowded my personal space, pressing me against the wall as he caressed the back of his hand against my cheek. "Does that sound a bit too serious? I own your *soul*, darling. And unlike some others of my kind, that actually means a significant amount to me. Do you understand?"

Breathless, I nodded.

"Perhaps I haven't done such a good job of reminding you," he said, looming over me as my world shrunk until it was only him and I. "That I own you, body and soul, and always will. Humans do have difficulty with the concept of forever, after all. Doesn't sit right in your sweet little heads, does it? But I'll set you right." He gave my chin a little nudge and grinned when my words came out as nothing more than a squeak.

Someone softly cleared their throat, and we turned to find Will staring at us.

"I've got the key," he said, face significantly redder than it was before. He kept shooting Callum distrusting glances. "Follow me. We'll take the staff elevator."

Being in a small, enclosed metal box with Callum was no easy feat. A thrumming tone reverberated from him, like the pulse of the universe itself. He put his arm around my shoulders, holding me close to his side, which only increased the intensity. My heart beat harder, my mouth salivated. The air was heavy, crushingly hot. Will's back was to us, and I cautiously lifted my eyes to glance up at Callum.

He had a nasty grin fixed on his face, staring at the back of Will's head. He was doing this on purpose.

By the time the short elevator ride had stopped, Will was rubbing his temples and wincing in pain.

"Just a little headache," he said when I looked at him in concern.

We were in a narrow hallway on the library's third floor. We passed a few open doorways, and although the interiors were not lit, they looked like offices: hulking wooden desks, leather chairs, walls lined with books.

We reached a solid wood door at the end of the hall. It was equipped with a pin padlock and a large metal keyhole. Will stepped ahead of us and withdrew a thick key from his pocket, turning it in the lock before he typed four numbers into the pad.

"This room doesn't get many visitors," he said. "Many of the books are delicate, so they're under glass."

The door creaked as it opened. North-facing windows allowed gentle light into the space, a tidy room with rows of display shelves holding books under glass. Filing cabinets lined the far wall, and a staircase led to a small upper level, covered with larger bookshelves.

"The plans are in here, supposedly," Will said. "They'll be in a folder, most likely. Unless they've been laminated, in which case, probably in a binder. Unfortunately, the computer didn't list a shelf number."

"Thanks, Will. We'll be quick, I promise." I clasped his arm in thanks and saw a storm cloud descend over Callum's expression. "We really appreciate the help."

"It's no problem." Will stared at Callum as the demon brushed past him, headed toward the filing cabinets. He lowered his voice, leaning toward me as he whispered,

"He's not really your fiancé, is he? You don't have a ring."

"It's complicated," I said. The less he knew, the better. "He's keeping me safe. You don't need to worry about me."

He didn't look convinced, but he nodded in acceptance anyway. "Okay. I guess I'll head over to the lounge and grab a bite to eat. I'll check back with you afterward. Just be careful with everything."

As he left us, shutting the door quietly behind him, I joined Callum at the filing cabinets. He already had a drawer open, rapidly flicking his fingers through the numerous papers within.

"That boy desires you," he said, shutting the drawer with a bit more force than necessary.

Surely he didn't think Will was any kind of threat to us—whatever "us" meant. Callum's affection for me was frighteningly obsessive but strangely sweet; I wasn't sure if he viewed me more like a pet, a toy, or a partner.

I wasn't even sure how to ask him. Considering he literally owned my soul, it felt silly to try to define "what we were" by human standards.

We were bound to each other for eternity. The sheer magnitude of that was hard to contemplate. But then Callum would do something like introducing himself as my fiancé, and suddenly I was left wondering what exactly he meant by it.

Was he merely being possessive? Or was he trying to use unfamiliar human terms to make a point he didn't have other words for?

"Will is sweet," I said. "And just a friend."

"I didn't say he wasn't sweet. I said he desires you. He wants to fuck you, darling."

Lightly swatting his arm, I gasped out, "Don't be so crude. Christ, Callum."

"Oh, is it *don't be crude* now?" His volume lifted, purposefully. In that small space, a regular speaking voice was like a yell. "That isn't what you were saying last night."

"You're being loud—"

"Good. I want him to fucking hear me."

Suddenly, Callum pushed me back against the shelves. He planted his arms on either side of me, the wood creaking under the force of his grip as he caged me in. I simply folded my arms as I looked up at him.

"Is this a tantrum, Callum?"

"Hardly. This is a reminder of who exactly owns you. And it's not sweet, friendly William." He brought his sharp teeth close to my ear as he said, "It's me. It's fucking *me* that's tethered to you. It's me that can mark you up, it's me that gets to touch you."

Then his teeth were on my neck. Kissing, sucking, and then biting. My determination to keep silent shattered in an instant, as a desperate gasp was wrenched out of me.

"I thought you weren't the jealous type."

"Oh, certainly not, love. I'm very welcoming and generous to guests. It's intruders I have a problem with."

"Will is hardly an intruder, he's . . . he's . . . Oh God—"

"Mm, what was that? I'm having trouble hearing you." The bastard gave me a sharp-toothed smile as he wedged his thigh between my legs. The pressure alone was enough to make my breath shudder. I ground down against him, hips rocking back and forth in a desperate attempt to chase more stimulation.

He'd made me like this. Desperate, lost in need, greedy for more.

"He'll hear us, Callum," I whispered urgently, shaking my head even as I kept grinding on him. He was barely touching me and it was driving me wild. His arms were still planted firmly on either side of my head, but I was grateful for the cage. I wanted it to tighten, to crush me, to force me to give in.

"We don't have much time," I gasped, and Callum chuckled.

"I suppose I'll have to make it quick and dirty then."

Phantom hands wrapped around my throat. Glaring into the demon's eyes, I tried to maintain my composure, at least as well as one could while grinding against his thigh. My attempts to control myself only made him laugh more.

"Look at that cute little glare," he teased as those phantom hands pressed all over me and pinned me to the shelves. "I don't blame William for wanting you. A beautiful woman like you . . . people should be crawling after you like dogs."

"That's what you did for me last night," I groaned.

He lifted my chin, capturing my lips in a knee-weakening kiss.

"That's right, darling," he whispered. "Last night I crawled for you, and tonight, I'll crawl for you again.

I'd drag myself through broken glass on my hands and knees if that's what you wanted. No matter the pain. Regardless of the degradation. The harder it is to please you, the more I'll try to succeed."

He turned me, face toward the shelves, his hands caressing appreciatively over my body before he gripped my hips, and said, "I'm going to fuck you right here in the library. You'd better pray to whatever God will listen that your *sweet* little friend doesn't walk in on us."

He peeled off my jeans and tossed away my shoes. He kissed every inch of skin he laid bare, his teeth leaving sharp, stinging bite marks everywhere he went. It wasn't long before I was covered in reddened marks, in little bruises left by his mouth and gripping hands.

He smacked my ass, and I moaned, looking back at him with wide eyes.

"Did that hurt?" He spanked me again.

Instead of whimpering in pain, I gave a lewd, exaggerated groan and arched my back toward him. His caramel-colored eyes instantly darkened, and his claws came out as he hurriedly turned me to face him again.

"Do you really think it's wise to taunt a demon?" he growled.

"It gets me what I want," I said, daring to be cheeky.

He lifted me suddenly, my back leaning against the shelves with my thighs gripped and spread by his hands. His claws pricked dangerously at my skin as he angled his cock, nudging his thick head against my entrance. He pressed in slowly, and every time I thought I'd taken his full length, I was wrong. By the time he was fully inside me, my toes were curled and every breath was a desperate pant. The stretch of him ached, every sensitive nerve consumed by a storm of exquisite pain.

"There's my good girl," he whispered. He shifted his hips back, easing out of me slowly. "How pretty you look with your poor little pussy so full. Remember to snap your fingers if you need to, darling."

A phantom hand pressed over my mouth, locking my lips together. Invisible fingers twisted in my hair, holding my head back so I couldn't turn away from the dark voids of his eyes. He thrust into me, hard enough to make the shelves behind me creak and several of the books jolt forward. My sharp whimper was muffled, but I froze when I heard the door creak open.

"Just checking in! Found anything yet?" Will's voice sounded muffled, as if he had a mouthful of food, and I held my breath in panic. God, if he came back here and saw me like this, I would die. Just melt into the ground and never recover.

Callum brought his lips dangerously close to mine, still fully sheathed inside me. The phantom hand over my mouth retreated.

"Answer him nicely, Everly," he said. "Tell dear William that everything is fine."

My words were a tangled knot, my brain incapable of cohesive thought. I couldn't meet Callum's gaze and speak without my words shaking, so I squeezed my eyes shut tight and said, "Not yet! We're, uh . . . working on it."

"All right, well, I'll help you look after I finish eating."

The door clicked closed again, and the invisible hand squeezed back over my mouth. I opened my eyes, only for them to roll back as Callum thrust inside me. Long, slow strokes that had me shaking with every inch, whimpers rising in my throat but stopped by my sealed lips.

"I'm sure you wouldn't want him to see you like this, would you? Legs spread, cheeks so pink. You're practically dripping on the floor." He brought his mouth even closer to my ear. "I'm not going to stop until you're a mess in every possible way."

More invisible fingers grasped at my throat and caressed beneath my shirt, teasing at my bra. My body jolted as my nipple was squeezed, then tugged.

I groaned before I could silence myself. The hand over my mouth tightened.

"Ssshhh, sshh, now. Don't be loud. William might hear you. I imagine the poor boy's face would be as red as yours if he saw this." His phantom touches were massaging my clit, his cock stretching me with every thrust. "But if he glimpsed us, I couldn't just let him walk away. Perhaps I'd have him use his tongue on your clit while I fucked you."

His lips brushed lightly along my neck, and he increased his speed. "You'd like that, wouldn't you? Such wicked thoughts in your deceivingly innocent mind. I would love to suffocate him with your pussy. Let him drown in it while I watch you fall apart. Perhaps I'll let him eat you after I've filled you with my cum. While he's busy with your pussy, I'll take your anal virginity too."

The fantasy his words were building was too good, too filthy. I'd always thought Will was too sweet for anything of the sort, but who could say no to Callum? Who could resist when he turned those eyes on them?

Callum kept talking, winding me up even more. "I'd have to punish him for snooping. I'd have to whip the poor boy while he ate you out. You'd get to feel every little cry with his mouth on you."

That broke me. I groaned shamelessly as I came, not even the phantom hand enough to muffle me. He laughed as he fucked me, every thrust drawing out my pleasure to a peak that stole my breath.

I became utterly limp as he used me, his movements more urgent now that I was weak with the afterglow.

"Fucking hell, you're more exquisite every time." His voice was little more than a breath as he eased me down from his arms. I leaned heavily against him, my legs shaking, my panties barely hanging around one ankle.

Callum leaned down, holding out my underwear so I could step into them. He pulled them up to my hips, saying, "I love the thought of you, so full of my seed. Dripping with it." His hand rubbed between my legs, teasing my overly sensitive clit. He kissed me softly, slowly. "Let's hurry up and find those plans before Will returns, or I might decide to make that little fantasy of yours come to life."

33

CALLUM

"IT'S LIKE A maze down there. No wonder so many men were trapped. When the elevator shaft collapsed, there was no other way out."

Everly shook her head at the building plans and old maps spread before her. She'd cleared off the desks within the vault, carefully organizing every note and journal as I dragged the remains of the Eld creature outside and dumped it in the woods. The vault had reeked of rotten fish when we entered, but Everly had found a book of beautification spells and was eager to use them at every opportunity.

Now, the room smelled like cinnamon and vanilla. Following Winona's careful instructions, Everly had enchanted a broom and a dustrag to get to work, tidying up the vault as she and I carefully studied the building plans we had found in the university library.

But there was a problem.

"Whatever part of the mine is underneath the house, they didn't map it," Everly admitted, having scoured the maps with increasing frustration for an hour. "God, did we really waste all that time . . ."

Nuzzling my face against her neck, I said, "I hardly think fucking you in a library was a waste of time."

She was deep in thought, chewing her lip as she nudged her body closer against my own. Even distracted by other tasks, she reacted to me, leaning into me, asking silently for more.

"Sybil must have created the tunnels under the house herself," she said. "They weren't part of the original mine, but were dug after. Where would they connect?" She tapped the end of her pen against her mouth. Finally, with a determined look, she circled a section of the mine with her pen. "There. It has to be. That upper level is the only one that could reasonably connect."

"We'll find out soon enough," I said, playing with her hair as she studied. "While you investigate Sybil's notes, I'll explore the tunnels. We'll have them mapped out soon enough."

She looked at me over her shoulder, her eyes bright with excitement. "There's something special in those notes, Callum, I just know it. Sybil found something important, and if I can translate her code . . ."

"You can. I have no doubt your clever mind can solve any puzzle it's given."

A blush rose on her face, and I brushed my fingers over her cheek just to feel the heat of her skin. My need for her grew more every day. It was a constant, insatiable desire to be close to her, touch her, listen to her speak.

Nothing else could satisfy me. Her body was a siren's song and I was its slave.

Everly rose excitedly from her seat, quickly gathering her maps. "Let's go down there now! You can explore, I'll start looking through her notes—"

She stopped when my head tipped curiously to the side, listening for the voice I'd heard calling me.

"It's Darragh," I said with a heavy sigh. "I'll go see what he wants."

Teleporting to the exterior of the greenhouse, I found Darragh lounging lazily between the boughs of his tree.

"There's intruders in the forest," he said before I could ask what he wanted. "A mortal woman and a demon." He opened one amber eye, giving me a thorny smile. "I have them walking in circles, and the flowers will put the woman to sleep soon. Shall I make them leave?"

A mortal and demon. My mind immediately went to Juniper, the woman who'd chased Everly. She'd told me to leave her alone, but . . .

"What do they want?"

"Oh, I certainly don't know," Darragh said with a dramatic yawn. "But the woman carries weapons."

Rage blanketed my vision. Then I had been right all along. This woman meant harm to my witch; she'd even brought a demon along to help her. No matter. They would both be destroyed, and Everly wouldn't have to fear them anymore.

"I'll take care of them," I said and returned to the library before the Woodsprie could reply.

Everly was waiting for me, clearly eager to get down to the tunnels. Her face fell when I said, "Darragh found intruders in the woods. But don't be afraid, they won't reach the house. I'll be back soon."

"Intruders? Who?" She gulped, her eyes widening with fear. "Are they humans?"

"You don't need to concern yourself with it," I said. "Find something to read in the meantime. When I return, we'll go down to the laboratory."

But that didn't satisfy her.

"Callum," she said slowly, softly. "Who is in the woods?"

But I didn't answer her. I vanished, reappearing in the yard and stalking out into the trees. It didn't take me long to catch the intruders' scent, and I shrouded myself in shadow as I pursued them. Everly would be angry, but her heart was gentle.

She didn't yet understand that violence was often the only answer.

The woman and her demon were walking in circles, confused and misled by Darragh's tricks. The air was thick with the scent of toxic flora, and as I stalked closer, the demon sensed my presence, warning the woman not to brandish her weapons.

But it was too late for that.

Creeping closer, I sniffed the air, inhaling the demon's scent. I didn't know him; he was younger than me but strong, not far off from ascending to an Archdemon himself. I didn't like killing my own kind. Perhaps with his woman dead, he would choose to simply be on his way.

But if I needed to destroy him too, I would. Murderous intent surrounded the woman, anger fueled her.

They shouldn't have come here. They shouldn't have come after my witch.

Wrapped in darkness, crouched low as the rain poured around me, I waited. They didn't even notice I was there until they were within just a few inches of me.

When he spotted me, the demon managed to get out a single word.

"Fuck."

Leaping from my perch, it took one swipe of my arm to send him flying back into a tree with an audible crack of wood. The woman scrambled to take out her gun, but I knocked her to the ground and the weapon was flung from her grasp. Bloodlust overtook me as the demon got up, charging for me with claws out, fangs snapping.

With a laugh, I plunged the forest into darkness, surrounding the three of us in swirling shadows. The demon was quick, but not quick enough. My claws ripped at him, tearing through flesh and cracking bone. My breath quickened with excitement, rabid energy filling me. The woman was still struggling for her weapon, but I seized her hair, my other hand wrapping around her jaw.

Her death would be quick, if not entirely painless. I could practically taste her blood in my mouth already. How sweet it would be to see the light go out in her eyes.

But her demon wasn't giving up. He slammed into me, knocking me off her, and we tumbled across the forest floor. His claws tore into me, teeth snapping viciously toward my throat.

"Why don't you fucking stay still?" I snarled and threw him off, and the moment he hit the ground, I slammed my foot into his face, crunching bone and sending blood spattering across the bright green grass.

Poor fool actually thought he could save the woman.

Comfortably cracking my back, I hummed a cheerful little tune as I approached the woman again. She looked at me as if she was witnessing Lucifer himself; eyes wide, mouth agape. The certainty of impending death settled coldly in her eyes. In an act of mercy, I knocked her unconscious before I wrenched her head back, extending my claws to rip open her throat—

"Callum! Callum, *STOP!*"

Everly's voice froze me. She was scrambling toward me through the trees, her feet bare, her hair wild and tangled from sprinting through the forest. Her eyes were wide with horror as she came upon the scene, a gasp leaving her as she saw the woman in my grasp.

"Put her down."

She didn't understand.

"Go back to the house, Everly," I said. "It isn't safe for you here."

"*I SAID, PUT HER DOWN!*"

The command in her voice was undeniable, and I winced, furiously baring my teeth as I refused to release the woman in my grasp. Snarling, I said, "They mean you harm, Everly. They came here with weapons. The woman brought a demon with her. They intended to kill you."

"You don't know that." Her jaw was tight, her eyes brimming with unexpected, angry tears. The sight of such emotion shook me, and my grip on the woman relaxed, her head dropping to the ground.

"My duty is to protect you," I said, shooting a cautious glance at the groaning, writhing demon. Stepping over my unconscious victim, I extended my hand to Everly, hoping to comfort her, to ease her fears.

But she stepped back from me and shook her head. Blood was dripping thickly from my fingers, drenching my hands, my arms. I could taste it in my mouth, sharp and delicious. I wanted more.

I wanted her in my arms. I wanted her understanding, her acceptance.

But she was looking at me in fear.

"Everly . . ." My voice was too loud, too fierce. "I'm protecting you."

"No," she said firmly. "You're *disobeying* me."

The words hurt. They pierced deep and sharp into my chest, tugging at the very strings of our bond. Anger and confusion wrestled within me as I stared at her. Her eyes kept darting around the scene.

I wanted to calm her, reassure her. But with every step I took toward her, she backed away.

"Stop," she said, and I went still. "Don't hurt them. We're taking them back to the house. I need to talk to Juniper. Just keep her demon restrained while I do, but *don't hurt him.*"

Her commands were a riddle I couldn't unravel. Restrain, but don't hurt. Let enemies into our house, let a murderous woman near my witch.

I wanted to defy her.

"Why do you wish to speak to her?"

"Because I think I know why she came back to Abelaum," she said. Her voice didn't waver this time. "She wants revenge against the people who hurt her, who murdered her brother. If she goes after the Libiri, if she keeps them distracted, we might gain a little more time."

Finally, I was able to see the sense in her words. But I still didn't like it. We didn't need anyone else's help. If she needed something done, I would do it. She only needed to give me the command.

Yet there I was, resisting her orders because I didn't agree. She wasn't backing down either. Her eyes still glistened with unshed tears, and frustration made me pace. I could kill them quickly, just get it over with, eliminate the problem.

But I couldn't disobey her. The idea of doing so repulsed me.

"Fine," I relented. "I'll take them back to the house."

EVERLY

CALLUM CARRIED THE intruders as he followed me to the greenhouse, the woman slung over his shoulder and the demon dragging behind him. His anger made the hairs on my arms stand on end. His eyes bored into the back of my skull, as if he could burrow into my brain and find the answers he sought.

I didn't have an answer; at least not one he'd be satisfied with. Juniper was an enemy, a threat. In his mind, there was only one way to deal with the enemies.

When I reached the foot of the great tree, I turned to him and said, "Leave them here with me. Let me talk to them."

He set Juniper down slowly. A muscle in his jaw ticked as he said, "I'm not leaving you alone with a demon. You can punish me later for disobeying you; I don't fucking care. I'm not leaving him with you."

"Fine. Just don't hurt him."

He looked confused, angry. His breathing became faster and sharper. "You shouldn't be alone with her either. She came here to harm you, Everly."

"We've taken her weapons, Callum. I'm safe in the house, and Darragh is watching."

He scoffed. "Darragh. As if that—" He shook his head. "At the least, take the demon's name. Give yourself a little more protection."

He sounded disgusted, and guilt bubbled inside me like a boiling pot. Part of me wanted to apologize, but for what? I'd done nothing wrong, even though he was frustrated, even though he didn't understand.

But I refused to perpetuate the harm my father had already inflicted on Juniper. I wouldn't carry on his legacy.

"I don't know how."

Callum's face softened, and he looked away from me before he knelt down and grasped the demon's wrists in his own.

"Come over to his side," he said. "Lay your palms against his chest, over his heart."

Crouching, I did as Callum said, but I couldn't bear to look at him as I did. I hated this feeling, this roiling tension.

He'd almost killed Juniper right in front of me. I didn't think he would stop, even though I ordered him to, even though I begged him. I'd felt powerless. Again. Helpless to the forces around me, unable to fight back against the will of others. Just like when I watched my parents cut Juniper, ignoring her cries in that dim, drafty church.

My fingers tingled, numb as cold panic swirled in my stomach.

Callum's hand came to rest gently on top of mine.

"Don't be afraid," he said. "I'm frustrated because I don't understand. I feel your frustration too. Now is not the time for a deeper discussion, but I assure you, I am no less yours than I was an hour ago."

My eyes stung with tears. But his assurance gave me the confidence to proceed. The demon's heart beat against my palm, slow and steady, and I focused on it like I would the ticking of a metronome. Glowing threads in a myriad of colors appeared behind my closed eyes, and I unraveled them like a ball of yarn. They took shape slowly, forming a sigil made of jagged lines.

"Zane," I whispered, and the demon twitched. Callum instantly tightened his hold on him, but the other demon didn't open his eyes.

His sigil stood out starkly in my mind. Part of me felt proud for having accomplished something new. But another part felt as if I'd crossed a boundary. I'd invaded a place where I wasn't welcome.

Callum got to his feet, dragging the demon up over his shoulder.

"If you need me, call," he said. His voice was strained, his mouth drawn down as he glared at Juniper. "I'll be listening."

Then he disappeared with a whisp of smoke.

Taking off my sweater, I folded it up and placed it beneath Juniper's head. Her head felt so heavy in my hand, and when I drew away, blood stained my fingers.

After all these years, she remembered me. She felt such hatred that she pursued me here, bringing weapons, a demon . . .

Callum was right. She meant me harm, she wanted to kill me.

"Why did you come here?" I wrung my hands as I paced in despair. "Why couldn't you just leave me alone?" My throat was swollen with panic, and I choked on my words, sinking into a nearby chair. "I don't want to hurt you. I don't want to hurt anyone."

A soft scent filled the air. When I looked up, a porcelain cup had appeared on the table beside me, filled with steaming tea. Although I couldn't hear her without a radio nearby, I could feel my grandmother's presence, warm and soothing.

"I don't know what to do," I whispered. "I don't know what I can say."

Juniper had come back to Abelaum to enact her revenge. Anger hung around her like a cloud; even unconscious, her bloodlust clung to her with undeniable fierceness. Her life had been destroyed thanks to my family. Only my mother's guilt-ridden betrayal of the Libiri had saved her. But that didn't erase what had happened. It didn't undo the harm.

She deserved her vengeance. Perhaps that meant I deserved to die.

Callum would have a fit if he could have heard me thinking that way.

From deep within the house, I could hear the piano playing. Its tune was light, soothing, intertwining with the birdsong around me. The house was trying to calm me, giving me a gentle song to guide me. Callum's answer to this was violence, and I didn't blame him for that. But maybe I could choose another way.

Juniper stirred, and tension shot up my spine. She groaned as she tried to raise her head, and I said quickly, "Be careful. He was rough with you."

She went still, her eyes widening as she slowly turned them toward me. Her expression was hard, guarded. Her gaze moved over me like a cornered wolf, trying to decide whether she could bite or flee.

"Everly Hadleigh?" Her voice was husky, deeper than when I'd last heard her speak. It gave me a sudden vision of long nights spent in desolate bars, the smell of cigarettes heavy in the air and the taste of whisky on my tongue.

"Everly Laverne, please." My hand shook as I sipped my tea, struggling to maintain eye contact with her. "My father never wanted me to have his name anyway."

Fury rolled off her in a wave as she snapped, "Where's my demon? Where the hell is he?"

"With Callum. He's alive. Callum won't allow him near me, so . . ."

"What the fuck is a Callum?" She got to her feet, her face contorting with pain. Regret that I'd sent Callum away suddenly seized me as I stared at her. She wasn't quite as tall as me, but she was muscular, and her hands were balled into fists.

My fingertips tingled as they grew warm, my arms itching as fire flowed through my veins.

"He's *my* demon," I finally said. "He's the guardian of this place. Of . . . me. I didn't mean for him to be so rough with you. With either of you. But your demon . . . Zane . . . he's fine. I mean . . . they heal quickly."

"Don't you fucking talk about him like it's not a big deal that *your* demon bashed his fucking face in."

Unbidden heat flared in my chest.

"Did you come here to kill me, Juniper Kynes?"

Her answer was obvious before she spoke. Her anger shimmered around her in a red haze. There was a pulse in the air that I could feel in my chest, shocking me with its fury.

In quick, unbidden glimpses, I saw visions of her life. Handfuls of pills and bottles of liquor. Tattoos to cover the scars on her chest. Her brother's pale corpse, wrapped in a sheet. Blood on her hands.

She avoided my question. Instead, she said, "You remember me. You looked terrified when you saw me in Abelaum. You looked like you'd seen a ghost."

A ghost of my past. The specter of my guilt. I said, more to myself than to her, "Memories are far more frightening than ghosts."

Her anger was justified. I envied her for having it, for being furious instead of frightened.

She glared at me. "You want to talk about scary memories? We share one: you, me . . . and your mother. Is she here? Is Heidi Laverne here?"

She yelled, as if hoping my mother would hear her. The red cloud of anger around her grew deeper, darker.

Maybe the truth would comfort her.

"My mother is dead," I said. "Her mistakes . . . I can't apologize for her. An apology probably isn't even what you want to hear. She regretted everything. She tried to make things right."

"She tried to *make things right*?" Juniper shook her head, lip curling in disgust as she charged toward me. "What have *you* done to make things right, Everly? You were there too, hiding in the shadows like a fucking coward!"

She lunged, but she didn't get far. Dangling vines snapped toward her, coiling around her arm and pulling her back. It wasn't my doing; Darragh was watching.

The plants rustled. Even the great tree creaked and groaned. A breeze whispered through my hair, and Darragh said softly, "Say the word, and I'll strangle her, my lady. You don't need to lift a finger."

"Please don't be violent." My hands shook as I grasped my teacup, but I couldn't make myself drink. My stomach was churning. My skin was on fire.

Juniper yelled, "Don't be violent? *Don't be violent?* You listened to me scream for help and did nothing! Was it *fun* for you, Everly? Did it make you happy to see some innocent girl suffer for your God? Did you—"

"I don't serve that God!"

Magic exploded from me in a wave as I raised my voice. One of the greenhouse's glass panes shattered, shards raining down like glittering rain.

Squeezing my eyes shut, I attempted to regulate my breathing. Somehow, I needed to convince Juniper that I wasn't her enemy, and losing control wasn't going to accomplish that. If only she would stop talking, stop blaming me, stop blaming my mother . . .

But she was right.

I couldn't change the past, I couldn't undo the evil my family had inflicted on her. But I also couldn't give her the justice she wanted.

My voice sounded so far away as I said, "I can't make it right. I was supposed to be inspired, that's what they told me. I was supposed to witness something beautiful and be left in awe of God's power."

I'd been petrified as I watched, all my horrified emotions locked up tight. That was the day I lost faith, the day blasphemy took root in my heart.

"All I saw was torture." I was still unable to meet her eyes, although I could feel her glaring at me. "There wasn't a day I could look at my mother after that and not see it. But she's dead. And I am not my mother."

"But you are your father's daughter."

Part of me wanted to laugh. Another wanted to weep. My vision was tunneling, my head throbbing. The magic pent up within me was making my skin itch as my emotions grew more erratic.

"He didn't raise me like them. He raised me, but not *like them*." Not like Victoria and Jeremiah. Not like the children he *wanted*. I was the extra child, the leftover, the mistake.

When I spoke, my voice didn't shake. "He was clear, always, that I was not the daughter he *wanted*; I was only the one he *needed*. I wish I could change it. I wish I hadn't been afraid. I wish I hadn't spent so many years *afraid*."

The teacup exploded. The noise startled me, and even Juniper flinched in surprise. We both stared in silence at the broken porcelain until, finally, I lifted my head and met her eyes.

She was looking at me differently now. As if she finally saw something she could understand. Something to connect us.

"What are you going to do, Everly?" she said. "Turn your demon on me? Or kill me yourself?"

I didn't have the right words to say. An apology wasn't enough. Excuses were a waste of breath, and she deserved better than that anyway.

Slowly, desperately, I said, "I don't want you dead, Juniper. I need you alive. I need you to finish what you set out to do."

CALLUM

MY PATIENCE WAS hanging by the thinnest of threads as I waited, listening intently to the conversation going on in the greenhouse.

The words wouldn't have been difficult to hear if this damn demon would stop talking. One would think being bound in chains and kicked in the face would inspire some silence, but this hellion didn't know when to shut up.

"You got a name?" he said, still talking even with my foot crushing his head against the stone floor. "I mean, since we're just going to sit here and get to know each other . . . I figured . . . an introduction might be nice. So . . . uh . . . I'm Zane."

My irritation rose. At least the voices in the greenhouse had grown calm; the raised tones I'd heard several minutes ago were gone.

Begrudging as I was to admit it, perhaps my witch had been right to spare them. If these two could handle some of the dirty work for us—namely, killing Kent Hadleigh—we'd be better off.

Still, the demon babbled on, "Have you been here long? Odd place, Abelaum. A little Hellish, isn't it? Where's that witch of yours? I mean, I'm assuming she's yours. I don't think a witchling could have summoned a lovely being like you. You two have made a deal, eh? Lucky you, getting a witch's soul. I've heard they're sweet as heaven."

If Everly hadn't ordered me not to, I would have ripped out his tongue for a moment of silence.

"You know nothing of witches, hellion," I said dryly. "You talk too much."

Everly and Juniper had left the greenhouse; their scents were growing closer. It was faint, but even at this distance, I caught a whiff of something that filled me with alarm: blood.

Everly's blood.

Seizing hold of the demon at my feet, I teleported through the halls, following Everly's scent. Her eyes widened when we appeared before her, and Juniper immediately shifted into a defensive stance despite having no weapon except her fists.

There was a tiny cut on Everly's finger, and she swiftly pressed it against the skirt of her dress, trying to hide it from me. "Let him go, Callum," she said. "They won't harm us."

I'd already forgotten about the demon dramatically gasping at my side. Being forced to teleport was certainly a bit discombobulating, but this bastard was playing it up for his woman's sympathy. Leaving him to Juniper's concerned embrace, I went to my witch's side.

She was uncomfortable. Restless. Her tension did not ease as I banded my arm around her, putting my body between her and the intruders. It made me want to hold her tighter, cocoon her within my wings.

She was watching the intruders as they embraced, their relief at being reunited fiercely obvious. The way they clung to each other, and how the woman positioned herself protectively in front of her demon, filled me with a strange melancholy feeling.

To my relief, Everly leaned her head against my side as she said, "Then we have an understanding, don't we, Juniper?"

Juniper faced the two of us with a cold gaze. "I kill the Libiri," she said. "You kill the God. And we stay the hell out of each other's way."

There was no forgiveness or comradery in her voice, but I was still impressed. Perhaps I had doubted Everly too much. I didn't know this woman, but her soul was strong despite being so damaged.

The other demon appeared impressed now too, looking me over with renewed interest. "A God killer, eh? Were you in the wars?"

Tightening my arm around Everly, I said, "I was. I've killed my share of Gods."

"But with an army at your back," he said. He sounded a bit smug for my taste, and it raised my hackles again. "Still so confident when it's just you and the witchling?"

He knew *nothing* of the wars. Like so many demons who had come into being after that time, he took his freedom and safety for granted. The lives of those lost were merely stories told by singers and bards to him, not flesh and blood that had suffered so Hell could be free.

Everly shifted her weight, pressing against me. She laid her palm on my chest. It was a warning—and a re-assurance. It quieted the fury in my head, the restless tingling in my limbs.

Kissing her forehead to reassure her, I said, "I don't need an army, hellion." Then laying my head atop hers, I lowered my voice. "Make them leave."

She bid them farewell, and we saw them out of the house and into the woods. Even after they had vanished from sight, we stood in the yard in silence, unspoken fears passing between us.

"I have angered you," I said, and she looked up at me in alarm.

"I'm not angry," she said, shaking her head at the word. "I'm just . . . all of this is . . . it's so much. I wronged her. She remembers . . ." She gestured toward the woods, where Juniper and her demon had disappeared. "She's going to kill my father, Callum."

Her voice was strangely void of emotion. She took a slow, deep breath in and didn't exhale.

Frowning, I said, "Is that not what you want?"

Still, she held her breath. She held it like it was the last wall between her and whatever invisible battle she fought.

"I never wanted to be the one who would decide if others lived or died," she said.

"That is war, Everly," I said. "It's a cruel thing. As many monsters as it destroys, it also creates."

She turned away with a solemn nod. "You're right. This is war."

IN THE TUNNELS under the coven house, the air was unnervingly still.

Behind me, there was a distant howl of wind, but ahead, nothing. Only the slow, cold drip of water. The smell of rot and mold.

The tunnel was narrow, the dirt soft and muddy. The path ahead had been sealed. A wall of wooden slats barred the way, runes carved into the wood to create protective spells.

But they hadn't been enough.

The planks were splintered, the wall broken. Thick slime clung to the broken slats and mushrooms grew from the wood. I rubbed some of the slime between my fingers, giving it a sniff. It had the odor of rotten fish and blood. Doubtlessly from an Eld creature. This was likely where the beast that had attacked Everly broke through.

Straightening up, I gathered magic around me, crafting it into rope-like braids of aether. The ropes were formed with the intention to protect, creating a formidable barrier the Eld would not be able to breach again so easily.

These tunnels were like a maze, and I'd been exploring for hours. For the past week, Everly and I had been coming down here every day. She would remain in the laboratory, studying Sybil's notes, and I would traverse the tunnels.

It was high time I returned to her.

Back in the laboratory, I could barely see Everly over the piles of books and papers surrounding her. She had conjured several small flames that floated around her, illuminating the handwritten book laid open on the desk. Her eyes were narrowed, and she chewed her lip in concentration.

It amazed me that she could sit in quiet stillness for hours, perfectly focused.

She stretched when I braced my arms against the back of her chair and leaned down, kissing her forehead.

"You've been in here all day," I said. "Studying. Reading." Pressing my face against the nape of her neck, I slowly inhaled. Her scent flooded my brain like the sweetest perfume.

The slightest glance from her—a breath, a word, a fucking giggle—and I was hard, forced to attention, ready to serve however she needed me.

There was a smile in her words as she said, "Is that your way of saying you miss me?"

I nodded. I traced my fingers down her spine, over her silky blouse.

"I do miss you," I mumbled against her neck. "Miss you every second I'm not touching you. Every moment I can't see you." My hands caressed over her, grasping her breasts and squeezing until her breath hitched. "I can hear you constantly, Everly. I hear you sigh when you turn the page . . ." I scratched my nails lightly down her arm, coming to rest on her hand. "I hear your tongue move over your lips as you're thinking. The beat of your heart . . . the chair creaking under you . . . the floorboards bowing when your feet move across them . . . You haunt me."

When I lifted my head, she was smiling at me. Her eyes were red around the edges from long nights spent reading by firelight.

Since her conversation with Juniper, she'd thrown herself into her work. It felt like she was withdrawing from me. Tension lingered between us that I didn't know how to address. In the past, if a fellow demon and I had a disagreement, we would simply fight it out.

Or I would leave. Running away from discomfort was a simple solution.

But I couldn't run from her.

"Have you eaten yet?" I picked up her hand and felt it shake. "What have I told you about neglecting yourself, eh? It's like you're trying to make me punish you."

She giggled as I growled at her, insisting, "I'll take a break! I am getting hungry. But it's so hard to stop." She surveyed the books spread around her, shaking her head in awe. "Sybil's notes are written in code. There's so much of it I can't decipher. But her journals, written in Latin . . ." She grasped one of the books, picking it up excitedly and flipping through the pages. "She was experimenting on flesh samples from the Eld, and from the God Itself. Her research seems to indicate that the Gods aren't carbon-based lifeforms—at least, They weren't in whatever dimension They came from. That's why They have such difficulty surviving on Earth, why it requires so much energy for Them to form physical bodies and move around. But They can imitate fungus. She believed that the God was using mycelial networks to expand the influence of its psychic energy."

She paused, ducking her head shyly. "What? Why are you staring at me?"

"Because you fascinate me," I said. "The sound of your voice. Your enthusiasm for what you study. It's soothing."

She laughed softly. "Kids used to tease me in school for being a know-it-all. I guess it was annoying that I was always the first one to raise my hand for the teacher's questions, or that I spent more time reading than playing outside."

I growled again, but it wasn't playful this time. "And who were these children?"

She shook her head. "Doesn't matter. You're not going to kill them, Callum."

"No." I folded my arms. "I'd merely take their tongues for being nasty to you."

She got to her feet, wrapping her arms around my neck. "Why don't you let my tongue distract you, instead?"

She rose on her tiptoes to kiss me. She tasted like Earl Grey tea and lemon cake, a feast for my senses. It was blasphemy for a creature like me to touch a being as heavenly as her, but I relished the sin.

"What do you say to a little game before lunchtime?" I said as she parted from me. "There will be a reward at the end, if you win."

"What if I lose?"

"That's the best part," I said, lowering my voice to a conspiratorial whisper. "You can't lose, my lady. It's impossible."

She looked confused as I leapt back from her, dancing my way to one of the branching tunnels. She shook her head, laughing when I took her hand and gave her a spin. She didn't know it, but I'd been reading her paperbacks after she went to sleep. The romance novels she would read in the brief spaces of time she wasn't researching or practicing were now my study materials.

These gallant heroes she read about weren't like me. Princes, dukes, and marquesses who could sweep a young woman off her feet with politeness and charm.

I found far more of myself in the villains, the shadowy figures determined to cause death and destruction wherever they went.

But if I was going to be a villain, I would be hers. Her protector in the shadows, her tool of chaos. If I couldn't charm her with poetry and politeness, then I would use the skills I *did* have.

I cupped her chin and peered with her into the darkness. The tunnel stretched ahead, dissolving quickly into shadow, and she gulped against my hand.

"Find your way through the dark," I said. "There are

candles along the way, so light them as you go. When you find the sun, you win."

"It sounds too easy."

"Does it? I wouldn't be so sure."

Her pretty lips curled into a playful smile. "Will you be hunting me?"

"Not this time, darling." I let her go, backing away from her into the tunnel. "This time, you'll be hunting me."

EVERLY

THIS WAS THE first time I had explored the tunnels so deeply.

Callum's laughter led me deeper, calling out to me in warning. "Don't lose yourself in the dark."

Then, silence. The light from Sybil's laboratory was distantly visible behind me, but it provided little illumination. Faintly, I was able to make out a cluster of white candles nearby, so I lit them with a wave of my hand. Onward I went, lighting candles as I found them, and soon, the camp vanished entirely, lost behind me in the maze.

The quiet was unnerving. The tunnels felt oppressively small, the weight of the earth piled above me. But I kept going, following my senses to discover my demon's path. He left no footprints, no marks of his passing.

Instead, I tracked him using the subtle vibrations in the air that he left in his wake.

The slim silver thread that bound our beings together was faintly visible in the dark. It could be seen most clearly when I meditated, but it was visible to me almost all the time now. When Callum was away from me, that thread was pulled taut and tugging, urging me closer.

Rounding a corner of the tunnel, I caught sight of a beam of light cutting through the darkness. The tunnel sloped upward, little green plants clustered thickly around the mouth of the cave. Clambering up the slope, I emerged breathlessly into the forest, smiling widely as I shouted, "I won! Ha! What's my reward?"

But the sight before me took my breath away, and I stared in disbelief.

The narrow cavern opening was in the middle of a meadow between the trees. The grass sloped away from me, toward a stream that trickled over a bed of smooth stones, its pebbly shore coated with dark green moss. Flowers bloomed in the grass, tall and swaying in the breeze, their yellow faces turned toward the sun. Insects flitted through the air, and birdsong filled the trees.

My demon stood waiting for me.

His expression was uncertain, almost embarrassed. At his feet was a large blanket laid across the grass, and on top of that was an open basket. There was a bottle of wine within and covered plates of various foods.

"Perhaps your idea of a reward was a bit different," Callum said, when my stunned silence stretched out. "I was uncertain if you liked red or white wine, so white may have been the wrong choice."

"This was your idea?" I said, and he nodded. "You . . . you made a picnic? For me?" He nodded again.

All I'd done was a simple training exercise, the kind of thing I needed to do every day anyway. It was too easy. What had I done to deserve this?

"Why?"

My question caught him off guard, and he frowned. Yet he still had an answer for me, and with every word my throat got tighter.

"I am not a gentle creature, Everly. I know my flaws; I've lived with them for centuries. I know the places I fall short and I see it in your eyes when I do." He paused, his eyes drifting off to scan the trees around us. Always searching for danger, always ready to defend. "You'll join me, won't you?"

The grass was tall enough to brush the tips of my fingers as I walked over to him, joining him on the blanket. His claws caressed my cheek, his thumb coming to rest at the corner of my mouth as I smiled.

"It kills me to disappoint you," he said. "I would cut off my hands if it would soften me enough to please you."

"You do please me," I whispered, looking at him with a sudden pang in my chest. But I couldn't deny his words. There were times when I looked at him in fear, when I felt overwhelmed by his sheer power and experience. I was merely a twenty-three-year-old witch, and he was an immortal being who'd seen kingdoms rise and fall, who'd watched modern humanity come into being.

Yet, *he* wanted to please *me*.

"I frightened you the other day," he said. "When the intruders came and I attacked them, I did it to defend you. But I still acted without thought as to what you would want, and for that, I'm sincerely sorry."

Shock cascaded over me, swiftly followed by a strange and unexpected panic. "You don't need to apologize. You did what you thought you had to, it's okay, it's—"

His finger pressed against my lips, silencing me.

"I offer you power, and yet when it comes time to relinquish mine, I struggle to do it because I fear what could happen to you. I worry about you, Everly, constantly. Not a minute goes by that I don't think of you. And I would sacrifice my own life to protect you, but I can't make myself into the creature you need."

It ached to see him look so uncertain. I laid my hand on top of his, pressing my face against his palm. Skin-to-skin contact with him felt electric, a current flowing between us.

"Callum, you are *exactly* what I need. When I found you, you were what I needed *most* . . ." My breath caught with unexpected emotion, and I fell silent, ashamed of myself.

"I didn't mean to make you sad." His thumb stroked over my cheek. "I can protect you from harm, but I can't protect you from what you feel. But I can give you shelter to experience the emotions you need to. If you need to speak, I want to listen. I want to understand."

He knelt and pulled me with him. I sat cross-legged, facing him, trying to gather my words. I was accustomed to keeping my feelings locked up, hidden away. If something bothered me, I would simply bear it and move on because there was no other choice. To admit how I felt was too intimate, too . . . honest.

But Callum looked just as uncomfortable as I felt. He knelt before me like he was awaiting something painful. His posture was stiff.

The last time he'd tried to apologize to me, he'd begged me to hurt him. Maybe pain was the only way he knew how to deal with his guilt. But he'd chosen another way this time, and he looked lost.

"When I met you, I was so afraid," I said. "Even now, I still feel so much fear, and *yes*—sometimes I'm afraid of you, Callum. You're larger than life. You're older and stronger than most beings I've ever encountered, and I've been surrounded by monsters every day of my life. But you gave me an opportunity to be brave and a reason to try. If I wanted to escape the monsters, I needed to be saved by one."

Edging closer to him on the blanket, I said, "I need you, Callum, exactly as you are. I don't need you to change. I need you to grow with me."

I'd never been given a clear vision of what romance was supposed to look like, or partnership, or love. It terrified me to even think of those things, to dare put some kind of relationship label upon whatever this was.

But *this*, regardless of what I called it, was special. It was intimate, it was raw. It wasn't something I wanted to change; it was something I wanted to explore, to nurture to see how it would grow.

Callum hesitated for a moment before he brushed his hand against my face. "The violence you've witnessed in your life is no fault of your own. Not your father's violence, or your mother's, or siblings' . . . or mine. But if I can, when this is over, I'll give you a life without violence. That's my promise to you."

Shaking my head with a soft smile, I said, "You've already promised me so much."

"But not enough," he said. "It will not be enough until you are at peace. I found my hope in you and I have no intention of letting that go. So if I anger you, if I frighten you, or make you sad—tell me. Yell at me if you wish, take out your anger if need be. But don't run from me." He leaned forward and rested his forehead against my shoulder before he turned his face, pressing into my neck. "Face me. Teach me. Let me learn how to take care of you."

I was thankful his face was lowered, so he wouldn't see the tears brimming in my eyes.

No one had ever *wanted* to take care of me. I had always been a burden to those around me, an unpleasant but unavoidable responsibility. When I wasn't being ripped between my parents, I was trying to make myself a shadow in Meredith's house to avoid her wrath.

This monstrous being claimed he wanted to keep me . . . protect me . . . *care* for me. The thought of allowing anyone else to take charge of my well-being was terrifying—no wonder Callum was tying himself into knots trying to please me. He saw the constant fear in my eyes, he saw me creeping through life like a hunted rabbit.

My reactions were my own responsibility to manage. As much as he wanted to, he couldn't steal the fear from my eyes or crush the distrust in my heart. I had to do that myself. I had to learn how to care for him too.

"It seems like you've already learned a lot," I said, smiling at him as he raised his head. The tears still lingered in my eyes as I was unable to choke them down, but he swiped his thumb over my cheeks and wiped them away. "Where did the picnic idea come from?"

"I read one of your books," he said and dragged the picnic basket closer. "Many years ago, I was told human women are fascinated by cheese, so of course . . ." He pushed open the basket, allowing me a glimpse at the goodies within. "I brought a variety."

My mouth dropped open at the sheer volume of food he'd brought. It looked like enough to feed an army. A large bottle of wine stuck out of the backside of the basket, and Callum drew it out, using one sharp claw to easily pop the cork.

"Where are the glasses?" I said, peering around in the basket.

"The wine is already in a glass. Why would we need more?"

Why, indeed.

He passed the bottle to me, and I giggled as I lifted the whole thing into the air for a sip. He took out the food, each plate carefully wrapped in a handkerchief. There was a whole roast chicken, a variety of dry sausages and cheese, and a loaf of fresh bread that was still warm as he unwrapped it. There were platters of sliced fruit and cream, roasted vegetables, cold salads. Then came the desserts, which Callum didn't bother to save for the end, but spread before me to pick and choose whatever I wanted.

I swiftly realized this monstrous pile of food wasn't even meant for the both of us; Callum didn't touch any of it except for the sausage, which he nibbled at as if it was an expensive whiskey to be slowly sipped.

"You really don't have to eat food?" I said while layering chicken, cheese, and salad on a thick slice of bread.

"I have no need for it," he said. "I do enjoy the taste of some things, however. Meat and sugar I find to be particularly tempting." He took a piece of chicken and a chunk of lemon cake, popping them both into his mouth and then nodding with pleasure. Despite my certainty that I wouldn't like it, I dared to try the combination anyway and proved myself right.

Callum smirked at my repulsed expression. He pulled me against his chest, resting his back against the massive tree we sat beneath. The position allowed me to lean against him, sprawled between his legs.

"Close your eyes," the demon said, and I obeyed with a little shiver of anticipation. "Open your mouth."

Something sweet and fruity dripped onto my tongue. A slice of fruit touched my lips, and I bit in, giggling as its juices filled my mouth.

"I love peaches," I said, my tongue tingling with sugar as I swallowed. His finger traced along my lip, following my tongue as I licked up the sweetness.

He brought something else close to my mouth. The

scent of strawberry wafted in my nose, and when I took it in my teeth, I groaned contently as I tasted the cream heaped on top.

"Are there fruits in Hell that aren't on Earth?"

"Yes. Many of them," he replied. "Entirely different species than what can be found on Earth. The evolutionary paths of our worlds are very similar, but Hell is infused with so much magic, it led to deviations."

"Mm, what kind of deviations?"

"That's a broad question, darling," he said, but he sounded pleased to be asked, not annoyed. "Where could I even begin? We have massive creatures, some of which are legendary even on Earth. We have species of plants as intelligent as primates. We have plenty of humans, but after a few years in Hell, they're practically indistinguishable from demons, save for their lack of magical abilities. Lacking for most of them, at least."

"There are other witches in Hell?" I said, my eyes popping open with unexpected excitement.

Callum laughed, reaching for a cracker and piece of cheese which I eagerly pointed to. "Yes, of course. Witches and demons have had a long and fraught history with each other. Among demonkind, claiming a witch's soul is the ultimate prize. A rush of power that most demons could only dream of having."

"Lucky you," I teased.

He kissed my neck, teeth and tongue coming to play teasingly close to my ear. "I'm very lucky indeed. I'm going to be completely unbearable when I take you to Hell. I'll be showing you off at every opportunity."

Every time he said such things, it caught me off guard. My cheeks turned hot as Callum's arms tightened around me, a possessively proud embrace that I never wanted to end.

"There's more to your reward," he said. "But you must promise me first that you'll tell me if it isn't right."

Confused but intrigued, I said, "I promise."

He reached for a parcel inside the basket, wrapped in brown paper and secured with twine. Setting it on my lap, he wrapped his arms around me again and rested his chin on my shoulder, clearly eager to watch me open it.

"Oh my God . . . Callum!" As I tore the paper away, I revealed a large leather-bound journal within. But that wasn't all. There were paintbrushes in a variety of shapes and sizes, and tubes of paint in numerous colors.

"I realized that you lost your artwork and tools when you left your father's house," he said. "Your days shouldn't only be spent working and studying. I look forward to seeing your creations."

I shifted around so I could face him, readjusting myself to straddle his lap rather than sit between his legs. A mask had come over his face, perfectly concealing his emotions.

"It's perfect," I said. "I never expected this . . . Thank you."

"I'll gladly continue to defy your expectations."

His eyes widened when I cradled his face in my hands.

"Close your eyes," I said, "and open your mouth."

His gaze darted around: searching the clearing, the

trees, even the sky for any potential threats. Gently, I laid the palm of my hand over his eyes. He drew in his breath sharply, spine straightening, nostrils flaring. But he didn't push me away.

"Relax," I said, remembering how he had talked me down the morning after he claimed my soul, guiding me through every moment of anxiety. "You're safe with me."

Slowly, his fisted hands relaxed, scratching lightly at the grass. His thighs unclenched beneath me, shaking slightly as he let go. He exhaled, a heavy sigh that deflated his chest and shoulders, and leaned against the tree again.

"That's better," I said, keeping my hand in place. Reaching back, I grabbed a piece of sausage and a small slice of a cherry tart. The combination didn't seem tasty to *me*, but I had a suspicion Callum would enjoy it.

Just as I'd hoped, he smiled after I put it into his mouth. Scrunching up my nose at the combination, I grabbed another bizarre duo of foods.

This time, my fingers brushed against his lips as he took it. He kept his eyes closed as I lowered my hand, his arms coming up so he could grip my hips. Taking a sip from the wine bottle, I pressed closer to him, bringing our mouths together. He drank from my mouth like it was a holy fount, messy and desperate, wine dripping from our chins as we parted, and I breathlessly laughed.

He opened his eyes, and they reminded me of the calm quiet depths of the deepest oceans.

"Thank you," he said.

I was quite certain *I* should have been the one thanking

him for going to all this trouble. Looking at him curiously, I said, "For what?"

With a heavy sigh, he closed his eyes again and leaned back. The sun kissed his skin, turning that pale flesh faintly golden. With the soft, airy tone of someone on the verge of sleep, he said, "For giving me peace."

EVERLY

"COME NOW, DARLING, is it really so bad? How would a sensitive little thing like you survive torture, if just a little rope makes you whimper?"

"I didn't—whimper—" I huffed, my chest straining against the ropes and against gravity itself to draw in a breath. "I growled. There's—there's a difference—"

Like a perverted, raven-haired bird, Callum bent his body to the side, turning his head upside down as he looked at me. It was a mockery of my current position: reddened face dangling toward the floor, my body trussed up in ropes as I hung, midair. One leg was extended up behind me, the other bent so my foot rested close to my opposite knee. My arms were bound together behind my back, and even my hair had been pulled into a ponytail and tied.

"You're right; there is a difference," Callum said sagely. "The difference being that growling at your torturer is very naughty." He straightened up, clicking his tongue in disapproval as he snapped his fingers to the music. We were in the piano room, the fire keeping my naked body warm as Frank Sinatra crooned from the record player and the piano magically played along.

Callum caressed his hand up my extended leg until he reached the curve of my buttocks. He patted my cheek like one would affectionately pat a horse, before he whipped his palm down with a sharp, stinging smack.

Sucking in my breath, I hissed, "I can't solve your puzzle if you keep distracting me!"

He circled me, clawed feet falling heavily with every step. "Yes, darling, that's what we dirty demons do. We distract, we redirect, we trick, lie, and corrupt. And I'm afraid that if you don't solve the puzzle, you're doomed to hang here forever. Although that certainly isn't a problem for me." His claws scratched along my thigh, and he kissed the red marks they left behind. "You look beautiful in my ropes."

God, how I longed to dissolve into submission, to beg him for pleasure, to whimper with abandon. Instead, I grit my teeth and tried to concentrate on the wretched puzzle he'd placed beneath me: a silver ball within an enclosed box, holding a maze of tunnels I couldn't see. I had to *sense* the maze within, focusing my magic to guide the ball through to the end.

But focus was nearly impossible when Callum kept touching me.

"I've never encountered a temptation as delicious as you," he said. His nose brushed against my thigh as he inhaled softly, slowly. His hands slid between my bound legs. Every inch of me trembled with tension as the ball rolled aimlessly within the puzzle box. "You smell like heaven."

"Callum—!" My words dissolved with a strangled sound as his forked tongue lapped over my clit. The ball thumped uselessly within the puzzle box as my brain dissolved, pleasure rendering me incapable of guiding it any further.

"Mm, you're failing your task, witch." His words were groaned between my legs. "I'll have to punish you for that."

Holding my breath, I waited for what he would do, but nothing happened. He'd suddenly gone completely still.

"Don't stop," I gasped desperately. "Please, Callum!"

But he darted toward the door. Swinging slightly from the ropes, I tried to look at him upside down. "W-what are you doing?"

He waited at the door, as still as a statue as he listened. "I heard something," he said.

In the space of a few seconds, the ropes dissolved from my body, and Callum caught me before I could hit the ground and turned me right side up, setting me on my feet. Then he was at the door again, head cocked to listen, nostrils flaring as he sniffed.

Dizzied by the sudden movements and still reeling from all the sensations, I immediately sunk into a chair. "What did you hear?"

He held up his finger, and my heart clenched. That look on his face was all too familiar; there was danger nearby. My hands tightened on the arms of the chair, magic rushing through my limbs and immediately bolstering my attention, bringing the world back into focus.

"Who's out there, Callum?" I whispered.

"A demon," he said, his voice soft. He turned his head, his black eyes pinning me with a heavy stare. "Stay here. Wait for me."

He slipped out the door, shutting it quietly behind him. The music kept playing, the piano softening as my worry grew. Callum could handle himself against any adversary; I'd seen him take down Juniper's demon easily. But it had also been a demon—Lucifer—who had separated the two of us, who had been strong enough to take Callum away from me and hold him captive.

What if Lucifer had returned? What if something had pissed him off again and he was here to take Callum?

Springing to my feet, I hurriedly dressed myself. Sybil's grimoire was on a small table nearby; I always kept it close at hand. Slipping it into my pocket, I rushed to the door. For a moment, only the house's usual soft creaks could be heard. But then—

Crack!

The floors shook with the force of the sound, a rush of adrenaline sending me sprinting down the hall. My magic wasn't perfect by any means, but I could summon enough power to cause damage and I wasn't about to allow Callum to be taken from me again.

The very thought filled me with fury as another massive crash shook the house. Doors flew open before me, sparks flying wildly from my fingertips. Pausing to take a deep breath and gather myself, I teleported to the top of the stairway above the foyer.

The entryway was in complete disarray. The tiles and columns were cracked, paintings fallen from the walls, tables and chairs overturned.

"What pretty teeth you have, hellion—"

My breath caught at the sight of Callum's claws tearing into Leon's face. Blood was splattered across the floor, the walls, even the columns. The two demons were locked together, muscles rigid and trembling, Leon's bloody teeth bared in a pained snarl.

"Callum, stop!"

They froze. Callum didn't turn, refusing to give Leon even an inch of room to move. But Leon turned his golden eyes toward me, and his snarl became a grin.

"Hello again, Everly."

MY FIRST THOUGHT was that Leon had been sent after me by my father. But the furious demon swiftly put those fears to rest. He'd come of his own accord, seeking only his sigil from within the grimoire.

His one remaining vulnerability, still tying him to the human world.

But the last time he'd seen me, the grimoire hadn't been in my possession; it had been in Raelynn's.

He'd spent time with her. He admitted as much. He even dared to admit he had feelings for her. It eased some of my fears, because my father would be hesitant to take Rae if he had Leon to contend with.

His sigil was no use to me. Enslaving other lives for my own power was repulsive; it would make me no better than my father, no better than every cruel generation that came before me.

"I'm willing to give you your sigil, Leon," I said. Callum stood protectively behind me, allowing me to take the lead but not taking his eyes off the other demon for even a moment. "But you need to promise me something."

"Demons don't make promises," Leon said quickly. He raised an eyebrow suggestively. "Unless you're trying to make a deal?"

The growl Callum gave in response made adrenaline shoot through my limbs. Reaching back, I immediately grasped his arm, pulling myself closer to his side and focusing my intentions toward him. *I'm yours and you know it. Body and soul, my demon. Don't be afraid.*

The tension eased out of him.

"I need you to keep Raelynn alive," I said, speaking to Leon but stroking my hand over Callum's chest to reassure him. "Time is running out. The Deep One is restless, and my father knows it. If he gets Raelynn, then I . . . I might not be able to kill the God."

A boisterous laugh escaped from Leon. "You— What? You're trying to kill the God? You can't be—"

"She means it. I've been alive long enough to see Gods die, hellion," Callum said, his voice harsh. "They're not above death."

Leon was still staring at me as if I'd declared I was going to fly to the moon and live there.

Taking the grimoire from my pocket, I flipped through the pages, searching for his sigil as I said, "I'm going to put an end to all this. The Deep One never should have been awoken, and It never should be freed."

At last, I flipped to the page with his mark upon it. Sybil had called him "The Killer": a demon who was known to destroy every summoner who'd ever attempted to enslave him.

Until Morpheus Leighman. Until generations of my family kept him bound in servitude, unable to leave, unable to fight back.

Carefully, I tore out the page and held it up.

There was more I wanted to say before he took his name and ran. "You say you *think* you love her, but it's clear that you do. It was clear the moment Kent told you to take her."

Leon looked away, but there was a softness in him I hadn't seen before, a crack in his viciousness.

"I'll do what I can," he finally said. "But I'm not a guard dog."

"You don't hide your feelings for the human woman very well," Callum drawled. He sighed as he turned to me, as if the entire situation was now horrendously boring and he couldn't bother to look at Leon for another second. Nuzzling close to my side, arms wrapping possessively around me, he lowered his voice and said, "He'll protect her. Send him off. I want to continue our game."

Our game. I'd nearly forgotten what we were up to right before Leon made his unannounced entrance. Hurriedly, I held out the torn page in offering, and Leon snatched it from my hands as if he thought I'd take it back at any second.

For a long moment, he simply stared at it, clawed fingers tightening on the page. How much of his life had he lived in constant fear of being summoned up until now?

Without another word, he folded the paper and tucked it into his pocket. He turned away, strode to the front door, and slipped outside.

"He's *obsessed* with that woman," Callum said, and I looked up at him in surprise. "Your father isn't going to have any easy time getting to his sacrifice with that young demon in his way."

He cracked his neck, rubbing his cheek where only minutes ago, Leon had sliced him open. The wound was completely healed now with only a faint red mark remaining.

"Haven't had a fight that good in a while," he said. "Got me worked up."

Suddenly, he lifted me off my feet and slung me over his shoulder, heading for the stairs as I shrieked in surprise.

"I need to build a wall around this place," he huffed. When he raised his voice, the house itself shook, and I laughed. "No more goddamn intruders while I'm fucking my witch!"

He was vibrating with unspent energy. We didn't even reach the bedroom before he was tearing my clothes off again. He slammed me against the wall at the top of the stairs, ripping so ravenously through my clothing that he left scratches across my chest.

"That hellion dared suggest making a deal with you . . ." He snarled, and gripped my hair to pull my head back as he kissed me. His forked tongue probed deep into my mouth and my knees went weak.

He drew back, mere centimeters from me. "My bloodlust isn't quenched yet darling. I want him to hear you scream my name as he flees this place. I want him to have no doubt of exactly . . . who . . . you . . . belong to."

He paused, staring at the scratches he'd given me. His grin spread, widening as he lowered his head. He licked the blood from my skin, eyes fluttering closed in ecstasy when I groaned.

He seized me again, flying me back to the bedroom so quickly I was dizzied. He pinned me to the floor, one hand around my throat as the other plunged between my legs.

"Callum! Oh my—God—"

"That's it, darling." I writhed on his fingers as he pumped them into me, panting with unbridled need. "You're mine. Mine to use. To fuck. To breed as I wish."

Tingles exploded over my entire body.

He got up suddenly, but I had no time to move. Ropes coiled around me, binding me tightly and dragging me into the air. I hung upside down, suspended, spinning slowly. With every rotation, Callum was closer, but I never saw him move.

The shadows were elongating, the room darkening. The fire shrunk down to smoldering embers. Callum was wrapped in darkness, a shroud of black mist enveloping him. It reminded me of how he'd looked in the woods when he'd gone after Juniper and Zane.

Finally, he stood next to me. He braced his hand against my leg to stop my spinning, and goose bumps exploded over my skin. There was a dangerous glint in his eyes as he peered down at me.

"I should stop feeding you that wretched tea," he snarled. He was referring to the birth control mixture I chugged down whenever he came inside me. My stomach was quivering, heat growing inside me. "I want to fuck you full of my seed and knock you up."

He caressed my belly, tracing the scarred lines of his sigil. For a moment, I dared to imagine myself swollen with child. The scars of our bond would cover my rounded stomach like a ward, allowing there to be no doubt that I was protected. Loved. Wanted.

It was only a fantasy. An impossible one, surely.

Callum stroked his hands along my inner thighs, squeezing my flesh. A throttled sound escaped my throat. The ropes held my legs slightly parted, so I could do nothing as he brought his mouth close to my core. His forked tongue extended, swirling deliciously around my clit until my legs were violently shaking.

"Callum, please! Please, that feels so—so good—I—"

"Are you going to come for me already? Mm, I can't allow that yet."

The ropes tugged, repositioning me. My arms were pulled behind my back, my chest drawn up so my stomach faced the floor. Another rope snaked around my head, pressing between my teeth like a gag and pulling my head up.

It was a strenuous position, similar to a hogtie. My

legs were still spread, my pussy at the perfect height for him to sink his cock into me if he wished.

His claws traced over my ass. Gently, at first, but then he dug in. His claws pierced me as he held my cheeks apart and plunged his tongue into me. Licking, sucking, and probing until I squealed, struggling helplessly. My teeth were clenched around the rope, my noises muffled.

"Scream for me, darling," he said, and pressed his tongue deep inside my pussy. My muscles squeezed desperately around him, my abdomen pulsating with pleasure. "Let Leon hear exactly what he interrupted."

Delicious humiliation washed over me. Not even embarrassment could keep me quiet. I cried his name, almost weeping with the desire to come. But he refused to let me tip over the edge. He would bring me close, then dig in his claws and drag me back.

The room was too dark to see anything more than vague shapes. Even the fire's embers were gone. The ropes wouldn't allow me to look back, but I knew that if I did, I would find Callum completely wrapped in darkness, a shadow brought to life.

"Mm, I can taste your fear," he crooned, claws scratching down my back. "And it so very good."

My legs were suddenly released, dangling toward the ground while my chest remained entwined in rope. Callum grasped my hips, and the head of his cock pressed between my legs. He rubbed himself teasingly over my clit, the ridges on his shaft making my toes curl with stimulation.

"You're going to come on my cock," he said. I cried out as he sheathed himself fully inside, my muscles clenching sporadically with the massive stretch. "You're going to come—dripping, screaming, and begging for more."

He drew back and slammed forward, and I saw stars. Saliva had collected around the rope in my mouth, and it dripped down my chin as I groaned. I was so close—so painfully close. The drag and pull of his cock had me gasping and clenching around him.

I tried to speak around the gag, tried to cry his name and tell him I couldn't hold back anymore, but all that came out were muffled whimpers. Ecstasy filled me, my body throbbing around him as I came. Mind-numbing heat washed over me, sparks flickering around me.

"Only you could take me so perfectly," he said. Every thrust was punishing, and I was lost in the sensation. Limp and moaning with abandon.

His cock swelled as he came inside me, pumping me full. I could *feel* the heat of it.

He pulled out with a groan. I was limp and trembling as he spread my cheeks, his cum dripping out of me. My thighs were sticky with it.

"That's beautiful," he murmured. Shaking, I moaned with overstimulation as he pumped his fingers into me. "So full. Warm and shaking. Just how I like you."

The ropes vanished slowly, allowing me to fall gently into his arms. He sank with me to the floor, cradling me, massaging me. He kissed my head as my aching body melted into him, whispering the sweetest nothings in my ear as I floated in the afterglow.

CALLUM

EVERLY WAS SEATED between my legs, hunched over Sybil's encoded notes like a gremlin. It was no wonder the poor girl's back was always hurting. I'd sheathed my claws so I could massage her, working my palms over her tight shoulders, inspiring the occasional contented sigh.

It was really just an excuse to touch her.

"You're ridiculously sexy when you indulge your sadism, you know that?" I said, and she chuckled as she glanced back at me.

"What makes you say that?"

"When you threatened that hellion yesterday. Very bold of you, darling. I thought you'd be scared of him."

"I mean, I am. Or was," she added quickly. "It's not really Leon's fault. He deserved his sigil back."

Her face tightened for a moment as guilt seeped into her veins, and I caught her chin before she could turn away. "It's not your fault either, that you need to protect yourself."

She smiled, nodding against my hand. "I know. I used to think . . . well . . ." She did turn away from me this time, her voice fading away. But I nudged her to continue, and she said, "I used to think that if I could just get away from my family, I'd never have to hurt anyone again. I'd never be . . . a threat . . . to anyone again." She pulled in her lips, pressing them tightly between her teeth. "But that was naive. Even if I hide myself away, people still think I'm a threat to them. So, I guess I am. If they want me to be dangerous, I will be."

"You are dangerous because you must be." I kissed the back of her neck. "The danger in you protects your gentle heart. And I adore that about you."

She turned and kissed me, pressing her body close to mine. Her fingers wrapped around the nape of my neck, caressing my skin. I wanted to toss that wretched book away from her and keep her attention for myself.

But of course, ever studious Everly would not be distracted for long.

"I'm trying to be good," she said, breaking away from my mouth and giggling when I chased after her. She settled between my legs again, pulling the notes back onto her lap. "You're so distracting. It drives me mad to be near you, without . . ." She trailed off, but her body did the talking. Her butt was pressed firmly against me, so when she gyrated her hips, I felt it intimately. My arms snapped tighter around her like a vise, and I muffled a snarl against her neck as I thrust against her.

"Without touching, I know," I finished for her. "It's torture not to fuck you. Can't you read and fuck at the same time?"

She gave me a smile that said she didn't truly mind seeing me tortured. It made me feel like an animal, salivating and desperate, a slave to my baser instincts.

A slave to her. To her whims and desires, whatever they may be. Whether it required me to top or bottom, I frankly didn't care. I aimed to please.

"Poor thing," she said, all mocking sweetness as she kept grinding her ass back against me. "But I need to concentrate. This language, this *code* . . ." She glared at the book as if it had offended her. "It makes me want to rip my hair out."

Peering over her shoulder at the lines of text, I narrowed my eyes at the strange markings. They didn't mean a damn thing to me.

"Can't demons understand all languages?" she said, and I shook my head.

"We can learn any language, and very quickly," I said. "But we need a fluent point of reference. That journal has me just as confused as you."

She groaned in despair, rubbing her head. She was so certain Sybil had discovered something important; even I suspected it, if I was to judge by the other bits of information we'd managed to glean. The old witch had been testing the reactions of various poisons on the flesh of the God. She'd been infusing weapons with experimental spell work, trying to figure out how to destroy the Gods from the inside out.

In all my years of fighting those creatures, I'd never found a hidden weapon or shortcut to Their undoing. They died as any other creature did, by slowly and relentlessly being worn down, injured, bled out, and ripped apart. Although They couldn't move around very well, Their flesh was incredibly strong and They could heal themselves swiftly. In all my years of hunting Them, I'd been fortunate to only encounter incredibly weak ones.

At least, until the Deep One. Even as weak as It was, It was still the most powerful God I'd encountered on Earth.

Whether or not my and Everly's combined power could take It down, I wasn't sure. Everly had no issue conjuring massive amounts of magic, and that gave me hope. But the reality was her grandmother didn't have time to give her the proper, thorough education befitting a witch like her. We were racing against time, trying to teach her all we could before we had to face the God.

Before the Libiri managed to offer another sacrifice.

Discovering Sybil's secret weapon could give us the upper hand. The engraving on the great tree in the greenhouse was Everly's only clue, an incomplete Rosetta Stone that she frequently referenced as she attempted her translation.

She sighed heavily, getting to her feet. "This isn't working. I'm going to go to the greenhouse for a while and try to meditate. My brain doesn't want to work anymore." She pouted her lip, looking down at me pleadingly. "Will you bring me tea?"

"And peach cake?" I offered, to which she excitedly nodded.

I headed to the kitchen as she teleported to the greenhouse. The radio was there on the table, Winona humming pleasantly as a watering can hovered over the herbs in the window box.

"Any luck with the old Grand Mistress's code?" she said, and I shook my head.

"Unfortunately not. Everly's gone to the greenhouse to clear her mind. She's exhausted."

A kettle was already steaming on the stove, the house having anticipated Everly's needs perfectly. There was a peach cake sitting on the countertop beneath a glass dome, and I took a slice for her before taking down several tins of tea and herbs. Her preference in tea depended upon her mood and the time of day. Earl Gray with a little milk and sugar in the morning when it was rainy outside, green tea with lemon if it was sunny. Black tea with cinnamon and clove if she planned on a late night in the library, chamomile and lavender with cream when she needed sleep.

Today called for something mild but sweet. Something that would awaken her mind but soothe her body.

Winona had been prattling away at me, although I didn't hear a word she said until she gave a soft laugh. "Well, I certainly never thought I'd see it."

Placing Everly's tea and cake on a tray, I glanced back at the radio. "See what?"

"An Archdemon serving tea to a witch." She chuckled. "My ancestors would never believe it."

Waving her off, I said, "You're not the only ghost in this house; just the loudest. The other old biddies watch in silence, but they do *watch*. They have no choice but to believe it."

The scent of rain greeted me as I stepped outside, headed toward the greenhouse.

"Ah, there you are!" The Woodsprie's face appeared from his tree, his expression perturbed. "Your witch is being strange."

Glaring at him, I said, "What do you mean?"

"Well, I thought she fell asleep," he said. "But she's . . . talking."

Alarmed, I quickly made my way inside. Everly's mind could sometimes drift when she meditated, wandering a bit too close to the Veil. But I'd watched her meditate many times now, and even when she had violent visions, she had not spoken aloud.

Before I saw her, I could hear her. She was whispering rapidly, the words running frantically together. Rounding a planter, I found her kneeling before the great tree, one hand extended, her palm flat against the tree's runic inscription.

I felt no emotion from her. When I reached for her mind, all I encountered was a cold void, like a breath of wind from a long-forgotten tomb.

Setting the tray aside, I knelt next to her. Her eyes were not closed; they were half-lidded and rolled back, only the whites visible. Her lips were moving, whispering, "Call his name, offering of sweetness, liquor and pain . . ."

"Everly?"

She didn't even flinch. Her lips kept moving, the whispers coming faster, "Blood of the dead, resentfully taken. Blood of the lover, willingly sacrificed. Bond made in feral night to call his name. Offer him sweetness, liquor, and pain."

Every time she said it, the words grew faster. Her arm trembled as it lay against the tree. In her opposite hand, clenched into her fist, were Sybil's encoded notes.

"Blood of the lover," she kept murmuring. "Willingly sacrificed—"

"Everly!" Grasping her shoulders, I wrenched her upright, and she screamed, thrashing against me. Her heart was pounding too hard, dangerously fast, while her body temperature had dropped frighteningly low. "Calm down, you're alright, darling. I'm here. Sshh."

She struggled for another moment before she went limp. Her chest was heaving, ragged, panting breaths wheezing out of her.

"Callum?" Her voice shook in terror. She grasped my arms, held tight against her chest. "I read it, Callum. I read it. I saw her write it."

"Take a deep breath," I said, stroking her hair. "Let your mind settle before you speak."

She clung to me as she shook. As I rubbed her arms, her back, her neck, the tremors finally stopped.

Her voice was hoarse as she said, "I can read the code. I had a vision of Sybil. I heard her speak. I know what we have to do."

EVERLY

"BLOOD OF THE dead, resentfully taken. Blood of the lover, willingly sacrificed. Bond made in feral night to call his name. Offer him sweetness, liquor, and pain. Hmmm."

Grams made a sound as if she was clicking her tongue, then the radio fell silent as she continued to think. We were in the greenhouse, Callum and I seated on the ground before the great tree, with the radio close by. My body was no longer trembling, not after I'd ravenously eaten the cake Callum had brought me, but my mind still felt hazy.

My vision of Sybil had felt so clear, so real. My hands had been hers and I could see through her eyes. Looking at her encoded language now, I still couldn't understand it any better than I had before. All I had was this persistent certainty that the words swirling around in my head were the ones I needed.

"I saw a knife in my vision," I said. "There was magic around it; the blade didn't reflect any light."

My grandmother hummed again. If a ghost had feet, hers would have been pacing. "I see. It would seem these are instructions for a ritual, doubtlessly intended to imbue a weapon with magical power. This is dark, dangerous magic; its use of blood makes that clear. *Feral night* and *to call his name* . . . now what could that mean?"

"Perhaps the night of a full moon," Callum suggested.

Suddenly, laughter rang out all around us, the plants shivering and shaking as Darragh appeared from the leaves. He burrowed up out of the ground, thin roots writhing around him.

"It's Halloween, you silly demon," he said, to which Callum growled. "That's what we fae call it. The Feral Night. When the Veil is thinnest, when all the strange worlds of this dimension come close enough to touch. And *to call his name*, that part is obvious as well. Who else would be summoned by sugar, alcohol, and pain?"

"Stop speaking in riddles!" Callum snapped, but at the same moment, Winona gasped.

"Of course!" she said. "I should have known. Sybil was referring to the fae king, the Lord of the Forest! Such offerings would be made when seeking his blessing."

"The Old Man himself," Darragh chuckled, the sound like rattling leaves. "You witches play dangerous games, making bargains with demons *and* the fae."

"It is *not* a bargain," my grandmother said firmly, the radio crackling. "That must be very clear, Everly. You are not making a bargain; you are beseeching him for a blessing." There was another crackle that sounded like a sigh. "As for *the blood of the dead, resentfully given* . . ."

"My father," I said, ignoring the way my stomach churned. "Juniper is going to kill him on Halloween. He would resent his blood being used for this." I swallowed hard, the taste of bile in my throat. "No one else should have to die."

There was a moment of silence, and I was thankful for Callum's hand on my back. Since Juniper had left, I'd done everything I could not to dwell on what she had to do. My father deserved what was coming to him.

But thinking about it made my chest feel hollow and cold.

Darragh rustled his branches, breaking the silence. "What about the blood of a lover then?" He waggled his leafy eyebrows. "I don't exactly have blood in the traditional sense, but I'm happy to offer—"

"Darragh." Callum's voice was dry, his lips pressed into a thin line. "Stop talking." His wing wrapped protectively around me. "I will sacrifice whatever you need."

"Then it's settled," Winona said. "We wait for Halloween night and make our attempt. You will need a weapon upon which to perform this ritual; Callum, perhaps you could search the old armory. I'm sure there's still many fine blades in there."

Staring at the radio in surprise, I said, "This house has an *armory*?" I'd explored many of the twisting halls and locked rooms over the past few weeks, but with every passing day, there was even more to discover.

"Naturally," my grandmother said. "The coven needed to defend themselves, and some preferred the sturdiness of a sword over magic. There are very few creatures that cannot be killed with steel and iron."

"There's something I still don't understand," I said with a frown. "An offering of sweetness and liquor is obvious, but an offering of pain? What does that mean?"

"It's a mating ritual," Callum said, his voice rumbling against my back as he pulled me closer. "Sex can conjure highly potent magic; the more heightened the sensations, the more powerful the magic. Pleasure and pain, as you know, can be very intense."

His claws scratched down my back, making me shiver, and my grandmother coughed loudly. "Well then! I'll be off before you two decide to start practicing. You too, Darragh! Come, we'll prune the rose bushes in the garden together."

Darragh sighed as if he was being terribly put out, but said dutifully before vanishing, "Yes, Grandmother."

Leaning back against Callum's chest, I stared at the boughs of the tree above, watching the colorful finches as they flew. His claws stroked over my arm, both his wings now drawn around me. Within them, I felt safe.

"Do you think it will work?"

"We won't know until we try," he said. "And it's always worth it to try."

My fingers tightened on his arm, my mind spinning in endless circles from everything I'd learned. "What if I'm not strong enough? Sybil was a Grand Mistress when she attempted this ritual. I'm nowhere near that."

"She entrusted you with her knowledge. Her spirit lingers in this house, although we cannot hear her. Would a Grand Mistress give you something you weren't ready for?"

"I don't know. Maybe she thinks I'm stronger than I am."

His claws scratched lightly over my scalp, and he gripped my hair, tugging it lightly. "If she does not doubt you, you shouldn't doubt yourself either. Regardless of whether the ritual works, whether we go into battle with a blessed weapon or not, your strength is a force the God fears. Don't forget that." He nuzzled against my neck and kissed me softly before playfully nipping my skin. "A powerful being from another world *fears you*. It has tried everything in Its power to destroy you, to keep you weak. But you are not weak, my lady."

A little red finch came to perch near my hand, chirping. It fluttered its wings and flew away, effortless in its flight. If only I had as much confidence to rise, to soar without a second thought.

"You must get tired of my worries," I said. "Of making the same reassurances day after day."

My demon growled. "Do I think I grow tired of embracing you? Holding you? Fucking you?" I shook my head, smiling at how tightly he gripped me. "Then why would I ever be tired of assuring you? When I can use mere words to make you smile, to give you joy. Why would I ever tire of that?"

My chest felt so warm. It ached in a way I never wanted to end.

40

EVERLY

THE AIR SMELLED of charred frankincense and pungent cinnamon. Smoke drifted before my half-lidded eyes as I inhaled, filling my lungs until they ached.

Distantly, a clock ticked. It was my lifeline, the measure by which I knew I was still alive and not merely a ghost drifting through the Betwixt.

The Veil was thin. Midnight was approaching.

There were whispers all around me. Some kind, some cruel. My vision was little more than a haze of white smoke, and the edges of my limbs felt fuzzy, almost incorporeal.

Tick, tick, tick. A countdown. But where it started, and when it would end, I had no idea.

The wolf was coming.

When I stretched out my mind, I could sense my father's energy. It presented itself to me like a bad taste in my mouth, a smell in my nostrils that made my stomach twist with anxiety.

Callum was close. In reality, where my body sat still and silent like an empty husk, he wouldn't take his eyes off me for even a moment.

If something went wrong, he would know. He would guide me back.

Tick, tick, tick.

The scent of blood flooded my nose. The wolf had arrived.

My father's energy churned, like the air before a storm. I sensed anger. *Rage.* It bubbled up inside me, like a pot boiling over. *Hatred.* It sunk its claws into my skin, it ripped and tore at my chest like a predator trying to force its way out.

With a sharp gasp, my eyes flew open. The world twisted and spun, and I slumped to the side. But Callum's arms swiftly wrapped around me from behind, holding me tight, squeezing me as I came back to reality.

"Deep breaths, darling. You're alright."

It was several moments before I could control my tongue enough to speak. And when I did, all I managed to choke out was, "He's dead. She did it. He's finally dead."

MY FATHER WAS barely recognizable.

His skin had a gray pallor, with a hardened sheen like porcelain. He was lying at a strange angle in the little garden shed outside his house, slumped against the wall, body broken. Blood had pooled beneath him, sinking slowly into the concrete floor. His glassy eyes stared into nothingness.

A pistol was in his hand. A weak attempt at making this look like a suicide. But a shot to the head didn't break one's legs in multiple places.

As the metallic stench of blood filled my nose, I felt as if I had stepped outside my body and was drifting through the Betwixt again. There but not there. Body and mind gone numb.

I withdrew a syringe from my pocket.

"Are you alright, Everly?" Callum's voice seemed far away. It shook the silence of the night, even though he spoke softly. The distant sounds of a party drifted through the air from the house—my family's house. Doubtlessly, Victoria and Jeremiah didn't even know our father was dead yet.

But when they did . . . when they discovered this . . .

All hell would break loose. Without Kent's careful control, no one within the Libiri was safe.

"I'm fine," I said. It felt like a lie as it rolled off my tongue, and I frowned. This wasn't sadness coursing through me, it wasn't regret. There were no tears in my eyes and no tightness in my chest. Before I could think too hard about it, I jabbed the syringe into my father's leg and pulled the plunger back, filling it with his blood.

"It feels appropriate that the man who wanted to free the God most will help make the weapon to kill It," I said.

After capping the syringe and tucking it into my bag, I hesitated to leave. If I was going to say good-bye, now would be the time. My father was gone, but his legacy was not. My thoughts kept swirling, round and round like water being sucked down a drain. I thought of all the cruel things he'd said to me. All the times he'd turned his back when he knew how Meredith was treating me. How he manipulated my mother, his children, his wife.

Surely, there was something good. A memory I could hold on to. Like the day when, as a child, he'd taken me to the pier at Pike Place Market. Just the two of us. We took the ferry across the lake, got ice cream cones and walked together through the bustling market. He took a photo of me sitting on top of Rachel the golden piggy bank, and there was a brief period of time where the photo was framed in his office.

But there were no more photos of me in the house when I left. Childhood memories, high school dances, accomplishments big and small—everything I did was forgotten. Inconsequential.

Maybe he loved me once. Maybe he tried.

Maybe I'd only ever been a means to an end.

That was close enough to a good-bye. If I had barely been his daughter, then he had barely been my father, too.

Callum was waiting for me outside the shed. Leaning my head against his shoulder as I came to stand beside him, I listened to the distant music emanating from the house. Victoria had been throwing those parties every Halloween for years, but I'd stopped attending after the last time she'd used the occasion to play a nasty trick on me.

Things were so different this year. In the space of just a few months, my entire life had been turned on its head. Everything had changed. *I* had changed.

"We should go back," I said. "We need to complete the ritual tonight."

"As my lady wishes." His arm wrapped around my shoulders. We weren't far from the house, and he was keeping a careful eye out for anyone snooping around. Juniper and Zane had already left, disappearing into the night once the deed was done.

"Do you grieve for him?" he said.

"No. I've spent most of my life grieving for him. Wondering why he didn't love me. Why I wasn't enough. Wondering how he could possibly look at his family, his children, like we were all just assets for his mission." Part of me wanted to cry. But those tears were behind a wall I couldn't seem to break down. "But I think my grandfather treated him the same way. And my great-grandfather before that."

Taking a deep breath of the crisp night air, a strange but comforting feeling washed over me. The magic in the air had shifted and the rot that infected this place had shrunk, if only a little. We were standing upon a precipice, our toes moving ever closer to the edge.

Either the edge would crumble beneath our feet, or we would leap into the unknown. But the events set in motion could not be undone.

"This family has been cursed for six generations," I said. "Passed down from parent to child, every generation sowing the same rotten seeds. But I'll break it. It ends with me."

CALLUM

IN THE DARK of night, my witch shone brighter than the moon. Her magic glittered around her like stars fallen to Earth, an aura of power that grew stronger every day.

She led me through the forest, following Darragh's sprouting flowers as he guided us, a flickering flame in her palm lighting our way.

"There's no guarantee the Old Man will show himself," the Woodsprie had warned us earlier that night. "I wasn't here when Sybil beseeched him previously, and I've never spoken to him myself. But he's been watching you, Everly. That much I know. I'll lead you to one of his haunts, but from there, it's up to you."

Had I been a younger demon, I would have balked at the very idea of beseeching a fae to help us. One couldn't trust those tricksters any further than you could throw them. But any power we could gain over the God, regardless of its source, was worth pursuing.

White flowers bloomed along the path before us, glowing faintly in the night. Spiderwebs glistened with droplets of dew, strewn across the flora like threads of jewels. Frogs croaked, the crickets chirped their song. Eld beasts watched us from a distance, their white eyes like tiny pale moons between the trees. They didn't dare approach.

With the aid of her grandmother, over the past few weeks, Everly had turned nearly all her focus to the study of ritual magic to prepare for this. She'd spent hours in meditation, honing her concentration, reading books of spell craft late into the night. She was pushing herself hard, determined that our attempt couldn't fail.

Her feet were bare, leaving soft imprints in the soil as she followed Darragh's path. She said she could feel the forest better that way, with her bare skin against dirt. The path sloped down, and branches pulled at her clothes as she squeezed through thick brambles and pushed low-hanging branches aside.

We emerged into a narrow ravine, the walls of which were completely overgrown with ferns and thick creeping plant life. The ground was soft, a thin stream trickling over the rocks nearby. Overhead was a clearing in the trees, allowing the meager light of the moon to shine through the drifting clouds. Darragh's flowers encircled us before wilting away, and Everly's eyes met mine.

Her pupils caught the moon's reflection, an opalescent

glow filling them as she said, "We need a fire, as big as we can make it."

As she cleared a space in the dirt, I collected kindling from fallen trees, snapping their branches and clawing pieces of wood from their trunks. We built a pyre, and Everly withdrew a knife from her bag. It was a well-made blade, light enough for her to wield but sturdy and deadly sharp.

She took out the syringe, filled with her father's blood. Pulling out the plunger, she carefully poured the liquid over the knife.

"The flames will cleanse the blade," she said, speaking low. Her words weren't for me; she was crafting her magic, speaking it into existence, weaving intent and power into action. "Any negative energy attached to this weapon will be burned away. Any curse placed upon it will be destroyed."

She placed the bloodied knife upon the pyre and stepped back, and I stood close behind her, my hands encircling her waist. Holding her was like cradling a spark, shocking and deceivingly delicate. She could disappear in an instant or flare to life like wildfire.

I held her with reverence, with care. As one would hold a holy artifact, subdued but awesome in its power.

She held her arms wide, and the pyre caught fire. The flames roared high above our heads, licking the night sky, twigs snapping and sap crackling. She circled the fire, reaching into her bag for a small handful of herbs that she tossed into the flames. A bitter, earthy scent wafted from the smoke as she murmured, describing a blade that was unbreakable, the sharpness of which would never fade. A blade that would imbue its carrier with bloodlust, with viciousness, with unshakeable bravery. A weapon that could penetrate any substance, that would cause pain and destruction for any being it was turned against.

Everly's eyes still held that opalescent glow, her expression focused but distant. She'd been meditating for most of the day. Even now, she had only one foot in the realm of the living.

As the blade reddened in the flames, Everly turned her back to the heat and faced the forest. She knelt on the ground, and as I stood over her like a sentry, she took a parcel wrapped in string and wax paper from her bag.

A small cake was within, drenched with honey. She set it upon a flat stone, then took out a jar of cream, and another of mead. She unsealed them and set them out.

"An invitation," she whispered. She sipped the sweet cream, and I was mesmerized by the thick white liquid as it slid from her lip. Kneeling beside her, I caught the drip with my tongue.

She responded to me instantly, her head tipping back so I could continue to kiss and lick her neck. Using the sharp inner edge of my claws, I cut the buttons on her blouse one by one, laying her bare.

"An offering," she said and brought the jar of mead to her lips before she lifted it to mine. It was sweet and slightly sparkling, flowers and honey coating my tongue.

She rose up on her knees, bringing our mouths together. She kissed me, her tongue tangled with mine as she moaned into my mouth. Tasting, probing, lavishly consuming. I seized her tightly, barely resisting the desire to rip the rest of her clothes off.

Sweet offerings weren't enough to draw out the fae lord. He needed something even more delicious to be coaxed into showing himself.

Something as delicious as my witch, as she shrugged her loose blouse off her shoulders and it fluttered to the ground. Her breasts were bare, her nipples pebbling in the cold night air as she stood. She unraveled the tie on her wrapped skirt, allowing the soft fabric to pool around her ankles.

She looked even more rapturous, even more powerful, standing naked before me. My eyes traced the lines of her scars, both the ones I'd given her, and the ones that had come before me. Leaning my head forward, I rested my cheek against her thigh, close enough to the apex of her legs that the soft, curly hair covering her pubic mound brushed against my nose. The scent of her was all-consuming, my mouth salivating with desire for her.

The mead was enchanted, crafted specifically for swift inebriation. It was a delicate balance as Everly took another small sip, walking the line between maintaining her sobriety and getting tipsy enough to sink into revelry.

There were few things fae liked as much as a party. Why would anyone show up if no alcohol was being consumed, if no indulgences were taken?

Everly swayed as she took another sip. She tipped the jar and allowed the honeyed liquor to trickle down her body. I caught it with my tongue, and followed the sugary trail up her thigh, her stomach, her breasts, until I captured her mouth with mine.

Her fingers splayed over my chest, her nails leaving red lines as she dragged them down my skin. I intended to make sure the entire forest heard her ecstasy. If the old fae wouldn't appear unless we gave him a show, we'd give him a proper fucking *show*.

Everly's feet left the ground as I scooped her into my arms. Her legs and arms wrapped around me—possessive, eager. Her nails dragged between my wings, and I shivered from head to foot, a low growl rumbling from my chest. She buried her face against my neck, her lips brushing tenderly over my skin. Her tongue traced my jaw, and when she reached my ear, she whispered, "Back on your knees, demon. Let me see what's mine."

Fuck, I loved that tone. Tugging my trousers down and tossing them away, I sank to my knees and gazed up at her. My cock throbbed, standing rigidly at attention as she touched my face. She brought the mead to my lips so I could drink, then placed the remainder beside the small cake and jar of cream.

She circled me, her fingers dragging over my shoulder and across my back before coming to rest on my nape. She leaned around me, one hand braced against my neck while the other wrapped around my cock.

"Spit on yourself," she said. "Get that cock nice and slick for me." I obeyed, and she kissed my cheek. "Good boy."

She stroked me slowly. My hips rolled, thrusting into

her hand, and she released my shaft to grip my balls instead.

"Fucking hell, you're wicked." I groaned, practically doubling over as she tightened her hold.

"Lie back," she said, her voice alone nearly making me groan again. "Make me come on your tongue."

I was flexible enough to remain on folded knees as I laid back, my back arching to accommodate the position. It kept my abdominal muscles tense, my breathing quick and shallow as Everly straddled my face. That perfect ass and pussy entirely filled my vision before smothering me, and my eyes rolled back as I sunk my forked tongue inside her. At the same moment, she gripped my cock again and stroked, fingers teasing over the sensitive ridges near my head.

"How does it taste, hellion?" she said. Her voice echoed in my ears, thrumming with magic, but I couldn't answer with my tongue inside her. Instead, I mumbled the words against her, every movement of my lips and tongue making her twitch and shake.

Wrapping my arms around her thighs to keep her in place, I splayed the forked sides of my tongue inside her, probing in and out. I closed my mouth over her clit, sucking as she stroked me, her hand trembling slightly as she edged me even closer to madness.

"Come for me, darling," I groaned.

As her body shook with the force of her ecstasy, a tremor of power went through the air. Goose bumps prickled over my arms—a reaction I seldom experienced, save when in the presence of extremely powerful beings.

My instinct was to rise up, to put my witch behind me and act as her guardian. But that was not my duty tonight. My witch's power was on full display, and who was I to get in the way of it?

The Old Man was coming.

He was already close.

His blessing would not be extended to someone who was incapable of wielding their own power, let alone the power of the fae. Everly had to prove herself. Prove she was immoveable, a force of nature as great as the waves, the rumbling Earth, the churning fire at its core.

Her flesh was pulsating against my lips, my tongue. The essence of her filled my head: her taste, her scent, her writhing magic.

My hips jolted upward as she stroked me, chasing her hand. She edged me mercilessly, pursuing my pleasure right to the edge of explosion before pulling back. She rocked herself against my tongue, groaning with abandon as she lost herself in the sensation. The words were muffled against her as I begged, mindlessly pleading for *more, more, more . . .*

She got up, leaving me dazed and twitching with overstimulation. With a wave of her hand, the fire she had lit fled from around the knife, and she withdrew it from the charred pile of wood. The blade was red-hot but cooled as she held it, the heat of it not bothering her at all.

She straddled my lap, positioning herself over my cock before sinking down, impaling herself. Her eyes fluttered, rolling back the deeper she took me. She made a sound like a wild cat in heat as I filled her entirely, and traced the tip of the still-warm blade down my chest.

"Are you ready to bleed for me?" she said in a voice that would have made me fall to my knees if I wasn't already flat on my back. She pressed the knife beneath my chin, giving me a smile that was dazzling in its beauty.

"Only for you," I said.

She laughed softly as it pricked my skin, the slight pain making me shiver with anticipation.

"Beg me," she whispered. The gentle part of her needed that. She needed the assurance I wanted this, I was willing, that I truly desired giving my blood and body to her.

"Please, my lady," I said. The knife was poised threateningly above my chest. "Hurt me. Use my body, use my flesh, make me bleed." My cock twitched inside her, so desperately turned on that I craved the sweet release that knife would bring. The blossoming pain, the heady feeling of blood loss, the magical rush that would ensue. "Cut me, please. Make it hurt. Make me feel every drop I give you."

She drew the knife down, carving a long, deep cut across my shoulder, and my eyes nearly rolled back. She moved her hand to grip my throat, keeping eye contact with me all the while. She made another cut, this time even deeper, ensuring my blood coated both sides of the blade.

I was suffocating and didn't even care. She traced her fingers through the blood, playing with it, creating designs of pleasure and pain across my chest before she cut me again.

Four cuts in total, two on either side of my chest, just below my collarbones. They were already healing, but I rather liked the placement of them and considered keeping the scars as a memento. All these thoughts floated through my feral brain as the fog thickened around us, roiling over the ground like a sea.

She leaned down to kiss me, and as she did, I took her wrist and pressed it down, encouraging her to dig the blade in one more time.

She did, and I groaned aloud to feel my body split open for her. Desperate, muttered words fell from my lips, switching rapidly between numerous languages because I couldn't keep track of where or when I was in that moment. The magic around us was a drug and my brain was wrapped in a haze, but one thing was perfectly clear.

As the knife sliced me again, drawing across my chest with gentle brutality, I said breathlessly, "Fuck, I love you."

She stopped. Stared at me. I'd promised myself words like that would never escape me again, and yet they had.

I didn't regret it either. Not even slightly. If anything, as I lay there drunk on magic and floating on pleasure, I wished I'd said it sooner.

But I would make up for that. Eternity was ahead, and I would spend all of it repeating those words in any way I knew how.

Her face was still so close to mine, and she whispered, "Say it again."

Smearing my hand through my own blood, I lifted my arm and traced my fingers across her chest, spelling out the words.

"I love you," I said. "I love you more than life itself, more than my own freedom. For you and you alone, I've stayed alive, Everly. For you, I would face everything I ever feared. I've lived a thousand lifetimes and I swear I've loved you in every one of them."

Her eyes welled up as she looked at me. I wasn't sure why those words had slipped out now, of all times. But when I saw her drenched in blood, silhouetted with moonlight, I fell in love all over again and couldn't stay silent.

"You mean that?" she said, her voice wavering on the edge of breaking. She was trying so hard to retain her composure. Words like that were terrifying and I knew it all too well, but I'd told her the truth: for her, I would face everything I feared.

Even this.

"I swear it," I said, cupping her face. She leaned into my hand.

"Oh, Callum," she gasped, catching her breath. "I love you so much."

From the dark depths of the forest, a drum beat. As the beating continued, vague shapes flitted through the fog around us. Whispers and soft laughter filled the air, accompanied by a sound that could only be described as the ringing of distant bells.

Slowly, Everly rose to her feet, staring into the mist. Her bloody hands hung slack at her sides, the knife still clutched in her fingers. Getting to my feet, I stood close behind her. Watching, waiting.

A figure slowly materialized from the mist.

He was tall and thin, with limbs as long and lanky as tree branches. His clothing might have been made of leather, but it was nearly impossible to tell with the amount of moss and lichens covering it. The skull of a horse shrouded his face, covered with an intricate design of bright silver paint. He carried a gnarled walking stick, and his white beard was so long he had to throw it over his shoulder to avoid it trailing on the ground.

The Old Man. The Fairy King.

Flowers grew around his bare feet as he walked. When he at last stood still and pushed back the mask, I had the urge to avert my eyes.

The fae controlled magic neither witches nor demons could touch. The air around the Old Man vibrated with unknowable energy, the scent sharp and earthy, like freshly crushed pepper. The length and pale color of his beard made him appear old, but when looking at his face, it was truly impossible to guess his age.

Doubtlessly, he was even older than I was.

"Long have the Laverne witches existed peacefully within my forest," he said, his voice rumbling the ground. "Generations of your family have come and gone beneath these trees. But it has been a very long time since one of you called to me. What is it you seek?"

"A blessing," Everly said, daring to take a step forward.

She held out the blade, and the Old Man regarded it with narrowed white eyes. "If you would be so generous to grant it."

The Old Man took the knife and examined it, weighing it in his hand. "The blood of the resentful dead, and the blood of your beloved." He sniffed, his nostrils flaring. "The blood of a demon. A most unusual aroma you've presented to me, Laverne witch."

Trudging over to the bottle of mead, he picked it up and took a long swig, draining the bottle. Fae creatures rarely showed themselves, Darragh being the rare exception. I'd seen them only a handful of times in my life, and never had I encountered fairy royalty such as this.

"I will honor your request," he finally said. "For the same reason that I honored Sybil's when she came to me. It is not because you've flattered me with offerings or tempted me with your revelry. It is because I know the purpose of it. I know your intent." He turned to us, nodding his head. "You mean to kill the Deep One. The poisonous Hellkite who sleeps in the mine, who has sought to destroy my power for decades. I've held it back, but the trees . . ." He laid his hand against the trunk of a gnarled oak, his expression suddenly sad. "They are tired. As am I. As the Deep One's power grows, it becomes ever more difficult to hold It back." He looked at Everly again, his gaze sharp. "It means to consume you. It whispers your name."

"I know," Everly said fiercely. "But I will kill It first."

The Old Man's eyes moved to me. He didn't say a word, but regarded me slowly, carefully. As if the answer he sought was written on my body but only lies would come from my tongue.

Then he took the blade and slowly plunged it into his own chest. He didn't flinch; he showed no outward signs of pain at all. When he withdrew it, dripping with his blood, he held it over the roaring flames until the blade turned red-hot once more. A peculiar scent filled the air, like burned grass and damp dirt.

"This blade can pierce the flesh of Hellkite. You must burn the beast from the inside out." He withdrew the knife and held it aloft. Within mere seconds, the reddened blade turned silver again. The blood was gone, but dark red swirls remained in the metal.

He held it out, and when Everly grasped it, there was a pulse in the air.

"The fae wish for your success, young witch," he said, covering his face once more. "We will be watching. If all else fails and hope seems lost, remember this, *the trees are always listening.*"

He stepped back, fog swirling around him. The leaves rustled, whispers and giggles echoing around us. With a final rush of wind, the Old Man vanished, and the whispers faded away.

EVERLY

THAT NIGHT, I did not truly sleep. When the drain of magic finally caught up with me and I couldn't keep my feet, Callum carried me on his back to the house. Dawn was creeping over the horizon by the time we returned, but I closed my eyes against the encroaching day.

Darkness still had its hold on me, and the growing light made me anxious. Callum pulled all the curtains closed, plunging my bedroom into beautiful, comforting shadow. Limp and exhausted, I let him wash my face with a cloth, then my hands, my arms, my feet. All the while I lay still and silent, relinquishing all control to simply trust in his care.

He sang to me as I drifted in and out of sleep, in a language I'd never heard. Or perhaps I only imagined the words, the sounds. It was difficult to differentiate between what I was dreaming and what was actually happening around me.

He held me close, and I sprawled naked on his chest, eyes so heavy I couldn't open them even if I wanted to. The smoke of the bonfire still swirled around me, and I could hear the echoes of the forest: the crickets, the rustling leaves, the trickling water.

For hours, I drifted in and out of dreams. While my body lay at rest, my mind was running through the trees. Running . . . running until my lungs burned, until my feet were cut and my arms covered in scratches from whipping branches. Deeper and deeper into the trees. Deeper into the darkness.

But I wasn't afraid. The darkness was my cloak, it was my protection. The darkness was the beginning. The darkness was the end.

But I wasn't the only thing lurking in the dark.

When I finally stirred from sleep, it was with a lingering feeling of trepidation. Pushing myself up from Callum's chest, I rubbed my aching eyes and paused, frowning as I tried to remember why I was feeling like this.

"Did you dream?" he said, rubbing his hand over my back. "What did you see?"

"Darkness. Only darkness. I was running, and . . ." I paused, trying so hard to remember. "Something was watching me. But it couldn't reach me."

He nodded. He balked at nothing. He listened to my worries and my fears and didn't judge me for them. And he . . .

He loved me.

The memory of him speaking those words suddenly filled my mind, making my heart beat faster and my chest feel as if it were full of fluttering moths. I laid down on him again, craning my neck to kiss his mouth.

"I love you," I whispered.

His dark eyes gazed into mine. His fingers stroked through my tangled hair, both of us laughing softly when he got caught on knots and had to tug through them.

"And I love you," he said. "You were divine last night. Not only your magic. Your confidence. Your bravery. You've faced so much, darling." He paused, holding me close. "I want to take you away from here."

Smiling, I said, "Where will you take me?"

He hesitated before he spoke, his lips parting and closing several times before he said, "To Hell. To Dantalion, the High City. The seat of the Council."

"That's not possible though, is it? At least not until I'm . . . well, not until I'm dead?"

"Witches can walk past the Veil and through the Betwixt. They can enter Hell, if they have someone to let them in. And you do."

When he grinned, a nervous laugh burst out of me. My smile faded, then reappeared, then faded again. "You really think I can? I could make it there?"

"I have no doubt. It's been a very long time since I've been in Hell. At least, since I've been there willingly. I haven't wanted to go back. But when I'm with you, you make me think of home. All the beautiful, magical places

I haven't seen in so long. You make me want to share a part of my life with you that I thought I would never return to."

"I want to see it," I said softly, even though the declaration made me shiver with nerves.

The cuts I'd given him last night were fully healed, but very thin scars remained beneath his collarbones, and I traced them with my fingers.

"There was a time when I never wanted to go back," he said. "Every familiar place caused me pain. There were memories everywhere, inescapable reminders of those I'd lost. It's still painful. I don't think mourning ever truly ends. But for a long time, Hell was all I knew. It's a part of me. It's part of you now too." He reached out, touching the scars on my stomach. "Hell considers killing a God to be an act of war. When the Gods were chased out of Hell, the Council demanded that if one was found and going to be killed, the hunter who sought to kill it would go to them first and seek their blessing. I never did." He grinned, but the expression wasn't joyful. "The war had never ended in my mind. My army was gone but I was still a warrior. But now . . . things have changed."

He had changed, and so had I. Things I had once thought impossible were within my grasp. A future without the terror of the God looming over us was closer than ever, and yet still so far away.

"When the Deep One is dead, my war is over," he said. "It's been too long. I don't want to run from the pain anymore. I want a life of peace. I want to know what it feels like to rest. I want to spend eternity learning how to love you."

The thought filled me with warmth. A life without the God, without the Libiri. We could stay safely in this house or we could travel as we wished.

I could have a life I'd thought was impossible.

But, between us and that life, the God still stood.

"We should seek the Council's blessing," Callum said. "They will give us an audience, and I want the royals of Hell to see the witch who is fighting in their names. It will help put an end to the bitterness between Lucifer and I, if I do something properly for once. And while we're there, it will give you a few days to rest. You've been working yourself hard."

With a heavy sigh, I said, "Some rest would be nice. My brain feels like soup. But even a single day I'm not practicing is a day too many."

"Time passes differently in Hell," he said. "A day on Earth is nearly three days there. You won't miss anything. Your body can rest while your spirit wanders with me. How does that sound?"

There was such eager light in his dark eyes that I nodded quickly, despite my fears. "It sounds amazing and terrifying. Of course I want to go!"

WHEN I AWOKE the next morning, there was only one thought at the forefront of my mind. I, a living, breathing human, was going to walk through the gates of Hell. A witch who'd only just learned how to control her power was going to stand before beings who had been wielding magic for thousands of years, and insist I could be trusted.

For several minutes, all I could do was lie in bed with a churning stomach. What did one wear when presenting themselves to Hell's royalty? A pencil skirt and blazer? A gown? Heels? Was I supposed to bow? Offer my hand? Hold my head high?

I wasn't ready for this.

Yet, I was also as ready as I would ever be.

Callum had left my room while I slept, which was no surprise. He'd been antsy last night, barely able to lay still in bed as I drifted off into sleep. Our nerves ebbed and flowed into each other, and only when I dragged myself on top of him, sprawling across his chest, did he finally lay still.

The scent of food wafted from beneath the cloche-covered plate on my table, but I couldn't tolerate eating when my stomach was determined to tie itself into knots. I was facing the task of leaving Earth, casting my spiritual self so far outside my body that I could walk in Hell. That wasn't a simple thing to do, even for experienced witches.

But Callum would be by my side. He would show me the way.

As I passed by the library, Grams called to me, "Looking for the demon? He's in his room. Been in there for hours!"

There was a question implied in her tone, but I didn't have an answer for her. Callum hadn't stepped foot in that room since I first stumbled through the door, so I couldn't imagine why he'd returned there now.

Making my way down the hallway, I could see the large doors were ajar. A smile came to my face when I remembered sprinting down this same hall, stumbling in terror, certain I was about to die at the hands of the monstrous beast I'd accidentally unleashed.

Now that monster was my prince. The beast was as loving as he was vicious, as loyal as he was dangerous.

"Callum?" I called his name as I slipped through the door. My demon stood at the far side of the room, in front of a large framed mirror. But something was different.

At first, I thought another demon had broken into the house. Callum's back was to me; he was naked, facing the mirror. But his skin, nearly every inch of him, was tattooed. Elaborate, detailed artwork, the likes of which I'd never seen on a human. The colors changed as I walked closer; even the lines themselves shifted, as if the art was alive.

But it wasn't only that. In the mirror's reflection, I watched as he slid a slim silver ring through his lower lip, adjusting it until a tiny crimson jewel was visible. Like a drop of blood in the center of his mouth.

His gaze shifted toward me in the mirror.

"Callum . . . you look . . . beautiful." It was the only word that could truly encompass my awe, my disbelief. Callum's expression was stunningly hard but somehow fragile. Softened, ever so slightly, by the visual acknowledgment of all the love he'd ever felt. All the love he'd ever been given.

It covered him like a tapestry. Jewels, ink, and metal. Lifetimes of love and devotion. But seeing it all, as beautiful as it was, filled me with sadness too. As I came up behind him and wrapped my arms around his waist to lay my head against his back, I felt him shake.

Every mark, every piece of jewelry, was a life lost. A soul he would never meet again, a voice he would never hear, a touch he would never feel.

"It's for you, Everly," he said. His voice was carefully controlled, but I felt the pain coursing through him. "Only for you would I go to war again. Only for you. But if I'm going to go, then I'll carry them with me. They deserve to see vengeance. They deserve to taste the blood of the Gods again."

"They do. And they will."

He turned to face me, and I reached up to lay my hand against his cheek. It made him look more human. Less like a being carved from marble and more like a creature of flesh and blood. A creature that could feel, so deeply and with such passion he'd locked it all away just so he could bear to go on living.

"This is it, isn't it?" I said. "We're going to war."

His fingers brushed gently against my face. "Yes, my love. We're going to war, and you will lead the way."

"I don't think I'm ready."

"I wasn't ready either. But sometimes, we're ready for far more than we believe."

We kissed. Soft and desperate, deep and ravenous. We kissed to drown our fear, to silence our doubts, to smother our pain.

WHEN WE WERE ready, we went to the meditation room.

My hands were clammy with sweat as the door clicked shut behind us and Callum set the metronome ticking. The sound made my brain feel softened, vulnerable even before I lit the incense. As fragrant smoke wafted around the room, the light dimmed. Soon, the only illumination that remained was the sparkling stars overhead, spread across the ceiling like diamonds thrown across velvet.

Callum took my hand, and together, we stood in the center of the room. Anxiety rose up in my throat, threatening to choke me.

"I don't think I can do it, Callum," I said suddenly. "I don't think I can cast out. I can't."

"Forget the lies you've been told, Everly." He lifted my hands to kiss my knuckles. "Forget everything that has made you doubt what you *know* you can do. I'll show you the way. I'll be right there with you, every moment. You've learned how to guard your mind, how to lock it up tight and let nothing in. Now, you need to learn how to let your mind wander again."

Sucking in a deep breath, I tried to convince myself this wasn't one of the most foolish, dangerous things I'd ever done. But I was not the same frightened girl who had stood in St. Thaddeus and felt the Deep One assault my mind. I was no longer the inexperienced witch who feared her own power.

I would walk into Hell with my head held high. A witch to be respected and feared.

Callum used the palm of his hand to cover my eyes, encouraging me to close them before he took my hands again. "When you walk through the gates of Hell, there won't be a single demon who won't feel your footsteps. They'll shake, woman. Relax now. I won't let go. Lower the guards, darling. Let your mind roam."

It felt wrong. Dangerous. Like touching a hot stove or stepping into the middle of traffic; instinct demanded I stop, that I turn back.

One by one, I relaxed my muscles. Even my eyes, twitching nervously despite being closed, were a point of tension I had to intentionally force to relax. As I exhaled, I imagined the unease seeping out of me, dissipating into the air like harmless vapor.

My body could be shed like clothing, stepped into and out of as I pleased. But I had to take care with it, like a dress made of expensive silk. If I wasn't careful, I might never find my way back to it again. Witches had lost their way in the Betwixt before, lost to that vast expanse forever. Unable to truly live . . . unable to die . . .

"Ev." Callum's voice was gentle. "You're pulling back. You're heavy as an anchor. Relax." His fingers brushed over mine, pressing harder against my palm. "Let go. Step into the Veil. Leave the weight behind."

I focused. I let all the nerves and fear rush over me like cold water over stone. And as it washed away, I did feel lighter. Softer. In my mind's eye, I envisioned myself like a willow tree, bending and drifting in a soft breeze, but so deeply rooted even a hurricane could not force me to break.

With every passing second, I felt more buoyant, less corporeal, my skin strangely numb.

Something cold and damp brushed my face, as if I had walked through a wall of mist. When I opened my eyes, I found I was facing exactly that: a sea of thick white fog in which Callum and I stood side by side.

The Veil.

We walked on, silent. The mist thinned; it twisted and swirled like smoke caught in a vicious wind. Streaks of color twined around us, like paint drifting through water.

"We are now betwixt and between all realities," Callum said. "All worlds. All universes. If you walk far enough, not even time is your barrier. The worlds as they are, as they were, and as they will be, are all accessible to you here."

The colors kept swirling, and if I stared at them long enough, I could see even more details within the fog. Visions of landscapes flashed before me, blown away like dust in the wind. Vast, craggy deserts. Thick, luscious forests. Unfamiliar flora and fauna, structures that were clearly not of human design.

Curiosity demanded I keep chasing those visions, that I pursue them even deeper into the mist. But that was exactly how wandering witches became lost. I had to stay focused.

"What should I look for?"

"A massive gate, of wrought black metal, that rises high enough to touch the clouds," Callum said. His hand, wrapped tightly around my own, was my greatest reassurance. "It's framed by great warriors carved in stone, with wings that cast shadows so large they can make the fields look like night. Can you imagine? Can you see it?"

"Yes. I can see it." I held the image in my mind. Staring hard into the swirling mist, I could see the iron bars rising toward the sky. The fields, rolling off into the distance, and perched above it all—a shimmering city, with towers that pierced the sky.

"Those gates will open for you, Everly. Walk toward them with confidence. Without fear. Hold your head high. Know that they will let you pass."

Although I couldn't see it clearly yet, I was certain the gate was there. I walked toward it, now leading Callum by the hand. Slowly at first, but with every step, I moved faster. It was there, it truly was. The gate, rising so high above I couldn't see its end. The demon warriors stood tall on either side, their hands braced against the gates.

The mist parted. Tall grass brushed against my hand as it dangled by my side, and I looked down to find that the blades were pale as pearls. A sea of white grass, bending slowly in the breeze.

I didn't stop; I didn't pause. The gate appeared sealed, but no one guarded it, nor was there a fence on either side of it.

"A gate without a fence?" I said. "Why?"

"The fence is there," Callum said. "Focus. Feel the crackle in the air, the heat? If anyone were to try to step around the gate, they would never enter Hell. They would wander through wastelands forever, with no way to return."

"And will the gates open for anyone?"

"No. The gates open for the powerful. Whether that power is greatly wicked or greatly good is irrelevant. Hell craves power, it craves strength. This world carries far more magic than the human realm, and all that magic is very hungry."

The magic was palpable, it was thick in the air and sweet on my tongue.

As the great gates opened before us, swinging back on hinges that groaned and howled like Hell's most wicked creatures, a smile spread over my face.

CALLUM

I WAS HOME. Of my own accord, of my own free will. I had finally come home.

My body was light, unburdened by all the flesh and blood required in the human world. Buoyed by magic and freed from the weight of Earth's gravity.

Hell was freedom; at least, it was always meant to be. That was what we'd fought for. We would not be ruled by Gods, we would not be subjugated to the rules and whims of any deity. The rules we had in Hell—and there were very few—were sacred, but they were sparing.

The air rippled as we stepped through the gates, thrumming like a plucked harp string. The pale grass rustled, brushing against my fingertips like the softest of feathers. Everly gasped as we passed the gates, the new world around her coming into focus. A forest of gnarled trees, with long, knotted branches that stretched low to the ground, spread out before us. Their bark was the color of ice, and deep green vines sprouting clear berries in tiny clusters coiled up the trunks.

Everly's steps slowed, her eyes wide with wonder as she looked around. "Oh . . . my god . . ."

She stopped walking entirely when she spotted a tiny fluffy creature scuttling up one of the trees. Eyeballs lined its back on little stalks, looking in every direction at once as it quickly hid itself among the leaves.

I allowed the nervous creature to climb onto my hand. It had suckered feet that stuck to my skin, and I brought it close so Everly could see. Her eyes were bright with wonder, her smile so wide it was like she had forgotten entirely why we were here.

Honestly, I hoped she had. I treasured every little moment of unbridled happiness I saw in her. Happiness that had been denied to her for so long.

"We call them pips," I said as she watched the little creature crawl along my arm. "Just be careful not to scare it. If they're startled—"

But Everly reached her hand out to pet the creature a bit too quickly. It vanished, leaving behind a sparkling golden cloud that made Everly begin to sneeze uncontrollably.

"I tried to warn you." I chuckled as she doubled over, leaning her hand against a tree as she continued to sneeze.

Once she'd recovered, I took her hand and said, "Hold tight."

Her fingers squeezed around mine, and I teleported, pulling her with me. By the time we touched the ground again, the sky was overcast and the sound of crashing waves filled the air. The ground beneath our feet was shining black rock, dotted with large crystalline structures the color of emeralds. Everly's mouth gaped open as she stared over the cliffside, where the waves of the Black Sea churned and crashed far below.

Gargantuan trees rose out of the sea, their trunks covered in green crystals that matched the same dark color of their massive leaves. Their roots reached all the way to the sea floor, creating a home for the numerous creatures that lived below the waves.

Everly's voice was breathless with disbelief. "Callum, it's beautiful."

It had been so long I'd almost forgotten, but it truly was. As we watched the waves, a spined iridescent fin rose above the water, glistening in the sun before the massive serpent beneath plunged back into the depths. Everly's breath stuttered as she silently took it all in.

I kept waiting for the pain to return. The memories, the grief. But when I looked at her, the ache inside me couldn't grow into agony.

"Turn around," I said. "There's more to see."

Her eyes were wide as she turned and saw Dantalion for the first time. The High City towered over the rocky plains, its towers formed of black stone and crawling with dark green vines. The Onyx Citadel rose above it all, shrouded in clouds and fog, its windows glowing with warm light.

"Can we go closer?" she gasped. "Can we go into the city?"

With a smile, I took her hand again and teleported us to the main boulevard.

Pale gray stones paved the road, bordered by tall willow-like trees that blossomed with bloodred flowers. Demons and human spirits lounged outside cafes, sipping liquors and herbal concoctions, the sounds of laughter and boisterous conversation echoing among the towering buildings. The shops here offered numerous things for trade: rare and uncommon plants, gems and jewelry, garments, furnishings, art, even beasts.

"Money" didn't have a purpose here. We used it only for our expeditions to the human world. Among our own kind, there was no reason for any of us to go without something we needed. Hell was a massive and bountiful place, and we were better off when we looked out for each other. What good was freedom if it was reserved only for those privileged enough to attain it?

Everly's head was on a swivel, trying to take in everything at once. As we walked, taking our time, it wasn't long before other demons took notice. A human soul in Hell was not unusual at all—there were plenty of mortal souls here, living out their eternity alongside us. But a *witch's* soul in Hell was rare, and Everly's scent was bright with life.

It swiftly attracted interest.

Claws shuffled and wings perked up. Horned heads craned up curiously to watch us pass. Whispers rippled up and down the street.

A witch in Hell?

A living witch?

Who's that with her?

He's an old one, isn't he?

"Callum. That's Callum."

We paused, my hand tugging Everly to a halt at the sound of a familiar voice. A demon was standing in the cavernous opening of a nearby tavern, staring at me with black eyes that sparkled with glittering gold. She looked different now—of course she did, it had been so long. She'd grown horns but no wings, her dark hair now long enough to brush the ground, her tattoos bright and colorful although they'd once been only black and gray.

"Kimaris." My voice struggled to form her name. She came closer, hesitantly, just a few steps at a time.

"You came home," she said. She laughed softly, her eyes moving to Everly. "I can't believe it. You really . . . you found your witch."

"I swore I would," I said. And then, in a flash, she'd crossed the distance between us to embrace me.

The painful memories bloomed, before wilting away. Kimaris gripped the nape of my neck, and I hers, our claws digging in enough to draw blood as we pressed our foreheads together.

"I thought you must have died," she said. "Killed on one of your hunts."

"If the Gods couldn't kill me in Hell, Kim, they certainly can't kill me on Earth," I said as we drew back from each other. Everly watched, smiling politely but also obviously confused. Kimaris turned to her, opening her arms for an embrace but then quickly catching herself.

"Ah, right. Human." She chuckled, extending her hand instead. Everly shook her hand and smiled sheepishly before opening her arms in acceptance of an embrace. Kimaris wrapped her arms around her, lifting Everly entirely off her feet as she said excitedly, "We all thought he was mad for chasing you! But you're real! Ha!" She set Everly back on her feet but paused for a moment, staring at my witch as she sniffed the air. "Your scent, it's . . ." Kimaris glanced at me, a question I couldn't read in her gaze. But she quickly looked away again, shaking her head with a chuckle. "That's a lot of magic you carry, love. A bit overwhelming."

"Tell me about it," Everly said with a jokingly dramatic sigh.

Kim laughed again, motioning for us to follow her. "Come, please, have a drink with me. It's been far too long."

"A GOD THAT'S being worshiped? Lucifer's balls, that's a bold one to pursue, Callum. Even with a witch at your side."

Kimaris took a long drink from her glass, draining it before she raised it in the air so the bartender could see. The human behind the bar gave her a nod before muddling some herbs in a glass, then pouring ruby-red liquid on top.

"Thanks, Willi," she said as he brought the beverage over to our table. The tavern was dimly lit, comfortable and cool. Day or night, places like this would be full of demons, drinking, socializing, fucking.

Everly kept getting distracted by the fact that demons liked to fuck in the open, like the three playmates in the opposite corner from us. She was trying so hard not to stare, but her reddened cheeks and quickened heart rate told me she kept sneaking looks in their direction.

"But you finally decided to do things properly, eh?" Kimaris said. "Asking the Council for their blessing?"

"It's time I buried the hatchet," I said, sipping my drink. Hell's liquor was far more powerful than anything that could be found on Earth, and I relished the burn as it went down. I'd warned Everly to sip her drink slowly, but she hiccupped and giggled after taking another gulp.

"Does Lucifer know about her?" Kimaris said, looking at Everly pointedly. When I nodded, she frowned. "But does he know that she's . . ." Her eyes darted between us.

"Inexperienced?" Everly said, finishing Kim's sentence. "He wasn't happy about me, but I'm sure he knows. Doesn't he, Callum?"

Kimaris lowered her eyes, and I had the strange feeling that wasn't the word she was going to say. But I didn't push it.

"Lucifer will be fine," I said. "Paimon and Bael will support our endeavor, without a doubt. And Lucifer won't go against both of them."

Kimaris leaned back in her chair, nodding her head. It was good to see her after so long, to see her healthy and happy. When I left Hell, she'd still barely been speaking.

The war took its toll on all who survived it.

"Well, I wish you luck," she said, raising her glass.

"Personally, there's not a bargain in the world that would make me face one of those damned Gods again. Not even for a thousand witch's souls."

"It's not for a bargain," I said. My hand trailed up Everly's thigh and she smiled at me. Her eyes were soft, tipsiness already taking its hold on her. "This is my last hunt. When It's dead, I want peace."

Kimaris reached over, easing Everly's glass away from the edge of the table as my witch leaned her head against my shoulder. "I think that may be enough for you, love. You don't want to overdo it." She winked and drained the glass herself.

She was right, of course. Dusk was only just beginning to fall, and Hell truly came alive at night. Everly couldn't enjoy it if she passed out drunk.

"What's the plan for the night then?" Kimaris said. "Surely, some revelry is in order before you go chat with the Council. Although, I imagine you'll cause quite a stir wherever you go."

"Somewhere we can get a bit of privacy to enjoy ourselves," I said, and Everly nodded eagerly. Even with me accompanying her, the presence of a witch made demons nervous. The ones here in the tavern were doing well to mind their business, but taking her somewhere crowded might draw more attention to her than she was ready for.

"You should go to the hot spring caverns," Kimaris suggested. "Used to be one of your favorite haunts, didn't it? They've changed since you've last been there; pretty damn luxurious now." She looked at Everly, giving her a wink. "The walk down the cliffside can be a bit frightening, but it's well worth it."

"I'm not afraid," Everly said. "Soaking in a hot spring sounds amazing."

Even sitting right next to me, she was still too far away for my taste. Hauling her onto my lap, I possessively buried my face against her neck, making it clear to every demon around that she belonged to me.

Keeping my voice low in her ear, I growled, "We'll be doing more than soaking, I assure you of that, darling."

EVERLY

KIMARIS WAS RIGHT; the path down to the hot springs was terrifying, but I did my best not to let it show.

Back at the cliffside near the sea, a narrow stairway led us down into a crevasse. Waves crashed far below, roaring as they echoed off the rock, foam churning in the water like the mouth of a rabid beast. The stairway wasn't so bad at first, with smooth black stone on either side. But then the crevasse widened, and the stairway clung only to one side of the sheer rock. There was no boundary, not even a rope. We edged our way along the steep stairs, with stone on one side and a straight drop to the sea on the other.

Callum wasn't bothered in the least. He led the way, holding my hand, glancing back at me occasionally and snickering.

"Do you think I would let you fall?" he said.

Keeping my eyes fixed on him so I wouldn't mistakenly glance at the massive drop beside me, I said, "No. But maybe we could have teleported there?"

He chuckled again, squeezing my hand. "We could have. But I enjoy the walk."

Of course he did.

Luckily, that demonic liquor was still buzzing in my veins, numbing most of my fear. I'd never drank much even in the human world, because my stomach was too sensitive for it. But whatever had been in the drink Callum ordered for me was delicious. Fruity and herbaceous, with a fiery burn I could still feel in my chest.

It was surreal to see so many other demons. Walking through the streets of the High City, seeing such a variety of wings, claws, horns, and fangs all around me, felt like walking through a dream. Even the humans here looked rather demonic. Their eyes were preternaturally bright, their faces youthful, their movements so relaxed they were almost feline.

Everything I'd once believed about Hell was wrong. I could have a future here. An *eternity*.

If the Deep One didn't consume me first.

Shaking my head to cast off those negative thoughts, I focused on the path ahead. The stairway finally ended, and we stepped onto a flat section of rock jutting from the cliff face. Glowing orbs were suspended from thin silver wires over the space, seeming to float in mid-air. A hammock was hung between two craggy crystal columns, and within it lay a demon who lazily raised his hand to wave at us but didn't bother to open his eyes.

That is, until his nostrils flared and he sniffed. Then his eyes flew open, golden irises darting to me with alarm.

"Damned mother of Bael!" he exclaimed. "That's quite a scent you have, witch. Fuckin' scared me. Thought I was about to have my sigil stolen." He stretched as he sat up, long legs dangling from either side of the hammock. It was difficult to notice at first because of the extent of his tattoos, but he was entirely naked. His eyes settled on Callum, staring at him for a long moment before he inclined his head. "Welcome to the springs, *dux*. Is there anything I can offer you?"

"Are any of the caverns unoccupied?" Callum said. For the first time, I noticed there was a cave opening in the rock, the path lit with more of those glowing orbs.

The demon nodded. "There should be a large pool unoccupied near the back. Just keep walking to the right, look for the sapphire stones. Libations are to the left." His eyes kept sliding curiously between Callum and I, as if there was a question he wished to ask but didn't dare. Slowly, he laid back down. "If you need anything, I'll be here all night. Name's Silas."

As soon as we passed into the tunnel, the air turned damp and warm. Humidity dripped from the sleek stones as we made our way deeper into the mountain. There were voices ahead, faint but boisterous, muffled by the distance. The scent of wet rock permeated the atmosphere, but there were also whiffs of marijuana, lemongrass, and something sweet, like sugar on the back of my tongue.

"He called you *dux*," I said, watching Callum curiously. "It's Latin, isn't it?"

"More or less," he said. "It's an honorific. The equivalent of *Master* or *Captain*."

"Did he know you? From before?"

Callum shook his head. "He's young. Likely wasn't even alive when I last lived in Hell. But certain demonic traits—wings and horns, for example—don't manifest until we're quite old."

Giving him a teasing look, I said, "So what he's really doing is calling you a senior citizen."

He laughed, then tucked me against his side and squeezed my ass. "Mm, keep sassing me, darling, and see what happens. There are plenty of demons around who would love to see a witch getting spanked."

Slapping his chest in mock offense, I said, "You wouldn't dare! Is that any way to treat your mistress?"

"It certainly is, when my mistress misbehaves. Besides, punishing you would inspire you to do the same to me later."

The tunnel opened, and I would have stopped in my tracks if it weren't for Callum's arm around me. The cavern we entered was massive, rising into a tall, peaked ceiling covered in stalactites. All around were hot spring pools. Clouds of steam rose into the air, strong with the scent of minerals and the vague aroma of salt. The stones beneath my bare feet were warm, covered with a thin layer of water that made my footsteps splash as we kept walking.

All around the cavern—sprouting from the ceiling,

the walls, the grounds—were gigantic crystal structures. Most of them were pale and faintly cloudy, like shards of ice, while others were tinted violet, pink, or blue. Paths had been cleared between them to lead to the various pools, but the size and thickness of the clusters allowed each hot spring to have a bit of privacy, partially sheltering them from view.

Dozens of demons bathed in the pools or lay on the rocks beside them. Sounds of laughter and ecstasy drifted through the air. Callum led me deeper into the caverns, following a winding path to the right that sloped upward and into a smaller chamber.

The crystals that grew here were clear at their base, but their sharp tips were vibrant blue. There was a subtle glow within them that lit the cave, bathing it in cool, soothing light. The pool was large, surrounded by smooth stone that practically invited one to stretch their body out and rest.

"We'll have the cavern to ourselves," Callum said, walking to the other side of the pool as I stood looking around in wonder. "The shared pools are enjoyable, but I'd much rather have you to myself."

As usual, Callum wasn't wearing much. Only loose trousers of soft, silky black material, which he quickly discarded. In the faint light, he looked ethereal. Skin tinted blue by the crystals surrounding him, the hollows of his eyes shrouded in darkness. Since he'd begun showing his tattoos again and wearing his piercings, I found it impossible not to stare. He'd always been beautiful, but to see him now was like looking at a classical masterpiece encrusted with gold and jewels.

"This was always one of my favorite places in the High City," he said. There were shelves carved into the stone wall, and he traced his fingers over the myriad of oddly shaped bottles upon them, with their brightly colored glass. "Whether I wanted company, or to be alone. I could come here and not have to think about the rest of the world for a while."

He selected a glass jar and unscrewed the lid, a pungent aroma emerging when he broke the seal. There was a variety of stone pipes hung on little hooks beside the jar, and he selected one that he filled with the marijuana-like herb. He sat at the edge of the pool, allowing his legs to dangle into the water.

"Go on, my love," he said. "Get rid of those clothes."

I was happy to do so. The air was refreshing on my naked skin, and I waded into the pool up to my waist, smiling at the pleasurable warmth.

"The water here is said to have healing capabilities," he said as I sank even deeper and allowed the water to come up to my shoulders. My feet could still touch the ground, but if I kept walking to the far end of the pool, the bottom was too deep to see. "Warriors often came here after training, to ease their sore muscles, to speed up the healing of wounds. Light?"

He held out the pipe, and I snapped my fingers to summon a little flame that I held close to the herb. He breathed in, held it a moment, then leaned back and closed his eyes as he exhaled, a little shiver going over his skin.

He slipped into the water beside me. He held the pipe to my lips so I could smoke and cradled me as I coughed on the exhale, my inexperienced lungs struggling to take it in.

My limbs floated to the surface as he carried me into deeper water. I could have slept there in his arms, perfectly safe and without fear.

That was the greatest gift he'd given me. A fearless existence. Freedom from the constant mind-numbing anxiety of my former life. It didn't mean I was never afraid. It didn't mean that terror never gripped me, or worry never plagued me. But those things didn't command me anymore, they didn't *control* me.

His wings tread the water, keeping us buoyant. We passed the pipe back and forth, lost in the physical sensations without any need for conversation.

Then, keeping his voice low as he spoke close to my ear, he said, "I have something to ask of you."

Turning to him, chest to chest, I looped my arms around his neck and said, "Anything you wish."

He seemed both larger than life and suddenly so small. The blue light tinted his eyes, the water reflected in their obsidian pools.

"Yesterday, I made the choice to wear my metal again. To remember the joy of those I lost . . . and the pain." His fingers traced over my cheek. "But there's a mark missing, and I cannot go to war without it."

My heart stopped. But as he kept speaking, it took off pounding again, a drumbeat in my chest.

"I want your mark, Everly. I want it given by your hands."

I stared at him for so long, at a loss for words. The jewelry adorning him carried such painful memories; I knew how hard it must have been for him to choose to wear them again.

But to accept a *new* mark after so long was on another level entirely.

His expression was vulnerable, unguarded. There was raw honesty in his voice as he said, "I swore to myself I would never accept a mark again. But that was when I also believed I would never love again. You proved me wrong on both counts."

He cradled my face and pressed his forehead against mine. That closeness said more than his words ever could.

"I'm terrified of losing you every second of every day," he said, his voice ragged. "I think of the task you have ahead and I want to rage. I want to take that burden from your shoulders and carry it alone. But I'm not enough without you. With or without a piercing from you, you've left your mark on me. I adore you endlessly." He gripped me, sucking in his breath like it physically pained him to not be able to have me closer.

"I'll mark you," I said. He made a soft sound—a laugh, or a sigh of relief, I wasn't entirely sure. "But you'll have to tell me how."

He grinned as he rose from the water. It dripped from him, streaking over his muscular form, and my breath caught as I admired every naked inch of him. "Gladly. Don't be nervous; we'll take our time. Now come with me. There's bound to be a jeweler here somewhere."

EVERLY

AT FIRST, AS Callum led me naked through the caverns, I was overwhelmed with self-consciousness. But the demons we passed didn't care. Not one of them even gave me a second glance, at least not until they sniffed the air and got a whiff of my magic.

Then they stared.

"There's always a jeweler around somewhere," Callum said as we entered another large cavern. Hot springs were scattered around the space, and there was a bar situated on a wide ledge where drinks were served by the tallest demon I'd ever seen. A few others lounged in hammocks hung around the cavern, and it was one of these beings Callum approached.

If he didn't care about being naked, I was determined not to either. Easier said than done when the demon sprawled in the hammock before us opened her eyes, giving us both a long look up and down.

Then she smirked.

"Well, well, if it isn't our runaway prince. How damn long has it been, Cal?"

"A few centuries, at least," Callum said, clasping the demon's hand with familiar comradery. She didn't bother to rise from her hammock. She wore a sheer skirt and nothing else, split at the hips so her long legs could sprawl freely. Richly colored, elaborate tattoos covered her; the colors shifted and moved as she did.

"Should've figured you'd return with a bang," she said, looking me up and down again as I tried desperately to keep myself from blushing. "Bringing a living witch straight into Hell, eh? Cheeky of you." She gave me a sharp-toothed smile. "Pardon me for not shaking your hand, love, but I can't risk my sigil ending up Earthside. Haven't had the best experiences with witches."

There was no judgment in her voice as she spoke to me, nor any dislike in her eyes. Although my first instinct was to blurt out that I wasn't a threat to her, I settled with, "I understand. My name is Everly. It's a pleasure."

"Oh, the pleasure is mine," she said, readjusting herself so that her legs were spread *very* wide. "Call me Niamh. Lovely soul-binding marks you have." She sat up, narrowing her eyes as she took a closer look at the scars on my stomach. Side-eying Callum, she said, "I've never known this soldier to have a very delicate hand; practically ripped his old claims to shreds. Aren't you a special one?"

Callum sighed heavily, fingers snapping repeatedly behind his back. "Niamh, please. That was a long time ago."

"You've still clung to other annoying habits," she teased, and his fingers began snapping a bit harder. "Fuck, that sets my nerves on edge. Hurry it up then, you didn't seek me out without purpose." She gave a lazy groan and closed her eyes again. "Tell me what you need so I can go get another drink."

"I'll bring you two drinks, if you'll allow my witch to pick a bit of metal from your collection," Callum said. Without opening her eyes, Niamh raised her eyebrows in surprise.

"Metal, eh? Last I heard, Callum doesn't wear metal anymore."

"Again. That was long ago."

She stared at him for a moment. Something changed in her face and she sat up, leaning against the rope holding her hammock aloft as she swung her legs. "I'll have a firewater and figberry wine. *Extra* fiery!" She shouted the last part, craning her neck to look back at the bartender and make sure they heard her.

Callum rolled his eyes and leaned down to kiss my head before he left. "Pick out whatever you'd like. Just consider location when choosing."

With my head buzzing, I barely managed an overwhelmed smile before he left for the bar. Niamh reached beneath her hammock, seizing a bag made of dyed red leather and holding it out to me.

"They're not organized, so you'll have to search

through," she said, before adding proudly, "Made 'em all myself. There's some real special ones in there, rare gems from the wastes. Wasn't easy to get them. There's even some dragon glass in there."

Opening the bag, I was instantly aghast. Numerous pieces of jewelry were within—studs, rings, barbells—all of them glittering in the light. Some were silver, some gold or black. Jewels of every cut and color adorned them.

"Did you say *dragon* glass?" I finally managed to sputter.

Niamh laughed. "Never seen a dragon before? I suppose they don't have them on Earth anymore, do they?" When I shook my head in absolute bewilderment, she shrugged. "It's pretty. Like milky glass with shards of charcoal inside."

As if my fingers were called to them, I swiftly found several pieces set with the gems she spoke of. There was a variety of sizes and shapes, some thick and heavy, while others were tiny and delicate.

"Where are you going to pierce him, hm?" Niamh said, waggling her eyebrows suggestively. "He's got an awful lot of them already. Not much of him left untouched."

"I'm not sure actually." The fact that I was about to give a piercing with my own hands was more than enough to occupy my brain, let alone choosing *where* to put it. I didn't know much about body modifications, the extent of my experience being my two sets of piercings in each ear. But Niamh's clearly suggestive tone gave me an idea.

"Niamh, is it possible to pierce the . . . uhm . . . penis?"

She immediately burst out laughing, rocking herself so hard she almost fell out of her hammock. When she finally calmed down, she said, "Aw, such an innocent little witch, aren't you? Adorable. I never would have expected it, but . . . I suppose that old soldier deserves a little softness."

She pointed out the jewelry that would work for such a piercing, even giving me a quick but thorough explanation for how I'd do it. "It's nearly impossible for you to hurt him, love, trust me. Just take your time and he'll heal perfectly fine. But what about *you*, eh? What's he giving you?"

"Giving . . . me?" I said, still trying to memorize the instructions she'd just disclosed.

"Yeah, piercings are usually a reciprocal thing."

That opened my mind to an entirely new path of possibilities as I rummaged through the jewelry. Callum returned to us right as I made my selections, handing off the beverages to Niamh before wrapping his arms around me.

"Clingy, isn't he?" Niamh said, before taking a long gulp of a clear, icy beverage sprinkled with little red petals. "Fuck, that's good. Properly fiery, Ro!" She lifted the glass in a toast toward the bartender before flopping back in her hammock and closing her eyes again. "Enjoy your new toy, Everly."

"New *toy*?" Callum said, eyes darting between us with instant suspicion.

"Never mind," I said, taking his hand. The jewelry I'd selected was hidden within my opposite palm, and I was eager for him to see it. But not here. "Let's go back."

He let me lead the way back to the cavern, winding through the glistening caves until we'd reached our private pool again. There were little alcoves carved into the smooth rock around the cavern, and Callum lounged on one of them, his toes dangling into the water.

For a moment, I stood still and admired him. How he sprawled himself across the damp stone, his naked body glistening with water, droplets clinging to the tips of his wings. His thick cock rested against his thigh, and I imagined the ridged head pierced with the jewelry I'd selected.

The thought made a smile spread over my face, and Callum immediately braced himself with anticipation.

"You know I love that smile, darling," he said. "Like you've thought of something naughty."

"I've thought of something *very* naughty," I said, approaching him slowly. Holding up the needle in a glass vial Niamh had given me, I continued, "In fact, I thought of something absolutely wicked."

"Don't keep me in anticipation," he said, shifting restlessly as I stood over him. Sitting on the stone between his sprawled legs, I showed him the jewelry I'd selected: a curved barbell of black metal, set with dragon glass. The gem was truly stunning, just as Niamh described it.

Callum somehow recognized what it was immediately. "Dragon glass? How did she ever—" He smirked, shaking his head. "Niamh is going to get herself in trouble collecting things like that. Dragons don't take kindly to intruders. Or to *anyone*, for that matter."

Glaring at him and pouting my lip, I said, "I can't believe you never told me dragons are real."

"Terribly sorry." He folded his arms behind his head, not looking sorry at all. "I suppose you'll have to punish me then."

"Brat." I smacked his thigh, and he caught my wrists and yanked me closer for a kiss.

"Where are you marking me?" he said.

Pressing my hand against his chest, I shoved him back against the rock and said, "I decided to mark you where we're most intimately connected. Your cock."

He blinked rapidly, looking surprised for a moment. The aforementioned body part twitched, swelling as if the thought of something being pierced through it was actually appealing.

"Fuck, I love you," he breathed out. "Do you want me to guide you through it?"

"Niamh told me what to do," I said and situated myself a bit more comfortably. "But, yes, please do. Just so I don't mess it up."

"You won't," he said confidently.

"I don't suppose there are any sterile gloves for me to wear?" I said, only half-joking. I didn't know much about piercings, but I knew enough about bacteria to cringe at the thought of doing this with my bare hands.

"There aren't, but I assure you, I'll be fine," he said. "Even if I were susceptible to infections, I would be extremely unlikely to catch one here."

As I removed the needle from its vial, his cock throbbed again, visibly thickening.

"How am I supposed to pierce you if you're hard?" I scolded. He was grinning like a cat with a canary in its mouth.

"Maybe you'll have to be rough," he said. "Or, you may have to force me to— Ahh, *shit*."

Grasping his balls in my hand, I gave them enough of a squeeze that he bared his teeth. He snapped them as his arms flexed, his body coiling as his muscles went rigid.

"You're fucking cruel, my lady. Absolutely goddamn merciless," he growled, gritting his teeth as I sweetly smiled.

"It's for your own good," I said. It certainly didn't calm his erection as much as it should have, but it did soften him slightly. The moment I took his length in my hand, it twitched again, no less eager to rise to the occasion than before.

With a heavy, mockingly exasperated sigh, I said, "I suppose I'll have to be rough with you then."

He groaned, hips thrusting sporadically into my hand. Smacking his thigh again, I told him to keep still as I carefully lined up where to push the needle through. Needles didn't frighten me, but the thought of shoving this one through such a sensitive spot made me slightly queasy.

But Callum was desperate for it. He was so tense he was shaking, his entire body locked with unbearable excitement.

As I lined up the needle, I lifted my gaze to meet his eyes. "Are you sure, Callum?"

"I've never been surer of anything in my life, Everly."

The needle went in, but it wasn't pain that contorted his face. It was pure bliss, melting over him as his eyes fluttered closed and his chest expanded with a massive breath. My hands were shaking as I fit the jewelry, a little blood marring the wound. But he didn't bleed for long, and opened his eyes to stare as I secured the jewelry in place.

"God, Callum, *really*?" I laughed as he throbbed in my hand again, having gone from semi-soft to rigidly hard in a matter of seconds.

"How can I help it with your hands all over me?"

Lowering my head, I kissed the tip of his cock, lingering with my lips against him for just a moment. "It looks so sexy on you," I said, and his eyes blazed with a fire that threatened to consume me. "I can't wait to feel it inside me."

He moved rapidly, faster than my eyes could see. One moment, he was lounging against the stone, devouring me with his eyes—the next moment, he'd seized me, taken me into the water, and held me tight as he claimed my mouth with his.

"If it were up to me, we would never leave this place." He left the words in kisses across my skin, trailing up my neck. "I would keep you here forever. A treasure all to myself. My holy, captive goddess. I would let humanity die, I would watch the world burn, if only to keep you safe. If only to shelter you. Guard you. But who am I to stand in your way?" The words were so full of pain my heart nearly broke. "Who am I to stifle your power? I am your eternal servant. I would deny you nothing. Not even danger. Not even . . ."

"Not even death," I whispered. My hands clasped his face, tracing the contours of his ears and the hard line of his jaw before I kissed him. For a moment, I had no idea how our mouths could part. I needed him to breathe, to *live*.

And for a moment, just the briefest moment, I wanted to beg him to do it. Keep me here forever. Hold me captive, give me no choice but to hide myself away and never return to the human world again. We could stay here, where it was safe, sheltered within our own little world.

But for how long would this world remain our own? If a God rose to power, what was to stop It from pursuing more and more? One world would never be enough. When the balance of our entire dimension was at risk, there was nowhere we could hide.

We could only face It. We could only fight.

It ached to pull away from him, even a little, but I forced myself to do it so I could look into those black eyes. The void stared back, and it was full of longing, full of love. But there was fear too, lurking in the depths of that endless abyss. Fear that wanted to drag me in and drown me, if only it meant he could keep me.

I wanted to let him. I wanted to drown in his darkness forever.

But I couldn't. God, I couldn't.

"Mark me," I said. He searched my eyes, lips parted slightly in disbelief. "I mean it. I want you to. I want to wear your metal, just like you're wearing mine."

His fingers traced over my stomach, over the scars he'd carved there. In blood and pain, we'd been bound together; in necessity, in fear. But I wanted a mark from him given purely in love, in devotion, in joy.

"Where do you want it?"

My stomach flipped over, tangled up like a writhing snake. I had no doubt of what I wanted. Drawing myself closer to him again, I spread my legs around his hips, straddling him in the water.

"Exactly where I marked you," I said. The smile that spread over his face was delightfully sadistic, giddy with disbelief.

"You honor me." I was stunned to see him duck his head, a small bow before he kissed me. It was addictive to have his hands on me; I never wanted it to end. "You'll heal swiftly, especially in Hell. But it will hurt."

He smiled when I presented him with the jewelry I'd already selected. It matched his, although it was slightly smaller, designed to sit snuggly through the hood of my clitoris. He retrieved a pillow, woven of soft fibers, and placed it under my head as I lay beside the pool, suddenly nervous now that he was between my legs with a needle.

But it was the best kind of nerves. The kind that roiled through my stomach, shuddered in my chest, made my hands shake and my head buzz.

"Nervous?"

I quickly nodded. I was turned on, I was intrigued, I was shivering with anticipation—and yes, I was absolutely terrified.

"I know you can take it for me."

Closing my eyes, I slowly exhaled. His words took me back to that night he saved my life and claimed my soul; how it had torn him apart to do it, how he'd broken his own heart to protect me.

We'd come so far since then, it felt like an eternity.

His fingers spread me open, and he moaned softly in admiration. "You're so fucking gorgeous, Everly. If there was anything I could ever worship, it would be you."

He lowered his head, and I practically levitated off the stone as he closed his mouth over me. Keeping me spread apart with his fingers, he sucked my clit while flicking the bud with his tongue, causing my legs to twitch with every caress.

"Be brave for me now, darling. Take a deep breath . . ."

Inhaling didn't stop my whimper as the needle slid in. The sting was sudden and sharp, but dissipated far more quickly than I expected.

"There's my good girl." He fit the jewelry in, and I winced at the discomfort, but couldn't deny the swell of heat in my abdomen. Every little touch of his fingers was a tease, egging me on.

"Jewels fit for a goddess," he said, admiring me before he lowered his head again, kissing my thighs. "You'll be tender for a little while. But your magic is bolstered by this place; you'll heal quickly."

He lifted me from the rock, holding me as we sunk back into the pool. As my bones turned to jelly, and I lay limp against him, my demon said, "I'd like to see how hard you'll come with that pretty jewel pierced through you. Glittering like a treasure . . ."

"You should find out." I wrapped my legs around his hips, his hard cock nudging against my entrance.

But he grasped my hips, hard, preventing me from impaling myself on him.

With a sardonic smile, he said, "You're too tender for it." I made a soft sound when his finger brushed lightly over my new jewelry. "You'll have to be patient and wait."

"No." I pouted, rolling my hips against him in a way that was undeniably demanding as I slid my fingers around his throat. "I don't want to be patient. I. Want. You."

Before I could get out another word, he grabbed my face, squeezing my jaw. He pressed me against the side of the pool, grinning hungrily.

"You want it that badly?" His voice was dangerously low. "Prove it. Beg for it."

My breath stuttered. "Please . . ."

His fingers tightened, digging in until I whimpered. "*Beg*. Show me how desperately you want it, darling. Convince me."

He let me go and sat on the edge of the pool with his legs spread, leaning back on his palms. Water streaked down his tattooed chest. His cock jutted up, monstrously thick and glistening with his new jewelry.

Positioning myself between his legs, I looked up at him with wide, pleading eyes. "Please, Callum." I stroked my fingers along his thighs, lowering myself until my mouth was only inches away from his shaft. "Please fuck me." I brushed my lips over him, flicking my tongue at the sparkling gem pierced through his head. "Treat me like your whore."

His breath caught, and he held it. I smiled.

"I know you want to." I traced my tongue from the base of his thick cock, up his shaft, caressing his balls in my hand. They were soft as velvet, and tightened as I closed my lips over his tip, swirling my tongue around him.

"Tempting little succubus, aren't you?" he said, still holding his breath. Struggling to control himself.

Popping my mouth off his cock, I sucked my finger instead, making it slick.

"If you're worried about hurting my piercing, I have another hole to fuck." I stroked my finger over his taint, pressing lightly. He leaned back, holding himself up on his elbows so he could watch me. "I want you to fuck my ass." I pressed my finger inside him, and his lips parted with a soft sound. "I want you to stretch me open with that big, thick cock and fill me with your cum."

Lowering my head, I stroked my tongue around where my finger was buried in him, probing at the tight ring of muscle. He growled, and his hand snaked around the nape of my neck to tightly grip my hair. He held my head there as I licked, probing my finger in and out. His wings were splayed out, twitching every time I pressed my finger in past the knuckle.

"I'd destroy you, darling," he said, his voice so dark that I shivered. "Is that really what you want? To get your ass ripped open by this cock?"

Unable to raise my head, I made an affirmative noise.

He smiled ravenously, arching his back to force my finger deeper inside.

"I'm not sure I believe you," he said. I begged, but my words were muffled as I pleasured him with my tongue. "Mm, that's it. Are you going to be a good whore for me? I'm going to take my time, stretch you open slowly. I'll make that tight, perfect ass *mine*."

He dragged me backward by my hair, slipping into the water and then shoving me toward the side of the pool. My knees came to rest on the low shelf along the edge, and he pushed my head forward so I was bent over the lip of the pool. His claws pricked into me as he curled over my back, possessively stroking his tongue along my spine until he could bite down on my shoulder.

"I get to claim your virginity yet again."

His long tongue caressed over my puckered hole before he spat, his finger swirling the saliva over me.

"So tight," he said, barely pressing inside. Groaning, I focused on keeping my muscles relaxed as he entered me. He worked his fingers, pumping them, stretching me open.

"It's going to feel even better with my cock inside you." He thrust his fingers in and out, saliva dripping from his tongue to keep me slick. "Let your magic help you. You're going to need it."

He added a third finger, taunting me gently as I whimpered and squirmed. He continued like that for several minutes, stretching me open, praising me as I relaxed for him.

"That's my pretty little whore. So tight for me. Take it nice and deep . . ."

His fingers withdrew, and I caught my breath as the head of his cock pressed against me instead. Glancing back, with my cheek still flat against the stone, I watched him stroke himself as he admired me. One hand gripped my ass, holding me open as he pleasured himself.

The sight of that pearlescent gem at the end of his cock made me shiver with anticipation. He met my eyes and spat on his length.

"I'm going to ruin you," he said. "There's no return from damnation."

"Why would I want to return?" I said, and my voice broke as he pressed inside me. I saw stars, the ache so sudden and sharp. "Fuck, wait—wait—"

He paused immediately, tracing his claws up and down my spine in a mesmerizing way.

"Breathe deeply for me," he said. "Let your magic fill your muscles and relax you."

It wasn't easy to do as he said. My thoughts were all over the place, buzzing like bees disturbed from their nest. But with every deep breath, the tension eased from my muscles. Callum was stroking himself with his head inside me, perfectly content to take his time. As I relaxed, I gyrated my hips, nudging myself back and pressing him deeper inside.

"That's it. You just can't resist, can you?" Callum praised me as I moved, one hand still rubbing soothingly over my back. "Such a good girl for me. How does that feel?"

"So . . . so good, Callum." I felt drunk and giddy. It didn't hurt as he entered me even deeper, but the *stretch* was mind-blowing. "Holy shit, you're so big."

"Or perhaps you are merely so very small," he said, arching over my back like a predator and driving all the way inside. I cried out—overwhelmed, stunned at how incredibly full I felt. If it weren't for the magic tingling in every nerve, I had no doubt the size of him would have injured me. But instead, I lay limp and trembling, rocking myself against him with lazy movements.

Too lazy for his taste.

He pulled me up and wrapped his arm around my neck, holding me pinned tightly against his body as he thrust into me. The groan he forced out of me was obscene, my body shaking as he slammed into me. My clit was so swollen it ached, but even that wound didn't feel as tender as it should have.

"Your body is a work of art," he murmured. "I should hang you on display and never let you go."

Never let you go. Every time he said those words, my heart swelled. Combined with the overwhelming sensation of him inside me, using me for his pleasure, my eyes rolled back.

"That's gonna make me come, Callum," I gasped. He snarled, hips slapping sharply against my wet skin.

"Fuck, you're glorious. Should be a sin—a fucking *sin* to feel so good, to look so irresistibly perfect. Every inch of you . . ." His hands trailed over me, grasping and possessive. My head fell back against his shoulder, my body beyond my control. "Mine. My witch, my goddess, my whore. In sickness and in health, in life and beyond death. Always and forever."

My bliss exploded into ecstasy. All I could do was breathe, swaddled in the tight grip of his arms, ravaged by the intensity of his body. His movements grew more urgent, messier, rougher—until he came inside me with a snarl, wet skin pressed tight to mine, his words still trailing in my ear, "I'll love you endlessly, darling."

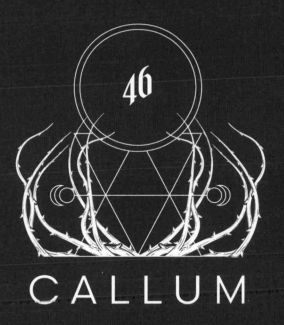

CALLUM

NOTHING COULD COMPARE to the sunrise in Hell. As Everly slept peacefully in my arms, I watched that massive fireball rise straight out of the churning sea, bathing the city in its light. It warmed my face, kissing my skin as it streamed through the open windows.

It had been so long since I'd set foot in this home, laid in this bed. Yet it remained unchanged, as if I'd never left. No demon in Hell was left wanting for shelter, so if a living space was abandoned, it usually remained untouched. But I'd spent so long on Earth that I still felt surprised when I walked in the unlocked door and found the suite exactly as I'd left it.

Some demons preferred massive living quarters. I did not. The suite was simple, occupying one floor of a great tower overlooking the sea. Demons lived both above and below, but I couldn't hear them. The walls were well-insulated, even for one with such sharp hearing as me.

A thousand years ago, I'd left this place because I couldn't bear the pain. Everywhere I went, every site, every smell, every poignant memory, was so filled with agony that I couldn't bear to remember. I cast it aside, I put it behind me. The work of a warrior is never done and that was what I clung to: the war in Hell may have ended but the war against the Gods had only begun. What else could I do except fight? It was all I knew.

Except it was different now. The memories were still there, and fuck, they still hurt. But like precious ancient relics, I could handle them with care. Turning them over in my mind, remembering with as much delicacy as I could manage. Happiness was sheltered in those memories, buried within them like seeds waiting for winter's frost to thaw.

Perhaps grief didn't ever truly end. Perhaps it only changed, growing with me. It no longer led the way, it merely existed beside me. Sometimes, in moments like this, I could forget about it entirely. The memories of those I'd loved and lost were as soft and warm as the rising sun.

This could very well be the last sunrise I ever witnessed. This journey to Hell could be the final time I set foot here. Death did not frighten me, nor did pain or suffering.

I feared emptiness. I feared the lonely expanse of a future without the one I loved. As I looked down at my witch sleeping soundly in my arms, I was filled with an emotion that wasn't rage, or terror, or desperation, but felt like all three at once.

I wanted to hoard her like precious gold, lock her away like a work of art to be protected.

But no art gallery, museum, or gilded cage could possibly be worthy of her. None of them could contain her. A life being sheltered and hidden away would be poison for her beautiful mind. She needed freedom. She needed to spread the wings of her power and fly as high as she could go.

I wouldn't stop her. I'd gladly risk my own life, if only to stand beside her every step of the way.

She stirred as the sun fell over her face. I sheltered her with my wing for a while, to give her a few more minutes of rest, before allowing the light to wake her. She lifted her head, her arm moving lazily to drape over my chest as she snuggled into my side.

She surprised me when she gave a long groan and swore under her breath. "My ass is so sore, Callum. It's all your fault."

"*All* my fault? Don't tell me my wicked witch won't accept some of the blame." She groaned even more, and I laughed. "I seem to recall you wantonly begging me for it."

"Oh, hush." She slapped my chest and leaned in for a slow kiss. "As if you're above *wanton begging* yourself."

She reached down, wrapping her hand around my cock. When she slid off the bed and onto her knees, she swiftly proved herself right that I wasn't above begging at all.

NO ONE, NOT even the eldest of demons, knew how the Onyx Citadel came to be built. It crested a mountain comprised entirely of black stone; its shining towers so tall they disappeared into the clouds on overcast days.

A long, steep stairway was carved into the mountainside, surrounded by a forest of moon trees, with their pearlescent white bark and emerald-green leaves. Thin streams of water trickled over their roots, spilling eternally from the wellsprings deep underground. The water flowed through the city below, nourishing our plants and churning the great waterwheels until it eventually reached the sea.

Standing at the foot of that stairway was meant to be intimidating, an experience of shock and awe at the sheer size of the castle above. It was impossible to look at those towers and not feel something: whether it was fear or awe, joy or comfort.

The first time I'd ascended those steps was when I'd been named the leader of Hell's army. When Lucifer promised me a seat on the Council if I returned victorious.

The last time I'd made this arduous climb, I had indeed returned victorious. But it was a poisoned victory, toxic and rotten. The accolades they'd offered me meant nothing. The praise for my strength and bravery were empty words.

None of it brought back the dead. The glory I'd thought I wanted was empty and cold.

Everly took my hand and squeezed, wrenching me back to the present. She was dressed in a sheer skirt that brushed her ankles and a short top that wrapped around her throat and exposed her stomach. It was difficult not to stare at my sigil, scarred beautifully onto her slightly rounded belly.

She'd been eating more since living in House Laverne, finally having access to enough food whenever and however she wanted it. Her scent had changed since coming here too, becoming even sweeter and brighter.

"Are you ready?" I said.

"Are you?"

Lifting my hand, I kissed her knuckles. "With you by my side, I'm ready for anything."

The moment we set foot on the stairs, the Council became aware of our presence. There was no visible change; no ringing of bells or sounding of an alarm. But high above, the Archdemons who watched over Hell were assembling, readying themselves for our presence.

As we neared the courtyard at the peak of the staircase, clouds billowed around us. The cool air shrouded Everly in a haze, making her appear ghost-like as she walked ahead of me, still holding my hand. We passed under a stone archway, dark red vines twined around its surface, and entered the citadel's courtyard.

On the opposite side of the clearing, six silhouettes were visible in the fog. Hell's Council was composed of some of the oldest and most powerful demons ever known, dwarfing me in their age and the magic they controlled. Bael and Paimon, the oldest of the six, covered their faces with red veils, pinned to their hair with metal circlets encrusted with jewels. In all my years of existence, not once had I seen either of their faces. Then there was Caim, with his long jet-black hair and coat of dark feathers. Murmur was his opposite, her hair as white as fresh-fallen snow and long enough to brush the ground like a cape.

Lucifer and Leaina stood in the center, both of them dressed in red from head to toe. Leaina's gaze was as sharp and observant as ever, but Lucifer's expression was unreadable.

If that dramatic bastard was still angry with me, we were going to have it out right here and now.

We stood for a moment in silence, facing each other across the courtyard. Then Everly stepped forward, without dropping my hand, and inclined her head. "Council, it is an honor to be granted an audience. I am Everly Laverne, daughter of Heidi, granddaughter of Winona. Grand Mistress of Laverne Coven." She lifted her chin, looking as calm and confident as a witch well beyond her years. "I come to ask your permission to execute an enemy of Hell."

It wasn't Lucifer who spoke, but Caim.

"It's been a long time since a witch set foot in this courtyard," he said. The other Council members nodded. "That is strange enough. But even stranger is that you do not come alone and are accompanied by a demon who is not in your thrall. A demon who is regarded very highly by all of us."

"An unusual witch indeed," Murmur said, her voice sweetly soft. She stepped forward, although she kept her distance, circling us as she tapped her chin with a long white claw. "Callum, our *Magni Deicide*. How very long it's been since I last had the pleasure of seeing you. It gives me joy to see you return so healthy. So strong."

The difference in my strength since claiming Everly was doubtlessly obvious to them. They would feel it when they looked at me, sense it when they smelled me.

Silently, Bael took a step forward, leaning toward Paimon. They whispered in the other demon's ear, far too softly for me to hear. Paimon nodded, and without removing their veil, said, "Why does a mortal witch seek to destroy one of Hell's enemies? Given the fraught history between our kinds, Lady Witch, it could be argued you are an enemy of Hell yourself."

"I am bound for Hell," she said. She laid her palm over her scarred stomach. "My soul will rest here for eternity. When Earth is done with me, Hell will have me, and I intend to protect my second home."

Leaina gave a small nod as she looked at Lucifer, who sighed heavily. Murmur suddenly stepped closer, extending her hand toward Everly.

"How very brave you are," Murmur said, clasping Everly's hand. Lucifer looked disgusted. Caim appeared intrigued. "A mortal woman, facing a God . . . and under such unusual circumstances. You are risking so much." Her black eyes narrowed slightly as she let Everly's hand go. When she touched my witch again, it was to trace her fingers very lightly across the scars on her body. "An Archdemon gave you his sigil and you did not use it against him. By the actions you've chosen, you've bound yourself even more tightly to our world. You are a witch of Hell."

Murmur stepped back, clasping her hands before her as she looked back at the other Council members. "But perhaps, Lady Witch, you do not understand how dire the situation has become."

The warning in her voice alarmed me. "What do you mean?" I said. Lucifer had averted his eyes from me, but looked back when I took a step toward him.

He said, "Last night, a Reaper tore through the Veil and arrived on Earth. It was summoned."

It was Everly who spoke up and said, "Summoned by who?"

"By the God," Leaina answered. "It has infected a host. A second sacrifice was made, and the third is in the hands of those who call themselves Libiri. She, too, will be offered soon."

Everly gasped, grasping her chest in alarm. Ripples of anxiety poured over her, although she struggled to keep her expression neutral.

"Raelynn," she choked out. "Did they—?"

In a voice like gravel, Paimon said, "That woman still lives. It was one of your bloodline that was consumed by the God, and it is your brother who now carries part of It within his flesh. His body cannot sustain It for long."

"The God is desperate," Caim said, fingers stroking slowly over his feathery robe. "It knows that It is under threat. It has become more aggressive in response."

Everly's emotions had gone cold. Her hands were clenched at her sides. "My bloodline . . . You mean my sister. Victoria. They killed her?"

Her words were steady, but her heart was pounding

erratically. Lucifer, ever-so-slightly, inclined his head toward her. "Yes. Your sister Victoria was killed, consumed by the God."

For a moment, Everly closed her eyes. Heat rolled off her, the air shimmering faintly around her until she took a deep breath and opened her eyes once more.

"The Libiri have Raelynn?" she said, and Lucifer nodded. "Then there is no time to waste. Once more, I ask for your permission to kill our enemy."

Lucifer said, "And if I refuse?"

Everly clasped her hands in front of her and said calmly, "I have my own free will. I ask for permission as a gesture of respect. But with or without your consent, Council, this God will die by my hand."

For a few long moments, the only sound on that cold mountaintop was the howling wind.

Then Murmur said, "I approve her request."

"If Murmur approves, I do as well," said Caim.

Leaina spoke up, "As do I."

"We have yet to hear her demon speak," Lucifer said, gesturing toward me. "Why does he believe that pursuing this execution is worthwhile?"

Leaina made a face as she turned to him. "Callum is bound to her. They made a bargain, as *you* demanded."

For a moment, Lucifer looked at her as if he wanted to bite her head off. Not that he'd have a very good chance of doing so—Leaina wasn't one to fuck with. None of them were.

But if Lucifer wanted me to speak, fine. I'd fucking speak.

502   HARLEY LAROUX

"I am bound to her," I said, speaking loudly enough for all of them to hear but looking only at Lucifer. "I swore my service, my protection, my guidance. By that oath, and that oath alone, I am compelled to kill the God that is terrorizing her. But I made another oath too, a long time ago. I stood before you in this very courtyard and vowed to defend Hell from all enemies, to destroy those who would destroy us. The Gods intended to wipe us from existence and succeeded in killing far, far more than they ever should have."

Everly stepped closer to my side, her fingers twining with my own.

"Perhaps you fear that I could die, Lucifer," I said. "Perhaps you fear it so much that you would drive me away, that you seek to take my free will. We've both lost so many, and I once thought you were callous and cold for attempting to forget that. But your pain is as great as mine. If I die, like the others, then I will die in their names. For all those we lost."

Bael once again whispered in Paimon's ear.

"Lucifer would do well not to allow his emotions to cloud his judgment," Paimon said, and Bael nodded in agreement.

Lucifer winced, his eyes darting away as his pride was stung. He'd loved me once. Perhaps he still did. But the end of the war had torn us apart. When I'd refused his mark and left Hell, he'd taken that rejection personally.

He hid his fears behind control and viciousness, but he was no fool. He knew there was no other choice.

"I give my consent," he said.

In unison, the Council members lifted their hands. They sliced sharp claws across their opened palms, allowing the blood to well and run down to their wrists. Everly and I did the same; Everly using a small knife on her belt to cut herself.

"First blood had been drawn," Paimon said in a voice that echoed with the vast ages of time. "Now go to war."

EVERLY

THE MOMENT CALLUM and I teleported back into the house, I knew something was wrong. The vines on the walls were shriveling and gray; the air was so cold I could see my own breath.

Callum growled, baring his teeth. "Something is in the house."

"We need to find my grandmother," I said. "Now!"

When I teleported again, he followed me. In the kitchen, I found the old radio sitting on the table and hurriedly turned up the dial. "Grams! Grandma, are you there?"

Static. Nothing but static.

"Winona!" Callum's voice shook the walls, and another wave of static poured from the radio.

Faintly, within the buzzing, I could hear a faint voice. ". . . infestation! Got in . . . night, It . . . Darragh can't hold It . . ."

"There's too much interference," I said. Rapidly turning the dial, I tried to find a station that had a clearer signal, but they all carried the same static. Except one.

The radio suddenly fell deathly silent. There was a faint sound, so soft I had to turn the volume all the way up and lean my head close to the speakers.

Drip. Drip, drip.

Chills went over my arms, and I looked up at Callum in alarm, but he was staring at the radio.

"Turn it off," he said softly.

Then, from the speaker, came a voice. It was ragged with pain, sharp with hysteria as it spoke in a grating whisper, "Everlyyyy . . . I miss you, sister . . ."

My stomach lurched. "Victoria?"

"It's so *cold* here . . ." She singsonged, breathy and shuddering. "Won't you come . . . down . . . down . . . down . . . into the dark?"

Callum lunged forward, turning the radio off. I sat there stunned, staring, stomach churning.

Finally, I managed to choke out, "We need to speak to Darragh."

As I carried the radio with me, Callum flew ahead of me through the house toward the conservatory, reaching the Woodsprie before I did. When I heard his shout, I sprinted. My footsteps squelched against the wet grass as I burst through the doors to the outside, crushing mushrooms underfoot. But when I reached the tree guarding the greenhouse, I stopped abruptly and gasped.

The bark had turned gray, the leaves brown and shriveling. The highest limbs still appeared healthy, their coloration normal, their leaves thick and green. Darragh was leaning his head back in the apex of the spread limbs, his honey-colored eyes dull and half-lidded.

"My lady," he said softly as I approached. I cradled his limp head and it lolled against me. His wood felt rough and dry; the bark flaking away.

"Oh no, no, Darragh!" I tried to hold his head up. He couldn't even keep his own eyes open. "What can I do? What do you need? Callum! What can I do?"

But the demon shook his head. "I don't know. We need to find a way to keep him alive. His roots protect this house. Without him, we'll be far too vulnerable."

In desperation, I seized the radio again and cranked the volume up, whispering, "Please, please, please . . ."

To my relief, my grandmother's voice came faintly through. ". . . needs nectar . . . go to my cabinets near . . . potting tables . . . large mason jars . . . green wax seals."

Callum vanished into the greenhouse. I could still feel Grams' presence close by. Focusing my magic toward her, I attempted to bolster her strength so she could speak to us more clearly.

"What happened, Darragh?" I said. There was a distinct outline of his legs within the trunk now, as if his very being was being pushed out of the tree he occupied.

"Infection," he said. "Parasitic . . . fungus . . . it reached my roots."

Callum returned, carrying a glass jar of pale-gold, syrupy liquid. He held it to Darragh's mouth, who for once didn't have a smartass remark to give. He drank deeply, desperately, the nectar running down his chin as he gulped.

It brought a little of the light back into his eyes.

"It came up from below," he said. "The mycelium. There's rot spread out all beneath the house. I can endure it . . . for now. But if it kills the other trees, I can't protect the house."

"It's the God," Callum said, and Darragh nodded.

"It carries the stench of ocean water," he said roughly. "So much salt. The soil is poisoned." He shivered, shaking loose a cascade of brown leaves.

"Ocean water . . ." I said. "But how? How could It have gotten in? Past all the trees . . ."

"From below," Darragh repeated. He bared all his thorny teeth in pain. "It got in . . . from below . . ."

He sunk back into the tree, soon vanishing entirely. When I laid my hand against the wood, it was freezing cold.

"It's killing him," Callum said.

"You need to move quickly," said Grams. Although static still distorted her voice, her words were stronger now. "The God's rot must have a source of power close by, a vessel to carry some of Its essence. It couldn't have overwhelmed Darragh so quickly otherwise."

"A vessel?" I gasped. "Jeremiah. It must be. The Council said It infected him. But how could he have found us?"

"It may not be him," Callum said grimly. "The God would only be able to contain a small fragment of Its essence in a human like him. His body will deteriorate quickly. But if the God has split Its essence between multiple vessels . . ."

He didn't need to finish his statement. Dread settled over me as I sensed a familiar prickling on the back of my skull. The sensation of being watched.

"It must be in the tunnels," I said. "In the vault." Getting to my feet, I handed the radio to Callum. "Meet me in the kitchen. I need supplies."

Teleporting first to my bedroom, I hurriedly opened the chest at the foot of my bed. I kept my most important positions in there: the grimoires I'd found within the library and around the house, including Sybil's, as well as the enchanted blade. I put Sybil's grimoire within a small pouch on my belt and secured the blade at my left hip in its sheath, before teleporting down to the kitchen.

Callum was already waiting for me there. I collected herbs, powdered fluorite, shards of quartz, and twigs of black laurel from the various jars upon the shelves.

My grandmother spoke again, sounding weary, "Be careful, Everly. There's no telling what's waiting for you down there. Even with Callum at your side."

"It doesn't matter what's down there," I said. "This is my house, and I will defend it. Nothing is allowed to enter here without my permission." I glanced over at Callum, my chest swelling when I saw the pride in his eyes as he looked at me. "Whatever is down there will be dealt with. This ends tonight."

48

E V E R L Y

THE LIBRARY HAD been overtaken by fungal growth. Mushrooms sprouted from the book spines, even bursting through the wooden floors. The silence around us was eerie as I opened the vault, greeted by a wafting smell of decay. Dust drifted through the meager light as I cast out my hand and lit the candles, illuminating the room. But the firelight was muted, the darkness was too heavy for it.

"This isn't a good sign," Callum said. He was staring at a web-like substance covering the books, desks, and chairs. "It's growing fast."

"Then we're in the right place," I said, spotting a puddle of water slowly seeping across the floor.

The hatch leading down to the tunnels creaked as Callum pulled it open. He went first, leaping down before I climbed onto the ladder. My feet squelched in mud as

I reached the bottom, greeted by the stench of mold and rotting fish.

Sybil's laboratory was in complete disarray. More pale webbing had grown over the tables, the specimen jars having cracked open, wafting the smell of ammonia into the air. The ground was soaked, mud swiftly caking my boots as Callum and I approached the tunnels.

The air was cold and stale. Distantly, I could hear dripping water. Taking a deep breath, I stepped forward, but Callum grabbed my arm.

"You should let me go first," he said.

But I shook my head. "You're the guardian of this house, but I am its mistress. An invasion like this is a challenge to me, directly. It's *me* the Deep One is hoping to get to, so it's me that will face It." He didn't look pleased, and I reached up to cup his face. "Trust me, Callum. You know what I'm capable of."

For a moment, it looked like he wanted to keep arguing. But he pressed his lips into a thin line and nodded once, releasing his grip on my arm.

He stayed close behind me as I made my way through the tunnels. He had explored them far more than I had, but it wasn't difficult to figure out which way to go. I only had to follow the mud and puddles of stagnant water.

"Shit—!" Stumbling forward as my boot hit something in the muddy soil, I would have fallen flat on my face if Callum hadn't grabbed the back of my jacket. Tugging my boot free with a wet squelching sound, I cast several balls of light ahead of us down the tunnel, illuminating what lay ahead.

Broken planks of wood jutted out of the mud like jagged teeth. The tunnel was completely flooded, wood and
debris floating on the surface. The water was murky and
still. Impossible to tell what lay beneath.

"There was a boundary here," Callum said. Although
he kept his voice low, it sounded so loud in the strange
stillness. "It's been broken."

Daring to take another step forward, I focused my
magic on my shoes. *Light as a feather, unburdened by
thick soil, resistant to the water flooding over them* . . .

The spell work was far from perfect, and every few
steps, I would sink into the mud again. But it was better than nothing, and the longer I clung to the spell, the
stronger it became. The water came up to my ankles, but
my magic prevented it from slowing me too much.

All the while, I kept the light moving steadily ahead of
us, my mind open but guarded as I tentatively searched
for any unusual magic nearby.

But everything felt so *cold*.

My light could barely penetrate the darkness ahead.
Despite trying my hardest to maintain them, one by one,
the orbs of light winked out.

Then, from the dark, a voice called to me.

"Everlyyy . . . Oh, Eeeverlyyy . . ."

The voice was familiar. Realization snatched the air
from my lungs and left me cold, eyes wide as I stopped
moving.

"Why won't you talk to your sister, Everly?"

The voice was distant and dissolved into laughter that
left me feeling nauseous. It was Victoria's voice, but it

was *wrong*. She sounded unnaturally high-pitched. Her words echoed through the tunnels in a lilting singsong. "I've missed yooouuu! Everlyyy!"

"Do not be afraid," Callum said. "You are strong. You know the power you possess. This is your house. Remember that."

The water was deeper here, coming nearly up to my knees. Every few steps, the sensation of something brushing against my legs would make me flinch, but I couldn't see anything below me in the tenebrous water. There was a distant dripping sound, and when I stopped to listen . . .

I could hear someone's harsh, gurgling breath.

Conjuring a flame in my palm, I grew its strength until the illumination reached deep into the tunnel ahead. There, standing hunched and swaying within the flickering light, was Victoria.

She was drenched in mud. It was soaked into her clothes, leaving them hanging wet and heavy from her limbs. Her head hung down, her dirty hair dangling in her face. Her feet were bare, and there was a strange scent emanating from her: slightly metallic and oddly fleshy. Like raw meat that had just started to turn.

"You're not welcome here," I said. It looked like my sister in every way, but that was impossible. Victoria wouldn't come seeking me in these tunnels. Victoria would never, ever claim to miss me.

She despised me. She always had and always would. And because I knew that, I knew it was impossible this was truly my sister.

This was only what was left of her.

"Not welcome?" A laugh, choked and thick, burst out of her. She still hadn't lifted her head. "Don't be so cruel, sister. Why, oh whyyy wouldn't you welcome me?"

Callum's hand clamped down on my shoulder as I stepped toward her. "We don't know what she is. The Deep One's stench is everywhere. It isn't safe."

Facing her swaying, shivering body, I said, "No one may enter here without my admission. You. Are. Not. Welcome."

Victoria went very, very still.

Shrugging off Callum's hand, I spread my arms, holding a flickering flame in each palm as I stepped toward her. The closer I came, the more of her I illuminated. That was when I saw the blood, a torrent of crimson leaking down from her slashed-open throat.

Jeremiah had gotten what he always desired. He'd killed our sister, murdered her and thrown her body to the Deep One. Its essence was burrowed into her flesh like a parasite, using her body like a puppet. The deep, mind-numbing thrum of Its power vibrated in the air.

About ten feet away from her, I stopped. Close enough to see her bulging, bloodshot eyes and the blackened rot that seeped from between her teeth as she bared them at me.

"So heartless, sister," she said, but her voice had changed. It was no longer high-pitched and taunting. It wasn't Victoria's at all. It echoed with an impossible timbre. "Turning me away when I am so desperately in need. Betrayal comes naturally to you, doesn't it?"

She lifted her head, and it lolled unnaturally to the side as a wide grin spread over her face. Whatever emotions she stirred in me—the disgust, the horror, and yes, the sadness—were quickly tamped down. I could mourn my sister when my house was safe once more.

"You betrayed your whole family," she said. "You betrayed your faith, your God—"

"How dare you speak of faith!" My flames burst forth with a shower of furious sparks that reflected in Victoria's dull eyes. "I have known good people with great faith in their God, but you . . . *you* are a trickster. A deceiver. A parasite." She twitched, as if my words needled her. "Without the people you deceive, you are nothing."

Her wide smile was still fixed in place. A slimy feeling ran up my back, but I bolstered the defenses around my mind, and it vanished. Victoria chuckled.

"Oh, but you see, I only need you pitiful humans for just a little while longer," she said. "One more sacrifice. Only one. Already my power is swelling. You can feel the difference, witch. I know you can. This rotten body may not serve me for very long, but I don't need it." Her eyes combed slowly over me. "How foolish you are to believe that you're brave, that you are beyond fear. You will always be afraid, Everly. Always. After all, you invited me into your head. I never left, you know."

"It's lying," Callum said, and Victoria's head jerked toward him.

"Silence, you vile, feral waste," she hissed. "You demons are only good when you're dead."

"As are your kind," he responded, his teeth snapping together.

"My kind . . ." She laughed. "Oh yes. My kind. Creators and destroyers of worlds. Consumers of souls. Beings far greater than any others in this dimension."

"Creators . . ." I shook my head. "No. You haven't created anything. But you'd love for the people you deceive to believe that you did. You need us to believe in your power. Your *stolen* power." I strode closer, my flames growing. "Hundreds of thousands of souls fed you, their power fused into you. You aren't powerful. You are weak. You are nothing. And *you are in my house*!"

A massive burst of flames sent her stumbling back. When the fire died down, her eyes were wide, darting side to side.

My smile grew.

"Oh? You weren't expecting this? Did you think you would come here and find a frightened little girl hiding away in the woods? Where is your Godly knowledge now? I thought you lived in my head?"

Victoria was swiftly retreating as I advanced. Stumbling, then crawling backward through the mud, she snarled at me as her body contorted, bulging and twisting as if something inside was trying to escape.

"If you lived in my head, then you would intimately know the power I wield. But you don't. You don't have the slightest *fucking clue* as to what I'm capable of!" With every word, I sent another burst of flame toward her. But with the last attack, I sent forth lightning. Sharp, crackling, blue pulses within the bright orange flames.

It struck her, rending her open like the body of a whale gone rancid. Thick black blood spilled out of her, tainting the water around her like ink. The smell was horrendous, gathering in my throat. But I kept striking, even as her bones cracked, her joints popping out of place as her body swelled, a ground-shaking roar coming from her gaping mouth.

"You can't kill me, witch!" The walls shook, dirt and pebbles shaken loose by the force of the God's voice. With every sweep and flick of my hands, fire and lightning swirled toward her, charring her flesh. "You're already too late! Raelynn Lawson is mine!"

I couldn't allow Its words to shake me. I couldn't allow the sight of my sister's deformed face to make me hesitate, not even for a moment. Callum was close behind me, but he didn't interfere as I fought, pushing Victoria further and further into the tunnels.

"They've brought her to me." She cackled, body writhing, unable to crawl any further. She kept talking, even as I unleashed a firestorm that swirled around her, stripping flesh from bone. "Her precious demon will die, just like yours. You're too late, witch. *YOU'RE TOO FUCKING LATE!* I have her . . . and her suffering . . . is so . . . sweet . . ."

When my flames finally died, I stood there gasping, swaying on my feet. All that remained of Victoria was a few blackened bones protruding from the water.

49

CALLUM

ELECTRICITY CRACKLED IN the darkness as Everly slowly lowered her arms. The charred remains of her sister sunk into the mud, the scent of burned flesh hanging in the air as the smoke slowly dissipated.

"It has her," she said. "The God has Raelynn."

There was no fear in her eyes. No despair. Nothing but grim resignation.

"There's no more time," she said. "We have to keep going. We have to kill It."

The air shimmered around her, waves of heat emanating from her. As I stepped closer, she wrapped her arms around me, and for a moment, I felt the dread in her heart. The bitter acknowledgment that after everything, this could be the end.

The end of our journey. The end of us.

My entire being demanded that I take her away from

here. Save her. Protect her. Even if it angered her, she would forgive me eventually. She would see that I had no other choice.

A snarl ripped out of me as I held her, and she looked up, meeting my eyes. "We'll face It together, Callum," she said. "As we were always meant to. You waited two thousand years for this."

"No," I said. "I waited two thousand years for *you*. To hear your voice again. To see your face. To touch you." My fingers stroked over her cheek, tucking back a strand of her long hair. Her scent surrounded me, and it was *different* than it used to be, but I couldn't determine why. Part of my own scent had melded with hers, becoming one and the same. "For so long, you haunted me. The familiar face of a stranger in a hundred lifetimes. As if we were always circling each other, two planets in cosmic alignment, thrown into a continuous loop by the power of one another. I waited for you, before I even knew it was you I was waiting for."

I kissed her forehead, and said, "To my last breath, I'll fight for you. Beyond this life, beyond death, I'll love you always."

"I love you. My guardian. My demon. My warrior. We'll find our way out of the dark. Your war will end. You'll lay down your weapons. We'll have peace."

ONWARD WE WENT into the dark depths of the mine.

Old wooden framing, covered with sprouting mushrooms, supported the narrow tunnels. There were bones, ancient and bleached, some still wearing the ragged clothes they died in. Miners, trapped here over a hundred years ago. Everly's fire lit our way, but even my sharp eyes couldn't see far in this oppressive darkness.

Strange cries echoed in the tunnels. The howls, clicks, and growls of numerous Eld creatures. The God's rotten magic made their existence possible, and they were gathered within Its den like vultures eager for scraps. Everly's flame would occasionally shine in the eyes of a beast lurking ahead, but they swiftly fled from us.

The ground rumbled around us, tremors running through the walls. Everly stopped, staring at the ceiling with wide eyes as pebbles dropped around us.

"How stable do you think these old tunnels are?" she said.

"Not stable enough. We need to keep moving."

The tunnels went on endlessly. Twisting and turning, up and down. We at last came to a massive shaft, stabilized with wooden framing. Old, rickety ladders led further down into the dark. The salty stench of seawater emanated from below.

With Everly on my back, I climbed down. Water dripped all around us, trickling into the unknown depths. Everly sucked in her breath sharply, her grip on me tightening, and I paused. "What's wrong?"

"I can feel the God," she whispered. "It's close. Like fingernails on the inside of my skull." She kept taking deep, slow breaths as she strengthened her mental defenses. "It knows I'm here."

We reached the next level of the mine, and as soon as Everly's feet were on solid ground again, she leaned her hand against the wall of the tunnel, clutching her stomach as she closed her eyes.

"It's just nausea," she said. "My head is vibrating. We're close, Callum. Very close."

She straightened slowly, swallowing hard. She reached for the enchanted blade on her belt and drew it from its sheath, before continuing determinedly down the dark tunnel ahead.

The path sloped downward, and Everly's light stretched ahead of us, illuminating a dead end. The tunnel had collapsed, massive rocks blocking our way. Everly frowned, stepping forward to lay her hand against the stones.

"There's something on the other side," she said, closing her eyes. After a moment, she opened them again and stepped back. She widened her stance, gulping in deep breaths.

She shoved her hands forward against the pile of rocks. They exploded outward, all but the largest boulders removed from our way by the force of her magic. I cleared the larger stones myself, bracing my shoulder against them to shove them aside and open the way into the cave beyond.

The cavern we stepped into was massive, filled with a strange gray light that didn't seem to have a source. A large pool of pitch-black water stood before us, the surface as still and smooth as glass. Old mining equipment, rusted and rotting, was discarded here. Wooden crates were stacked in a pile, stained with age, covered with fungal growths.

"Someone else was here," she said. "Do you smell them?"

I did. The scent of human fear hung heavily in the air, along with the subtle smell of blood. As we rounded the pool, Everly crouched down beside a small pair of boots and wet, bloodstained pants. Partially buried in the mud beside them was an old folded piece of paper, and Everly carefully held it up.

"Leon's sigil," she said. "From the grimoire." She clutched it against her chest, eyes closed, her head shaking slowly. "Raelynn was here . . . she was *here* . . ." She stood, looking all around the cavern. "Where could she have gone? It must have . . . fuck, Callum, It must have already taken her."

"Stay calm," I warned her. "And keep your voice down."

This entire space felt eerie, like something suspended outside of reality. The more I looked around, the more certain I was that something was very wrong here. The air was too still; the silence was uncanny. Even the smells that should have been present—wet dirt, stagnant water, damp rocks—were absent.

This place was a mockery; a stage without all its props.

Everly walked to the edge of the pool and knelt, staring into its depths. She turned her head, leaning down, frowning as she listened.

"What is it?" I said. I didn't like her being that close to the pool. I didn't like being here at all. I'd faced numerous Gods, but I hadn't felt like this since I last faced them in Hell. "Be careful, Everly."

"I can hear something. It's . . ." She leaned closer to the water, and alarm shot through me.

"Everly . . ."

Her nails dug into the soil, her fingers clenching as her eyes widened. "Screaming. I hear screaming."

With a shrieking sound like metal being torn apart, the pristine surface of the pool burst. Gargantuan tentacles burst from the water as a massive form filled the cavern. The walls cracked as reality fractured around us. I leapt forward, seizing her before she could be struck, and curled my wings around her as we hit the ground and skid through the mud.

A roar, loud enough to feel like it would split my head in two, shook the ground. Above us, the mutated body of the God flailed, tentacles writhing. Its limbs clawed at the stone as hundreds of eyes blinked and rolled across Its repulsive form. With every howling shriek, the very fabric of this dimension shuddered, ripping like wet paper, exposing swirls of iridescent color that undulated with microscopic strings.

"Brace yourself, Everly!" I shouted, but my voice barely carried over the God's roaring as we scrambled to our feet. Its body was constantly changing, morphing; Its interdimensional being unable to fully manifest.

Everly flung up her arm and the boulder beside her jutted upward, barely shielding us both from one of the tentacles as it whipped toward us. It shattered the rock, sending shards flying.

"You've come to me at last, witch!" The God's voice was contorted, as if hundreds of voices were all screaming at once. "You'll make a fine vessel when your soul is consumed!"

Its mouth gaped open, revealing a horrifying sight: a bulbous growth within Its throat, comprised of writhing, shrieking bodies. Contorted faces screamed, rotten hands grasped at the air, broken limbs stuck out at every angle.

Everly sprinted, dodging flailing tentacles as I took to the air, manifesting two large blades of aether, one in each hand. I flung one first, then the other, aiming toward the mass in Its gaping throat. The blades struck their target and the God bent backward, roaring in pain.

As Everly ran around the pool, she kept one hand outstretched toward its surface, rapidly muttering under her breath. The water was swiftly freezing solid, the frost creeping up the God's slimy gray skin. As she dodged under the undulating tentacles, she slashed her knife toward them, opening vicious but shallow wounds in the God's limbs.

"Petulant cunt!" the Deep One roared. "You will join your kin in my belly, hellion! Even your bravest warriors beg for release from their suffering." It laughed, the sound echoing around the chamber as I dipped and dodged through the air. A distorted limb swiped toward me, claws the size of tree trunks slicing through the air.

Searing pain ripped through my wing and suddenly I was falling, crashing to the ground as my blood spattered across the dirt. My wing was torn open, my skin swiftly knitting itself back together, but the God's claws were still descending.

Fire blazed over my head, the heat of it so great I had to turn my face away. Flesh was seared away, melting into putrid black slime that dripped around me like tar. Everly stood only a few yards away from me, arms outstretched, teeth bared as she conjured her fire. She maintained it until I leapt up and away, flinging herself to safety behind a boulder as the God's attention turned to her.

"Foolish girl!" Its voice reverberated through the cavern. "Your petty magic cannot harm me." Its flesh was rapidly reforming, but Its skin was still reddened and raw.

It was a liar.

Despite my aching wing, I took to the air again, determined to distract the creature so Everly could have her chance.

"Channel your magic through the blade!" I shouted, swooping over her head as I dodged another attack. The walls shook, massive stones falling from the ceiling. Everly had to move quickly, teleporting across the chamber before a boulder could crush her.

But she teleported directly into the path of one of the creature's whipping tentacles.

She couldn't move quickly enough.

Nor could I.

The tentacle struck her with an audible crunch of breaking bones. She flew back, hurtling through the air until she struck the wall and tumbled limply to the ground. The enchanted blade flew from her hand, spinning end over end until it struck the rocky ground and slid to the edge of the pool—then fell into the black water.

"Everly!" I flew to her side, dragging her out of the way before another tentacle could crush her completely.

Her skin was . . . cold.

"Everly!"

Her head lolled in my arms. Her blue eyes were dull, glassy as they stared at nothing.

The God's laughter was like claws ripping through my ears.

"Her soul has fled, hellion!" It cackled. "Her body will be repurposed for my own ends. Can you smell it? Can you *feel* it?" The God leaned down, Its gaping jaws spewing hot laughter in my face. "Can you feel your spawn dying inside her?"

"You're a liar!" My chest felt like it was caving in. This couldn't be.

No.

No, no, fucking no!

The God's massive tentacle descended, and I had to move too quickly to carry Everly with me. I flew into the air, an agonized scream tearing out of me as my fangs elongated, my veins running black as my body was consumed with shadow.

It couldn't be true. It couldn't.

She couldn't be . . .

The cry that roared out of me shook the cavern walls. It stripped my throat raw. I couldn't bear the pain—I wanted to tear my own heart from my chest to make it stop. All sense left me; my desire for self-preservation fled.

All that remained was fury. Agony. Hatred deeper than the cosmos.

I perched on a massive column of stone, facing the God as I conjured a blade in my hand, twice as long as I was tall. It felt as if I was splitting apart, my mind and body in disarray. All I could see was Everly's eyes, the light gone from them, blood staining her lips.

The God was shrieking with laughter as the walls of the cave dissolved. Nameless colors swirled around us, sparking with long streaks of lightning. In the chaos, silhouettes of impossible architecture flashed—nameless shapes, imperceivable expanses.

Survival did not matter. My life was already gone.

Death was calling, and my time had come to answer.

But I would not go alone.

EVERLY

IT ALL HAPPENED so fast. One moment, I was standing, catching my breath after teleporting, my legs tensing to sprint again, and then--

Pain, splintering through me like nails in my flesh.

Then darkness.

Nothingness.

I didn't feel afraid; I felt nothing at all. I could have stayed like that forever. Cold. Content. Unfeeling.

Slowly, a feeling of urgency grew inside me. Uncomfortable, clawing in my chest, blaring in my head like an alarm.

Get up, get up, get up.

I remembered who I was.

Lurching to my feet in panic, I spun around in confusion, trying to determine where I was. This wasn't the mine. There were no walls around me, there was no dirt beneath my feet. It was just dark, like it had been when Callum guided me beyond the Veil. The scent of damp dirt and mildew was gone, the stench of rot and seawater had vanished.

"Callum?" My voice didn't echo. It sounded muffled, as if I was surrounded by an invisible buffer that swallowed my words the moment they left my lips. "Callum!"

With a sudden gasp, I clutched my chest as searing pain seized me. When I dared to look down, there was a growing red stain on my shirt. Blood covered my palm when I pulled it away from my side, revealing a gaping wound ripped deep into my flesh.

But I still felt strange—detached, like a balloon cut loose from its string. My body was injured. I was still alive enough to feel the pain; but I was beyond the Veil, my soul ripped loose from my body.

I sat, cross-legged on the floor, and closed my eyes. Envisioning the cavern I had stood in, I reached for the familiar warmth and weight of my body . . . but I couldn't find it.

My breath came faster. Was I bleeding out? Was my body dying? Callum was alone against the God, and if he . . .

If he died . . .

No, no. I couldn't think of that. I couldn't consider the possibility of the Deep One consuming him, severing our bond.

It wasn't too late. That was the only hope I could cling to. I was alive, I could move, I could feel my magic still close at hand.

I needed to find a way back to my body.

Getting to my feet, I started walking. I held my intentions firmly in my mind: return to the mine, return to my body. Find Callum.

I had to find Callum.

My sense of time was warped. Only seconds may have passed, but it felt like hours of darkness. Hours of walking without any visible progress.

My heartbeat was growing weaker, my breathing more labored.

With growing horror, I realized I could feel myself dying.

Then, I became aware of vague shapes moving around me. Swaying, like long stalks of kelp in a gentle ocean current. There was dampness on my skin, and the air was cool. There were no stars overhead, there was no whisper of a breeze. It was so eerily silent.

Swallowing around the lump in my throat, I looked down to see the silvery thread dangling from my chest. It wound away from me through the strange grass, disappearing into the darkness. With no other choice, I followed it.

With every step I took, my heartbeat grew weaker. It became increasingly difficult to remember what I was doing, why I was doing it, who I was looking for.

Who was I looking for?

I stopped.

There were faint lights around me, glittering gold as they floated in the darkness like dozens of fireflies. The scent here was so familiar. Patchouli and vanilla, freshly ground coffee.

"Mama?" My voice was so tired, so small. Like I was a tiny child again, lost in the dark. "Are you there? Please . . ." I stumbled, falling to my hands and knees. The ground was damp beneath my palms, and I realized I was kneeling beside a small, very still pool.

It was one of dozens. Glass-like pools dotted the landscape, partially hidden by the swaying grass. The glittering lights were reflected in them, and I leaned forward, peering into the water.

"I don't know what to do," I choked out. "I'm so lost." Tears dripped into the pool, sending ripples cascading across the pristine surface. "I'm not strong enough, Mama."

There was a sensation like a hand resting gently on my shoulder, and I looked back in alarm. But I was still alone. Turning back to the water, I stared at my own reflection, but I barely recognized myself. I looked faint and hazy, a mere ghost in the fog.

"Show me what I have to do," I whispered desperately. "Show me the way."

My reflection disappeared. The water grew dark, shadows swirling beneath the surface like slithering eels. A vision appeared within the water, and at first, I had no idea what I was looking at. Grotesque writhing flesh, numerous blinking eyes, a gaping maw. My stomach lurched as I realized I was looking at the God. It had someone in Its tentacles, flailing and screaming.

"Raelynn!" I gasped as the small woman struggled to free herself from the Deep One's hold. Suddenly, she lifted her hand, a dagger clutched in her fingers. The blade shimmered with familiar magic; the design of the weapon was different, but it carried the same enchantment as the one I'd created. Raelynn plunged the knife down, spearing one of the God's numerous eyes. She swung back, and stabbed the knife down again, ripping it deeply into the tentacle that gripped her.

The God loosened Its hold, and she squirmed free. But her lips were turning blue from lack of air.

The vision faded.

"No, no, no." I leaned desperately over the water. "Please! I need to go home, I need to know the way!" I focused all my concentration on what I could remember of the cavern: the large pool in the center, the craggy rock walls, dilapidated mining equipment.

And Callum. My demon, my love. I held his face in my mind, willing all my magic toward him.

The water swirled, and a new vision appeared. But it wasn't the mine, and it wasn't Callum. It was *me*.

I was sitting in the garden behind the coven house, a paintbrush in my fingers. The scene was calm, serene. I turned my head, smiling as I opened my arms and a little blonde-haired child rushed toward me, embracing me. The girl lifted her head, smiling at me, and her pupils were *golden*.

That . . . that wasn't possible. It couldn't be. I'd dutifully taken the tea my grandmother made every day, which was supposed to prevent . . .

But that night in the forest, when Callum and I came together to call to the fae king. I hadn't drunk the tea that day, or the next morning, or any day since. I'd felt a little strange since then, but I'd been stressed, working myself hard.

A sudden sharp feeling in my abdomen made me gasp. It felt almost like . . . a kick? But that couldn't be. It *couldn't*. It had been only days. I was showing no physical signs at all.

But this wasn't a human child. Not entirely.

My body shook violently. Why had I seen our child in that vision but not Callum? I searched the water, my eyes straining to see anything in the shadowy depths.

"I know you're still out there," I whispered. "It can't be too late, please, it can't."

The water remained still. The shadows within stopped moving. In fury, I slammed my fist down, splashing cold water everywhere. "No! Show him to me! He's still alive, I *know* he's still alive, he—" My words caught, shuddering on a sob. "He's still fighting. I know he's still fighting. Please, Callum."

Shuddering, I doubled over until my forehead lay against the ground, my eyes burning with tears. Beneath me, the silver thread that bound my soul to my demon still shimmered faintly. Clutching it, I climbed to my feet. My limbs were numb with cold, but I forced myself to trudge forward, one painful step at a time.

"Keep fighting, Callum. Please. I'm coming back. I'll find you again."

THE MIST WAS so thick it was impossible to see my own hand in front of my face. Fog swirled around my feet, cold and damp on my skin as I trudged onward, following the shimmering trail of the thread.

My strength was fading. Despite my attempts to ignore it, that numb feeling was spreading up my legs and arms. When I looked closely at my fingers, I could see a blackness under my nails.

Death was taking me slowly, one piece at a time.

It was impossible to tell if I was walking in a straight line or going in circles. Everything looked the same. The same white mist, the same dull gray light, the same damp cold. The injury in my side was throbbing in time with my weakly beating heart.

"We're going to get back, little one," I said. I wasn't sure why I felt the need to address the little spark of potential life inside me. I hadn't even been aware of it an hour ago, or was it a day? How long had I been wandering in the mist?

Why was I wandering at all? I was so tired. Everything hurt. Perhaps I could lie down. Just for a little while. Just a little rest.

I stopped abruptly, shaking my head as if to cast off flies and cobwebs. Holding tight to the silver thread in my hands, I pulled it through my fingers as I kept walking. Clinging to that semi-solid reminder of what I was searching for helped my focus, but confusion still battered me. My thoughts were like startled birds, fluttering away from their roost with nowhere to land.

"We're coming back, Callum," I said. "We're coming. Keep fighting. Please keep fighting. We'll find you."

I stopped again, staring down in disbelief. Because

there, at my feet, vaguely visible through the mist, were long stalks of brown grass.

It was a vast field. The grass rippled slowly around me, a churning sea that rattled as the dry stalks brushed together. The thread's silvery light was brighter now, and it felt heavier in my hands. Emboldened, I walked faster, then ran. Although I had no idea where I was, I felt like Callum was close. Far closer than he'd been before.

I nearly tripped face-first into a massive dark lump that appeared before me out of the mist. Stumbling, I caught myself with my hands planted against the massive thing, only to immediately recoil in horror.

It was a mass of quivering, rotting, blackened flesh. It was slashed open in places, revealing muscle that was pink and coiled, like the outside of a brain. The muscle seemed to be crawling, quivering, twitching. As if it were made up of thousands of squirming pink maggots. The body was the size of a whale, and smelled so repulsive I had to cover my mouth and nose with my shirt before I gagged.

But then, in the cold and confusion and the awful stench, I felt him. Callum was here.

He stepped out of the mist as I looked up. He was about fifty yards away from me, and the moment his eyes fell on me, he froze. His wings were limp, dragging on the ground. They were ripped and bleeding; his body bruised and torn.

"Callum!" I tried to call out to him, but my voice was so weak, my mouth so dry. It hurt to speak. "Help me . . ." The pain flared, sharper and deeper than before. "Help me, please!"

But he didn't take a single step toward me. He stared at me as if I were a stranger, as if . . . as if I was an enemy.

Stepping around the massive dead thing, I stumbled toward him. "I don't know what happened. Where are we? Where is the—"

He leapt back, fangs bared, wings flared back, claws out and ready. A vicious snarl roared out of him. "Stay back, witch! Don't come a step closer!"

His words slapped me in the face. I stared at him, unable to understand. "Callum? It's me, it's . . ."

"How do you know my name?" he hissed. "Answer me truthfully, human, or I'll strike you dead where you stand. How the fuck do you know my name?"

His words dripped with venom, with an undeniable hatred. My weakly beating heart throbbed, while the pain in my side grew worse. This had to be a nightmare. Why didn't he know me?

"Callum, you claimed me." I didn't dare take another step closer. "Please, we marked each other! We've slept together, we've fought alongside each other!"

His eyes widened, and I was stunned to realize his irises weren't black. They were glittering gold, so bright and intense it was like staring into the sun. But black veins were shot through the gold, like burned cracks in a gilded surface.

I looked at the lump of rotting flesh beside me, the

monstrosity that had only recently been killed. And suddenly, I knew where I was.

Not only where. But *when*.

"Callum, please listen to me . . ." He flinched as I reached for the laces on my shirt, loosening it slowly, painfully. It peeled away from my side, sticky with blood, and the demon's eyes fixated on the injury. His nostrils flared, and I wondered if he could smell the truth of what I'd told him. Could he smell himself on me?

"I'm not supposed to be here," I said. "I'm in the wrong place, the wrong . . . time. I found you too soon. But I know your name because you gave it to me. You carved it into me." I shrugged off my shirt, baring myself to him. Even now, even here, centuries before he knew me, I trusted him not to hurt me. He gave no vocal reaction as I showed him the scars on my stomach, but I saw the conflicting emotions on his face.

Horror, confusion, suspicion.

"How is this possible?" he whispered. The silence in this vast field felt so heavy, so full of grief. He'd lost everything here. Here, in this field soaked in blood, he had watched countless die. And there, beside me, rotting in the open air, was a dead God.

One of dozens. One of hundreds scattered around us. Yet somehow, in the midst of all this death, my frantic search for life had led me here.

"Witches wander where they will," I said. "And I've wandered very far. I need . . . I need your strength, Callum. To keep going. To get back to you. Please."

"Back to me . . ." He stepped closer, his entire body coiled as if to leap away at any moment. It was truly strange to realize he was afraid of me. "And where, exactly, do you think you will find me, if not here?"

"In the future," I said, desperately hoping he would understand. "Please, Callum, you need to remember this, please. I'm coming back. I promise you, I'm coming back. Don't stop fighting, don't . . . don't give up." I reached for him, and he didn't flinch away when my fingers brushed against his chest. "Please don't give up. I'm coming back to you. It's not over, please . . ."

God, I wanted him to hold me. I wanted to sink into his arms, I wanted to feel safe with him and know he was safe with me too. I wanted to tell him the truth, that the future we had together was already better than either of us could have imagined.

I stepped closer, and he flinched but something made him stay. He sniffed the air, his expression morphing from anger, to confusion, to shock.

He was staring at me now as if I'd revealed to him the secrets of the universe. But he didn't truly understand, not yet. It would be centuries before he understood.

For so long, you haunted me. The familiar face of a stranger in a hundred lifetimes. As if we were always circling each other, two planets in cosmic alignment, thrown into a continuous loop by the power of one another. I waited for you, before I even knew it was you I was waiting for.

His eyes softened. Tears poured down my face, but I couldn't reach for him, I couldn't stay.

I backed away.

"Wait." He reached out for me, his viciousness gone. "What's your name?"

"Everly," I said. "Everly Laverne. You'll find me someday, Callum. And I'll find you again. Please don't forget. I'm coming back to you. I will get up. I will. Please . . ." I didn't want to leave him. It hurt; it was terrifying. It felt like ripping myself away from the one being I wanted most, with no idea if I would ever find my way to him again.

But I had to. No matter how far or how long I had to wander, I would find him again.

He called my name as I stepped back into the mist. But I had to keep following that thread, pulsing and pale as it snaked ahead of me.

I would find my way back to him again.

THE MIST WAS never-ending. I had been walking for an eternity. Time and space meant nothing.

Was I already dead? My heartbeat, erratic as it had been, had stopped. Or become so weak I could no longer feel it.

Now and then, my surroundings would change. Cities would loom around me, ancient and strange, full of shadowy faces. But one face was always clear: Callum. I would spot him in a crowd, a brief glimpse before I walked on. I walked across decades, across centuries, and I found him again and again.

But it wasn't right. Dipping back and forth between the Veil, in and out of time, my brain felt continuously more unhinged. The vision of the cavern that I tried so hard to hold in my mind was fading. My memories of who I was and where I was trying to get to were so tangled, so weak.

But the throbbing pain in my side reminded me I was alive. I didn't belong here; I wasn't merely another blank face in the mist.

"We'll find him, little one." My voice was faint; it sounded so unfamiliar. "Your papa is fighting for us. He won't give up. I know he won't. He'll wait for us. He'll be so excited to meet you. He'll protect you, always, like he protected me."

My vision blurred.

"He'll be so kind to you, little one. He won't be like my father at all. He'll love you endlessly; we both will."

There was no more mist. No more light. Only the darkness, and my faint silver thread.

"You'll get to see so much. You'll have so much to learn. Don't . . . don't be afraid of your father. He's kind. He's gentle. He would never . . . never hurt you . . ."

The air stunk of mold and rotten fish.

The pain was so bad I swayed on my feet, and there was a strange, faint thrumming in my ears. I was tired. So very tired. I needed to rest, only for a little while. Just close my eyes.

Lying down, I let my cheek rest against the cold, muddy earth.

"He'll protect us, little one," I whispered. "Until we get back . . . until we find him . . . he'll protect us. So that when . . . when we find him . . . we can protect him too . . ."

Everything hurt. I felt sick and faint and so, *so* heavy.

I opened my eyes.

EVERLY

REALITY WAS FRACTURED around me. Light and sound, shape and distance were all muddled together in swirling chaos. Lightning flashed, bursting with unnamable colors. Rocks and columns of stone floated around me, and I was lying on a chunk of earth that was floating unanchored through the turmoil.

I was still so numb, so cold.

But I could remember what I'd seen. My child.

Our child.

There was an awful sound, like the screaming of a thousand voices in agony. A shadow loomed above me, tendrils writhing. Barely managing to turn my head, I beheld the God, massive and grotesque. Its clawed hand was clutching something, and I saw limp wings, pale skin webbed with black veins.

"Callum . . ." My arm was so heavy I couldn't even

lift it off the ground. The God's jaw gaped open, and the screaming grew louder.

It was going to consume him, and I couldn't even lift my head. I couldn't call his name.

Inches away from my hand, a tree root was sticking out of the mud. In this chaotic place, it stood out to me as one of the last beacons of reality, and my fingers inched toward it until I grasped it weakly. It felt warm in my hand, and my vision flashed, fluctuating rapidly between pandemonium and the real world.

The Old Man said the trees were always listening. If that were true, even here, even now—perhaps they would hear me.

"Help me," I whispered. My fingers tightened around the little root, its wood rough against my palm. My weapon was gone, but I'd seen Raelynn leave another blade behind, buried in the God's flesh. If I could only reach it. If I only had the strength to get up, to get to Callum . . .

"*Help me,*" I snarled, pouring every last shred of magic I could into my demand. "Lend me the forest's strength. Help me destroy this thing. Help me, before it's too late. Please. Please, if you can hear me."

It may have been only my imagination, but the root grew warmer in my hand.

Everything shattered. Stone, rock, and water crashed around me, the swirling colors vanishing as the cavern rematerialized. The God roared, Its massive body slumping over for a moment as if caught off guard by Its own weight. Callum dropped from Its grip and lay limply where he fell; eyes closed, limbs sprawled across the muddy ground.

"What is this?" The God roared, Its tentacles writhing.

Roots were sprouting from the ground around It, growing up and around Its body. It tore at them, swiping them away like strings as It looked around in confusion.

Then Its eyes fell on me.

"The witch *lives*?!" It snarled. "You were cast beyond the Veil, you fucking bitch! How did you—"

More roots were sprouting around me, and around the God too, thicker than the last ones. They gave me a handhold to climb to my feet as the warmth seeped back into my body, and I stood to face the God.

An inferno was growing in my chest. My vision was drenched in red. I needed weapons. Claws and fangs. I needed a body that could move with speed, that could leap and bound. I could *feel* my muscles swelling, tendons elongating, teeth growing as the forest fed me its strength.

I had no idea what I would become. It didn't truly matter. All the magic I could gather into myself, I did. I swelled with it, my own strength threatening to overwhelm me.

"Do you really think calling the fucking fairies will help you?" the God roared. Thick roots, as large as Its own tentacles, were coiling around Its body, bursting from the ground, the walls. Holding It in place. "They will bow to me like all the rest! Your forests will rot, witch, and your world will choke in its own decay!"

"No," I said softly. My teeth were too long and sharp

to close my own mouth. When I looked at my hands, I had sunk sharp claws into the root I still gripped. I had made myself into a weapon, and felt nothing but blood-lust. "You think you can destroy without consequences. You would lay waste even to the very beings you need to survive. You're only alive because of the power you've stolen! Demons, humans. Countless lives. You are no God. All you're capable of is destruction. But I . . ." I lifted my hands, flames billowing from my palms. "I can create. I can destroy. I am far more a God than you will ever be."

The God lunged toward me, but I was quick. The wind flew through my hair as I sprinted, my claws rip-ping into the soil. I put myself between Callum and the God, hunched over him like an animal as the God de-scended.

"Your power is mine!" Rocks were shaken loose from the ceiling with the force of the God's voice. "You are weak! *WEAK!* A shame upon your own bloodline, a bas-tard child!"

"Liar." Callum's voice was a mere whisper below me. "It's a liar, Everly."

He was alive. He was still alive, and I—I *laughed*. I laughed with the force of the joy overtaking me, the sheer euphoria, as power and hope collided inside me. From between my sharp teeth poured fire, swelling into a storm that swirled around the cavern.

The cave roof suddenly gave way, mud, rock, and pouring rain streaming down, but my fire allowed none of it to touch me. More roots burst from the soil, thick and coiling as they wrapped around the God, constricting and piercing into Its flesh.

As the God roared, tearing at the roots, I dragged Callum out of the way. He was so heavy; my muscles trembled violently as I used all my strength to move him. Only magic kept me standing. Alarming pain pulsed through my chest, my shattered ribs aching.

I just had to stay on my feet. I feared that if I allowed myself to falter for even a moment, I would collapse and not get up again.

Callum grasped at me, his grip surprisingly strong even though he could barely open his eyes. He tried to speak, but the words were too quiet to hear.

I had to move. I had to keep the God's attention away from him.

I kissed him before I fled, sprinting to the opposite side of the cavern. Tentacles whipped after me, smashing rock and cracking the cavern walls. I leapt over roots and clambered over boulders, moving with unnatural speed.

"This world is mine! *MINE!*" The God's scream nearly burst my eardrums. A tentacle slammed down in front of me, blocking my path. Water rushed toward me, sloshing over my shoes and swiftly rising toward my knees.

This was it. I couldn't run anymore.

The God loomed over me. Pain pierced through my head, but I grit my teeth and faced the beast. It leaned down, laughter reverberating as It bared Its monstrous teeth at me.

"I will relish your eternal suffering, witch," It said. "You should have stayed beyond the Veil. You should have hidden in the darkness forever. Instead, you have run straight back into the arms of your fate: to be mine."

"I was never yours!" The words poured out with my fire, and I sprinted forward. I leapt upon one of the God's tentacles, my claws allowing me to grip as I scrambled up the slimy surface. I cast billows of flame toward the God's face, and It thrashed, nearly throwing me off.

"Fate does not command me," I snarled. The trees' twisting roots were holding the God captive; It could barely move now. "I will not spend my life hiding in fear!"

There, jutting from the God's flesh, was the knife Raelynn had stabbed into It. The blade called to me, twisted threads of light tangled around it. I scrambled toward the knife, claws rending into the God's flesh to prevent myself from plummeting to the rocks below.

"All those souls you've stolen will be set free to rest! And you"—I seized the handle of the knife, gripping it with all my strength as the God fought, Its limbs swiping at me furiously—"you will rot away and be forgotten!"

When I channeled my fire into the blade, the weapon latched onto it as if it was a living, ravenous thing. It drew my magic in like a funnel, so fast and intense that my head swam. But I kept holding on, I held my concentration even when waves of dizziness made my vision sway.

Lightning crackled around me as the God made a wretched, agonized sound. Its flesh split open, revealing a river of fire burning within. My claws receded, my teeth shrinking, my body returning to normal as all my power was poured into burning the God from the inside out.

There was a deep, ear-shattering boom. The force of it was so great I was flung to the ground and tumbled across the stone. The God was dissolving into ash, Its charred remains melting into the mud. It gave an awful, gurgling cry as Its body slumped down, water sloshing around Its writhing limbs.

Far above, around the edges of the cavern's gaping ceiling, Eld beasts yipped and cried as they flung themselves down in panic, the massive amounts of magic making them crazed. They were reduced to nothing but worms and bones before they even struck the ground.

The great tentacles lay still, flames crackling across their surface. All that remained of the God was ruined flesh, quivering and twitching. It blackened as my fire kept burning, even as the rain poured down from above.

Weakly, I crawled back to Callum's side and lay beside him, facing him. His eyes were closed, but when I laid my hand against his face, his skin was warm. Too weak to speak, I lay there in silence, drenched by the rain, still and cold beneath the gray night sky.

I wasn't sure how much time passed. Minutes or hours. Days or an eternity.

Time had changed, or my perception of it had.

Soft footsteps made me open my eyes. Over Callum's shoulder stood the Old Man, a horse skull covering his face, red flowers blooming from his walking stick. He walked around us, and everywhere his bare feet touched, grass and flowers rapidly grew.

He walked behind me, toward the God, and said, "Scars will remain, but even the deepest wounds will heal, Lady Witch. Thank you. The fae will not forget."

When I managed to turn over, he was gone.

Plant life was growing around Callum and I. Grass, flowers, moss and lichens. Sapling trees shot up from the dirt, reaching eagerly toward the sky. The God's body was rapidly rotting, mushrooms overtaking and consuming It. I watched it all, grasping Callum's limp hand, a weak smile on my face despite the rain.

Slowly, Callum stirred. He drew closer, his arms coming around me as he buried his face against me. Neither of us spoke; holding each other said everything we needed to.

Softly, he said, "You came back. I hoped . . . I remembered what you told me . . ."

He opened his eyes, and I gazed into the void. I guided his hand lower, laying his palm over my stomach.

"Do you feel it?" I whispered. As he looked at me and smiled, the expression was both full of pain and full of bliss.

"Our future." His voice was tight with the sweetest heartache as he crawled to his knees, helping me stand. As he knelt, I used his shoulders to balance, and he kissed my stomach before he laid his cheek against me. "Our eternity, darling. Our peace." He chuckled softly. "Or our new terror."

I laughed with him. My hands tangled in his hair as I clutched his head against me.

"The war is over, my love," I said. "It's finally over."

Epilogue

EVERLY

IT WAS THE last hour before sunset, and the garden was bathed in gold. Light streamed through the blooming roses, kissing the soft spring grass. It warmed my hands as I swirled my brush in dark green paint, carefully adding tiny leaves to the vines around the edge of my canvas.

Biting the end of the brush in thought, I leaned back on my stool. I'd been hunched there so long my back was aching, but I couldn't resist staying outside as long as I could. The day was too lovely to miss even a moment.

Even after the sunset, when my light was gone, I'd sit out here and listen to the crickets and frogs, the screech of the owls and clicking bats. Perhaps I'd ask Callum to lie with me under the stars until I fell asleep; he'd carry me back to bed after that, tuck me into the blankets and lie by my side until morning.

There was nothing to fear in the dark. Not anymore.

Or so I thought.

Something was creeping through the garden on nearly silent feet. But it announced itself in subtle ways, with quick breaths and barely suppressed giggles. Although my eyes remained on my canvas, I was perfectly aware of where the little monster was as it snuck up behind me.

I was also aware that behind that little monster was an even bigger one.

Tiny footsteps sprinted across the grass, a war-like screech splitting the air before it ended with an abrupt "Oof!" Setting down my brush, I turned to see Callum standing behind me, holding our child in midair by one ankle as she clawed at his hands, snarling, "Not fair, Papa! Not fair!"

"What have I told you about sneaking up on your mother?" Although his voice was stern, the corner of his mouth twitched as he looked up at me and winked.

Our daughter groaned, folding her arms and scowling. "Don't scare Mama when she's painting," she grumbled.

"And what exactly were you doing?" Callum insisted. The child started squirming again, grabbing at his arm like a monkey.

"She knew I was there! Didn't you, Mama?" The child turned her bright golden eyes to me, giving me a not-so-innocent grin. "So I couldn't *really* scare her, huh?"

Grabbing her hands, I helped her flip upright as Callum released her ankle. She jumped up into my arms, laying a dozen kisses against my cheek as if that was what she'd planned all along. She was only three, but her size and maturity had already outpaced her young age. So had her cleverness.

"I knew exactly where you were from the moment you stepped foot in the garden, Heidi," I said. "But you still need to obey the rules."

"Rules are boring," she sighed, already squirming to get down again. She climbed up her father's back instead, to perch on his shoulders between his wings. "Right, Papa?"

"They're not rules," he said. "They're guidelines, to ensure you don't get burnt to a crisp when you startle your mother." He reached back, ruffling her wild mane of curly blonde hair. "Why don't you go to the kitchen and help your Granny with dinner?"

"Okay!" She leapt to the ground and sprinted across the grass, climbing directly over the garden wall rather than simply going around.

Shaking my head as she ran, I said, "You know Grams is going to feed her sugar. She'll be up all night."

"She can run around in the woods then," Callum said, wrapping his arms around me and resting his head atop mine. "It will get her out of the house for a while and give us some time to play."

He squeezed my ass, and I laughed, "I don't think I'll ever get used to that. Letting my toddler run around in the forest by herself after dark . . ."

"There's nothing out there she can't handle," he said, the pride obvious in his voice.

"I'm not sure I'll ever get used to that either."

He cupped my face in his hands and kissed me deeply. All the worries in my head, the unspoken fears, melted away as my knees grew weak, and I was smiling like a fool as he drew back from me.

"What was I saying again?" I joked, and he nodded toward my canvas.

"You were about to show me your latest creation," he said. "The light is beautiful."

I'd captured the sun's rays right as they were dipping below the trees. The silhouette of the forest was dark, but the light shone through in golden beams, making the colors of the garden's flowers even more vibrant.

"I swear your skill grows every time you pick up the brush," he said. "One for the Art Festival this year, perhaps?"

I shook my head. "No. This one . . . well . . ." Rubbing the back of my neck as I gazed toward the setting sun, I said softly, "I had a vision last night during meditation. A silly one, I suppose."

"None of your visions are silly," Callum said. He sat on my stool, drawing me onto his lap. "What did you see?"

"Raelynn."

He widened his eyes in surprise. "You haven't seen her since . . ."

"Since we faced the Deep One," I said softly. Neither of us particularly liked talking about that time. Although it had been years since I'd last felt the evil creature's eyes on me, there were still some days when I grew paranoid, fearing that I could feel Its slimy presence in the back of my mind.

It was only paranoia. The God was long dead.

"I didn't even know if she was alive," I said. "But she is. She and Leon both. He's still with her. They're in Europe now, in France. Apparently, they've moved into a haunted old château." I laughed softly. "Of all things, I saw Raelynn complaining they didn't have any art for the walls. So I think I'll send her this one when it's finished."

"Perhaps we can hand-deliver it," Callum said. "It's been too long since I took you traveling. Kimaris can help your grandmother look after Heidi."

"Mm, it would be nice to have some time alone with you." I turned to straddle his lap. "I have a whole list of places we need to see."

"Do you? Give me the list and I'll ensure we see them all. It may take us quite some time though. It won't be enough to simply see and explore these places."

"What else did you have in mind?" I shivered as he kissed my neck, nipping my shoulder.

"I'm going to fuck you in every single place on your list. Worship you. Pleasure you. I'll make the world your temple."

His dark eyes stared into mine as my arms came around his neck. Softly, I said, "To whom do you belong, my demon?"

"To you, darling. You will have me in life. I will keep you in death. For eternity, I am yours, and you are mine."

Bonus Chapter

JUNIPER

HELL—SEVERAL YEARS LATER

THE TEMPLE HAD been there since time immemorial. Its history was even more ancient than my demon's, who didn't know when the massive stone structure had been built.

"It was a different age of demons," he said as we hiked along the winding path toward the temple entrance. "Before man settled the Earth."

I'd begged Callum to show me a dragon for my birthday. It was all I wanted, but it wasn't easy to persuade him. We had traveled deep into Hell's wilds to find this place, avoiding monstrous beasts and trekking over strenuous terrain.

It was worth the difficult journey. Here at the temple—tomorrow, at sunrise—the dragons would fly.

It was night as we approached. Despite the temple having been abandoned for many thousands of years, the windows glowed with silvery-violet light. Wild magic was bursting from this place; the air was charged with it. The old dark-gray stones glittered beneath the vines growing over them, as if diamond dust was infused into the rock.

There were no doors, no fences. Nothing barred our way as we walked through a gargantuan stone archway into a courtyard. It was once home to a beautiful, manicured garden—but the plants had grown wild. Their limbs were long, their leaves massive. Tendrils grasped cracks in the stones and roots squeezed between the tiles, twisting toward the sky.

An eerie silence fell as we passed from the courtyard inside. A chamber surrounded us, carved from the solid rock. Milky-white crystalline structures grew from the walls, and a dry, dusty perfume hung in the air. The remnants of burnt incense were scattered across the floor.

Before us was a round stone dais, raised about a foot above the floor. A skylight far above allowed a shaft of moonlight to fall upon the altar, illuminating the intricate carvings upon it.

"What was this for?" My voice echoed in the vast space, seeming to carry on into eternity.

Callum circled me, and his clawed finger traced across my bare shoulders.

"Offerings," he whispered, and a shiver went up my spine. "Legends say the demons who built this place would offer sacrifices to the dragons to ensure the creatures would stay and protect the temple."

"And who did they sacrifice?"

"Witches." His teeth clipped together menacingly on the word, but I laughed.

"You're lying. Demons would never let a witch have all the fun of being sacrificed. You're too selfish a species for that."

Callum sighed heavily. "And this is why witches are so dangerous: you understand my kind too well. You're right, darling. Only willing offerings were made here. The belief was that the dragons would be entertained by cries of pain and pleasure. So that is what was offered."

Stepping to the edge of the dais, I raised my hand and slowly curled my outstretched fingers into a fist. Ropes descended from the high ceiling, shimmering slightly with the magic I'd used to create them.

"It seems only right," I said, "that we, too, should offer a sacrifice, if we wish to see the dragons fly."

IN THE SHAFT of moonlight, dangling above the dais, my demon hung for me.

Taut ropes bit into his flesh. The position was strenuous; his muscles flexed, tight and shivering. His head dangled toward the ground, his mouth gagged with my panties.

They were his favorite pair of mine. White lace and

satin. The fabric looked so delicate between his sharp clenched teeth.

Reaching up, I dragged my nails down his thigh. His head hung at the same height as my waist, and every time I came near, his nostrils flared as he deeply inhaled. Consuming my scent, torturing himself with it.

"I love seeing you like this," I said. Circling him, I admired every inch of his massive form—almost human, yet monstrous, too. His wings hung limp, the only part of him I'd left free. He stretched them now, groaning as I teased my nails along the shaft of his cock.

The organ twitched as I wrapped my fingers around it. Back and forth, I flicked my finger slowly over the glittering jewel pierced through him.

"A sacrifice must suffer," I said, stroking him slowly, barely touching. I brought my mouth close enough so he could feel the whisper of my breath. "Don't you enjoy suffering for me, my love?"

Callum made a muffled sound of affirmation. I kissed the swollen head of his cock, then brought my lips around it. Delicately, I lapped my tongue over the thick organ. My demon's entire body went rigid, veins bulging. I moaned softly and he responded in kind, huffing desperately as a pained sound escaped him.

With slow licks and soft touches, I teased him until he was shaking. I talked him through the struggle until my words had lulled him into a state of pleasure-drunk acceptance.

"Such a good boy," I whispered. I kissed the hollow near his hip bone, his abdomen, his chest. I knelt so I could cradle his head, kiss his cheeks, his mouth, his forehead. His breathing was deep and slow, almost as if he was asleep.

"My beautiful demon," I murmured. The ropes dropped, lowering him gently to the ground. He was laid out on the dais, bound and gagged as I rose up and stood over him.

"You'll have gorgeous marks when I untie you," I said, placing one foot on his chest. "Your body is my canvas, isn't it?" He nodded, with a desperate groan. I lowered myself until I was straddling him. The apex of my legs came to rest on the throbbing shaft of his cock, but I didn't take him inside, not yet. "I can play with you like a toy. Bend you to my will . . ." He writhed as I slid myself over his length, giving him a small tease of what was coming next. "Are you going to be a good sacrifice for me?"

Reaching down, I pulled the lacy panties from between his sharp teeth. His forked tongue licked quickly over his lips as he said, "Yes, my lady. Please—"

"Suck." I placed two fingers against his lips and he obeyed, taking them into his mouth. His forked tongue twined around the digits and I shivered at the sensation, biting my lip as he made eye contact. He bobbed his head, opening his mouth so I could see his tongue as it slid over me.

Withdrawing my fingers, I reached back and slid them between his legs. As I gripped his cock, impaling myself on it, I pressed my fingers inside him. He shuddered and groaned, breathing deeply as I pumped my fingers in and out.

"Thank you, my lady." His voice was tight, his black eyes half-lidded. The full feeling of him inside me was glorious, the weight and heat of his member causing me to gasp with abandon as I rode him.

"How does that feel?" I said. My fingers were pressed into him up to the knuckles, massaging over his prostate. Although his arms were still bound, I could hear his nails rending scratches into the stone as he struggled to control himself.

"So—fucking—perfect—" He choked out the words as I gyrated my hips, slowly building the heat inside me. I'd picked up a few magic tricks over the past few years; I'd learned how to surround his cock with heat, or subtle vibrations, or a rippling squeeze. I edged him with the unexpected, taking my time, savoring my own pleasure.

When he began to beg, it sent me over the edge.

"Please, my lady, let me—let me come—"

"You sound so sweet when you beg," I said. Pumping my fingers into him, I used my other hand to touch myself. "You want to come? Do you want to see your seed dripping down my legs?" A trembling breath escaped me, my pleasure peaking. Inescapable heat exploded through me, sparks bursting from my mouth as I came.

Callum groaned, watching me as if in agony but never looking away. "Please. Let me fill up that sweet cunt and lick it clean, Mistress. I want your taste on my tongue. I want to drown in you." His words carried me through, guiding me over waves of bliss.

"Come for me," I said, the words barely a whisper.

There was a sudden, rapid snapping sound as Callum tore through the ropes binding him. They broke like mere threads as he seized me, claws digging into my hips. He thrust into me, hard and fast, snarling like a beast. His cock swelled as he came deep inside me, whispering to me all the while, "Thank you, Mistress, thank you."

WE WERE STILL entwined as the sun rose.

First, it was just a sliver of red on the distant horizon, before the land was drenched in orange and gold. Warmth crept over my skin, melting into the stones. Callum's face was bathed in a shaft of sunlight, serene and soft, eyes closed.

Then the temple rumbled, and he looked toward the horizon.

"They're coming, darling," he said. He lifted me in his arms, cradling me close as he carried me into the courtyard, up a stone staircase and onto the parapets atop the temple. Cold wind whipped around us, but the sunlight was warm, almost blinding . . .

Until a shadow passed over its light.

It was bigger than any creature I'd ever seen, with leathery feather-tipped wings that stretched over the landscape as it flew. It perched on a distant craggy cliff, onyx scales shining in the sun, its lizard-like armored maw stretching wide as it yawned.

Then, with a raptor-like cry, another shadow covered us. But this dragon wasn't alone. As the massive beast wheeled through the sky, I spotted a smaller creature

at its side. A young dragon, with azure scales t.
shimmered like the ocean, and fluffy fledgling feather
shedding from its wings. It remained close to its parent,
landing with them atop the cliff. They stretched out their
wings, raising them high to catch the sunlight.

My mouth was agape. I couldn't find the words,
couldn't manage more than a disbelieving gasp of,
"They're real . . . oh my God . . . dragons are real..."

We watched them in silence, careful not to draw attention to ourselves. The dragons sunned themselves,
twining their necks together and nibbling each other's
feathers. Occasionally, one would lift their head toward
the sun and cry out, a piercing roar that shook the landscape and made goose bumps cover my arms.

Sometimes, another roar would answer back, far
away, but powerful enough to carry over great distances.

It took several minutes before I realized that as I was
watching the dragons, Callum was watching me.

The morning sun bathed his skin in its light, and I
took a moment to admire him. When Heidi was still an
infant, Callum had an old friend come to the coven house
and tattoo a replica of his daughter's handprints on his
chest. It was unusual, apparently, for demons to have
close relationships with their offspring. Most demonic
youth preferred to explore rather than stay with their
parents.

But part of Heidi was human, and that part of her
needed us. She was Callum's pride and joy. I saw it in his
eyes whenever he looked at her, how he grinned every
time she did the impossible.

Ours was an eternal family. Even if time separated us, it would also bring us together again. It was the family I'd hoped and dreamed of having.

I leaned my head against Callum's shoulder, nuzzling into the crook of his neck. "Are the dragons boring you?"

He kissed my head, his wing wrapping around me like a blanket. "I could never be bored with you at my side. I didn't come here for the beasts. I came for you." Then softly, as if confiding in me a secret, "It's thanks to your wonder at this world that I can see its beauty again. Your happiness is the only map I follow."

He kissed me as the dragons took to the sky once more. Unbidden sparks surrounded me, and the longer we kissed the hotter they grew, until wisps of flame spontaneously licked the air around us. The dragons wheeled overhead, and as if in response to my fire, they roared their own bursts of flame into the morning's pale golden light.

The life I'd longed for, wept for, fought for, was finally mine.

ACKNOWLEDGMENTS

It's remarkably bittersweet to have this trilogy come to an end.

To my husband, thank you for being there for me always. You're my number one supporter, my greatest adviser, and my most incredible muse. Callum's enduring love for Everly was inspired by you, who supported me through my lowest of lows while celebrating my highs. I love you.

To Z, my incredible editor: What an amazing journey it's been together! You've been there for every book in this trilogy, and it's been such a joy to know you, and to see you grow so much both professionally and personally. You're so skilled at what you do and deserve every success. Thank you for showing such love and care for these books; they wouldn't be what they are without you.

To Cassie, who designed every gorgeous cover in this trilogy, thank you for sharing your magical talent. You made these books into absolute beauties!

To Bethany, thank you for being an absolute force of nature and invaluable partner in this crazy publishing world.

To the amazing ladies of JLCR Author Services, thank you! From managing the ARC team and sign-ups, to blasting teasers and always offering your support, it's been wonderful to work with you.

To everyone in the Wicked Dark Desires reader group, y'all know I love you! Thank you for all your support and incredible love for these books.

To every reader, blogger, and creator who shared their excitement for this trilogy, who created amazing posts, wrote thoughtful reviews, and in any way shared their support: Thank you. The fact that I am able to continue writing these books would not be possible without you.

Until next time,
Harley